Praise for the novels of Jude Deveraux

"Deveraux spins an intriguing and unorthodox romance...
An entertaining page-turner."
—*Kirkus Reviews* on *Met Her Match*

"*Met Her Match* is vintage Jude Deveraux from start to
finish, a joy to read."
—*Fresh Fiction*

"Deveraux's charming novel has likable characters and
life-affirming second chances galore."
—*Publishers Weekly* on *As You Wish*

"Jude Deveraux's writing is enchanting and exquisite."
—*BookPage*

"Deveraux's touch is gold."
—*Publishers Weekly*

Praise for the novels of Tara Sheets

"This was adorable! Enemies-to-lovers romance, and
magical house you'll never forget."
—*Kirkus Reviews* on *Don't Call Me Cupcake*

"The first in Sheets' new Holloway Girls series is funny,
sexy, charming and full of practical magic. Fans of
Sarah Addison Allen will love this novel."
—*RT Book Reviews* on *Don't Call Me Cupcake*

JUDE DEVERAUX

AND TARA SHEETS

CHANCE OF A LIFETIME

mira

Recycling programs for this product may not exist in your area.

ISBN-13: 978-0-7783-3183-4

Chance of a Lifetime

First published in 2020. This edition published in 2021.

Copyright © 2020 by Deveraux Inc.

This edition published by arrangement with Harlequin Books S.A.

For questions and comments about the quality of this book, please contact us at CustomerService@Harlequin.com.

Mira
22 Adelaide St. West, 40th Floor
Toronto, Ontario M5H 4E3, Canada
www.Harlequin.com

Printed in Lithuania

MIX
Paper from responsible sources
FSC® C021394

For all of those who believe in the power of love

CHANCE
OF A
LIFETIME

PROLOGUE

For an angel as old as Agon, there was nothing new under the sun, or above. After thousands of years studying the human condition, he'd pretty much seen it all. Time didn't lie. It proved over and over again that human beings were flawed. They led messy lives. They didn't always learn from their mistakes. And yet, as he swooped into the Department of Destiny and prepared for another day of judging souls, he remained ever the optimist. Because time also had a way of proving that even in the face of all odds, love would prevail.

He landed silently in the misty chamber and slapped his associate on the back. "What's up, Samael?"

The shorter angel jerked, fumbling for the clipboard in his hands. He gave Agon a scathing look of disapproval. "How many times must I tell you not to sneak up on me like that?"

"Oh, yes. Sorry," Agon said breezily. "Who's up next?"

Samael checked the clipboard with a heavy sigh. Pale curls framed his round face. Next to Agon's imposing figure and dark hair, Samael looked almost boyish. But he'd been in charge of the Department of Destiny for over three hundred years, and he ran it with a stoic sense of justice that made him seem much older. "A grave disappointment, to be sure. The soul of Liam O'Connor stands judgment today."

"Ah." Agon shook his head sadly. "Poor Irish ruffian. Such a tragic love story, Liam and the fair Cora."

"Those two should *never* have fallen in love," Samael said with a scowl. "It shattered all of our plans. For over a century! So many destinies were ruined because of it." He tucked his wings neatly behind his back, then glanced at Agon. "Are you ready to call him in?"

"Yes." Agon turned toward the wall of mist and pasted an encouraging smile on his face.

"I told you not to do that," Samael said. "This is serious business. We must reflect the gravity of the situation through our appearance and mannerisms."

"But humans like smiles," Agon said. "I thought perhaps it would make him feel more comfortable."

"His soul hangs in the balance between heaven and hell, and we're about to judge it," Samael said flatly. "Who could possibly be comfortable with that?"

"Right." Agon arranged his features to appear as bleak and unyielding as the surrounding chamber.

"Much better," Samael said with a nod. Then he raised his hand and called into the void. "I summon the soul of Liam O'Connor."

Like a cannonball hurled through a cloud, a man shot out of the mist, tumbling head over heels to land before the angels in a tangle of curses and grunts. Unlike other souls who were called to the Department of Destiny, Liam did not rise on unsteady feet, shaking with fear, terrified to stand judgment for his past life's choices. Instead, he jumped up, slapping at wisps of fog still clinging to his hair and clothing, dark eyes casually scanning the room.

Samael regarded him coolly. "Do you know why you've been summoned to the Chamber of Judgment?"

Liam raised a dark brow. "Judgment day, I'd imagine?" For someone who stood on the brink of eternal damnation, he was far too nonchalant. But the angels knew this was part of his act. Liam O'Connor was no stranger to deception.

"We have reviewed your past life and found you wanting," Samael said. He flicked his hand, and moving images suddenly appeared in the misty wall. Liam picking pockets. Breaking into houses. Liam running through the forest carrying a bag of stolen jewels. A stagecoach in the background with victims shouting after him. A musket ball shattering the branch of a tree near his head. Liam laughing in the face of danger.

"You were a thief," Samael said. "And you stole from innocent people. Often."

"Well…" Liam crossed his arms and leaned against the wall of mist. "Crops were failing. I only stole to help put food on the table. Simple as that."

"Do not attempt to lie to us," Samael said coldly. "We can see into your soul, Liam O'Connor, and we know the truth. You enjoyed stealing. You *reveled* in your life as a thief."

"Fine." Liam pushed off the wall and began to pace, dragging the tips of his fingers through the roiling fog. "I did enjoy thieving, and I was good at it, too. I was never any good at farming. But I kept my brother's family from starving, didn't I? That has to count for something."

Samael gazed at him sternly. "You didn't only steal objects." He flicked his hand and another image appeared, a sweet, innocent young woman with glossy blond curls and rosy cheeks. She had a round, pretty face with a nose just a little too prominent, and a smile just a little too trusting. She was holding out a rose.

"Cora," Liam breathed. He stepped closer, but the image of the young woman vanished. "Bring her back!" He grasped at the fog with both hands. "Let me see her again."

"She wasn't meant for you, ruffian," Samael said. "You stole her from her fiancé."

"But I loved her," Liam shot back. "And she—"

"You interfered with her destiny," Samael interrupted. "She was supposed to marry that man, and together they were going to raise a child who would someday help the world."

Liam scowled. "Her fiancé didn't deserve her. She wanted *me*. It was me she loved in the end."

"Ah, yes," Samael said icily. "The *end*."

Liam glanced away.

"Things ended very badly for her, as you well know," Samael continued. "For both of you. And now, because of you, Cora's soul has never found peace. In every new life we've given her, she's afraid to fall in love. She never lives long enough to fulfill her destiny." He flicked his hand again.

This time, terrible images appeared. Cora as a young nurse, caring for soldiers during an outbreak of scarlet fever...dying in a hospital bed. Cora as a nanny, rushing to save a young child from the path of a runaway horse...dying in the street. Cora working in a factory during WWII...dying in an explosion.

The angels knew Liam wouldn't understand some of the things he was seeing, but the message was very clear. Cora's life always ended in tragedy.

"Enough!" Liam flung his hands up, scrubbing his face. "Just tell me my fate. Is it to be hell, then?"

The angels exchanged glances.

"It is true you've done much wrong in your life," Samael said. "But you've also done some good. For this reason, we're going to give you a chance at redemption."

Liam's head shot up. He glanced back and forth between the two angels.

"Cora is on earth again in this twenty-first century," Samael said. "You must make sure she fulfills her true destiny in this life."

"But...how?"

"There is a man named Finley Walsh. He is her true soul mate—the man she must marry. The man she *was* destined to marry until you ruined everything. This time, you will see that Cora falls in love with the right man."

Liam scowled and kicked the floor, displacing wisps of fog. He grumbled under his breath, then glanced up. "Will she remember me?"

"Of course not," Samael said. "Certainly not as you remember her. The role you play this time will be...much different."

Liam narrowed his eyes but remained silent.

"You have three months to complete the task," Samael continued in clipped tones. "We will bestow upon you some knowledge of the current century, but it won't be an easy transition. If anyone questions your struggles with modern technology, just explain you're from a very rural town."

Liam raised his chin. "What if I tell them the truth?"

Samael let out a huff of amusement. "That you're a transplanted soul from 1844 Ireland? Good luck with that." He slid the clipboard into a pocket of mist. "Three months, Liam O'Connor. Get Cora to fall in love with Finley. It is imperative that this happens. If you fail—and that includes sleeping with her—you will be sent straight to…"

All the light in the chamber vanished, plunging them into icy darkness.

"Hell." Samael's voice echoed off the chamber walls like a war drum.

"And if I succeed?" Liam whispered.

The light snapped back on.

"Heaven," Samael said matter-of-factly. "Now, off you go." He started to lift his hand.

"Wait!" Liam cried. "If Cora's been on earth living all these different lives, where have I been the whole time?"

"Suspended up here," Samael said. "Waiting for us to decide if you deserved a chance at redemption. I do hope you are worthy of it. Goodbye, ruffian." He waved his hand a final time, and a hole opened in the mist beneath Liam's feet.

They could hear him yelling for a long time as he fell, even after the hole closed.

Agon chuckled. "That was a rather dramatic exit, don't you think?"

Samael shrugged. "I thought the moment could use a bit of theatrics."

"And the flickering lights with the echoing voice?" Agon elbowed him in the ribs. "Nice job."

Samael pressed his lips together and tried to look stern, but Agon could tell he was pleased.

They turned to the wall of mist as the image of Liam appeared. His body floated to earth, landing softly on a bed of leaves on the forest floor. He glanced around in a daze, his lips slowly curving into a smile.

"He always loved the forest," Agon said wistfully.

"I thought he could use a moment here to reflect on his past, before we send him to work," Samael said.

Liam's eyes drooped. His dark lashes fluttered once. Twice. And then he slipped into a deep, dream-filled sleep.

"You didn't tell him the truth." Agon turned to Samael. "About the child."

"He's not ready to hear that—and neither is she."

Agon glanced back to the image of Liam's slumbering form. "Do you think he'll succeed?"

Samael frowned. "What's that human saying about a snowball's chance?"

Agon shook his head. "It eludes me."

"No matter." Samael expanded his wings and stretched. "Time will tell."

"Yes," Agon mused. "Time always does."

1

Kinsley, Ireland,
1844

The fight inside the Goose & Gander tavern was nothing new. Flying fists and hurled insults were as common as the daily swill served there, and in Liam O'Connor's opinion, sometimes preferable. If a fight poured into the street, a tipsy farmer ended facedown in the pig trough, or someone lost his teeth—or worse—the poor villagers of Kinsley barely noticed. A potato blight was ravaging the country. Crop yields were low and spirits were lower. If a man died drunk and surrounded by friends, well… There were worse ways to go.

Liam leaned a broad shoulder against the wall outside, waiting for the right moment to enter. It had been a long day, and he wasn't in the mood to get tangled up in another brawl. Tonight, he had far more important things on his mind. Important, expensive things that sparkled and gleamed exactly the way the Goose & Gander didn't.

"Rat bastard!" a man roared. "May the milk spoil in your cows and a pox take you!"

A moment later, two men came flying through the tavern door, cursing and punching and kicking up mud.

Liam yawned and pushed his way past the drunken spectators who were already spilling into the street and making wagers.

"O'Connor!" A man yanked at Liam's shirt, ripping a seam.

Liam craned his neck to see a gaping hole in the shoulder of his sleeve. *Hell and damn.* His brother's wife was going to have his head for that. It was the third time this week he'd torn it, and he only had the one shirt.

Liam scowled at the barrel-chested man who stood near the door, weaving on his feet. "What do you want, Angus?" The old man was a regular at the tavern and known to make bad wagers whenever he was drunk, which was most days.

He squinted at Liam. "You still owe me fer last week's ale."

"Aye, that's why I'm here, you big oaf," Liam lied smoothly. "Come inside after the mud fight and I'll pay you back."

Angus eyed him suspiciously. Even deep in his cups, he was skeptical, which proved he wasn't quite the pudding brain people believed he was.

Liam gasped and pointed to the men fighting in the mud. "Would you look at that! They're really going at it now."

When Angus teetered on his feet and turned his attention to the fight, Liam slipped quickly into the tavern. If luck was on his side, Angus would be snoring facedown in the dirt within the next few minutes. Knowing him, the odds were good.

The tavern was smoky and dimly lit, which helped hide the occasional rats on the floor and the questionable food. Wooden tables and chairs were crammed so close together that a person had to turn sideways to avoid bumping into people, which was probably the reason fights broke out as often as they did. And if an optimistic soul ever tried to pretend the place wasn't as bad as it looked, well…the smell of unwashed bodies, spoiled stew and mangy dogs snuffling under the tables took care of that delusion.

But as unsavory as the place was, it suited Liam and his gang just fine. In his line of work, it was just the place he needed to carry out plans without worry of being overheard. No magistrate would willingly step foot in there, so that made it just about perfect.

"Liam," his best friend called from the corner table. Boyd was a short, stocky man with dark curly hair and a shrewd gaze that missed nothing. "Over here."

Liam joined the table. Beside him sat the O'Malley brothers. The Bricks. They were as dumb as their nickname, but what they lacked in brains they made up for in brawn. They were identical twins with blunt, blocklike features and powerful fists. Liam didn't know them like he knew his childhood friend Boyd, but it didn't matter. The Bricks were always up for shady business, especially if it paid well.

"What's the news, then?" Boyd asked.

Liam signaled for a tankard of ale. "A baron travels this way in a week's time. He's taking his wife to visit friends, so there should be a nice bit of jewelry traveling with them."

Boyd let out a derisive snort. "Hang your bits of jewelry, Liam. The boys and I have far better news."

One of the Bricks grunted and took a swig of ale.

A serving girl brought over a tankard and set it down in front of Liam, leaning over a little farther than necessary. Her smile was big and her cleavage, bigger.

"Thank you, Betsy." Liam winked.

She giggled, sliding a hand over his muscular shoulders before sashaying away.

"How do you do it?" Boyd asked irritably. "Every woman within five miles of you can't resist shoving her tits in your face. Even rich Margaret Brady gives you calf eyes whenever she rolls by in her grand carriage, and I can only guess what else she's giving you when that husband of hers is out of town."

Liam shrugged, but said nothing. He'd been in a casual dalliance with Margaret for months, now. Being unhappy in her cold marriage with her ancient husband, she'd lured Liam in with her sleek black hair and lush figure. He sighed dramatically. "Everyone has a cross to bear, my friend. I endure it as best I can."

Boyd snorted. "One of these days you're going to get tangled up in something, Liam O'Connor, and your pretty face and even prettier lies aren't going to save you."

"You've no need to be bellyaching," Liam said. "Your wife is the best-looking girl in the village."

Boyd's scowl smoothed out. "True. Alice is the best. She's got the loveliest—"

"Enough," one of the Bricks muttered. "Tell him about the house."

Boyd leaned in. "We just found out Squire McLeod and his daughter left town for some fancy party today. They'll be gone for three days, leaving that big house on the hill all alone." He braced his arms on the table. "Think of it, Liam. The squire's house. They say he keeps a treasure trove of his late wife's jewels in there. Jewels like none of us have ever seen." His small eyes glittered with greed. "It'll be our grandest haul yet."

Liam gripped his mug, unease prickling the back of his neck. He liked the squire. The man was an understanding landlord, and he'd been kind to his brother and family when their crops began to fail. Liam was never one to shy away from easy profit, but to steal from a man who had been so generous to them… It did not sit well with him.

"Boring." Liam tried to bluster. "I'd much rather rob the rich coach when it comes through the woods, or have you all lost your balls for a real adventure?"

The twins growled in unison.

Boyd looked at Liam in disbelief. "Did you fall and hit your head out there during the street fight? I'm talking about the squire's legendary jewels. They'll be sitting in that house unprotected. Ours for the plundering."

"Not just plundering," one of the twins said in a voice like gravel. He gripped his hand into a fist and smacked it against his open palm.

"Aye," Boyd said. "We're not just going to steal the squire's jewels. We're going to destroy his house. All of it. See how the lofty pig enjoys having nothing, like the rest of us."

"Burn it to the ground." The other twin growled.

Liam struggled to keep his expression neutral. He hooked an arm over the back of his chair and took a long, slow drink of ale, trying to figure a way out. He and Boyd had been stealing from the rich for years, scheming and picking pockets and robbing the occasional stagecoach. In a world where the next meal might not come for days, they'd learned out of necessity. But this plan of Boyd's tasted wrong. Not just because Liam liked the squire, but because there were too many unknowns. Boyd often let his greed overrule his common sense, which was why Liam usually made the final calls, and why they'd survived as long as they had.

"It sounds like a hassle," Liam finally said.

Boyd turned to the twins. "I think our fearless leader here's gone daft."

"Look." Liam set his tankard down on the table with a *thud*. "Robbing a stagecoach in the woods, you can run for miles in any direction. If we're chased, no one will be able to outrun us. We know all the hiding places and all the hidden trails. In a house like the squire's..." He shook his head. "None of us knows our way around. The squire and his daughter may be gone, yes. But what about the servants? There are bound to be many in a house that big. We'd be trapped like fish in a barrel if we get caught, and there'd be nowhere to run."

Boyd's mouth flattened in annoyance. "Listen to yourself, Liam. Spouting off about running from danger like some wee lassie hiding behind her nursemaid's skirts. This is a foolproof plan. The twins heard it from the dressmaker that the squire's servants have been given the time off, as well. They'll be leaving tomorrow, and the house will be empty. So we go in tomorrow night, simple as that. The only danger to us will be the danger of getting too fat from overeating and overdrinking because we've all become rich as the devil himself." He pounded his fist on the table and roared with laughter.

The Bricks joined in.

Liam gave a reluctant smile and took another drink of ale. He knew Boyd well enough to know there was no stopping him when he got like this. Boyd was a loyal friend, but his greed was boundless.

As the men discussed the following night's plan, Liam came up with a secret one of his own. If Squire McLeod's house did have a treasure trove of jewels, he would break in tonight and steal them before his friends had a chance. Then he'd present the jewels to them tomorrow. He'd say going it alone was easier than having them all risk their necks. Boyd and the Bricks would likely be so dazzled by their good fortune, they'd forget their plan of setting fire to the house. It was the only way Liam could think to keep it safe.

He gritted his teeth with determination, mind spinning with what he was about to do.

Men from the outside brawl began pouring back into the tavern, and Liam caught sight of old Angus in the crowd. Perfect timing.

"Damn," Liam said, scraping his chair back. He moved to the window behind Boyd's head and unlatched it. "I'm out of here, boys. When Angus comes by, just tell him I couldn't wait for him any longer and I'll be back tomorrow with his money."

"We'll cover for you." Boyd slapped Liam on the back. "Off you go, then. Meet us tomorrow at dusk, right?"

Liam nodded, then jumped out the tavern window, sticking to the shadows as he made his way down the street.

It was cold as a witch's kiss, and well past midnight when Liam found himself clinging to the side of the squire's house, praying to St. Nicholas. While it crossed his mind that St. Nicholas was the patron saint of *repentant* thieves, Liam decided it couldn't hurt. He'd be especially repentant if he fell and broke his bloody neck.

He was aiming for a second-story window above a tall rose trellis. The first part of the climb up the trellis had been easy enough, but the last few feet were proving to be brutal.

Shaking with exertion, sweat trickling down his back, Liam gripped the jagged stones and pulled himself up. His jacket, a castoff from his brother, had been too tight around the shoulders for him to climb freely, so he'd left it behind in the bushes along with his boots. Now, with the damp fog rolling in and the walls growing more slippery by the minute, he was beginning to regret his plan of going alone. Unfortunately, it was too late to back down, so he continued the treacherous climb, muscles straining as he inched toward the window.

Seven Hail Marys and one near-fatal slip later, Liam finally reached the ledge. He pushed the window open with one hand, hooked a leg over the sill, and hauled himself inside.

When his bare feet touched the stone floor, he rested his head on the frame, breathing heavily and sighing with relief. *God's teeth*, that had been a close call.

"Hello," a soft voice said behind him.

Liam whirled. Something sharp stabbed into his right heel. He let out a curse, grabbing at his foot as he bounced on one leg, staring in shock. The hard, sharp pain slicing through his foot was completely at odds with the soft, sweet vision in front of him.

A lovely young woman sat watching him from the middle of her bed. Surrounded by pillows and lace, she looked like a fluffy pink tea cake.

She had a pretty, round face, with a long nose and golden curls cascading around her shoulders. In one hand she was holding a half-eaten apple, and in the other she held a book. A single candle burned beside her bed, casting just enough of a glow for Liam to see that she was more surprised than afraid. Odd. Most women would be screaming down the house by now.

"Oh!" Her delicate brows drew together. "Did you hurt your foot?" She tossed the apple and book aside and slid from the bed.

She was concerned for *him*? He almost laughed, but he was too busy staring at the little cake who was now kneeling on the floor in front of him to examine his foot.

"I'm so sorry." She blinked up at him with big, round eyes. "I'll just get a towel." She jumped up to fetch a towel and small bowl of water from the washstand, then gestured to her bed near the candle. "Sit on my bed so I can see better."

On her bed? Liam didn't move. Was the woman daft?

"It's all right." She gave him an encouraging smile, pointing to the poufy white bed covered in lace. "Just a few steps over there."

Liam slowly walked to the bed, briefly wondering if perhaps he had fallen from the stones and died, after all. Except she looked far too much like an angel, and he wasn't entirely sure he was headed in that direction. She had big blue eyes fringed with dark lashes, and a plump, rosebud mouth that could make a man think sinful thoughts. She was not an angel, then. Otherwise he'd be tossed into hell for what he was imagining about her mouth.

"I'm so sorry about your foot," she said, tearing the towel into long strips. "It's my fault for leaving my seashell collection on the floor. The one you stepped on is very sharp and spiky, I know, but isn't it a beauty?" She held up a wicked-looking shell with brown spotted spikes. *Beauty* was not the word that came to mind.

Liam raised a brow, but said nothing. She didn't seem to notice.

"My father's steward brought it from a ship in port," she continued, setting the shell on the nightstand and dipping a washcloth in water. "He said it was from some far off, exotic place where the air was filled with spices. What do you suppose that must be like? Spices in the air?" She laughed as she gently cleaned the wound on his heel. "I imagine it could be nice, if the spices were cinnamon mixed with sugar or maybe nutmeg, but I'm not partial to black pepper. I think visiting a place where the air was filled with black pepper would be quite dreadful, don't you?"

Liam nodded, because a young woman was washing his foot in her bedroom. In the middle of the night. After he'd just broken into her bedroom. The situation was entirely new to him, and he was rather at a loss for words. She, on the other hand, did not have that problem.

"Collecting seashells is one of my favorite hobbies." She smiled up at him, and it felt like sunlight on his face. "Nanny always yells at me for leaving things on the floor. Well, she's not my nanny anymore, because I'm seventeen, of course, and that would just be silly. But she used to be my nanny, so I still call her Nanny, even though she's now my lady's maid. Do you know...?" She looked at him thoughtfully. "She's become very bossy and grumpy in her old age. I can't decide if it's my fault, or if she's just upset because life here is so dull." She began wrapping a long strip of fabric around his heel. "She says I'm always walking around with my head in the clouds and wasting time on silly hobbies when I should be doing better things like learning embroidery. But what's a needle and thread compared to the wonders of the ocean, I ask you? Have you been?" she asked suddenly.

Liam blinked. Nodded.

She let out a breath, stirring a soft curl that had fallen in her eyes. "Well, that's luck, isn't it? I've never been to the seashore. I've never seen anything but Kinsley and the surrounding countryside. My father, the squire, says it's too dangerous for me to go anywhere else. Sometimes I wish I were a sea captain, so I could go on grand adventures and see all the amazing things." She sighed heavily, tying his bandage in a tight knot.

Liam flexed his foot, testing the bandage. Not bad work for a pampered lady.

"I've seen you before, you know," she said conversationally. "In town, with your friends."

He eyed her carefully. Had she seen him with Boyd and the twins? Did she know what kind of life they led?

She waved a hand in dismissal. "I'm sure you didn't notice me. I've always been with Nanny, or in the carriage. But father speaks very fondly of his tenants, and I listen. I've seen your family's farm, too. It's to the west, isn't it? Such a pretty farm, with the lovely fields against the blue sky." She was smiling at him again, only this time Liam's thoughts were far from sunny. He was thinking of his brother's farm, where he lived. The tiny cottage with the cramped straw pallets. The bone-deep chill seeping through the thatched roof in winter. His brother's wife screaming about the rotten potatoes on the table. Three small children crying. One of them sickly. There was never enough food. Never enough of anything.

The squire's daughter stood and put away the washcloth and basin of water. Then she walked over to her vanity and lit another candle, which allowed Liam to see her more clearly.

She was dressed in a lump of a gown. Pink ruffles cascaded down the high-necked bodice, obscuring most of her chest and waist, the style lost somewhere between childish and matronly. It wasn't the type of dress most young ladies her age would wear. Not that Liam had seen many fancy ladies, but he knew enough to recognize the oddity on a pretty young woman like her. He'd never noticed her in the village before. But then, he wasn't in the habit of frequenting the places the squire's daughter might go.

"I'm Cora, by the way. Cora McLeod." She marched over and held out her hand.

Liam stared at it, then at her. What did she expect him to do? Shake her hand like two men who'd just struck a deal? Or worse, kiss her hand like they were being introduced in some ballroom? This time, the humor of the situation got the better of him, and his shoulders began to shake with laughter.

Cora tilted her head, watching him curiously. "What's so funny?"

Liam rose from the side of her bed, still laughing. He walked to the wall and leaned against it. "You," he finally said with a grin. "You are very funny, Cora McLeod."

Her face fell and she turned away. "Yes, well… I've been told that a time or two." She smoothed the skirt of her gown.

Liam suddenly felt the need to explain. He didn't want her to be upset. "I don't mean to offend. It's just that I climbed the wall of your house in the middle of the night, broke into your bedroom, and you don't seem at all bothered."

She turned back, brightening. "Well, I'm not afraid of you. You don't seem like a bad person. Are you?"

He chuckled, tipping his head back to gaze at the ceiling. "If I were, I wouldn't tell you."

"No,.I suppose not," she mused. "But you're very big and tall. And you must be incredibly strong to climb up the side of the house. So even if you were planning to do something bad, I wouldn't stand much of a chance against you, would I? Therefore, you might as well tell me the truth. Are you planning to do something bad?"

Liam's gaze fell to her lush mouth, then back up to her wide, inquiring eyes. "What do you mean by 'bad'?"

"Well…" Cora hesitated, wringing her hands in front of her. "Nanny says wicked men try to take advantage of young ladies and do their worst."

His lips quirked up at one corner. "Which would be?"

She swallowed visibly. "I suppose you might try to… kiss me?" Her cheeks flushed with color and she looked scandalized, just for mentioning it.

He laughed again. She was truly an innocent if she believed that's the worst a man could do. "You have my word that I did not come here to kiss you."

"Good." Cora smiled in relief. "I'm glad to hear it."

Liam wasn't sure how he felt about that. Usually the ladies fell at his feet, but it was late, and he was off his game. He shifted on his feet, grateful that the cut on his heel hadn't been deep. Cora's bandage was tight and efficient. Walking—or running, if necessary—would be easy enough, if it came to that. He hoped it wouldn't.

"Have you come to rob me, then?" Cora asked with wide-eyed interest.

Liam considered lying, but what other reason could he have? "I don't suppose you'd believe me if I told you I was doing a routine check of the house's window latches?"

She shook her head, blond curls tumbling over her shoulders.

"I was setting traps for rats?" he offered hopefully.

Her eyes sparkled with humor and she shook her head again.

Liam wrinkled his brow. "Sleepwalking?"

"Up the side of a stone wall?" Cora giggled. "Sorry. I may not get out into the world much, but I am a good reader. I've read *Robin Hood*. I know what thieves do."

"Then I'm afraid you've caught me." Liam bowed and gave her his most charming smile. The one he used with ladies when he needed to get out of a sticky situation. "I am a thief, but I also wanted to see inside your great house." He lowered his voice in a conspiratorial whisper. "Please don't tell."

She sighed. "To be honest, this is the most interesting thing that's happened to me in ages. Life around here is frightfully dull." She lowered her voice. "Your secret is safe with me, er... What is your name?"

He should lie. He knew it, but for some reason he didn't want to. "I'd rather not say."

"Oh." She blinked in surprise. "Yes, of course. It wouldn't be wise for a thief to reveal his name after being caught mid-robbery."

"No." This time, Liam's smile was genuine. She was such an intriguing bundle of contradictions. With the dress and the golden curls, she looked like a fragile porcelain doll—like she'd crack at the first sign of trouble. But she wasn't that way at all. This woman had spirit. He liked it.

"Shall I take you on a tour of the house, then?" Cora asked. "It's terribly drafty and old, but there's a library downstairs. I can show you the great book of seashells."

For the first time since he climbed through her window, Liam thought about the squire's legendary jewels. He glanced around her bedroom, noting the washbasin, a painted silk screen in the corner and the vanity table. There was a large fireplace on one end of the room, but nothing that looked particularly grand or fine. No jewelry boxes or objects of great value. If the squire did keep jewels in the house, Cora's room wasn't the place.

"Yes," Liam said smoothly, pushing off the wall. "But what about the servants? Won't they talk if they find you wandering the halls with a stranger in the middle of the night?"

Cora lifted the candle beside her bed. "No one's going to hear a thing. Most of the servants have taken time off, and Nanny's half-deaf, anyway. There's Cook, but he drinks too much. The house could burn down around him and he probably wouldn't notice."

Liam's gut tightened at her mention of the house burning. She had no idea how close she'd come to the truth about what Boyd and the twins were planning to do. Liam felt more determined than ever to find the jewels and save Cora's home.

"As long as we're quiet, no one will discover our secret adventure." Her blue eyes sparkled with excitement, and her rosebud mouth curved into a mischievous smile.

It was impossible not to smile back. "All right, then, Captain Cora. Show me your great house."

She led him out into a dark, cold hallway. "There's not much to see up here, I'm afraid," she said in a hushed voice. "Just old bedrooms nobody uses."

"Still." Liam stopped at the first door. "Let's have a look. We are on an adventure, after all. You never know what ghosts could be lurking behind closed doors."

Cora opened the door, leading him into a musty room. Dusty sheets were draped over what little furniture there was, and it was clear nobody had been inside to clean in a very long time.

"Ghosts, indeed," Liam murmured, taking a quick inventory of the room. No jewels in there, to be sure. He turned to Cora. "Onward, Captain."

She led him through the rest of the rooms on her floor. All the same. All in varying states of neglect. It was odd to him, that a grand man like the squire would allow so many bedrooms to lay dusty.

Cora led him down a curved staircase to the first floor of the house. She pointed to a narrow hall and whispered, "That's the kitchen and the servants' wing."

He followed her in the opposite direction through a set of ornate double doors. The grand drawing room had soaring ceilings, but the stale, musty air made the room feel cramped and lifeless. As Cora led him through, Liam was shocked to see how threadbare the furniture was. All of the chairs and settees were faded, and none of the pieces had been polished in ages. There were blank spots on the walls where some paintings were missing. The whole scene made no sense.

"This way lies the hall of portraits," Cora said, leading him out into an immense hall with long, narrow carpets. "I used to be afraid of this place when I was little because I imagined *he* was watching me." She held up the candle and pointed to a large, grand painting in a gilded frame. "The Black Duke," she said in a dramatic whisper.

The painting showed a handsome, proud man with dark, wavy hair and dark eyes. He was tall and broad shouldered, with a muscular build that seemed at odds with his satin and lace clothing. It was a typical formal portrait, but the artist had managed to capture a roguish gleam in the man's eyes that was anything but common. Something about the way he stood, surrounded by the three wolfhounds, made him seem restless and a little bit wild.

"The infamous Black Duke is one of our ancestors," Cora said in a low voice. "He's said to have stolen the money and land that was the basis of my family's fortune." She looked at the portrait, then at Liam. "He looks a bit like you, actually."

Liam ran a hand through his shaggy hair. No one had ever compared him to a duke before. He glanced at Cora to see if she spoke in jest, but it was clear she meant it.

"Though I can't imagine you sitting in a drawing room wearing satin and lace," she said with a laugh. "You seem like more of an outdoor man."

Liam thought of his last robbery. The stagecoach footman hollering after him. Heart thumping as he ran like mad through the woods. The scent of foliage and damp earth mixed with the hot rush of adrenaline. "I am definitely an outdoor man."

Cora chatted sweetly as she showed him the rest of the house, and everywhere Liam looked, things had fallen into disrepair. The rooms were dusty and ill kempt. There were faded areas on the floor where rugs had once been, and all the rooms had peeling paint and crumbling millwork and threadbare curtains. Liam couldn't believe what he was seeing. He and his friends had often imagined the squire's house to be magnificent, with gold ceilings and silver staircases, but the inside of Cora's house was a wreck. No wonder nobody from the village had ever seen the inside.

She shivered as they moved toward the back of the house and Liam wished he had a coat to offer her.

"It's always drafty here," Cora said. "I've never much liked it. If I could live anywhere, I would choose that lovely cottage in the village. The one by the great tree. It seems like such a warm, happy place. Do you know it?"

"Yes." Liam knew just the cottage she was talking

about. Situated near a babbling brook at the edge of the village, it had a sturdy roof and cheerful flowers by the garden gate. Everything about it was sunny and bright. A place like that suited her.

"And now, we come to the library," she said in triumph. She pushed open two double doors and led him inside. "This is my favorite room in the house because this is where all the great stories are. Nothing amazing ever happens in my life, but whenever I come here, it's like the whole world cracks open." She gestured to the floor-to-ceiling bookcases that lined the walls. The air smelled like dusty parchment, old leather and tea roses. There was a writing desk near the far wall and comfortable reading chairs near the fireplace. Liam could just picture Cora settled there to read.

A painting of a beautiful woman hung on the wall behind the desk. She had black hair and stunning blue eyes, and she wore a pale silk dress adorned with roses.

"My mother," Cora said wistfully. "She was a great beauty, and so charming. My father said she could charm a selkie right out of its skin. When she was alive, the house was always full of music and friends. I was very young when she died, but I still remember her rose perfume and her colorful gowns and all the parties."

"What happened to her?" Liam asked softly.

She turned away from the portrait and leaned against the desk. "She caught a cough. And one day she went to bed and never woke up. It devastated my father, which is why he's so strict with me. If I so much as sneeze, he practically wraps me in cotton wool and sends me to bed. It's the reason I had to stay home today." She walked over to the fireplace. "I was pulling books from a shelf this morning to take on the trip, and I started sneezing from all the dust. My father overheard me, and became convinced I'd caught a chill." She shook her head, running her fingers over a carved wooden box on the mantel. "Nothing I could say would persuade him otherwise. So I've been in my room all night, reading." Cora lifted the box's lid, and a soft melody began to play. She shut it firmly and turned to face him. "And that's when you found me." She forced a bright smile and gestured to her gown. "Alone and dressed for a ball I won't attend."

Something sharp twisted in Liam's chest at the injustice of it. He eyed her gown with distaste. No wonder it was so concealing. Her father was overprotective. It was a crime to leave such a lovely, intelligent, kindhearted woman alone in a dusty old house like this. She should be dancing. She should be at parties full of laughter and light, not hidden away like some rare jewel in a dark cave, shining for no one.

On impulse, he closed the distance between them and drew his knife.

Cora gasped.

"Don't be afraid," Liam said, his dark eyes searching hers. "I won't hurt you."

Cora stood frozen in place, but gave a tiny nod.

Liam grabbed the offending ruffles on the neckline of her gown and began cutting. His knife parted through the silk fabric, altering the childish style to expose her graceful neck and shoulders. Then he bent to slice away some of the flounces on her gown until, at last, he was satisfied. "Now," he said firmly, "you're dressed for a ball."

Cora's stared down at her exposed cleavage and bare arms. Her chest rose and fell quickly, and a deep blush stained her cheeks.

For a moment, Liam wondered if he'd gone too far.

But then she looked up at him with a brilliant smile and laughed.

He reached over her head and flipped open the box on the mantel. The melody began to play again, filling the library with sweet music.

He stood back and bowed deeply, a mischievous gleam in his eyes. Then he held out his hand. "May I have this dance?"

Cora's gaze flew to his bandaged foot. "But—"

"It's fine," Liam assured her. "I barely feel it." It was almost true, too. In that moment, he was so enchanted with the lovely woman in front of him, nothing could've stopped him from dancing.

Cora curtsied and placed her hands in his.

He led her around the library, his body thrumming with exhilaration. He didn't know much about parlor dancing, but he knew about women, and Cora was very much a woman. Her skin was so soft, and her laughter irresistible. She smelled like sweet lavender and fresh linen. When he lifted her off the floor and twirled her in a circle, he could feel her soft curves pressed against his hard chest, and it lit his blood on fire. Everything about the moment felt clandestine. Forbidden. A man like him should never be dancing with a fine lady like her. Somehow, the knowledge just stoked his excitement more. He felt as if he could fly.

When at last the music died, they both stood in the darkened room, breathing heavily and smiling at one another.

"I think," Cora said, panting, "I'm so very glad you're a thief."

Liam tenderly brushed a loose curl off her face. "No one's ever said that to me before."

"I am," she insisted. "Otherwise you'd never have

climbed through my window, and I'd never have met you." She glanced down at his large hands, still holding hers.

Slowly, with reluctance, he released her and stepped back.

Cora spun away, smoothing her skirts. "I'm engaged to be married." Her voice was hollow and resigned.

Disappointment gripped him, but he shoved it aside. Of course a woman like her would have a suitor. Why should he care? This moment between them was stolen out of time. It would go no further, and he knew that. But the stab of melancholy he felt was just a ripple effect of something that went much deeper. Liam wanted a better life. Would he always be destined to scratch and scrape? Would he never have more? *Be* more? For a brief moment, when he was dancing with Cora, he'd imagined what life could be like if he was a better man. A man worthy of someone like her.

"You don't sound happy about your engagement," Liam finally said.

"Oh." Cora shrugged. "Finley is a nice enough man, I suppose."

Liam frowned. Terrible name, Finley. Most unfortunate. He'd never known anyone named Finley, but it was surely the name of a fat, pimply man with gout.

"He's my father's solicitor," Cora continued.

Old, then, too. A decrepit old man with a monocle and a limp. Liam disliked him already.

"I don't dislike him," Cora said kindly. "It's just that he's so very quiet. He never even talks to me. Whenever we're in a room together, he just sits and stares at me."

A lecher, too. It just wasn't right. "I'm sorry," Liam managed.

"I just don't think he and I have anything in common,"

Cora said in frustration, pacing the room. "I want to go places and *do* things. I don't want to sit beside the fire and embroider cushions for the rest of my life."

Liam wanted to run and sweep her up and dance her around the room again, if only to see her smile.

"You lead an exciting life," Cora said, face shining with admiration. "I imagine you've gone on many wild adventures. Just the idea of it is so romantic. Do you steal from the rich to feed the poor, like Robin Hood?"

Liam's gaze slid away, and he ran a hand through his hair. His memory flashed to that morning when he'd tossed a bag of coins on the table at home. His brother's wife picked it up, glancing at her hungry children. His brother hadn't been able to look him in the eye, because they all knew the money was stolen.

"Sure," he said lightly. "I steal from the rich and give to the poor." It wasn't a lie.

"Well, I think it's wonderful you do that," Cora said with feeling. "I wish I could help people and be brave and daring like you." She studied him thoughtfully for a moment. "Come with me. There's something I want to give you." She lifted the candle again and led him out of the library.

Liam followed her to a smaller room down the hall. The faint scent of cigars and brandy lingered in the air.

"This is my father's study," Cora told him, walking to the tall bookcases built into the wall. She held the candle up, searching the shelves.

Was she going to give him a book? Liam didn't have the heart to tell her he didn't do much reading. During the day he was either helping his brother in the fields or roaming the countryside with Boyd and the Bricks. And at night, he didn't have the luxury of burning candles just for reading.

Cora's delicate hand settled on a large leather book. She pulled it forward and Liam heard a *click* inside the wall. The bookcase opened out to reveal a hidden compartment behind it.

A rush of excitement rippled over Liam's skin, his senses suddenly on high alert. This was the kind of thing he and his gang lived for. Yet, as Cora drew out a large jewel box, he felt a strange mixture of elation and…shame. For the second time that night, he wished he were a better man.

Cora set the box on her father's desk and opened it. Large, chunky pieces of jewelry sparkled in the candlelight. They were not delicate pieces, as Liam would've imagined. Thick gold chains with red and green and blue stones. An ornate brooch. Several gaudy rings. Cora placed the necklaces into Liam's hand. "I want you to have these. For the poor people." Her expression was so earnest, so full of kindness, it made Liam's chest tighten.

He lifted the necklaces up to the candlelight. The settings were rough; the stones oddly placed. He quickly assessed the rest of the jewelry, then glanced at Cora's sweet, shining face.

"Go on, then," she said. "Take them. I can't imagine a better person who should have them."

Liam thanked her and slid the necklaces into his pocket.

She led him to a side door that opened into the garden. "You're safe to leave this way. No windows overlook this part of the garden."

He stepped over the threshold into the yard, his feet squelching in the muddy grass. Turning to face her, Liam felt as if he were leaving all the happiness and hope behind with her, where it belonged. Now he was an outsider again. Only a few feet separated them, but it might as well have been a thousand miles.

"I'm so very glad we met," she said softly. "I wish…" A deep blush suffused her cheeks, and she bit her bottom lip.

Liam's gaze lowered to her mouth. His throat went dry, and his fingers ached to pull her toward him. "What is it you wish?"

"I wish…" Her voice faltered for a moment, and then she seemed to catch herself. She straightened her spine and lifted her chin. "I wish you well."

Liam swallowed hard. "And I, you." He turned and marched across the grass before he did or said something foolish.

"Farewell, thief." Cora's soft voice floated on the breeze.

He spun around without thinking and called out, "Liam."

Cora blinked in surprise.

"My name is Liam O'Connor." Maybe he was a damned fool to tell her, but he didn't care. His name was all he had to give, and he wanted her to have it.

"Liam." Cora smiled. "I'll keep your secret." Then she closed the door and was gone.

A dull ache settled in his chest as he made his way home in the dark. The realization that he'd probably never speak to her again left him feeling hollow inside. What irony! He'd gone to the squire's house that night to steal something, and he left feeling as though something had been stolen from him.

Liam crossed an open field and climbed over the low stone wall that bordered the edge of the squire's land. Stopping for a moment, he reached into his pocket, gripping the tangle of necklaces she'd given him. He drew them out, studying the crudely cut stones with a mixture of

wry amusement and uneasiness. Even in the weak moonlight, it was clear they were just cheap replicas made of
paste. He'd known it the moment she'd placed them into
his hands. Cora's father must have sold the original jewelry long ago to keep his estate running. And Cora had
no idea. She thought she was giving him a fortune to help
the poor, and Liam didn't have the heart to tell her they
were worthless.

He shoved the jewelry back into his pocket and continued walking. Boyd and the Bricks were going to be
furious when they found out the legendary jewels were
worthless. There was no telling what they'd do. A prickle
of fear slithered down Liam's spine, and he picked up his
pace. The sun would rise in a few hours, and he needed a
plan. After tonight, he was more determined than ever to
keep the squire's house safe. Because it wasn't about the
squire anymore. It was about *Cora McLeod*.

2

Providence Falls,
Present Day

Police investigator Cora McLeod crossed her arms and stared in exasperation at the lanky teenager who was doing his utmost to impress her with his street swagger. "For the last time, Billy, this isn't about *me*."

She'd been grabbing lunch at her favorite diner in downtown Providence Falls, just minding her own business—sort of—on her day off, when she happened to see the kid. Billy was a wealth of information, and on more than one occasion he'd tipped her off and helped put criminals behind bars. If she'd been driving past the seedier end of the city today specifically looking for him, she'd never admit it. Hey, it was a lovely summer afternoon. Why not take the scenic route home? But now that she'd finally found him outside the Gas n' Go, she might as well try to get some information.

Billy MacCarron, or "the Mac" as he liked to call himself, was wiser than his fifteen years. He'd been in and out of foster homes his whole life, and he was no stranger to the streets of Providence Falls. As a police investigator, Cora often relied on her connections to help track down people of interest, and even though it was a Saturday and officially her day off, the previous week had been a headache. Three reports of aggravated assault on Friday, and still no one could find the attacker. Nero Polinsky, a petty criminal with an ever-growing rap sheet, was in the wind. But Cora was determined to change that.

"Nah, girl. It's about you and *the Mac*." Billy wagged a finger between them with a crooked grin. "When're you going to admit we got something going on?" His boyish face, along with the peach fuzz on his chin and freckles across his nose, reminded Cora just how young he really was. He drew a cigarette from behind his ear and pulled a lighter from his pocket. With an expert flick of his fingers, he lit the cigarette and took a long drag.

"Billy, I'm practically old enough to be your mom." It wasn't exactly true, since she was only ten years older, but it sounded good. She gave him her best stern-parent face, which might've worked better if she wasn't so much shorter than him. At five feet three inches tall, the top of her head barely came up to his chin. "And I don't have time to talk. I'm looking for Nero Polinsky. He's been on a rampage since last week, and we need to bring him in before he does any more harm."

Billy's gaze slid away, and he shrugged a bony shoulder. "I ain't seen him."

Right. The kid might smoke with the practiced ease of a Vegas slot machine addict, but he sure as hell didn't have a poker face. "You sure about that? Because I just came from Rock & Bowlers and the manager saw you talking to him an hour ago."

Billy took another drag on the cigarette. "I guess I saw him earlier, yeah. But that don't mean I know where he is now."

Cora fought for patience, knowing from experience she'd get a lot further with Billy if she gave him a little time. At heart, he was a good kid, even though he tried his best to portray the image of a tough bad boy. "Look, this isn't the first time Nero's been in trouble, and you know it. He hit up a convenience store yesterday. Beat the owner with a baseball bat. Did you know that?"

Billy's face blanched, making his freckles stand out even more. He shook his head.

"He's been getting worse, and if you have any idea where he is, you need to tell me. It could be a matter of life or death, depending on whose path he crosses next."

Billy swallowed visibly. "I didn't talk to him for very long. He just wanted to know if I had any weed—" He glanced up sharply. "Which, I didn't. I swear."

Cora nodded encouragingly. "Okay. Did he say where he was going?"

Billy looked worried. "If I tell you, do you promise not to rat me out?"

"I would never do that," Cora said with feeling. The last thing she'd ever do is put a kid like Billy at risk, or anyone in her city, for that matter. Cora had lived in the small North Carolina city tucked in the Appalachian foothills her entire life. It wasn't nearly as big or as cosmopolitan as the larger cities to the east, but what it lacked in glamour, it made up for in charm. Providence Falls had a small university known for its creative arts programs, and the town was often a summer vacation destination for state residents who wanted to go "glamping." It had all the benefits of city life, with the perk of being surrounded by forests, lakes and state parks. Cora couldn't imagine living anywhere else, and her job of keeping the peace and protecting the people meant everything to her.

"He said he was going to The Lusty Lady to talk to his ex-wife," Billy said. "Something about her owing him money."

Bingo. The Lusty Lady was a gentleman's club several blocks away near the old warehouse district. Every city had its shady side, and The Lusty Lady was smack-dab in the center of it. Cora knew Nero was as slippery as an electric eel, and just as dangerous. He seemed to have a sort of sixth sense when it came to cops, so he'd probably be long gone before she even showed up. But with any luck, she could talk to his ex and maybe get some useful information. While it crossed her mind that she wasn't on the clock, she didn't see anything wrong with driving by The Lusty Lady, just to check things out. Hey, she was in the neighborhood, after all. And people could do whatever they wanted on their days off. Some people liked to go shopping or see a movie. Today, she just happened to feel like heading down a dark alley past stinking dumpsters to a shady strip club with questionable, sticky floors. Yep.

Cora gave Billy a brilliant smile, snagged the cigarette from his mouth and crushed it on the pavement.

"Hey!" Billy looked mournfully at the ground. "That was my last one."

"Good. You're not supposed to be smoking, anyway. Here." Cora opened her tote and pulled out a take-out bag from Munchies Diner. She'd just bought lunch, but Billy probably needed it more. "Crispy chicken with all the fixings. Plus curly fries." She handed it to him.

His face lit up, but then smoothed out like he was trying to play it cool. "I'd rather have my cigarette."

She raised a delicate brow. "Just be glad I don't slap a fine on you for underage smoking."

He gave her a wounded look. "You wouldn't."

"Oh, I so totally would." She grinned and jerked a thumb at her chest. "Police, remember?"

"After all we've been through? I thought we had a thing going, you and me." Billy's dejected expression morphed into eagerness as he yanked the warm sandwich out of the bag.

"We do," Cora said, turning toward her Mini Cooper parked along the sidewalk. "We've got that thing next Tuesday afternoon, remember?"

"I wasn't talking about no internship at the Teens in Action club," Billy called over a mouthful of sandwich.

"I was." Cora gave him a cheery wave as she got into her car. Billy could make a great mentor for younger kids like him. It would give him a sense of confidence and purpose to help out; he just didn't know it yet. All he needed was a bit of a push in the right direction. Luckily, Cora had a connection at the teen center, so she'd set him up for an interview. Teens in Action was mostly run by adult volunteers, but they could always use kids to help with the daily after-school activities. So far, she hadn't had much luck getting Billy involved, but she wasn't going to give up.

Her stomach growled and she lifted her lukewarm coffee from the cup holder, took a sip and grimaced. Sighing in resignation, she took another sip as she pulled onto the main road. It wouldn't be the first time she dined on nothing but caffeinated sludge. As a police officer, it was practically a rite of passage. How many times had she watched her father wolf down bowls of cereal at the end of a long day because he'd neglected to eat on the job? Cereal for dinner was a standard operating procedure in her house growing up, at least until Cora was old enough to cook. Since her mother had died when she was little, it was always just her and her dad, which meant lots of pancakes and Pop-Tarts for dinner. Even now that he lived a few hours away in Charlotte, Cora sometimes visited during long weekends or holidays with homemade meals. Old habits died hard, and she'd gotten used to taking care of him over the years.

Cora's phone rang and she answered as she pulled onto the busy street. "McLeod."

"Are we still on for drinks at Danté's tonight?" a familiar voice demanded. "Because last time you bailed on me in the middle of my crisis."

Cora smiled at her friend Suzette Wilson's disgruntled voice. "Suze, I hardly call not fitting into your skinny jeans a crisis. Besides, I didn't bail willingly. I had to work."

"Yeah, well, someone else can be the hero this time. You can't single-handedly take down all the villains in Providence Falls. Let someone else have the limelight for a change. Anyway, it's the weekend, and you promised. I'm in dire need of a girls' night. Jimmy's been getting on my nerves ever since he started hanging around those bikers. He called me his old lady yesterday." Suzette's voice rose up a notch. "His *old lady*, Cora."

Cora wanted to laugh at her friend's outrage. "I think it's a term of endearment."

"Maybe when you're in a biker gang," Suzette pointed out with a huff. "Which, Jimmy isn't."

"True." Suzette's current boyfriend spent his days working at the Artists Loft, drinking soy decaf lattes and creating "art" on canvas via splattered paint. Mostly he just angsted around wearing fingerless gloves, doing his best to look world-weary. As he'd yet to hit it big as an artist, he tended to try on new personas.

"So I went nuclear on him, and now we're not talking," Suzette said.

Cora was glad Suzette couldn't see her grin. Her friend was always having a meltdown about something. They'd met in high school and bonded over their mutual dislike of the cafeteria food and old Mr. Sleazak's bell-bottom pants. Suzette had been new to Providence Falls High, and since Cora pretty much knew everyone and everything about her beloved city, she'd taken Suzette under her wing. Later, when everyone else graduated and moved on, both of them had stayed in town. Suzette had gone to aesthetician training, and Cora had taken the fast track toward her lifelong dream of becoming a police officer. Since she was five years old, she'd dreamed of following in her father's footsteps. Cora and Suzette's chosen career paths couldn't have been more different, but over many years and countless dating disasters, the two of them had remained fast friends.

Suzette was still going off when Cora pulled into the gravel parking lot behind The Lusty Lady a few minutes later. The building was old and weathered, with peeling pink paint and a faded sign showing a pair of legs with fishnet stockings. The parking lot wasn't even half-full, which was a good thing. A slow day meant Nero's ex-wife might be more inclined to talk. From reports yesterday, Nero was tweaking on something, and the baseball bat made him more dangerous than usual. The sooner Cora could track him down, the better. With any luck, she'd be able to find his ex with minimal effort.

"Get your hands off me!" A bleached blonde woman

came teetering out of a side door wearing a micro mini-skirt and a halter top the size of a postage stamp. Her enormous breasts were heaving in fury, and she was spewing curses at the glowering man who had a death grip on her arm. *Nero.*

"Thank you, Lady Luck," Cora murmured.

Suzette, still ranting on the other end of the phone, halted midsentence. "*Old* lady," she corrected. "Which is just stupid, since I'm only like, one month older than him."

"Suze, I have to call you back. I'm in the middle of something." Cora didn't wait for her friend to respond, but quickly disconnected and yanked a pair of handcuffs from her glove compartment. Unfortunately, she wasn't carrying her sidearm, but she'd had enough self-defense training to take him down without the threat of a gun, if it came to that.

Nero Polinsky looked like a walking stereotype as he shoved his ex and charged toward a black Dodge Ram. He was in his midthirties with a closely shaved head to hide his receding hairline, and he was wearing a Tapout shirt like an MMA fighter, except Cora doubted he'd entered a gym in over a decade. His truck had a CB whip and four headlights across the top, with a bumper sticker that read, "Gas, Ass or Grass: Nobody rides for free." And if that didn't indicate his hard-core manliness, the dangling aluminum testicles attached under the rear bumper really brought it home. *Charming.*

"I said, don't touch me," the woman screeched, tripping along behind him in her six-inch platform heels.

Nero spun around and shoved her, sending her sprawling onto the ground.

Cora inched closer, ducking behind the parked cars to stay undetected.

"I want my money, Starla," Nero shouted. "And I know you took it."

Starla wobbled, pushing herself to her feet. She scowled at her fingers, then at Nero. The look of fury on her face was hot enough to melt the aluminum balls on his truck. "You broke my nail."

Nero dug into the back of his truck and withdrew an aluminum bat. He hitched it over one shoulder and smirked at Starla.

Showtime. Cora's muscles tensed. She had to move fast before he hurt her.

"That's not all I'm gonna break, bitch." Nero spun toward the rusted Camaro beside his truck and swung the bat, shattering the taillight with a loud *crack*.

"Not my car!" Starla screeched, but Nero was on a mission, and he showed no signs of tapping out. He lifted the bat again and swung, smashing the bumper. Then the driver's side window.

"Freeze!" Cora shouted, keeping several feet of distance between her and him. It was disconcerting not to have a gun to back up her command, but she'd work with what she had. She dug into her pocket and flashed her badge at the incredulous Nero, who was blinking at her like she'd just materialized out of thin air.

"Police," Cora said in the monotone voice she'd adopted early in her career. "Drop the weapon and step away from the car."

Nero's eyebrows rose, and he let out a raspy laugh. "No can do, blondie. Why don't you head on inside and climb a pole? Do something useful with yourself."

"You're the police?" Starla gave Cora a skeptical once-over.

"I am," Cora said calmly.

Starla looked unconvinced. She pursed her cherry red lips, and said, "Girl, if you're really a cop, you're going to have to do something about your look."

"Oh, yeah?" Cora said conversationally, keeping her gaze trained on Nero. "What do you suggest?"

"For starters, you gotta lose those ringlets." Starla placed a hand on her hip and snapped her gum. She seemed to have forgotten that her unstable ex was standing just one swing away with a baseball bat. "The goldilocks thing isn't going to win you any intimidation points. And, maybe drop the mascara. It makes your blue eyes look too big and, I don't know. Blinky."

"Blinky," Cora repeated. "Got it. Thanks. Can you do me a favor, Starla, and stand just a little farther over there? I don't want you to break any more nails when I take him down."

Nero let out a bark of laughter. "You offering to go down on me, blondie? I'm game if you are."

"Just stand over there, okay?" she said to Starla, ignoring him. "This will only take a minute."

Starla glared at her broken fingernail again, then held her hands up with a look that said, *It's your funeral.* She backed away toward the wall.

Nero slapped the aluminum bat into his beefy hand, leering at Cora. "What's it gonna be, blondie? You want a piece of me?"

Cora's muscles tensed, preparing for whatever came next. "I don't suppose you'd do the smart thing and just toss the bat and come with me quietly?"

His oily gaze slid over her body, taking in her tennis shoes, dark denim jeans and fitted T-shirt. Up close, Cora could see his dilated pupils and the slight shake of his hands. Whatever Nero was on, it wasn't weed. He licked his lips, leering at her chest. "Let Nero take you for a ride, doll. I guarantee *you* won't be coming quietly."

Starla let out a derisive snort. "Because she won't be coming at all."

Nero sent Starla a murderous glare. He tightened his grip on the bat, then spun and took out the windshield of her car.

Starla shrieked, spewing more profanities that mostly called his sexual stamina into question. Apparently, this was a hot button with Nero, because he roared, raised the bat and bolted toward Starla.

Cora burst into action. She blocked his path, falling back on her twelve years of karate and self-defense training.

He wound the bat, ready to swing. She shot forward, closing the distance between them, using a chop block on his arms before he could gain any momentum with the bat. Lightning fast, she slid her hand underneath his arm and grabbed the bat above his grip. Yanking back hard, she pulled it free and tossed it behind her.

Nero blinked in thunderous surprise.

Cora quickly grabbed his hand, pulling him down into a wrist lock, twisting with just the right amount of pressure. He yelped, his face contorting in pain as he dropped to his knees.

Cora grimaced. She had him now. "Down on the ground."

He toppled face-first, his foul curses muffled in the gravel.

She drove her knee hard into his kidney, then pulled her cuffs from her back pocket and slapped them on his wrists. It was over in less than ten seconds.

Then Cora glanced at Starla, who was gaping at her as

if she'd just grown a pair of horns. "Call 911," Cora said calmly.

Starla swallowed visibly, then nodded. "Dang, girl. Never mind the ringlets. You've got moves."

It was seven o'clock that evening when Cora found herself ordering another round of margaritas at a university pub. She'd been only half listening to Suzette gush over the new laser machine at the medical spa where she worked. She was obsessed with all the latest and greatest beauty trends, and even though Cora was interested in "fighting the good fight," as Suzette put it, she could only take so much talk of skin care and facial treatments.

"But enough about injectables. I think I found you a roommate," Suzette announced, licking residual salt from the rim of her glass. Her red hair was pulled back into an artfully messy bun, and with her hazel, kohl-rimmed bedroom eyes, she looked like she always did—over-the-top glamorous. "He's one of Jimmy's friends, and he needs a place to stay right away."

Cora gave Suzette a look and stirred the slush in the bottom of her margarita glass. Her gut instinct was to turn away any friend associated with Jimmy, but she was in dire need of someone to help with the rent. Ever since her previous roommate decided to move to Sri Lanka, Cora had been struggling to cover all the bills. If she was ever going to save up enough money to put an offer on her dream house, she needed to find someone soon. "Is he an artist like Jimmy?"

"Well…" Suzette's gaze slid sideways, which was never a good sign. "He's definitely artistic, but he's more like a musician."

"*Like* a musician," Cora repeated, growing suspicious.

"What kind of musician are we talking? Symphony orchestra, or drummer in a band?" Her current rental house was in a cramped neighborhood where the homes were practically shoulder to shoulder. She could almost reach out her window and touch the house next door. If her new roommate was going to be a drummer in a band, she wouldn't be winning any points with the neighbors when he practiced in the garage.

"He's very talented," Suzette said with too-wide eyes.

Cora leaned back and crossed her arms. "Let's hear it."

"Okay." Suzette took a deep breath. "He just moved to Providence Falls, so he doesn't have a full-time job yet. But he's currently a one-man-band performer over in the town square." She held her hand up because Cora was already rolling her eyes. "But he's really talented and he has this amazing harmonica attached to a—"

"Save it," Cora said, grateful for the fresh margarita the server set in front of her. "The last thing I need is a guy whose income relies heavily on the mercy of tourists."

"Fine." Suzette couldn't suppress a giggle. "I'm just trying to help, and I've exhausted all my resources."

"Hey, ladies," a quiet, masculine voice said.

Cora turned to see the perfectly refined, perfectly polite defense attorney, Finley Walsh, standing beside her. He was a friend of her father's, and Cora had met him a few years ago when he was working on a case she'd been following. Occasionally they ran into each other at the bar, and a couple of times her dad brought him to her house on their way to go golfing. Even though Finn was only a few years older than her, he always just seemed so reserved and, well…a little bit on the stuffy side. He was attractive enough—that wasn't the problem. With his sandy-blond hair and broad shoulders, no one would argue that he wasn't easy on the eyes, but he reminded Cora of one of those guys on the BBC channel. The kind who sat in leather armchairs drinking brandy and saying things like, *Now, see here, my good man.* Maybe it was the meticulous way he dressed, with the designer suits and ties. Or maybe it was his hair that was always so neatly arranged. It made Cora want to reach out with both hands and muss it up sometimes. Like now, after she'd had a few drinks.

"Hi, Finn," Cora said, sitting up straighter. Why did she always do that in his presence? He made her feel like she needed to be on her best behavior. It was annoying. "You know my friend Suzette."

Suzette gave a cheery wave. "Good to see you again, Finn. For some reason, Cora can't remember that we've all had drinks together before, but don't hold it against her. She's tipsy right now. Had a tough day arresting bad guys."

"I am not tipsy," Cora said indignantly, even though she was feeling a little fuzzy around the edges. "And I only arrested one bad guy."

"Did you?" Finn smiled down at Cora and she blinked, because the warmth in his eyes made him seem suddenly less stuffy and more...something else. Alluring, maybe?

She glanced away sharply and took another sip of her margarita. The drinks must be strong tonight.

Finn looked like he was about to say something, but her phone rang. It was her father again. He'd called twice in a half hour. "Excuse me. I need to take this outside." She slid from her chair and made her way across the crowded pub, exiting the side door where it would be easier to hear over the muted street traffic. She pressed one finger to her ear and answered her phone. "Hey, Dad. What's up?"

"Cora, there you are." Her dad's voice sounded stern

and determined, the way he always did when he was on a mission. "I've been trying to reach you for over an hour."

"Believe it or not, sometimes I do crazy things like go places with my friends on a Saturday night."

"Where are you?"

"I'm down at the docks searching for my next drug hit. You know, the usual," Cora teased, leaning against the wall. "There's this guy here in a white unmarked van who says he has puppies and candy in the back. He seems really nice, so I'm going to go check it out."

Her father didn't take the bait. "Cora, I've found you a roommate."

She straightened her spine and pushed off the wall. It wasn't like her father not to joke with her, at least a little. Ever since she was a kid, he'd been overprotective of her, and now that she was a cop, she sometimes teased him about it. But tonight, he sounded carefully controlled. Serious. "What do you mean?"

A slight pause. "Are you aware that there's a new transfer in your department?"

"I heard something about it." There was talk all last week at the station, but she didn't know much beyond that. "They're pulling bets to see who gets stuck with the new guy. How'd you know about it?"

He made a huffing sound. "I'm retired, kiddo. Not dead."

Cora smiled. Even though her father lived hours away and was no longer the police chief in Providence Falls, old habits died hard with him. He still had friends in town and kept his finger on the pulse. She shouldn't have been surprised.

"He can be your new roommate," her dad stated. "He's moving there from Raleigh, and he needs a place to live."

Cora raised her brows. There were several reasons why

that wasn't a good idea, but she decided to address the most surprising one. "Wow, Dad. A *guy*? I never would've thought you'd be on board with me having a male roommate, even if he is an officer of the law."

"This is different," he declared. "It'll be a win-win situation for both of you." She got the feeling he'd already made up his mind for her. Sometimes he still treated her like she was a little girl in pigtails who needed him to solve all her problems.

"Dad," she warned. "I don't need your help with this."

There was a long pause. "Remember back when you were ten, and there was a shooting at that bank on Twenty-Fourth?"

An old feeling of unease tiptoed down Cora's spine. "Of course, I remember. Your partner took a bullet in the chest and almost died." She hadn't slept well for weeks after she found out. They'd even visited his partner in the hospital afterward. Cora remembered how the man looked, lying there on the bed, skin as pale as the sheet covering him. He'd had dark circles under his eyes, and he was hooked up to an IV and machines that beeped. Even though the man rallied and forced a smile during their visit, Cora had hated being there because it reminded her of her mother dying from cancer when she was much younger. It reminded her how easily it could've been her father in that room. "What does that have to do with anything?"

"I never told you this, but he saved my life. It would've been me in the line of fire, but he jumped in the way to block the bullet."

"Oh, my God." Shock rippled through her. "Why didn't you tell me?"

"You were ten years old," Hugh said, as if that were all the explanation he needed to give. "I wasn't going to give you any more reasons to worry. Not after you'd already lost your mother."

Cora shook her head in annoyance. "But you could've told me later. I'm twenty-five, for God's sake. It never occurred to you to bring that up?"

"Frankly, no. It wasn't relevant, but I'm bringing it up now." Hugh's voice took on an authoritative edge.

Cora gritted her teeth. Yet another thing that drove her crazy about her dad. He was always trying to shield her from things, even though she was a grown woman who could handle her own emotions. She'd been five when she lost her mother. It had been hard, and Cora secretly believed her father never really recovered from it, but she'd been in kindergarten back then. That was decades ago, and she didn't need him to shield her anymore.

"Remember how my partner retired after that and moved away to Raleigh?" Hugh continued. "Well, he had a son back in Ireland from a previous marriage. His son moved to the US years ago and ended up becoming a cop like his dad. His name's Liam O'Connor. He's been on the force in Raleigh for the past few years, and he's the one transferring to your station. I promised his father I'd look out for him, so I mentioned you having room at your house—"

"Dad!" Cora flung a hand up in exasperation. Already miffed at him for not telling her about the shooting, this just added to it. "You shouldn't have said anything without asking me first. I get that you want to do your old partner a favor, but it's not your call. Choosing a roommate is personal. I'll take care of it myself."

"There's no need for you to go looking when I've already found the perfect solution," he insisted. She could tell he felt strongly about it, which had to be a manifestation of his old sense of loyalty toward his ex-partner, but that didn't mean she had to fall in line with his plan.

Cora sighed heavily as her dad launched into a detailed explanation of all the reasons she should take his advice. She suddenly felt like a bristling teenager again, and it only made her more determined to do things her own way. Her father tended to roll through life like a bulldozer. He was the type of man who said or did whatever he needed to, without worrying about the aftermath. When it came to giving orders and getting his way, Hugh McLeod took no prisoners. But what made him good at his job didn't always transfer well to parenting. He used to drive Cora nuts growing up, until she realized his overbearing and protective nature stemmed from a combination of love and fear. He'd already lost his wife, and he couldn't bear the thought of losing his daughter. But she was a grown woman now, with a career and a life all her own, and she would make her own decisions. Besides, the last thing she needed was a roommate who both lived *and* worked with her. That was just way too close for comfort. If this was her dad's mission tonight, then he was going to be sorely disappointed. She lifted her chin and prepared to butt heads with the bulldozer.

3

Waking up to birdsong in one's ears was normally a pleasant experience, but this bird sounded like a harpy. Its rhythmic squawking grew louder with every passing moment until Liam felt like it was screeching from inside his skull. He cracked open one eye and stared at the flashing electronic clock on the table next to him. Not pausing to wonder how he knew exactly what it was, he slapped the alarm off and rolled onto his back with a groan.

A familiar floral scent enveloped him. Liam rubbed his face and slowly opened his eyes. The ceiling above him was pristine, white and perfectly smooth, like the surface of a frozen pond on a winter day. He shifted on the plush mattress, recognizing at once that it was nothing like any bed he'd ever slept in before. The robin's-egg blue sheets were soft, and the warm body beside him, softer. He squinted at the woman's lush black hair fanned out on the pillow, taking in the delicate slope of her bare shoulder and the supple curve of her hip under the sheets.

His mouth curved in appreciation. Sure, he'd been thrust into the future with a ridiculous task, and he was in danger of suffering the eternal fires of hell if he didn't succeed, but he had to give the angels some credit. Waking up with a lovely woman in his bed was a damned fine way to begin. Maybe they were giving him some encouragement. Maybe they just wanted him to embrace this new life with passion and enthusiasm.

Rising to his elbow, he peered at her sleeping face, instantly recognizing the woman as his on-again, off-again mistress from his former life. Margaret Brady wasn't the type of woman a man could easily forget. She'd been beautiful back then, and clearly her reincarnated self hadn't changed. He wondered if she still had that same come-hither smile, or those skillful hands, or—more importantly—if she was married in this life, too. The memory of Margaret's cold, calculating husband was like a bucket of ice water over his head.

Liam rubbed a hand over his throat, confused and somewhat frustrated at finding himself in bed with Margaret. Was it some kind of joke, then? Were the angels watching him, laughing from up above in their mist-filled room? He sat up and took in his surroundings.

The plush furniture and lustrous fabric were distinctly feminine, with soft colors and ruffled cushions making it clear to Liam he was in Margaret's bedroom. In the past, she'd loved flowers and plants, and she'd been renowned for her beautiful gardens. It seemed her love of nature was still strong. There were floral paintings on the walls, and the cushioned chairs near the windows were covered in a leafy vine pattern. One of the side tables held a huge crystal vase filled with blooms. A framed photograph on the wall caught Liam's attention. It showed Margaret as a bride in a white lacy gown, standing beside a smiling, older man Liam recognized. It was her same husband from the past, only this man in the picture seemed more relaxed and happy.

"Liam," Margaret's sleepy voice murmured. "What time is it?"

He glanced over at the clock on the nightstand. Strange how he knew about things like digital clocks and photographs. The angels had said they'd give him some knowledge of this century. "Eight thirty." He leaned against the padded headboard.

Margaret's throaty sigh and soft hand on his shoulder made his body stir. Even after all that had happened, he wasn't immune to her charms. Although he was in love with the sweet Cora, Margaret Brady was a veritable siren, and he was a man, after all. A man who'd spent several lifetimes without the finer pleasures so tantalizingly displayed in front of him.

"Come back to sleep, early bird. Since I don't have to work today, I plan to waste my entire morning in bed." She rolled over and rose on her elbows, revealing the soft swell of her breasts. "With you."

Liam cocked his head in surprise. In the past, Margaret had been a wealthy, married woman. She'd never had to work a day in her life. "Where do you work?"

She peered up at him from beneath dark lashes, her wide gray eyes sparkling with humor. Her lush, full lips slowly curved up at the corners.

Well, that answered that. Liam swallowed hard. She still had the come-hither smile.

"You know where I work, silly." Margaret reached out and gave him a playful shove.

"Aye, I do." Liam scooted down and draped an arm over her. "But let's pretend I don't. Tell me the story of how we met."

Margaret stifled a yawn and laid her head on his shoulder, running a manicured hand over his broad chest. "Once upon a time, there was a drop-dead gorgeous, total hottie."

"I'm glad you think so."

Margaret lifted a delicate brow. "Who says I was talking about you?"

Liam gave her a sudden, tight squeeze and she laughed.

"As I was saying," Margaret continued. "Once upon a time there was this total hottie who worked as a botany professor at Providence Falls University."

"Ah, that would be your job," Liam said with a nod. "You're the botany teacher. You've always loved plants and flowers, so it makes sense."

Margaret lifted her head. "Will you stop interrupting? I thought you wanted the story."

"I do." Liam took the quilt and drew it over them. "Go on."

"So, this hot botany professor had to go to a business conference in Raleigh for a few days. One evening while she was at a bar, she met a tall, dark—"

"Incredibly fit and handsome—"

She covered his mouth with her hand. "*Annoying* man. This tall, dark and annoying man was named Liam O'Connor. At first, all he did was send her hot, smoldering looks from across the room. Then he sent her a drink, and finally, he walked over and tossed her the old 'Do you come here often?' pickup line. She was not impressed."

He gave her a wicked grin. "Liar."

"She wasn't," Margaret insisted, laughing. "He was a shameless flirt. But they got to talking, and over the next few hours, he unleashed his avalanche of charm. She found out he was planning on moving to Providence Falls, too, which was an intriguing coincidence. So, before the poor botany professor had a chance to order a third vodka tonic, he was taking her by the hand and leading her out the door."

Liam raised a brow. "And then?"

"And then…" Margaret slid her hand lower to trace the defined ridges of muscle on his abdomen. "Then the botany professor took him back to her hotel room and was so blinded by his godlike physique, she decided it didn't matter that he wasn't smart or interesting."

Liam gave her a warning look and slid a hand teasingly over her rib cage. He let it hover just over her ribs with a wicked gleam in his eyes.

Margaret's mouth twitched as she struggled to keep a straight face. "And she didn't care that his hair was a shaggy mess, either." Margaret shrieked with laughter as he began to tickle her. "Because his hot body was—was—" she gasped for breath "—all that really mattered."

He flipped her onto her back with expert precision and rolled on top of her, until her laughter eased and she began placing sinfully delicious kisses along his neck.

"That's quite a story, Professor," Liam murmured, trying to focus. It wasn't easy when she was sliding her talented hands over his backside. "How does it end?"

She wrapped her long legs around his waist and rolled until she was on top again. "I could tell you, but I'd rather show you."

Liam was just about to throw caution to the wind and embrace his new life with passion and enthusiasm, when a shrill ringing sound came from the bedside table. He tried to ignore it, instead focusing on Margaret's mouth as she lapped her way down his chest. The ringing continued, and Liam muttered a curse under his breath.

Margaret giggled. "Did you just say, 'bollocks'?"

He blinked down at her. "No." If he was going to fit in, he'd need to adapt his manner of speaking. The angels had undoubtedly taken care of most of it, but they wouldn't be instilling modern curse words in his head, which was a pity because curse words were often quite useful. Those, he'd just have to learn on his own.

"You should probably answer that," she said, rolling away and sliding from the bed. "And since we're both up now, let's go get breakfast."

Liam watched her rise, gloriously naked, to tread lightly across the plush blue carpet. She flicked on the bathroom light and it highlighted the enticing curves of her body. Before, he'd never actually seen her naked in full light. They'd always had clandestine meetings late at night when her husband was away.

"Liam?"

He dragged his gaze up to her face. "Mmm?"

"Your phone?" She pointed to the still-ringing phone, then closed the door behind her.

"Right." He fumbled for it, automatically knowing which buttons to press. That was convenient. For a moment he just stared at the device in his hand, testing its weight and marveling at the vivid, flashing lights. He wondered what other skills the angels had bestowed on him to navigate this new world. The ringing continued until he finally swiped the screen and answered. "Yes?"

"Liam, it's Hugh McLeod."

Liam's hand trembled as he held the phone to his ear.

The squire. This was unexpected. He needed to tread lightly to figure out his role here.

"I told Cora," Hugh continued. "She knows about you needing a place to stay."

Liam struggled to sound neutral. It was disconcerting to hear Cora's father speaking so plainly in his ear. Squire McLeod's voice still held that quiet ring of authority. Liam fought for composure. "Hello…" My lord? Sir? Best just to skip it. "How are you?"

Cora's father made a guttural sound of dismissal. "I'm fine, Liam. Fine as can be, but it's your situation we need to figure out."

"All right." Liam stared around the room as if the floral curtains and dainty objects could give him answers.

"I think you should live with my daughter," Hugh declared.

Liam choked a little, uncertain if he'd heard the man correctly. "Come again?"

"It just makes sense. You're new to Providence Falls. You're both police investigators. Heck, you'll even be working at the same station together. And Cora's been looking for a roommate for a while now, so I say, why not you?"

Liam struggled with the knowledge that he was now supposed to be an officer of the law. The irony there was laughable, but first things first. "You want me to move into Cora's house," he said, incredulous. "To live and eat and… *sleep* there under the same roof? With your daughter?"

"Of course, Liam, what else would I mean—"

"Sounds great." Sounds bloody damn well *fantastic.* He grinned like a lunatic, never one to look a gift horse in the mouth. He was beginning to like this assignment more and more. "When can I move in?"

"Well, that's the problem," Hugh continued, "Cora's not on board yet. I brought up the idea with her yesterday and she flat out refused. I asked her to take you in as a special favor to me since your father and I were partners, but she doesn't think that's enough justification for her to have to... How did she put it? Ah, yes, 'bring a potential creep-a-zoid under her roof.'"

Liam flinched. He felt as if he'd been hit over the head with a river rock. Cora thought he was a creep. He'd almost forgotten. They were complete strangers in this life.

Hugh chuckled, then added, "I assured her you're a fine upstanding man, just like your father, but she's not convinced since she's never met you."

Liam gritted his teeth. "Fine and upstanding" may be a bit of a stretch, but he wasn't a creep. Never mind the part where he'd crawled through her bedroom window in the dead of night the first time they'd ever met. And the fact that he'd intended to rob her blind. And the fact that he'd ruined her destiny. "I'll just have to do my best to prove I'm trustworthy."

"You shouldn't have to, but Cora can be a bit stubborn," Hugh said with a note of apology in his voice. "Still, you can't stay in that crap motel forever. I told your father I'd look out for you, and I'm going to do my damnedest."

It was odd to hear Cora's father take such an interest in his well-being. Liam made a noncommittal sound, hoping it was enough. He had no idea what his background story was, so it was safer to say nothing. There was so much he didn't know, and the angels certainly hadn't been forthcoming with their information. As frustrating as it was to have to piece together his role in this life, it was even harder to have to accept that Cora didn't know him, trust him, or even like the idea of him. His fingers clenched on a feather pillow, and he flung it across the room.

"Don't worry about it. She's one tough cookie, my daughter. I didn't raise her to be reckless." There was a note of pride in Hugh's voice. "But she's smart, and she'll come around. As far as roommates go, I told her you're the safest bet she's got."

Safe. Liam scoffed. Of course, he was safe. He *loved* her. But she wouldn't know that now, would she? He sent another pillow hurtling across the room. The bed comforter followed, narrowly missing Margaret's vase of flowers. He was so irritated, he could barely focus on what Hugh was saying. Surely, the love they'd shared still meant something. It didn't matter that this wasn't the same world anymore. She would remember him, wouldn't she? Some part of her *had* to. He felt certain of it. The angels might have set everything up to their perfect specifications this time around, but they couldn't just expect him to shut his feelings off. Maybe they were wrong about everything, and he'd be damned if he'd just follow along like some mindless—

A draft of frigid air suddenly blew across his skin, sending a chill down his spine. It radiated outward, sending crackles of freezing energy along his nerve endings until it was difficult to move. Liam tried to draw in a steadying breath. After several terrifying seconds, the cold dissipated and he could breathe normally again. It was clear the angels were sending him a message. He'd be well and truly damned if he *didn't* let this scene play out the way the angels wanted, and he needed to remember that. "Point taken," Liam murmured, running a shaking hand over his face.

Hugh paused, then said, "So, anyway, I'm driving in to town, and I'm taking you to meet Cora this morning."

Liam jackknifed off the bed. "Now? Today?" Elation gripped him, followed quickly by anxiety. He ached to see her again, but he'd be a complete stranger to her. How would he bear it?

"Yes, she agreed to meet you, but only because she already had plans to make me breakfast today, and I told her I was bringing you along. She assured me she doesn't plan on changing her mind about you." Hugh chuckled again. "So, you'll have to charm her into liking you enough to keep you around."

Liam clenched his jaw as he paced the room. "I'll see what I can do." Charm was never a problem for him, especially when it came to the opposite sex. But Cora wasn't just any woman, and he'd never been in a situation like this before. Not when his heart was involved. He suddenly felt like a newborn colt on unsteady footing.

"She's got her sights set on some fancy cottage house that's supposed to go on the market before the end of the year, and she's trying to save money," Hugh continued. "With her gunning to find a roommate, it's perfect timing, you transferring there. Kind of funny, the way everything just fell into place."

"Aye," Liam said grimly. "Very funny." He could just imagine the angels kicking back on their misty reclining couches with their gilded feet propped on poufy clouds, grinning as they watched this all play out. He scowled. Why couldn't they have given him some kind of magical shield to dull his emotions, so he wouldn't feel so raw? Did they *want* him to fail? Angels were supposed to be helpful and good. But maybe people like him only got the doom-and-gloom, fire-and-brimstone kind with the scary ultimatums.

"So, I'll swing by the motel and pick you up in twenty minutes," Hugh was saying.

Liam snapped back to the moment. "I'm not at the motel."

"Where are you, then?"

Liam walked to the curtains and drew them open. The downtown streets of Providence Falls were teeming with traffic. Somehow, he knew all about automobiles and bicycles and modern-day conveyances, but it was still startling to see the cars speeding by. There was movement everywhere, and smooth pavement in the place of mud and dirt. Neatly groomed hedges and trees lined the streets, with shops as far as he could see. The only things that looked remotely familiar were the hills and forest off in the distance. Everything in the town seemed sleek edged, orderly and clean. A far cry from his village in Ireland. Across the street was a park with an iron statue of a lion by the sidewalk.

"I'll meet you at the lion statue," Liam said. "Near the park."

"Belltown Heights? What are you doing over in that ritzy neighborhood? Hopefully not looking for places to live, unless you plan on robbing a bank."

"Not anytime soon." Liam located his clothes in a heap on the floor. "I was just going to have breakfast with... a friend."

"Ah. I see." From the way Hugh's voice rose slightly, it was clear he did see.

Liam's knee-jerk reaction was alarm, until he remembered that this was a different life. Hugh didn't think of him as a poor tenant farmer anymore, and he certainly had no reason to suspect him of foul play with Cora, so Liam had no reason to worry. If Hugh assumed Liam was involved with someone, it wasn't his business to comment on it.

"I'll be ready when you get here," Liam assured him.

They got off the phone and Liam dressed quickly. The black, short-sleeved shirt was luxurious and soft, and he marveled at the stretch as he pulled it over his head. He hitched on the sturdy, dark blue pants, then pulled on a pair of leather shoes that molded perfectly to his feet. He was striding back and forth, enjoying the bounce in the shoes and the ease of movement the new clothes afforded him, when Margaret emerged from the bathroom wrapped in a towel.

"What happened in here?" She stared at the jumble of bedding and pillows strewn across the room, then at him. "And why are you doing lunges?"

Liam scooped up the bedding and tossed it back on the bed. "I've just had a call from the—" he stumbled over Squire McLeod's old title "—from…an old friend of my father's. He's taking me somewhere this morning, so I can't stay."

Margaret's full lips formed a sensual pout that Liam remembered well. She lifted a bare shoulder and let the towel slide off her naked body. "Have it your way." She ran a hand across his back as she sashayed over to a chest of drawers against the wall. "Now that you've moved here, we'll have plenty of time to get together. It'll be nice living in the same town, don't you think?"

Did he? He wasn't so sure. Margaret was a complication he hadn't expected. He cared for her, yes. But he had Cora to focus on now. And, of course, the small matter of his soul facing everlasting damnation. *Aye.* He nodded. That's where his focus needed to stay.

It seemed to appease Margaret, because she gave him a sultry smile. Then she took a chemise from the drawer, raised her slender arms and pulled it slowly over her head.

Liam watched as the pale blue satin slid over her naked curves. Margaret Brady had the body of a goddess, and she knew how to use it. That much hadn't changed. In another life, he'd have taken her hard and fast, throwing her body to the bed and caution to the wind. But that was before he found out the wind could retaliate. And it was merciless.

Several minutes later, Liam found himself leaning against the stone lion near the park, trying to remind himself that caution was a good thing, and he'd been wise to walk away from the warm and willing Margaret. He'd made his excuses to her and she'd been quietly accepting, which had been a big surprise. Back in his time, Margaret had been hotheaded and prone to sulking if she didn't get her way. On more than one occasion, Liam had been the recipient of her rants, and he was grateful to avoid one today. Small mercies, and all that.

A dark SUV pulled up to the sidewalk. Hugh McLeod waved from the driver's seat.

Liam placed a steadying hand on the lion's mane, taking a moment to ground himself. Cora's father looked very much like the squire he remembered, but there were distinct differences that were impossible to miss. Squire McLeod had had pasty skin, a few missing teeth, and a round, paunchy belly. This man was the complete opposite. He had a muscular, compact frame, gray, cropped hair and what appeared to be a full set of healthy teeth. He was also tanned from the sun, as if he spent a lot of time outdoors.

The difference was remarkable, and it reminded Liam just how far from his comfort zone this new world was.

Hugh rolled down the window. "Are you getting in, or are you waiting for that lion to give you courage?"

Liam squared his shoulders and quickly got into the car.

"Don't worry about meeting Cora," Hugh said with a chuckle as he pulled onto the busy street. "She's going to love you."

Liam's heart squeezed. "I hope so." But as he stared at the buildings, the shops and the people rushing by, a sinking feeling settled in the pit of his stomach. If he was going to save his soul, then she could never love him again. The angels had set him up for torture. He clenched his fists and wondered—not for the first time—if this was all some joke and he'd really been sent to hell, after all.

Hugh drove through the busy neighborhood, then pulled onto a highway. The bustling streets gave way to a sleek road flanked on either side by gently sloping hills, thick with trees.

Liam rolled down the window and stuck his hand out to feel the wind on his face. Thanks to the angels giving him some basic knowledge of the modern world, he was comfortable with automobiles, but he still marveled at the speed. No conveyance he remembered could match this. He breathed in the balmy morning air, letting it soothe his senses. Even though the landscape was different from the Ireland he remembered, he loved the scent of damp earth and green things growing. It gave him a sense of comfort to know that nature didn't change, even when the rest of the world did.

"Cora's making us breakfast, so you're in for a treat," Hugh said. "She's a wonderful cook. Had to be, poor thing. Ever since her mother died when she was little, she sort of took over the role of housekeeper, and all that. Which is a damned good thing, since my cooking skills are terrible."

Liam wondered just how much of the past the angels had reorchestrated. There was so much he still didn't know, so he'd need to tread carefully. "It's a shame Cora lost her mother so young."

"Yes. The cancer was…" Hugh's knuckles whitened on the steering wheel. "We thought she was going to beat it, but then she contracted pneumonia and couldn't recover." His voice was too matter-of-fact. Too carefully neutral. Cora's father still mourned his wife.

"I'm sorry," Liam said. Even though he never knew the woman, he knew how deeply the loss affected Cora, too. She'd lived a very sheltered, uneventful life in the shadow of her mother's death.

"Damned monster, cancer. Not right for a mother to die so young," Hugh said, taking an off-ramp that led into a quaint residential neighborhood. The houses were small and close together, but the streets were clean and easily accessible. "But you'd know all about that, yourself. I'm sorry about your mother's passing. A car accident, and you just eighteen…" He shook his head and trailed off.

Liam remained silent, frantically piecing together his backstory based on their conversation. His real mother back in his time had died in childbirth, along with the baby. His father followed a few months later, leaving only Liam and his brother to work the land.

Hugh took a deep sigh and thumped his hand on the steering wheel. "Well, you know how the song goes. Only the good, and all that."

Liam glanced at Hugh. "What song?"

"'Only the Good Die Young.'"

When Liam didn't respond, Hugh looked shocked. "Billy Joel?"

Liam shook his head, and Hugh muttered, "Jesus, I'm old."

"Ridiculous, at any rate," Liam said. "I know plenty of sinners who've died young." Himself, included. He raked a hand through his hair and stared blindly out the window.

"Well, I know your father was thrilled when you left Ireland and moved to the US. The day you decided to become a police officer, he called me up to brag. When he was my partner back in the day, he used to carry your picture around in his wallet. I bet he still does, doesn't he?"

Liam struggled to come up with a vague answer that would appease Hugh, and instead shrugged. How the hell would he know what his fake father did or didn't do?

"I know your parents split when you were a baby," Hugh said kindly. "But your father always talked about you. He was proud of you, you know."

A flash of anger spiked through Liam, surprising in its intensity. "Sure," he said through clenched teeth. Everything about his presence here was built on a foundation of lies. This was all just a charade, and it felt wrong. Strange, when he'd never had a problem lying in the past. As a thief, spinning a tale had always come as naturally to him as breathing, but this felt different. He wasn't in control of this mess of lies, so there was no way for him to navigate through it with confidence. He felt like a fallen leaf caught in a stream, bumping into every jagged rock as it was pulled helplessly forward.

Before Hugh could comment further, something up ahead caught his attention. "Ah." He slowed the car and broke into a smile. "There's my girl."

Liam looked up and suddenly felt as if all the sunlight in the sky had coalesced into one perfect spot. *Cora.*

She was digging through the mailbox when Hugh parked the car across the street from her house. A riot of blond curls floated around her head, and Liam was both shocked and captivated by the skintight black pants and fitted top she was wearing. Her body was leaner and more toned than he remembered, but she still had the soft curves he'd admired over a lifetime ago. When she turned toward them, Liam's mouth opened on a shaky exhale. If she'd been lovely before, she was downright breathtaking now.

Her eyes were the same bright blue, but there were subtle changes in her face. Her luminous skin had been kissed by the sun, there was a light sprinkling of freckles over her slightly smaller nose, and her lips seemed fuller and a deeper pink than he remembered. When he knew her before, she'd been only seventeen and just on the cusp of womanhood. Now she was all grown-up and more vividly beautiful than ever. This was a version of Cora he'd never seen, but greatly appreciated. And it wasn't just her face. *Christ.* She was wearing a thin, short-sleeved top that clung to her curves, leaving nothing to the imagination. Except Liam still took a moment to imagine, in great detail, what she must look like underneath—

"Come on." Hugh's gruff voice snapped Liam back to the moment as he cut the engine and got out of the car.

Liam followed Hugh across the street until he was standing before the woman he loved. The woman he'd risked everything to have. The woman who was staring at him right now with barely concealed distrust, like he was a goddamned stranger.

4

Cora watched the tall stranger get out of the car with her father. Her skin instantly pricked with physical awareness, and her stomach fluttered as he approached. She had the strangest sense of déjà vu. His gaze was so intense, she couldn't look him in the eyes. At least, not yet.

She took an involuntary step back to stay grounded. He was at least a foot taller than her, with broad, muscular shoulders, tanned skin and a body that indicated he was no stranger to exercise. He moved with the easy, casual grace of an athlete who was comfortable in his own skin. She'd guess he was a runner, like her, except the thick ropy muscles on his arms and chest meant he must spend a lot of time in the gym. Strange. For some reason, Cora couldn't imagine him lifting weights indoors. He seemed more like a rock climbing, extreme sports type of guy. A crease formed between her brows. Then again, how would she know? She never even knew he existed until her father told her about him last night.

She glanced at her dad, whose overeager smile made it obvious he was still hoping to change her mind about the roommate thing. Cora gave an inward sigh and waited as they approached. She loved her dad. He'd always been a strong and steadfast presence in her life, raising her to believe in justice and honor and all those heroic things a good police captain would. But all her life, her father had been overprotective and controlling. Not letting her go camping with friends because it was too dangerous. Not letting her go on the beach field trip because she could get a cramp and drown. Heck, he hadn't even let her go on dates until she'd begged him for months. And even then, she'd had to text him every half hour to let him know she was safe. It was no wonder she didn't get asked out much. Nobody wanted to deal with Captain McLeod. He was a formidable presence in any given situation. To a teenage boy, he must've seemed like a holy terror. All of that could be forgiven, though, because she loved him. But at times like this, his meddling really got on her nerves.

Now that Liam O'Connor was standing before her, Cora studied him with reluctant interest. Okay, so he was definitely not a "golden boy." The way her father talked him up, one would think Liam was single-handedly responsible for pulling the sun across the sky. But this guy looked more like a dark, sexy highwayman. The kind in stories who accosted innocent women in carriages with their sinfully wicked ways. He had glossy dark hair that waved around his tanned face. A firm jaw with a shadow of stubble. A straight nose. Strong, masculine features and full, sensual lips. Yep. This man was what her friend Suzette would call "*GQ* magazine hot." Utterly, undeniably handsome.

And his eyes… Cora bit the insides of her cheeks, fighting the crazy urge to either move in for a hug, or back away. *What the heck?*

The intensity in his deep brown eyes was unsettling. He looked like a man dying of thirst who was standing before an oasis. His expression was an odd mixture of disbelief, joy and longing, and she suddenly felt as if he were speaking volumes to her, though he said nothing. Cora took a tiny step back, shocked to realize how eager he was to be there. Clearly, he'd anticipated this meeting far more than she had. He must really need a place to stay.

"Liam, this is Cora," Hugh said with forced cheer. "Cora, meet Liam O'Connor."

She waited.

Liam stepped forward and began to raise his hands, almost as if he were going to reach for her, then thought better of it. "Hello, Cora. I'm pleased to…meet you." Something flashed across his face. Frustration? She had no idea. This guy was handsome, yes, but something felt off. Suzette would probably love him. She had a thing for the weird ones.

"Hi," Cora said, holding out her hand. She wasn't thrilled that her father brought him to breakfast, but she could rally. She'd just have to find a good way to make it clear she had no intention of taking him on as a roommate. Unfortunately, he seemed even more eager than her dad.

Liam stared at her outstretched hand, then his mouth curved up at the corners. When he closed his large, calloused hand around hers, Cora felt a sudden *whoosh* of vertigo.

She stumbled back a step, then straightened. Damn the uneven sidewalk. "Should we go inside?"

Liam was scowling down at his palm in confusion, muttering something under his breath.

She spun and hurried toward the house, trying to shake off her ridiculous reaction. She was slightly hungover from the night before. That would explain the momentary dizziness. All she needed was breakfast and everything would be fine. She glanced over her shoulder at the dark highwayman. Totally fine.

They followed her inside the old tract house. Like the rest of the homes in her neighborhood, it was built in the late '70s with the dark wood paneling and harvest gold kitchen counters. She'd tried to spruce the walls up by painting them a soft, sky blue, and adding colorful art prints, but Cora had no love for the place. It was just a rental, and she had her sights set on something far better.

"This is a lovely home," Liam said as he stood in the middle of the tiny living room. He turned in a circle, and if Cora didn't know any better, she'd say he looked completely charmed. Huh. Either he was a fantastic actor, or he was into La-Z-Boy furniture rejects and glittery popcorn ceilings.

Her dad began telling Liam about the neighborhood, the easy access to the highway and how Cora's roommate moved away a few months ago. He glanced at Cora a few times to try to rope her into the conversation, but she pretended not to notice. She knew exactly what her dad was doing, and it was almost laughable, at this point. Didn't he know her by now? The harder he pushed, the harder she'd push back. She was Hugh McLeod's daughter, after all, so she knew all about stubbornness and standing her ground. She'd learned from the best.

"I hope you guys are up for waffles," Cora said, walking into the kitchen. She pulled the pan from the oven where she'd kept them warming. "I made enough to feed an army." She placed the pan in the middle of her kitchen table, along with maple syrup and a pitcher of orange juice.

Liam was staring at the pile of waffles with an odd expression on his face.

"What?" Cora took a seat at the head of the table as they joined her. "You don't like waffles? There are Pop-Tarts in the cupboard. And bagels."

"No, this looks great." Liam took the seat to her right, and her dad sat across from him. "It's just a lot of food."

She shrugged. "If you guys don't finish it, I'll just feed it to the ducks when I go running tomorrow morning."

"Feed the ducks?" Liam grinned. "You're funny, Cora McLeod. I love that about you."

When he smiled at her like that, she felt a familiar warmth bloom inside her like a caress, spiraling through her limbs until her toes curled. It was completely unexpected, and unsettling as hell. She didn't like it. "You haven't known me long enough to love anything about me," she said sharply.

Liam looked startled, and then...sad, for some reason.

Guilt washed over her. She shouldn't have blurted it out like that. But it was true. He didn't get to just breeze into her life and say he loved things about her within the first twenty minutes of meeting her. Whatever the odd sensation was inside her, it made no sense, and she didn't trust it. She cast a guilty glance at her dad. He gave her a disappointed frown.

"Yes, of course. You're right," Liam said carefully. "I only meant that I enjoyed your joke."

"I wasn't trying to be funny," she mumbled, pouring some orange juice. "But okay."

"So, Liam," Hugh said brightly. "Are you looking for-

CHANCE OF A LIFETIME   81

ward to starting work tomorrow? Protect and serve." He smiled and handed Liam the syrup. "The Providence Falls police force will be a lot smaller than you're used to in Raleigh, but it's a great group."

"Sure." Liam was holding the syrup like he didn't know what to do with it. Weird. He set it down in the middle of the table.

"You must be looking forward to working with your old friend," Hugh continued. "How long's it been since you've seen each other?"

"My old friend?" Liam looked confused. "It's, uh, been a while." He lifted his waffle and absently took a bite.

Weirder. Cora watched him from beneath her lashes. Who eats waffles with their hands?

"I was surprised to learn Captain Thompson was a buddy of yours back in Ireland," Hugh said. "And now he's going to be your boss. Such a small world."

Liam choked. Coughed. She reached over and thumped him on the back, then she poured him some juice and handed it to him. When her fingertips brushed his, he jerked his hand away, nearly spilling it. He muttered something under his breath with a shocked look on his face. Cora thought she heard him say *angels* and *killing me*. She narrowed her eyes. Something was up with this guy.

"Boyd doesn't even have an Irish accent," Hugh continued, "so I just assumed he was born in the US. Apparently he moved here when he was still young, so that's why he sounds like a regular American."

"But your own accent's pretty faint, Liam," she pointed out. "Practically nonexistent. What's up with that? My dad says you were raised in Ireland and only moved here after you turned eighteen."

"Uh, yes." Liam took a drink.

Was he stalling?

Suddenly his eyes flew wide and he stared in wonder at the orange juice in his glass. "This is bloody marvelous!"

Yeah, he was stalling. No one got that excited about store-bought OJ. She watched as he took another gulp, and then another, smacking his lips in delight. His child-like glee was so diverting, she almost forgot to be skeptical. *Focus!* "So, you were explaining about your accent. Why don't you sound Irish?"

"Right." He set down his empty juice glass. "I just acclimated to the language here very quickly. It's a talent of mine, I suppose." He switched to a thick Irish brogue and gave her a wicked grin. "But my Irish accent still pokes its head out once in a while, ye ken?"

Cora tried not to smile, but failed. Oh, she *ken'd*, all right. Too bad he'd acclimated. The accent really suited him. He could wield it like a secret weapon, and the ladies would come running. Did he know it? Probably. Even though he was acting all polite now, he had a roguish streak inside him. She could tell. Suzette was seriously going to love this guy.

Cora was quiet as they ate, letting her father take the lead on conversation. He filled Liam in on some of the city's summer festivals, the best local restaurants and the university baseball team's sad losing streak. Even though her father now lived in Charlotte, he'd spent most of his life in Providence Falls, and he still enjoyed relaying all its many attractions to whoever stood still long enough to listen. Liam seemed happy to soak up all the information, asking pertinent questions around enthusiastic bites of his breakfast.

Cora sat back and watched as Liam put a fourth waffle onto his plate. Or was it his fifth?

"You know you can use your fork, right?" she asked, half joking.

He shrugged. "This way's faster." He took another bite. Chewed. Swallowed. Then another. He ate like a starving man.

"Geez, when's the last time you ate?"

He blinked, then asked around a mouthful of waffle, "What year is it?"

She rolled her eyes and jerked a thumb at the wall calendar behind her.

"Ah." Liam studied the calendar for a few moments, his brow furrowed. "One hundred and sixty-six...no that's not right." He paused. "Seventy. I haven't eaten in one hundred and seventy-six years."

Hilarious. "Well, in that case, keep eating."

"These are truly delicious," he said with feeling. "Your father was right. You are an excellent cook."

She glanced at her dad. "Well, I've had to be. If it were up to my dad, we'd have gone to Shakey's Burgers every night. Either that, or The Pizza Pirate."

Liam stopped mid-chew. "Pizza pirates?"

"It's a restaurant near the police station," her dad said. "Best pizza in town. You'll have to try it one of these days after work. Speaking of that, Cora can introduce you to everyone and show you around tomorrow."

"Dad, it's not preschool. I'm sure he can manage just fine." She didn't even want to think about tomorrow. It was weird enough having her dad try to force the new guy into her house, she had a feeling her boss was going to make her babysit him, too. Cora was driven, she worked hard, and Captain Thompson knew it. He was stoic and not one to dole out praise, but he had a shrewd eye, and he knew Cora was one of the best investigators they had. He'd even told her once at last year's holiday party. It was a slurred, *Cora, you're an asset to this team. Maybe even the best we've got.* Sure, he'd had one too many beers when he'd said it, but the unexpected praise had been enough to have her floating on cloud nine for weeks afterward.

"But you can give him the scoop on everyone at the precinct," her dad said. "Captain Thompson's a good boss, wouldn't you say, Cora?"

She tried to think of a diplomatic way to answer. Was he a good boss? Captain Boyd Thompson was as prickly and tenacious as the weeds growing on her front lawn. He was one of those people who looked unassuming, being short in stature, with a forgettable face, and brown, curly hair. The only remarkable thing about him was his shrewd eyes, which seemed to look right into you and glean all your secrets. Even though she'd known him for five years, she still never felt connected. But maybe that was the sign of a good boss. Never get too close, and keep everyone on their toes.

"Captain Thompson demands excellence, and doesn't tolerate mistakes," she finally said. "Sometimes that can be daunting, but no one can argue that it isn't effective. Providence Falls hasn't had any major crimes in years, and I think he likes to take credit for that."

There was a sardonic twist to Liam's mouth, as if he found it amusing.

Cora poured some orange juice into her glass, then offered the pitcher to him. "So you two knew each other in Ireland when you were kids. You reconnected here a few years ago?"

Liam paused to fill his glass with more juice. "Aye, I knew Boyd a long time ago. He sounds a bit different than I remember him. Very enterprising, was Boyd. Always searching for opportunities to get ahead. I'm… I was surprised to learn he'd become a law enforcer."

"Why is that?" Cora asked.

"He was just always so…restless. I never imagined Boyd would settle into a role with such regimented structure."

"You make him sound like he was a wild child," Cora said with a grin. "Was he? I really can't imagine Captain Thompson doing anything crazy. He's so gruff and militant."

"Oh, I could tell you stories about him that might surprise you," he said with wry amusement.

"Okay, then." Cora put her elbow on the table and dropped her chin into her hand. "Tell me."

His expression clouded for a moment, making Cora wonder how bad the stories were. Then he flashed her a brilliant smile that sent her thoughts scattering like leaves on the wind. That was some powerful stuff. Liam's mother must've been an absolute knockout, because he certainly didn't get his looks from his father. From what Cora remembered of her dad's old partner, he'd been bald and heavyset with a weak chin. Liam looked nothing like him.

"Once, when Boyd and I were very young, around six or seven…" He leaned forward and lowered his voice like he was about to divulge something scandalous. "We crept onto my neighbor's land in the middle of the night and stole a chicken."

Cora couldn't help grinning. "I thought little boys were more into snakes and snails and puppy dog tails."

He scoffed. "Why eat those, when we could eat a whole chicken?"

"Wha—" She frowned. Surely, he was joking. "You *ate* it?"

Liam nodded proudly. "Roasted it ourselves in the woods. We tried to go back on the next moonless night, but old Fergus was waiting for us. He caught us and threatened to nail our ears to the fence as punishment."

Cora's mouth fell open.

Liam gave her a charming wink.

She snapped her mouth shut. Oh, he was good. With the earnest expression and the lethal smile, he almost had her believing him. "Nice try." She reached for her drink.

"You don't believe me?" His face was all innocence, which, paired with his dark good looks, really worked for him. It was a wonder he ever became a police officer at all. He could have made a fortune selling snake oil. "It's completely true."

"Uh-huh," Cora said. "Because little boys love to steal pet chickens in the middle of the night, slaughter them, then consume their carcasses over an open fire. I think there's even a Boy Scout badge for that."

Confusion flashed across his face, then he finished the last bite of his waffle, murmuring "pet chickens" under his breath. "I can assure you," he finally said. "Old Fergus Maguire never had a pet in his life. That would imply he cared, and the only thing he cared about was his whiskey. He was as mean as a wounded badger, but he wasn't an idiot. Keeping a pet was an extravagance few could afford. A waste of resources."

Her father smirked. "The angel might disagree."

Liam's shoulders tensed and his face grew pale. "What?"

"Angel," her dad said. "He's far loftier than us lowly humans, isn't he, Cora? He'd never consider himself a waste of resources."

Cora continued to study Liam. Something had rattled

him, but she couldn't figure out what it was. Now she was almost certain his easy charm was just an act. This guy was hiding something. She could *feel* it, and her instincts were never wrong.

"There he is now," her dad announced.

A furry white cat sauntered into the kitchen with as much pomp and circumstance as a movie star walking the red carpet.

Cora pointed at her cat. "That's Angel. Don't be alarmed if he hisses at you. He pretty much hates everyone, at first."

"At first?" her dad said with a laugh. "He still swats at me if I get within clawing distance, and I've been trying to win him over for three years."

Angel padded over to Liam's chair and sat at his feet, staring up at him. Cora frowned. That was unusual. Her cat avoided most people. Angel's tail twitched back and forth. Cora was about to jump up and grab him before he used Liam's leg as a scratching post.

To her utter shock, a low, rumbling sound began to fill the room.

"Is he—" her dad began.

"Yes." Cora looked at Liam in astonishment. "He's purring. This is insane. Angel never does this with strangers."

Liam locked eyes with her. "Guess I'm not a stranger, then, am I?" He slid his chair back and Angel jumped into his lap. Jumped. *Into his lap.* Liam began to pet the purring cat, but he kept his gaze steady on Cora's face.

The hairs on the back of her neck prickled with awareness, and she had the sudden feeling they'd met before. The way he looked at her was so...familiar. She sucked in a breath. Ridiculous! She'd never seen him before in her life. Of that, she was certain. Liam O'Connor wasn't the type of man a person could easily forget. She leaned back in her chair and shifted her gaze to her cat. "I promise you, Angel never acts this way. It's like you've bewitched him."

Liam smoothed the cat's back, then scratched him behind the ears. Angel nudged his nose affectionately against Liam's hand. "Maybe he just has good taste."

"Or hell just froze over," Cora said.

Liam's mouth curved into a wicked half smile. "If it did, I'd be the first to know."

She shifted uncomfortably and rose from the table. It was his damned smile. It tugged at her insides and made her stomach flutter in recognition. Or confusion. Or something. She walked into the kitchen and placed her plate in the sink. Then she filled it with warm, soapy water, grabbed a kitchen towel and began wiping down a counter. What was going on with her? She felt split down the middle, equal parts skeptical and charmed by this man. Her usually keen instincts were in a tailspin because she wanted to remain calm and clinical in her assessment of him. Her plan that morning had been to keep him at arm's length and be cool and aloof. But she was undeniably drawn to him, and it wasn't just his sinful good looks. She couldn't remember the last time she'd felt this uneasy around a man.

Cora spent fifteen minutes milling around in the kitchen until she felt more grounded. When she returned to the table, her dad was discussing the upcoming charity ball at the famous Davenport Estate just outside the city.

"It's a big black-tie event the local businesses host every year. They raise money for different charities. This year it's for… What is it, Cora? I can't remember." He glanced apologetically at Liam. "Ever since I moved to Charlotte, I'm not as up-to-date on Providence Falls' society news. Cora usually fills me in when she comes to visit."

"Bread for the Hungry." She began to clear the table. Liam lifted the now-empty pan to help her. When their fingers accidentally brushed, he sucked in a pained breath and drew his hand back.

"What's wrong?" Cora asked, eyeing him warily. "Did Angel just claw you?"

He blinked, then said in a strained voice, "It's fine."

Cora glanced at her cat, who was draped across Liam's lap, kneading his claws and purring in contentment. She shrugged and carried the pan to the kitchen sink. If Liam insisted on risking his limbs by petting the dangerous feline, it was his loss.

"The gala is basically just a big, fancy party where we ply rich people with too many drinks and get them to part with their money so we can help the less fortunate," Cora said, returning to the table.

Liam gave her a roguish smile. "Like Robin Hood."

"I guess. Except instead of wearing tights and slinging arrows, we're wearing formal clothes and slinging alcoholic beverages. Also, we don't actually steal. And we're not fugitive outlaws. But other than that, sure. Just like Robin Hood."

Liam slapped a hand on the table. "I like the sound of this party. When is it? I want to go."

"Excellent." Her dad beamed at both of them. "It's in a couple of weeks. You guys can go together."

Cora clamped her mouth shut, struggling to keep her expression neutral. She needed to have a talk with her father before he got carried away. Scratch that, he already was. At the rate he was going, they'd be off on their honeymoon in no time flat. This had to stop.

"Dad, can you help me in the kitchen for a moment?" Cora asked through gritted teeth. Then she glanced at Liam and said, "Why don't you take Angel into the living room and kick back on the couch?" It wasn't a question; it was a command.

In the kitchen, Cora dropped the last of the dishes into the sink and turned on her father, keeping her voice low so Liam wouldn't overhear. "Look, I get that you're loyal to Liam's father and you feel you owe him, but you have to stop trying to force him on me."

"I'm not trying to force anything, honey. I just think he's a very nice man, and—"

"Believe me," Cora said, holding up her hands. "It's abundantly clear you think he walks on water, but please allow me the courtesy of making my own decisions."

Hugh's voice softened. "It's just hard for me to think of you living alone out here, now that I live so far away."

"Dad, this is not Antarctica, and I'm not alone. I can literally hear old Mrs. Gilmore next door snoring at night when she leaves the window open."

He shook his head. "I just like the idea of having someone close by to protect you. Can you blame me for that?"

"Yes! When are you going to realize I'm not a little girl anymore?" Cora said in exasperation. "I can protect myself. I'm a cop, for God's sake."

"But, I'm your father." Hugh smiled, his blue eyes crinkling at the corners. "To me, you'll always be that little girl crying at the bus stop on your first day of school."

Cora rolled her eyes. "I was crying because I wanted to walk to the bus stop myself, and you wouldn't let me. And don't try to change the subject." She jerked a thumb at the living room. "You're trying to manipulate me into letting him move in here, and it's not going to happen. Stop trying to control me."

Her dad's face fell, and even though she was annoyed, it

tugged at Cora's heartstrings. "I'm sorry, honey. I just want to see you happy. I know you've been saving up to make an offer on that house you've always wanted, and I thought if he took over half the rent, it would be a quick solution."

Cora sighed, absently playing with the gold rose pendant she wore around her neck. It was one of her mother's only pieces of jewelry, and Cora never took it off. It reminded her of a time when her family was blissfully happy together, before cancer tore everything apart. She slowly shook her head. Her father had a point. After her former roommate moved away, Cora hadn't been able to save as much money as she'd hoped. And she *needed* to save if she was ever going to make a competitive offer on her dream house.

The cottage at the edge of town wasn't grand or palatial or fancy, but in Cora's mind, it was as close to perfection as she'd ever seen. It was a beautiful two-story home with flower boxes in the windows, shady trees, a picket fence and a rose trellis. The location was perfect, close enough to shops but tucked away near the edge of the woods beside an honest-to-God babbling brook. There was even a tire swing in the side yard where Cora used to see children playing. Ever since she was a little girl, her dad would drive by that house and she'd imagine what it must be like to live someplace that looked so warm and inviting. She always thought the house felt like it was smiling. Like laughter and happy traditions and wonderful memories had seeped into the walls so deep, any person lucky enough to live there would live a charmed life. The kind of life where you were surrounded by loved ones who celebrated together, supported each other and shared every precious moment, no matter how fleeting.

She gave her dad a reluctant smile. As annoyed as she

was, she could never stay mad at him for long. He was her rock, and he always had been. She knew he meant well. "Just don't rent a moving truck and try to shoehorn him into my life anytime soon, all right?"

Hugh gave a single nod. "I'll cancel the U-Haul."

She narrowed her eyes. He'd better be joking. "And stop being so pushy. I barely know this guy, and when I do get a roommate, he or she will be someone of *my* choosing."

Her dad stopped smiling. "You wouldn't choose some random man, surely? Cora, that's not safe."

"Dad," Cora said in exasperation, pointing in the direction of the living room. "*He's* a random man!"

Her dad gave her a look that said she was being overly dramatic. "He's my good friend's son, Cora."

"So what?" She jammed her hands onto her hips. "Contrary to popular belief, sometimes the apple falls far, far from the tree. *You* don't even know him that well."

"I know he's going to be working with you."

She crossed her arms and lifted her chin. "Not by choice."

Hugh's brows drew together. "Aside from my involvement, what do you have against him?"

Cora's gaze darted around the kitchen as if she could find a good answer somewhere in the room. "He's... I don't know. He's just..." She walked past her dad and peeked around the corner. Liam was holding her cat Angel as he browsed the photographs on her mantel. It was odd to see such a tall, muscular man snuggling her fluffy, prima donna of a cat.

She turned back to her dad and whispered, "He's weird."

"Your last roommate hung crystals in all your windows to balance her cheese."

"Chi."

Her dad made a face. "She piled garbage in the backyard."

"She was trying to make a compost heap." Although Cora was pretty sure a compost heap shouldn't include soda cans and Burger King bags.

He rocked forward on his heels and brought out the big guns. "She sang *opera* all the time?"

Cora blew out a defeated breath. "Okay, yeah. That was tough."

"See?"

Cora stared blankly at the wall, remembering. "She was so loud."

"My point," her dad said triumphantly, "is you could do worse. Liam's a good guy. I'm not going to bug you anymore about taking him in as a roommate, but just don't rule him out yet, okay?"

She gave a reluctant nod, which was the best she could do, at the moment.

Her dad joined Liam in the living room and Cora listened to their easy conversation as she put the kettle on the stove for cinnamon tea. She didn't even really want it, but it gave her a chance to linger. Hugh said something that made Liam laugh. It was a deep, rich sound that seemed to resonate straight through Cora's bones, tickling the back of her memory. She peeked around the corner again, unable to tear her gaze away from the sight of him laughing. The curve of his mouth. The smooth arch of his throat as he tipped his head back. Once again, she had that weird sense of déjà vu, like she'd lived this exact moment before. With him.

The teakettle whistled.

Liam glanced over and caught her staring. A jolt of physical awareness seemed to crackle in the air between them.

Cora spun away and went to turn off the stove. She poured hot water into her teacup and slowly stirred in sugar. Whatever was going on with her, this wasn't normal. She felt shaky and uncertain, like she was standing in the eye of a hurricane, and any second that hurricane was going to come swirling through her normal world and turn everything upside down, sweeping her along with it.

The hurricane stepped into the kitchen and leaned a broad shoulder against the doorframe. "Are you coming?"

She placed the spoon in the sink. Did she have a choice?

5

The Providence Falls Police Department was only twenty minutes from Liam's motel, but he spent the better part of an hour on Monday morning just trying to navigate through rush hour traffic. By all that was holy, if he survived the drive to work, it was going to be a bloody miracle.

When he'd woken that morning, there'd been a black duffel bag filled with clothes and toiletries on the motel chair, along with a set of car keys. He'd been eager to see what car the angels had arranged for him, until he walked into the motel parking lot, and he knew. He just *knew* when he saw it, it had to be his. Because he was beginning to realize the angels had no intention of making things easy for him. There were five vehicles in the lot. Two sleek black trucks, a sporty red two-seater that looked fast as the wind, and a wicked, steel gray motorcycle that appealed to him on every level. The last car looked like the equivalent of an old, swayback mare put out to pasture. Liam pressed his key fob and, sure enough, the faded beige sedan with the dented fender blinked its headlights at him in greeting. Of course.

The car was so nondescript, he had to concentrate lest it fade into the background beside the other options. When he walked closer, he noticed a silver charm dangling from the rearview mirror. A pair of angel wings. He tipped his head back and grumbled at the sky. "Are you enjoying yourselves?"

The angels didn't reply. They hadn't said a word to him since he'd arrived, and not for lack of him trying. Yesterday, after visiting Cora, he'd returned to his motel practically growling. He was furious at the angels when he'd discovered their latest surprise. Every time he'd touched Cora yesterday, an unpleasant shock of electricity zapped through his body. When he'd first shaken her hand, he'd thought it was a one-time thing. He hadn't been pleased with the angels for that little surprise, at all, but he'd thought they were just sending him a simple reminder to stay on track. But later, when Cora handed him the glass of juice, it happened again. He'd felt a snap of pain along his skin. And then again, when their fingers touched by accident as she was clearing the table.

He'd arrived back to the motel, seething. He'd paced the room for hours, muttering at the angels for setting him up with so many obstacles, but the only answer he got was the steady sound of the dripping faucet in the tiny bathroom. Eventually he'd fallen asleep on the bed, wrapped in a stale-smelling blanket and a deep sense of melancholy. He'd felt certain Cora would sense the connection between them, but she plainly didn't trust him in this life, let alone care for him.

Today he vowed to change that. Liam gripped the steering wheel tightly as he navigated the creaky car through rush hour traffic. He was putting his newly acquired driving skills to the test, and—if that lady honking in the lane next to him was correct—doing a piss-poor job of it. His car barely missed hitting hers as he switched lanes. She glared at him before speeding ahead, offering him a hand gesture through her window. That was a good one. He'd have to commit it to memory. If nothing else, driving gave him the opportunity to pick up fresh, modern-day insults.

Fifty minutes later, he steered into the police station parking lot and cut the engine, taking a moment to appreciate the fact that all his limbs were still intact. Then he took another moment to be grateful he knew how to use the global tracking system in his car. A talking map! Who'd have ever dreamed it? This modern world was filled with fascinating things. Unfortunately, the Providence Falls Police Department didn't appear to be one of them. It was an unimpressive brick building in the old part of the city across from a public park and the local community center. He harbored no delusions that enforcing the law was going to be a barrel of fun, but at least he'd be with Cora every day. That made it worth it.

He walked inside to the reception desk where a heavy, middle-aged woman sat. She was wearing a purple blouse, gold dangly earrings and a sweet, sugary perfume that was so strong, he suspected it came around the corner before she did. Her face lit up when she saw him. She patted her hair, batted her eyelashes and broke into a toothy grin.

Finally. A familiar situation. He started to introduce himself but didn't get the chance.

"Oh, I know who you are." The woman was bubbling over with excitement. "Liam O'Connor, right? Captain Thompson said you were coming in this morning. I saw your picture on the announcement." She stood, yanking the hem of her blouse to straighten it. "I'm Mavis. Office administrator extraordinaire. Candy?" She held up a bowl of red-and-white-striped mints.

Liam smiled and took one. "Lovely to meet you, Mavis."

She let out a self-conscious giggle that ended on a bit of a snort. "Captain Thompson told me to send you into his office when you arrive. It's this way."

He followed her down a hall past a kitchen, and into a large open pen. Several officers sat working at their desks, a few others milling in conversation. Liam's gaze was drawn to Cora like a magnet. She was seated at a corner desk, dressed in black slacks and a tailored jacket. Her thick blond hair was pulled into a messy bun, and she was deeply engrossed in paperwork. He still wasn't used to the shock of seeing her, of standing in the same room and being so close to her. He suspected it would take a long time before he stopped feeling that pang of exquisite joy every time he saw her face.

"O'Connor," a familiar voice called. Boyd Thompson stood in his office doorway with the same calculating expression Liam remembered. But instead of threadbare clothing and worn-out shoes, his old friend now wore a suit and tie. His hair was cropped very short, and his body appeared softer, with a slightly protruding belly. It was odd for Liam to see Boyd with extra weight. They'd been hungry for so long, the idea of being fat had been nothing but a fantasy back then.

Boyd shook Liam's hand. "You're late this morning."

Liam blinked in surprise. Odd that Boyd, of all people, would point out the rules. He'd always been the one most eager to break them. "I had a difficult time with the traffic."

"No matter. I'm sure tomorrow you'll be right on time." It was less of an observation and more of a command.

Liam worked to appear agreeable. "Of course."

Boyd led him into the office, took a seat at his desk and gestured to one of the chairs opposite his. The room had a window overlooking the parking lot and the community baseball field beyond it. The dusty metal window blinds were crimped in various spots, and an abandoned coffee cup sat on the window ledge. Two framed accolades depicting Boyd's credentials took prime space on the wall above him. But aside from that and a plastic plant in the corner, there wasn't much to personalize the place, save for a couple of framed photographs on his desk.

Liam leaned closer to one of the photos. It showed Boyd with a flaxen-haired woman who he instantly recognized. Boyd's wife. She had the same pinched smile she had back in his old life. Liam still wasn't used to seeing people he recognized from the past. Even more unsettling was the realization that none of them would remember the *real* him. It was as if his real life had never existed, and it only served to emphasize how truly alone he was now.

"My wife, Alice," Boyd said, gesturing to the photo.

"A fine-looking woman," Liam managed.

"Yes, well. She should be, considering all the money she spends shopping and going to the spa." Boyd forced a chuckle, his smile not quite reaching his eyes. "I work really hard, and she spends really hard. But happy wife, happy life, right?" He paused, then gave Liam a condescending look. "You're unattached, but someday you'll understand. How are you settling in?"

"Still looking for a place," Liam said. "I met Cora yesterday."

"And how'd that go?"

Terrible. She doesn't want me around. Touching her burns like hot coals against my skin. "Just fine."

"Excellent." Boyd leaned forward and steepled his fingers together. "I still can't believe how well this worked out. Talk about coincidence that you'd ended up moving to the US and living in the same state as me. And becoming a police officer, no less. When you emailed me out of the blue last year, I never thought you'd end up working for me."

"Neither did I." Liam kept his expression neutral, but it wasn't easy. Just the thought of having to answer to a cocky bastard like Boyd scraped along his pride like a rusty nail. Boyd had never been a good leader. He was too hotheaded and prone to fighting, and his emotions got them into trouble more times than Liam could count. Liam had always been the leader.

Boyd lifted his coffee cup and took a drink before saying, "Truth really is stranger than fiction, isn't it?"

"Boyd," Liam said with a solemn shake of his head. "You've no idea."

Boyd's shrewd gaze narrowed a fraction. "Listen, Liam. I know we knew each other as kids, but you'll want to call me Captain Thompson in the office. Proper protocol, you know."

Liam clenched his jaw. Since when had Boyd ever been concerned about propriety?

"You wanted to see me, Captain?" Cora stood in the doorway like a sudden spark of light. The whole station was cloaked in a palette of dull, shadowy grays, from the painted walls to the cold, tiled floors, but Cora seemed to emanate a glowing warmth with her presence. It made Liam smile.

"I want the two of you to work together this week," Boyd said.

She flicked an annoyed glance in Liam's direction before addressing Boyd. "You sure that's a good idea? I'm in the middle of—"

"It's a great idea," Boyd interrupted. "You're one of our best officers, born and raised here. You know this town better than anyone, and it makes sense for the two of you to pair up." His phone rang, and he placed his hand on the receiver. "That will be all." Boyd dismissed them both by tipping his head in the direction of the door before answering his phone.

Cora led Liam out into the pen, looking none too pleased. "I was just on my way to make some inquiries on a robbery that happened yesterday, so I guess you're coming with me." She pointed to an empty desk at the far end of the room. "When we get back, you can take that desk over there near Otto."

A fat, balding officer glanced at Liam. He had squinty eyes magnified by thick glasses, a ruddy complexion, and a face like the full moon. He heaved himself out of his desk chair and offered Liam a sweaty but firm handshake. "Otto Simpson. Good to meet you." He gestured to a thin man with a sharp, sullen face sitting at the next desk. "That's Happy Blankenship, my partner."

Otto's partner gave Liam a tight-lipped, barely perceptible nod. The two men were exact opposites. Where Otto looked like a smiley, squishy marshmallow, his partner, Happy, looked like the charred, brittle stick it was roasted on.

"The man's name is Happy?" Liam asked under his breath as Cora led him out into the hall.

"Yep. And he rarely smiles. I think it was a nickname he got when he was a kid, and it just sort of stuck." She pushed through a door and stepped into a spacious kitchen. Three vending machines lined the far wall along with a sink and a refrigerator. A few round tables and chairs filled the rest of the room.

Cora made a beeline for the coffee maker and spoke to a man sitting in front of a box of doughnuts. "Looking pretty lonely there, Hopper. Where's your partner?"

Unlike Otto and Happy, this man looked strong and athletic. He had brown hair, blue eyes and an arrogant smirk. He sized up Liam, then turned his attention to Cora and drawled, "I wouldn't be so lonely if you'd come sit with me, McLeod."

Liam bristled. He didn't like the overly familiar way the man spoke to her. She didn't seem to notice, though. Or if she did, it didn't seem to bother her.

Cora made the introductions as she filled two paper cups. "Rob Hopper and I went to school together," she told Liam.

Rob pushed the carton of doughnuts toward them. "You want?"

Cora shook her head. "We're heading out. I heard you guys found the carjacker last night during that store robbery."

"Yeah, but he got away."

"What? I thought it was a done deal." Cora walked over to Liam and handed him a cup of coffee.

"We had him cornered," Rob said around a mouthful of doughnut. "But he gave us the slip. Hey, try one of these. They put cream *and* jelly in them."

Cora frowned. "I don't understand."

"I know, right? Who puts jelly and cream together?"

"No. How'd he get away? There were three cops on him."

"He jacked a car from the Gas n' Go parking lot and took off before we could catch him." Rob took another bite. "A hybrid."

"The car?"

He held up the half-eaten pastry. "A creamy, jelly hybrid."

Cora let out a frustrated breath. "You're impossible, Hopper. Did you at least get the make and model?"

Rob slouched back in his chair. "Relax, Peaches. We're on it. It's not even nine o'clock yet. Why don't you take a load off and have a cup of coffee?"

She lifted her cup. "Having it. And if you call me Peaches one more time, I'll—"

"Okay, okay." Rob held up his hands. He gave Liam a conspiratorial look. "She's feisty, this one."

Liam pierced him with a glare. "She's a lady, and I'll thank you to keep a respectful tongue in your head."

Rob leaned back in his chair in surprise. "Whoa, there, my man. I was just kidding around." He glanced at Cora with a barely concealed smirk. "No hard feelings, right? *Lady?*"

Cora turned to leave. "Come on, Liam."

"Where are you going?" Rob called after them.

She spun around. "Did anyone talk to the pawnshop owner to see if he noticed anything?"

"I don't think so."

"Then that's where we're going. He lives upstairs from his shop, and he watches the neighborhood with the same level of dedication that you watch *Real Housewives*."

Rob sucked in a breath. "You know about that?"

Now it was Cora's turn to smirk. "Everyone knows, Hopper."

"Damn," Rob muttered. "Joe promised not to tell."

"Your partner's not the one who let it slip," she said. "Remember last week at Danté's when you had too many shots of tequila?"

He nodded.

"You sang like a bird." With that, Cora opened the kitchen door, and Liam followed her into the hall.

"Who is that man to you?" he asked as she led him out of the building. "I didn't like his tone with you. Why did he call you Peaches?"

Cora glanced at him sideways. "It was just a nickname he gave me a long time ago. He knows it bugs me, which is why he does it. Rob and I go way back. We used to date in high school, but that was when we were young and foolish."

A flash of jealousy spiked through him. "That man used to call on you?"

She gave him an odd look. "I mean, yeah. He called me all the time. Teenagers and their phones, you know."

"But you're not together anymore," he said, just to make sure.

"God, no." She laughed as she stopped at a shiny sedan and unlocked the doors. "That ended a lifetime ago."

Good. One less obstacle to worry about. "Yet, he still calls you Peaches," he grumbled, getting into the car. "I don't like it."

"Hey, ease up there." Cora gave him a strange look. "Rob's actually a decent guy. He just likes to tease me. Besides, it was a long time ago and there's nothing there, trust me. He's like a brother." Cora pulled the car out of the parking lot and onto the busy street. "I was barely seventeen when we dated," she explained. "We were just dumb kids."

His scowl deepened. That was the same age she'd been when she fell in love with him. "Seventeen is plenty old enough to know your mind."

Cora scoffed. "Hardly. If I still had to be with the guys I dated when I was a teenager, I'd die of embarrassment."

"Oh, is that so?" He didn't like where this conversation was headed. He certainly didn't like thinking about Cora being courted by other men. Hugh was supposed to be a good father. What kind of a man would let his daughter go all over town with multiple suitors? "Exactly how many were there?"

"Guys?" Cora seemed oblivious to Liam's growing annoyance. "Not nearly as many as I'd have liked. My dad was ridiculously protective, and most boys were too afraid to date me."

Thank God for small mercies, Liam thought darkly. Hugh was a decent father, after all.

"Some of them were real winners," Cora said with a laugh. She hit a yellow light at an intersection and slowed to a stop, then flashed him a smile filled with scandalized glee. "One guy was even a thief."

Liam's gut clenched.

"Ironic, isn't it? Me being a cop, and all."

If only you knew.

"He lied and told me he went to a different high school and worked at the local gym, but really he just stole hubcaps and ran scams with some of his buddies. It turned out he wasn't even a high school senior. He was twenty!"

"What happened to him?"

Cora let out a huff. "My dad used to be the police captain in this city. What do you think happened? They threw the book at him for being with a minor."

Liam swallowed hard. He knew the basics of the law,

thanks to the information the angels had bestowed on him, but it was strange to think how different things were in this modern world. Back in his time, most women were married with children by the time they were seventeen. And a boy was considered a man even before that age.

Cora drove them into the older part of the city. As she pointed out landmarks and chatted about her high school days, Liam grew increasingly miserable. It was hard enough to accept that Cora wasn't exactly the sheltered, innocent girl he remembered, but to have to sit and hear about all her past boyfriends? Remaining silent, he did his best to appear unfazed. He had an understanding of the mechanics in this world, but no true context to help him acclimate to the new social norms. And they were a far cry from those of his old life.

He took a gulp of the drink she'd handed him earlier, then froze. *Holy mother of—* He forced it down. Sputtered. "What is this?"

Cora glanced at his cup. "Coffee. I was on autopilot when I made it, so I added my usual cream and sugar without asking. You don't like it?"

He took another sip just to be sure, then made a face. It was worse than the swill at the Goose & Gander tavern. "I'd prefer a cup of tea."

"Tea, huh?" Cora looked like she was trying to keep a straight face. "Like in a china cup, or...?"

He shrugged. "Doesn't matter."

Her mouth twitched. "And crumpets?"

Liam perked up. Now, he wouldn't say no to that. A nice fat crumpet dripping with melted butter and honey. "Have you any?"

Cora just laughed and shook her head. Then she pointed out a community swimming pool and launched into an account of her and her friend Suzette's high school escapade involving boys and secret midnight swimming.

Liam grimaced, plunked the coffee in the cup holder and glared out the window. One way or another, this task was going to be the death of him.

6

Cora pulled up along the sidewalk next to Perry's Pawn-shop. Like most days, she ended up in the older, less savory part of town, but that was to be expected. Many of the reported robberies took place along Front Street, which was filled with hole-in-the-wall bars, pipe and tobacco shops, dry cleaners, and various other small businesses. The pawnshop had been there since before Cora was born, and Perry never missed an opportunity to remind her. Like many of the older locals, he'd known Cora's father, and he considered her to be a good egg, despite her willingness to use government mind control devices like cell phones and computers. For a guy who sold electronics, Perry was unusually old-school. He insisted on only using a land-line phone and an old-fashioned cash register with paper receipts.

Liam had grown quiet in the car, and she had no clue

why. From what she'd witnessed, his moods seemed mercurial. One moment he was fascinating and engaging, and the next he seemed uncomfortable and withdrawn. She still couldn't get over the feeling that he was hiding something, but everyone had their stories. Maybe he just wasn't ready to share much about himself. Come to think of it, she wasn't normally the type of person to talk a lot about herself with people she'd just met. She'd always been more of a gathering-of-information type. But with him, she had no problem telling him personal stories. How was it possible to feel simultaneously unsettled, yet strangely comfortable with a person?

She cut the engine and unfastened her seat belt. Liam was giving her that intense, almost pained look again. Her skin prickled, and this time, rather than ignoring it, she faced him. "Okay, what?"

He blinked. "Nothing."

"No. You've got something on your mind. Just tell me."

He looked away and mumbled, "How am I supposed to do this?"

"Easy," Cora said, opening her door. "We go in there and ask Perry what he saw last night during the robbery. Standard routine. Just follow my lead."

Perry's Pawn Shop smelled like cash, dust and broken dreams. The shelves were filled with odds and ends in no particular order. Musical instruments were piled beside outdated electronics. Designer handbags of questionable authenticity and random crystal tableware jockeyed for space beside old gym equipment, baby strollers and vacuum cleaners. There was a glass case along one wall filled with knives and guns, and two more cases filled with jewelry. Some of them were old estate pieces, but there was a section of engagement and wedding rings that seemed to outnumber the rest of the jewelry, which always struck Cora as sad. All those symbols of hope, traded away for something else.

She absently fingered the gold pendant around her neck.

Liam came to stand beside her, his dark eyes fixed on the jewelry display. "So many jewels," he murmured. "This Perry must be a very wealthy man."

"Ha!" Perry cackled as he stepped into the front room. He looked like a grizzled sea captain, with white hair and skin like leather left too long in the sun. "From your lips to God's ears, son. Been waiting for my ship to come in for decades. Figure it must've sank at sea, by now." When he saw Cora, his wrinkled face splintered into a grin. "Little Cora McLeod!"

She grinned back. He'd been calling her that for as long as she could remember and, if nothing else, Perry was a creature of habit. He wasn't big on change, but Cora didn't hold it against him. "Hi, Perry. This is Officer O'Connor. He's just transferred here from Raleigh, and he'll be working with me this week."

"You're in good hands, then," he said to Liam, hooking his thumbs into the pockets of his jeans. "Cora knows everything about this town. I've been running this shop since before she was born. She used to come in here with her dad when she was this high." He held his palm low, parallel to the floor. "When she was five years old, she asked me to sell her a gun, so she could protect people from bad guys." He cackled again. "Can you believe it?"

"Cora wanting to protect people?" There was a thread of pride in Liam's voice. "Aye, I can believe it."

"Aye?" Perry squinted at Liam. "You Irish?"

He nodded.

"Your accent's not too noticeable, though. How long you been away from Ireland?"

"Feels like centuries." Liam looked down at the jewels in the case, smoothing his hand over the glass.

"I bet you miss the good stuff." Perry made a motion like he was tipping back a drink. "That Irish whiskey's liquid gold, I tell you. I used to know me a girl from Dublin who could drink anyone under the table. She was my kind of lady, you know what I mean?" He wiggled his bushy white eyebrows.

"Aye, Perry." Liam gave him a crocodile grin. "I surely do."

Cora decided to change the subject before they started breaking into bawdy limericks. "We're here to ask you a couple of questions about the robbery last night. At the Gas n' Go on the corner? I just wanted to follow up to see if there's anything you might have seen. I know you're a few stores down, but is there anything you can think of that might be useful?"

"It's like I told the cops last night, I was watching TV, so I missed the whole thing." Perry looked truly disappointed, and even a little embarrassed. For a renowned neighborhood busybody, he probably felt like he'd been slacking on the job.

"Did you maybe hear anything unusual?"

Perry scratched his beard. "Sorry, no. But why don't you ask little Billy Mac? He's always out and about. I saw him on the street near the Gas n' Go yesterday evening."

Cora murmured her thanks for the lead, though it wasn't much to go on. After a few more questions, she realized Perry was a dead end. She and Liam spent the next couple of hours checking in with all the shop owners on the street, but all she found out was that Mrs. Minniver's cat had kittens in the front window of her thrift store, somebody spray-painted #JusticeForDolphins in the sushi restaurant bathroom, and Liam O'Connor had an annoying, overprotective streak that rivaled her own father's.

They were walking past a liquor store when a street person leered at her. He was slouched on the pavement, leaning against the wall, eyeing Cora like she was a new bottle of top-shelf whiskey. She fully intended to ignore him, until he made a lewd comment about her backside.

She turned and opened her mouth to say something, but before she could form words, Liam flew at him.

He slammed the man up against the wall.

The man made a surprised, gurgling sound that ended on a choked cough.

"You don't talk to her like that," Liam said fiercely, shaking him. "*Ever*. Do you hear me?"

"Liam!" Cora shouted, grabbing his arm. "Let him go."

Liam didn't budge. A muscle ticked in his jaw. He shook the man again.

"I said, let him go," Cora repeated, gripping his rock-hard arm with both her hands. "Now."

Very slowly, Liam released the man, who stumbled off down the alley as fast as he could.

She glared at Liam, incredulous. "What the hell were you thinking?"

"Me?" He looked at her like she was insane. "That man insulted you. He was one foul breath away from laying his filthy hands on you. I know for a fact there are laws against assaulting a police officer—"

"But he didn't. And anyway, I would've handled it," she interrupted. "I am very aware of the laws. Just like I'm aware of when it is, and isn't, appropriate to use force on a civilian. You can't just go around slamming people against walls like that because you don't like what they say."

"I can and I will," he said stubbornly. "That man should be locked up and—"

"It wasn't up to you," Cora interrupted fiercely. "It was my problem, do you understand? *My* call." Just because her dad seemed to think Liam would make a great roommate-slash-bodyguard, didn't mean Liam got to play the savior whenever it suited him. Before he spent another minute in her presence, she needed to hammer that home. "I didn't need you to intervene, O'Connor." His eyes narrowed at her use of his last name. She had no idea why, and at the moment, she didn't care. "I can take care of myself, and I've been doing it a lot longer than you may think. I am not a victim. I don't need a hero."

"And you won't be getting one." Liam stepped close enough that she could see thin streaks of amber in his dark brown eyes. He bent down until they were almost nose to nose, and the tension seemed to crackle in the air between them. "I'm no hero, Cora McLeod, and I've never claimed to be. But you're getting my protection, whether you want it or not."

"Daang," a young voice drawled. "You got balls, man. *Balls.*"

Cora spun around to see Billy "the Mac" staring at Liam in awe. The kid was so thin, he appeared to be all angles and bones in the baggy T-shirt and jeans he was wearing. "That was hard-core, man. I just saw you jump that guy, all defending Cora's honor, and stuff."

"Billy," Cora said as calmly as she could. "Why aren't you in school?"

He shrugged his bony shoulders. "No school. Teacher Field Trip Day, or something."

Cora eyed him suspiciously. Was that even a thing? "We actually have some questions for you."

Billy didn't seem to hear her. He jerked his chin at Liam. "Man, that was a badass move you did back there. What else you got?"

Cora saw Liam mouth the word *badass*. Then he smiled and reached out to shake Billy's hand. Before Cora could blink, he had Billy in a headlock.

She gasped. "Liam! What the—"

"You're making it easy for me, kid," Liam said with a laugh. He gently released Billy, and thumped him on the back. "I'm Liam O'Connor, Cora's…friend."

Oh-ho, she wouldn't go that far. "Officer O'Connor is new to Providence Falls," she said coolly. "He'll be working at the station, and I've been assigned to show him around. We just met yesterday." She threw Liam a glance to see if he got the message. They were *not* friends. They were barely even acquaintances.

Liam gave her a long, searching look. His odd expression seemed brimming with secrets she had neither the time nor the inclination to decipher.

"Just met yesterday, huh?" Billy nodded and gave Cora a cocky grin. "That's good to hear. Wouldn't want some rando coming between us, know what I mean?"

"Hey, watch it, kid. You saw what happened to the last guy." Liam held up a worn leather wallet with exaggerated, wide-eyed innocence. "Is this yours, by any chance?"

Billy's mouth fell open. He reached into his jacket pocket. "How did you?"

"Slip of the hand," Liam said, handing back the wallet. "If you answer a few questions for us, I'll show you how it's done."

"Seriously?" Cora jammed her hands on her hips. "You're going to teach a minor how to steal wallets, now?"

"It's not stealing," Liam insisted. "It's just a magic trick. Like this." He waved a hand and produced a quarter out of thin air. Then he waved his hand again, and the coin was gone. "It's a great way to impress the ladies."

"Sweet!" Billy looked so eager and happy to learn, Cora didn't have the heart to intervene. It wasn't often she saw him smile like that. She sighed heavily, and for the next few minutes, she questioned Billy about the Gas n' Go robbery while Liam taught him the coin trick. When Billy didn't have anything useful to offer, Cora checked her phone messages and answered a few texts from Suzette. By the time Liam started showing Billy how to pick pockets, she figured it was time to go.

"This has been fun," Cora announced. "But I think you've corrupted the minor for long enough."

They said their goodbyes and got into the car. She pulled onto the busy street as Liam waved to Billy. The kid's face was filled with hero worship.

"You guys seemed to hit it off pretty quickly," Cora observed. She was still annoyed at Liam for pulling that macho bullshit move with the street person earlier, but it was hard not to admire the way he'd interacted with Billy. The boy had so few positive role models in his life, and it was clear they had a connection. "I think you made quite an impression on him." She stopped the car at a red light and glanced over at Liam.

He was staring out the window, his gaze a million miles away. "He reminds me of some kids I used to know."

"Who were they?"

Cora saw him tense.

"Just some kids from my village back in Ireland," he

said quietly. His expression was so bleak and haunted, she suddenly wanted to do whatever she could to lighten his mood.

"Well, I think you've got yourself a new friend," she said brightly. "I guess those cheap tricks are good for more than just impressing the ladies, huh?" She waited for his reaction. Hoped…

Liam ran a hand through his hair and glanced sideways at her. Then he flashed a brilliant smile that would make any Hollywood heartthrob green with envy. "They're not cheap tricks." Was that a dimple in his left cheek? Of course it was. "They're *badass*."

7

The following night, Liam lay staring at the ceiling, reciting all the modern swear words he'd been learning. Given the fact that he was a police officer and, in the past couple of days, he'd spent a considerable amount of time driving through traffic or working with Cora out in the city, his list of curse words was getting off to a right good start.

"Dick off," he murmured. No, that wasn't it. Something piss, and then head, or… Ah, yes. "Piss off, dickhead."

"Eloquent," a smooth voice said from the darkened corner.

Liam jackknifed out of bed, his hands balled into fists.

The shadows dimmed, then melted away in bright sparks of light as the tall, dark-haired angel moved into the room. The shorter blond one appeared beside him. Their wings glowed at their backs, the feathers softly rippling in a breeze Liam couldn't feel.

He stumbled back and sat down hard on the bed. Even knowing these celestial beings were on his side, they were awe-inspiring and fearsome to behold.

"I see you've been working at blending in, ruffian," the blond one said stoically. "What with all your attention to certain aspects of the modern language."

Liam struggled to find his voice. His initial shock at seeing them morphed slowly into frustration. He had questions, dammit. And he needed a lot of answers, but he'd settle for the biggest issue first. "Why does it hurt whenever my skin touches Cora's?" he demanded. "That's your doing, isn't it?"

The blond angel looked bored. "Of course, ruffian. It was necessary to keep you focused. You're like a starving mongrel at a buffet when it comes to her, and we didn't want you to fail within your first hour here. Think of it as…" He turned to the other angel. "What's it called, again?"

"Training wheels," the dark-haired angel said proudly. His encouraging smile did nothing to alleviate Liam's escalating frustration. "From what I gather, they're often very helpful."

"I don't need training wheels," Liam snarled. "There's little chance of me failing because Cora remembers nothing of the love we shared, thanks to you."

"True," the blond angel agreed. "But you forget we're familiar with your tactics when it comes to charming women. This way, it won't be easy for you to fall into old patterns. As long as you keep your hands to yourself, you'll have a better chance of steering Cora into the arms of the right man."

"Finley Walsh," Liam almost spat the name. He still couldn't say it without grimacing. He scrubbed his face with both hands, then clenched his fingers into his hair and tugged. "How can I influence Cora to fall for that milksop of a man if she doesn't even care for my opinion? And as for him, I haven't even seen him yet. I've no idea where he is in this godda—uh—in this city. And then there's Boyd as my boss. *Boyd.* Really? It's bad enough I've got to deal with Margaret, too. Why have you thrown me into a relationship with her? I don't see how it can help my situation in the least. Everything is so screwed up here, I feel as if my mind is cracking. And Cora…" He trailed off, a bleak, overwhelming sense of hopelessness settling over him, then finished on a whisper. "Cora doesn't know me anymore."

The dark-haired angel glided closer and reached out. He touched the tip of his finger between Liam's eyes, Liam suddenly felt as if he'd been dipped in sunlight. He was as weightless as a song on the wind. Blinking in awe, he rolled his shoulders, no longer crushed by heavy emotions.

"Have patience, Liam O'Connor." The angel's voice was like a balm to his frazzled nerves. "There are things you must learn in your own time."

Liam took a calming breath and dropped his head into his hands. "It's just hard seeing her after missing her for so long. And then coming back to this motel alone, each day. She won't have me at her house."

"We've taken care of that," the blond one said.

He glanced up sharply. "How?"

Neither of them answered. They began to slide back into the shadows.

"Wait!" Liam stood up in alarm. There were so many things he still needed to know. He tried to step closer, but an invisible barrier stopped him. He pressed both hands against it. "Can't you tell me more? I thought you were supposed to help me."

"Tomorrow you'll meet Finn." The dark-haired angel said kindly.

"Perhaps then, you will stop wasting energy trying to learn curse words, rogue," the blond one added. "And you will focus, instead, on saving your endangered soul."

They spread their shimmering wings, burst into a thousand pinpoints of light and then disappeared.

Liam sat alone in the dark for a long time. When he was certain they were well and truly gone, he slumped back onto the bed and whispered, *"Balls."*

On Wednesday evening, Liam felt like a wild horse chomping at the bit. He had to get out of the office. He had to move his body. Sitting still for long periods of time had never been easy, and he didn't understand how these people did it. He'd been fake-working at his desk all day, still incompetent at computers. Apparently, the angels hadn't thought it necessary to fix that aspect of his knowledge. Since Cora had to write up some reports, they hadn't spent any time out in the field, and he felt like he was going to explode.

It didn't make things easier that his desk was across the room from Cora. All he had to do was glance up to see her lovely face. Watch her lick whipped cream off her fancy coffee drinks. Witness as she absently played with the gold necklace nestled in her V-neck shirt.

He shifted uncomfortably in his chair, then shot to his feet. Enough sitting.

Otto swiveled his balding head in Liam's direction. "Everything okay?"

"I'm just going to grab some…coffee." Grab some coffee *never*, because that stuff was bad enough to curdle a man's insides, but everyone in this place seemed to consider it one of life's necessities, so he played along.

In the hallway, Liam walked quickly, gaining speed until he shot past Mavis at the entrance and bolted into the parking lot. Unwilling to stop there, he took a lap around the perimeter of the building, grateful for the stretch of his muscles and the familiar burn in his legs. When he came full circle, he did it again. And again. By the time he made it back to his desk fifteen minutes later, he felt much better. How these people could stand to sit in front of computers for so many hours out of the day was a mystery to him. It wasn't natural.

"You coming to Danté's with us after?" Otto asked, turning in his overstuffed office chair. "They have great microbrews on tap."

Liam glanced over at Cora. "Is everyone going?"

She was shuffling papers on her desk, so she didn't make eye contact when she said, "Not everyone. It's just a local bar down the road. It's not a big deal."

"*I'm* not going," Happy said with his usual pinched expression.

Otto swiveled to face him. "Come on, Happ. Just this once. You might actually enjoy it."

"I'm surrounded by you people all day long," Happy said, adjusting his jacket before standing and pushing in his chair. "Some of us prefer to find enjoyment in more meaningful ways."

"Oh, yeah? Like what?" Otto asked.

Happy just shook his head, checked his phone and left without a backward glance.

When Rob Hopper breezed into the room, he swooped

up to Cora's desk, grabbed the back of her chair and spun her in a circle.

Cora let out a little shriek, but she was smiling.

Liam wasn't. The man took too many liberties with Cora. He needed to change that. If he dared call her Peaches today, he'd drop the sorry bastard on his ass.

"It's hump day," Rob announced. "You're going to Dan-té's, Cora, because I need you to bring your friend Suzette. I'm still trying to win her over with my razor-sharp wit and hot body."

Cora shoved at him, then adjusted her chair. "Suzette's too smart to fall for you. Besides, she's dating someone else, so don't get your hopes up."

"Nonsense," Rob said. "I like a little competition. A good fight once in a while really gets the blood flowing, amirite, Liam?"

Liam gave him an assessing look. "Sure." Rob was a couple of inches shorter than him, and even though he looked strong, Liam felt certain he could beat him at anything. He'd been in drunken fights with the Bricks a time or two, and he'd survived to tell the tale. This man was soft as porridge compared to them. "Anytime you need a challenge, let me know."

"Excellent!" Rob made a show of bouncing on the balls of his feet and punching the air a few times. "How are you at boxing? We should go a few rounds sometime."

Liam stood up fast. He was itching to expend some energy, and Rob was a damned fool if he thought he could best him. "I'm ready."

"Ignore Rob," Cora said in exasperation. "Nine times out of ten, he's screwing with you."

"True," Rob said. "Except when I asked Suzette out last week, Cora. I wasn't screwing around then."

She stood and tugged on her jacket. "You've asked out every woman in the city, Hopper. I'm pretty sure screwing is exactly what you had in mind."

He slapped a hand to his chest and turned to Liam. "She kills me."

"You deserve it," Liam threw back.

Rob stuck his tongue between his teeth and grinned. "Probably."

Cora was halfway to the corridor before she glanced back. "If you want to go, Liam, you can follow me over. Unless you're busy tonight." She looked like she didn't care, either way.

It cut deep, this casual disregard. Liam wasn't used to it, especially not from her. He steeled himself with a renewed sense of determination as they left the station. No matter what his task was here in this lifetime, he and Cora were connected. One way or another, she was going to care for him again. He'd make sure of it.

Ten minutes later, Liam stood outside of the bar staring at the sign that read Danté's Inferno. It was surrounded by dancing orange and red flames that blinked back and forth. The letter *T*, upon closer inspection, was a black pitchfork. A traveling bard back in Ireland had once talked about the seven circles of hell, so the irony was not lost on Liam. He tipped his face to the sky and barely refrained from muttering one of his favorite new words. Either this was a bad omen, or the angels had a wicked sense of humor.

A tall man with light brown hair rushed forward to open the door for Cora. He said something that made her laugh.

"Liam, this is my friend Finn Walsh," Cora said over her shoulder. "Finn, meet Liam O'Connor."

Finn's smile was automatic, but it didn't reach his eyes

until Cora added, "Liam's a new officer on our team. He just started this week."

Relief washed over the man's face. "It's great to meet you."

A slight incline of his head was all Liam could manage. He was glad to finally meet his target, but the feeling was overshadowed by a hot spike of jealousy. Finn Walsh was certainly nothing special to look at. Cora could do—had done!—so much better than a man like this. For one thing, he had an extremely forgettable face. His suit and shirt looked as stiff as his posture, and he was wearing a red striped tie that Liam wouldn't be caught dead in. And if history truly repeated itself, Finn was going to be as dull as a box of rocks.

Liam clenched and unclenched his hands as he followed them into the bar, doing his best to seek reason. No matter how tempting, it would not do to accidentally slip and punch the man in the kidney. That would be very hard to explain later.

It was dark inside, with intimate lighting and plush red velvet booths in the corners. Glowing sconces lined the walls casting soft pools of light on the ceiling, and round tables with leather chairs took up the main floor. A glossy wood counter ran along the far wall where two bartenders were serving drinks to a clientele far different from any tavern regulars Liam used to know. Most of the people here were dressed in sophisticated, well-tailored clothes, and the air was thick with the scents of cologne, aged leather and alcoholic drinks. Everything about this place was alluring and decadent and—Liam gazed at the shelves behind the bar filled with hundreds of liquor bottles—intoxicating. Designed to draw a man in and keep him there. Danté's Inferno, indeed.

Cora took a seat in one of the booths, and Liam squeezed in beside her, leaving Finn to sit opposite them. Liam slung an arm over the back of the booth behind Cora and stared stonily at Finn.

The man gave him a nervous smile, tugged at his tie, then glanced away. Coward.

"There you are," Cora said to a woman approaching the table.

A fiery redhead swooped into their booth on a cloud of spicy perfume, her silver bracelets jangling. The intrigued look she gave Liam was as wicked as her low-cut black dress.

"Liam, this is my best friend, Suzette Wilson," Cora began. "Suze, meet—"

"Liam O'Connor," the woman exclaimed, glancing at Liam like he held the answers to the universe. "Cora told me all about you on the phone." Before Liam could respond, she slapped her hand on the table. "It's high time we got a newbie in town. It gets boring when you grow up in the same place with the same people and everything's just same old, same old, you know?"

"I—" Liam began.

"Tell us your whole life story," Suzette blurted, pinning him with a cheeky smile. Her kohl-rimmed eyes roamed over him with blatant appreciation.

"I'm not sure you'd believe me if I did," he said. "And most of it's not fit to mention in the polite company of ladies."

Suzette let out a delighted, throaty laugh that was pure feminine pleasure. "Damn, Cora, when you told me about him on the phone, you left out some very important details."

Liam cocked a brow. "Like what?"

"Don't ask," Cora warned, throwing Suzette a look.

Suzette cupped her hand to the side of her mouth and told Liam in a stage whisper, "Like, she never mentioned you were all tall, dark, and…" She let out a giggle that ended on a hiccup. "Piratey looking."

Liam gave Suzette an amused smirk. He wondered how many drinks she'd had. The glass in her hand was almost empty.

"Ignore her," Cora said with a begrudging smile. "Suzette was dropped on her head at birth. We try not to talk about it."

Suzette gave Cora an air kiss, then turned to the box of rocks beside her. "Oh. Hey, Finn. How are you? You're so quiet, I didn't notice you."

Ha! Liam was beginning to like this friend of Cora's.

"I mean I saw you," Suzette said with a laugh, "but I was distracted."

Before Finn could answer, Rob Hopper suddenly appeared at their table. "I'll give you a distraction, Suzette." He gave her a toothy grin and ran a hand through his hair. Liam was almost certain the man flexed his biceps on purpose.

Suzette made a show of sizing Rob up, unimpressed. "Sure thing, Rob. Let me know when he gets here."

"Aw, come on, Red," Rob pleaded. "Let me buy you a Long Island iced tea."

She crinkled her forehead. "Hell, no. You know those things knock me flat on my ass."

His grin became positively wolfish. "And the problem with that would be…?"

Suzette pressed her lips into a hard line, but it looked like she was trying not to smile. "I have to get up early for work tomorrow, so just forget it."

"Fair enough," Rob said. "A glass of wine, then. Please?"

"Fine. But only because you owe me." She slid out of the booth to join him. "The last time you offered to buy me a drink, I watched you flirt with that flight attendant and then you left with her and stuck me with the bill."

"I told you, I hadn't seen her in a long time," Rob insisted. "She was my cousin."

"Kissing cousins?" Suzette punched him on the shoulder as they disappeared into the crowd.

Liam watched the red-haired woman walk away, noting how she clung to Rob's arm. She seemed outspoken and very at ease around men, unlike the shy, guileless Cora he remembered from his past. "That's your best friend?"

"Don't worry," Cora said with a smile. "She grows on you. Right, Finn?"

"Sure." Finn looked at Cora as if she'd just given him the deed to a gold mine. Jesus, this man was transparent. Liam wouldn't be surprised if a puddle of drool formed on the table in front of him.

Cora seemed clueless. How the hell was he supposed to urge her in Finn's direction? It would take a herculean effort. No woman in her right mind would be interested in *that*.

"So," Finn began, tugging at his tie. "Are you guys planning to go to the charity ball next Saturday?"

Plain as day, Liam could see where Finn was going with this. The man wasn't even looking at him; he was focused only on Cora.

She was waving her hand to get the server's attention. "I haven't decided yet."

Liam braced himself. This was a perfect opening, and he really ought to take it. He could almost feel the angels watching him, and he'd not be forgetting their warning anytime soon. When the floor in that chamber of mist opened up and he'd started to fall, he thought he would surely die. And they were angels. The good guys. If that was the fear *they* inspired, he didn't even want to imagine the alternative. He balled his hands into fists, crossed his arms and said, "Are you planning to go, Finn?"

Finn kept glancing at Cora. "I think so."

"I swear the server looked right at me and then turned around," Cora said absently.

Liam nudged her with his shoulder, grateful that the barrier of their clothes kept the pain at bay. Apparently, the only danger was in their skin-on-skin contact. He probably ought to thank the angels for that small mercy, but he wasn't going to. "You're attending the gala, right?" he asked Cora. "I'd like to go, and it would be great if you were there since I don't know many people yet."

She looked at him in surprise. "*You* really want to go?"

Liam tried to appear sincere. "Of course. I believe you said it was a charity event with the main purpose being to drink a lot and rob rich people of their money. Sounds like my kind of party."

"I guess you just don't strike me as the tuxedo-wearing type, that's all," Cora said. "It's a formal event. You know that, right?"

"Yes," Finn chimed in.

"Not you, Finn," Cora said with a laugh. "You're totally the penguin-suit type."

His face fell for a split second, but she didn't seem to notice.

Liam wondered if Cora had any idea she'd embarrassed the man. A tiny voice inside him was chanting a little victory tune, but he forged on. "I do want to go. Both of you have lived here for a long time, so you can introduce me to people." He opened his arms wide and said in his best jovial voice, "The three of us can make a party of it!" There, angels. How was that for playing his role?

Finn glanced up in surprise.

"Fine, fine," Cora said, preoccupied again with getting the server's attention. "I'll go if it's that important to you."

"Should I swing by and pick you up, Cora?" Finn asked. "I mean, your house is on my way, so it wouldn't be a problem." Of course, it wouldn't be a problem. If Finn lived on the other side of the planet, he'd find a way to *swing by* and pick her up. Liam barely refrained from kicking the man under the table. Instead, he sat up straighter and forced himself to think of the consequences if he failed to get them together. Nothing like the thought of eternal hellfire to snap things back into focus.

"No, you don't have to pick me up," Cora said. "I can catch my own—"

"Actually," Liam interrupted. "If there will be a lot of drinking going on, it seems like a good idea."

Finn sat up straighter, looking as if Liam had just granted him a knighthood.

"What about you?" she asked Liam.

He paused, then forced out, "I nominate Finn our designated driver."

"That's great," Finn blurted. He looked grateful just to be included. "No problem, at all."

"It's settled, then," Liam said flatly. Conflicted, he leaned back in the booth and crossed his arms. He had no desire to go to that gala in a penguin suit, but if he was supposed to get Cora and Finn together, it seemed like the easiest way to do it. Part of him felt a smug sense of satisfaction at the way he'd maneuvered things. The angels couldn't have missed that. Extra halo points for him, surely.

But a larger part of him was annoyed beyond reason that Cora was going to be going anywhere with Finn. He let out a frustrated groan. This was madness.

"I know, right?" Cora said, glancing at him. "I've been trying to get the server's attention, but it's not working. Maybe I should just go to the bar."

"I'll go," Finn offered. Because he was Finn. And if Cora suddenly decided she wanted the moon, he'd probably start building a ladder on the spot. "What do you want?"

They gave him their drink orders, and then it was just Liam and Cora left in the booth. They were sitting so close, Liam could feel the warmth of her arm next to his. He wanted to lean closer and breathe in her scent to see if she still smelled like lavender and sunshine. He wondered if her hair still felt as silky and smooth in his hands, if her lips were as soft.

The torch above their booth suddenly flared, casting ominous, flame-like shadows on the ceiling. Liam grimaced, then forced himself to slide out of the booth to sit across from her so they could converse more easily. "So." He braced himself. "How long have you known Finn?"

She got a far-off look in her eyes. "Years, I guess."

Hot jealousy spiked through his veins. He'd never been lucky enough to have that much time with her. "Years?"

"I mean, we only really got to know each other a couple of years ago when he was working on a case I was following, but my dad knew him before that. They used to go golfing together, and they still do sometimes. I guess Finn's always kind of been there in the background, but I never paid attention."

Satisfaction washed over him. "That bad, huh?" He shouldn't have said it, but he couldn't help himself.

The torch flared ominously again, and Cora glanced up

to watch. Liam tried not to stare at her slender throat, remembering all too well how soft her skin was right there, where her neck met her shoulder.

He tore his gaze away and tried again. "Finn seems like a nice guy."

"He is. He's just…" She trailed off, smiling to herself.

Stuffy? Cowardly? A wimpy excuse for a man? "Well, if he's friends with your father, I'm sure he's a good man." The words tasted like ashes on Liam's tongue, but he was proud of himself for getting through them without choking.

Finn returned with their drinks and placed them on the table. He gave Cora another sappy smile. "Suzette said to tell you to meet her over at the bar for a minute. She said she has some good news."

Cora went off in search of her friend, leaving Liam alone with Finn.

They sat across from each other in silence. Liam studied the man, cataloging every flaw he could find. Finn had nondescript beige hair. And it was too artfully arranged with some kind of pomade. He wasn't out of shape, but he didn't look like the type of man who spent his time outdoors. He was probably one of those dapper types with more clothes and shoes than days in the year. Yes, he could just imagine Finn standing in the middle of an enormous closet every morning, carefully deciding which stuffy suit he'd wear for the day. They'd all be nondescript and beige, of course.

Liam's lip curled.

Finn gave a nervous smile.

Right there. That was another flaw. The man was far too smiley. In Liam's experience, men who smiled too much were trying to swindle you. He took a long drink, watching Finn over the rim of his beer glass with suspicion. *Whatever you're selling, dullard, I'm not buying. I'm no fool, and neither is Cora. It's going to take a miracle to get her to fall for you.*

Finn was beginning to look uncomfortable. He tugged on his stupid tie. "Good weather we're having."

Kill me now. The man truly was a perfect bore. "Perfect." Liam took another drink of his beer, which was surprisingly good. At least there was that.

"Okay, we need to talk about this new guy of yours." Suzette grabbed Cora's hand and tugged her down the hall toward the bathroom.

"He's not my guy," Cora said with feeling. "If it were up to me, I wouldn't be hanging around him at all."

Suzette spun to face her with dreamy anime eyes. Cora could practically see stars twinkling in them. "But he's *so* gorgeous."

Cora waved a hand. "He's not that… He's just a basic…" She blew out a frustrated breath. Because no matter how she spun it, Liam O'Connor was undeniably gorgeous.

"Um, are you feeling okay?" Suzette asked. "Because on a scale of one to ten, with ten being like shirtless-Jason-Momoa-holding-a-puppy hot? That guy is a solid eleven. Don't even try to tell me you haven't noticed." She gave Cora a challenging look.

Cora squirmed. Suzette had always been able to see right through her. "Okay, sure. I've noticed, but so what? We're both going to be working together at the station. *Every single day.* I don't date guys at work. That's just way too close for comfort. And not only that, I'm not even sure I like him. At all. He's overbearing and controlling. His first day on the job, he almost beat up a guy for catcalling me on the street, for God's sake! Like I was some damsel in distress who needed someone to defend my honor. I mean, what the hell?"

"That's kind of romantic," Suzette said in a swoony voice.

"No, it's reckless and irrational." Cora shook her head in exasperation. "The guy is like my dad with the overprotective thing, and you know how much I hate that. So, nothing's going to happen between us because I'm not interested, okay? Just let it go."

Suzette pursed her lips to the side, considering. "Meh, for now. But you and I are going to revisit this topic at a later date. Now, *get this*." Her hands began to flutter with excitement. "I just ran into my friend Jacquie from the real estate office, and guess which house is going on the market toward the end of August?" She didn't wait for Cora to guess. "Your dream house!"

Cora pulled to an abrupt stop in the hallway. "The cottage?"

"Yep," Suzette said triumphantly.

Cora's insides clenched. *Her* cottage. The house she'd been in love with as long as she could remember. She automatically reached for the gold rose pendant she always wore.

"End of August," Suzette repeated. "So, you better get your butt in gear because you'll need to save up to make a competitive offer."

Suzette kept talking, but Cora wasn't listening. She grappled at her neck in shock, realizing her necklace was gone. *"No."* She frantically searched her blouse. Her jacket. The floor. "My mother's necklace! It's not on me. It must've fallen off." Dread whipped through her at the thought of losing it.

Suzette started scanning the hallway floor. "When was the last time you remember seeing it?"

"I don't know." Cora's voice began to rise. "I never take it off. It's just always there." The panic snaking through her stomach made her almost queasy. "I have to find it!" She strode down the hall and plunged back into the crowd near the bar.

Suzette found her a moment later, crouched low and searching the area under the barstools. When nothing came up, Cora began asking everyone within hearing distance, "Has anyone seen a gold necklace?" She held her thumb and forefinger close together. "It has a rose pendant on it about this big?"

Some of the more polite patrons helped her search for a few minutes. Others just ignored her and carried on with their conversations. Cora and Suzette continued searching under every chair and table, but it was nowhere to be found.

Cora returned to the booth where Liam and Finn were sitting.

Liam took one look at her and his brows snapped together. "What's wrong? What is it?"

"My necklace," Cora said miserably. "The gold rose pendant I always wear. I lost it and can't find it."

"Could it be at your office?" Finn asked with concern. "Or maybe in your car?"

"No," Liam said. "I saw it on you when you were sitting across from me earlier. You were fiddling with it."

"I'm always fiddling with it," she said. "I think it must've broken and fallen off somewhere in here."

Finn slid out of the booth quickly. "I'll go look for it." He took off toward the bar and Cora did a cursory search under the booth before slumping down in the seat. "If I don't find it…" She trailed off and dropped her head in her hands. It was silly, really, for her to place so much importance on a piece of jewelry. Her father hadn't raised her to be overly sentimental, but Cora couldn't help it. The necklace was one of the only things she had left from her mom, aside from some old family photo albums. To anyone else, it probably wouldn't be worth much, but to Cora, it was one of her most prized possessions.

Liam offered to help search, and together they retraced her steps, but it soon became apparent that the necklace was gone.

"Maybe someone will find it later and turn it in," Suzette said soothingly. She patted Cora on the back.

"Or maybe someone stole it," Liam said, glowering at the crowd like he was ready to do battle.

Suzette threw him a look. "Can't you see she's upset? If you're trying to help, that's not really working."

"No." Cora shook her head. "He's right. Someone could've found it and decided to keep it."

"Or like I said, someone might turn it in later," Suzette insisted. "We'll look around one more time, and if we don't find it, you can call and ask tomorrow."

"I can't believe I lost it," Cora whispered.

"I'm sorry, Cora." Liam touched her shoulder gently. The warmth from his large hand felt reassuring through the fabric of her shirt, and strangely familiar. "I'll come with you tomorrow to ask in person. Don't lose hope, okay? We'll do whatever we can to get it back. I promise."

She nodded. He looked genuinely bothered that she was so upset. It surprised her how strongly he seemed to care. Maybe her dad was right about him, and he really was a good person. Maybe she just needed to give him a chance, especially now that her dream house was going

up for sale. Time was running out. She needed a roommate more than ever. All her finances were in order, but
if she could save up just a little more money over the next
few months, she'd be able to make a competitive offer on
the cottage if there was a bidding war. In the current real
estate market, it often happened. She had to be smart. It
was now, or never.

"Liam, do you still need a place to live?" she asked in
a rush.

He blinked at her sudden change of subject, then hope
flickered across his face. "I do."

"Well, I need a roommate. Right away. I have to save up
money and I need someone to help with the rent as soon
as possible. So, you can move in on Friday, if you want."
There. She said it, and now there was no going back.

Some strong emotion flickered across his face, then he
nodded. "I'd like that."

"It's settled, then." So that was that. Roommate problem
solved. At least one good thing came from this disaster of
an evening. She slid out of the booth. "I'm heading home."

Finn walked up to the table after an apparently fruitless
search. He looked like a sad kid with a popped balloon.
"Leaving so soon?"

"Yes." She hoisted her purse onto her shoulder. "I'm
not up for hanging out anymore."

"Let me walk you out." Liam started to stand, but Cora
waved him down.

"No. Stay and enjoy yourself. I'll see you all later."

She wove through the crowd and into the parking lot,
automatically reaching for the necklace that was no longer there. *Don't lose hope, okay?* Liam's words rang in her
head as she drove home. Having him as a roommate was
going to be a big change. She hadn't had the best first im-

pression of him, but there seemed to be a deeply caring side of him that couldn't be denied. And he'd been kind to little Billy Mac the other day, hadn't he? Maybe living with him would turn out to be a good thing. Maybe her dad was right, and he would be good for her to have around. The sudden memory of him roughing up the man outside the liquor store flashed across her mind. Then again, maybe this was a huge mistake, and she was going to kick herself later. Either way, she was about to find out.

8

Kinsley, Ireland,
1844

"I should pound your skull in for this," Boyd growled through clenched teeth. He stood outside of the Goose & Gander tavern as twilight fell, glowering at Liam like an angry boar. In his fist he clutched the paste jewelry Cora had given Liam the night before. "You and I are practically brothers, but—"

"He's not *my* brother." A sharp crack exploded against Liam's face, and his head snapped back. One of the Bricks—Liam could never tell the twins apart—had just walloped him upside the head with a fist the size of a Sunday ham. "We were supposed to raid the squire's house together." Spittle flew from the man's flattened lips, and his blunt face was twisted in anger. "You had no business goin' off on yer own last night."

Liam rubbed his aching jaw and pointed at the large hulk of a man. "I'll give you that one, but if you touch me again, you'll spend the rest of your days looking even uglier than your identical twin here."

The Bricks squared off together, facing Liam like a pair of angry bulls, but neither of them made a move. No one would ever accuse them of being smart, but at least they knew enough to be wary of Liam's threat. Liam wasn't as strong as they were, but he was much faster, and he knew how to fight dirty when he had to.

"I'll tell you again, and try to get it through your thick heads," Liam said, swiping a fleck of blood from his mouth. "Squire McLeod is as broke as a swayback mare. His house is falling apart. Anything of value has been sold off or traded away, and if there ever was any treasure, *that*—" he pointed to the tangle of necklaces Boyd clutched in his fist "—is all that remains. The squire's been keeping up appearances for a long time, and from the looks of it, he won't be able to carry on much longer."

"But I've seen the squire's daughter drive through the village with that old maid of hers," one of the twins snarled. "Riding high in that fancy carriage, snooty as you please. She doesn't look hard up."

"An illusion," Liam said quickly. A bolt of alarm shot through him at the thought of these men even thinking of Cora. They were unpredictable, and he wanted to keep them as far away from her as possible. "All of it's for show. The squire is deeply in debt. I overheard the servants talking. Most of that place goes unused, with rooms full of nothing more than dust and shadows. I'm telling you, there's not a single thing in that house of value." Nothing except the lovely Cora, whose value had become immeasurable to him.

Boyd swore foully and shoved the necklaces against

Liam's chest. "Maybe we should take a look for ourselves tonight, just to be sure. You might've missed something."

Liam took the jewelry and pocketed it, never taking his eyes off Boyd's angry face. Even the tips of his ears were red. "You know I'm better at stealth than any of you, and I searched the entire house from top to bottom, which was no easy feat. There are more servants on the premises than we expected. It's not worth the risk." He gave Boyd a pointed look. "Your wife, Alice, will be none too pleased to see you dangling at the end of a hangman's noose for nothing if you were to get caught."

Boyd spat on the ground and cursed again. Then he began to pace. "She's been nagging at me to bring in more money, and this was going to be our big break. Now what am I supposed to tell her?" He raked his hands over his head, yanking at tufts of his hair. For a moment, Liam pitied his friend. Alice had a sharp tongue, and they'd married very young. She was as bawdy and loose in morals as her husband, which made it an easy match in the beginning, but the harder times got, the more bitter and angry Alice had become. Liam knew things at home weren't good for Boyd, but he also knew not to mention it. Boyd was a prideful man, and he'd never admit he couldn't keep his wife happy. It was surprising he'd mentioned her at all.

"You go home tonight and tell Alice to be expecting a great pile of riches before the week is over," Liam said, launching into his new plan. He'd been sitting on it all day, and he prayed it would divert their attention away from Cora's house.

"What are you on about?" Boyd demanded.

Even the Bricks looked more alert, which was saying a lot.

Liam jumped right in. "I overheard the servants talking

last night. The grand party the squire attends is north of here, off the main highway. There are dozens of wealthy families in attendance there for the next few days. All we'll have to do is wait it out. We can camp in the woods, and as the carriages make their return trips home after the party..." Liam held out his hands in a foregone conclusion.

"We pick them clean," one of the Bricks said.

"Like raptors on a fresh carcass," the other twin added. Both brothers glanced at each other and a silent communication passed between them. Then, in unison, their craggy faces broke into identical leers.

One of them gave a curt nod. "Hang the squire's house. We'll go where the real money is. We'll go after the carriages."

Thank God and all that was holy. The Bricks were on board. Liam waited for Boyd to chime in. It didn't take long. Once the twins began speculating about the piles of riches in store, the excitement caught, and soon Boyd became just as motivated. By the time they all parted ways, a new plan was underway, and more importantly, Cora's house was safe again.

Relief flooded Liam as he walked down the main road toward the path leading to his brother's farm. The night sky was brilliant with stars and the full moon shone like a crown jewel, but he barely noticed. He was too blinded by the dazzling memory of Cora's sweet face and soft voice from the previous night. Now that the crisis was averted and his friends no longer wanted to raid her house, he had the luxury of replaying the precious moments he'd spent with her. He hadn't slept a wink since meeting the beguiling young woman who'd made him feel more alive than he had in ages. Even though he knew he shouldn't, he was already devising a plan to see her again. He wasn't sure how or when; he just knew he had to find a way.

A carriage rumbled up the road behind him. Liam stepped into the weeds to let it pass, but it slowed to a stop. He recognized the crest on the door and swore under his breath. This wasn't going to go well.

An elegant, gloved hand pushed the carriage door open, and Margaret Brady's regal face appeared. She was a beautiful woman, with porcelain skin, wide gray eyes, and a long, graceful neck. Her shiny dark hair was arranged in perfect curls high on her head, and as always, she was impeccably dressed in a pale silk gown and gleaming jewelry.

"Liam. I haven't seen you in a while." Her throaty voice was low and sultry, and there was a time not long ago when it would've worked like a magic spell. "You haven't answered my messages this past month." Whenever her husband had business out of town, she'd leave a note tucked into the hollow of a tree at the edge of her property to alert Liam. She'd tell him when it was safe to visit, and he'd steal away in the dead of night and meet at the designated hour. Their clandestine affair had been mutually satisfying for a while, but Liam had begun to suspect Margaret was growing restless and wanting more. She'd been careless the last few times her husband left town, sending servants to approach Liam with notes to meet more often—sometimes even during the day. It wasn't safe, and her husband was a cold, jealous man with enough wealth to do Liam serious harm if he ever found out. Liam had been wanting to break things off with her for some time, and now he was more determined than ever to end it.

"Margaret, we must talk." He kept his voice low so the coachman wouldn't overhear, though he suspected the servants at her house knew everything that went on behind closed doors. The danger was in not knowing whether they were loyal to Margaret or the master of the house. "We can't carry on anymore. It's too dangerous."

She let out a soft, melodious laugh. "Since when has my brawny Liam been afraid of a little danger?"

"It's more than a little if your husband were to find out about us. He'd see me flogged or hanged. You know it as well as I do."

Her delicate brows drew together. "You're seriously worried. What brought this on? It's never been a problem before, and the risk has always been there."

That's because before he'd never had much to live for. Now that he'd met Cora, he suddenly wanted to do better with his life. To *be* better. "I'm sorry, Margaret. It isn't right, what we've done, and it's best if we end it."

Her mouth opened in surprise. It was obvious Margaret never expected him, a peasant who had to scrape and scratch just to survive, to break things off with her. For a moment her calm expression crumpled, revealing genuine hurt and disappointment, but she quickly masked it with the chilly aloofness she reserved for servants and shopkeepers. Liam had never been on the receiving end of it before, but maybe it was better this way.

"You're certain?" she asked calmly, leaning forward until the moonlight fell on the perfect rise of her pale breasts above the neckline of her gown. The scent of expensive French perfume wafted in the air between them. "I've grown rather fond of our arrangement. It would be quite tedious for me to have to look..." her eyelashes fluttered coyly "...elsewhere." If she was trying to make him jealous, she needn't bother. Since the moment he'd climbed through Cora's window last night, he was a changed man.

"Do what you feel you must," he said gently. "It's not my business."

She jerked back. "You're not acting like the man I know."

"Perhaps I've changed."

Margaret regarded him shrewdly, then sucked in a breath. "There's someone else, isn't there? You've met someone." It sounded like an accusation.

He dipped his head. "Aye, I have. But—"

"Who is she?" Margaret demanded. "Surely not the baker's daughter? I've seen her making calf eyes at you and every other man on the street. Tell me you're not that stupid. Her giggling alone is enough to drive a man to drink."

"It's not her."

"Then who, the bowlegged laundress? The widow who runs the dress shop?"

Liam shook his head. "It doesn't matter. You and I have never had a future together, Margaret. We were just having a bit of fun, after all. It's time we both moved on from whatever this…thing was between us."

She pulled back farther into the shadowed carriage, but not before Liam saw the glimmer of unshed tears in her eyes.

Liam felt a sudden pang of guilt. He knew she was deeply unhappy in her marriage. Her husband was decades older than her, and he treated her like one of his possessions. "I'm sorry, Margaret."

"Do not apologize again," she said quickly. "I quite agree, anyway. We were just having a bit of fun, and it's better to end it now before it grows dull."

"I do hope we can still remain—"

"Friends?" She let out a derisive huff. "What would we do, meet for tea in the village? Go on picnics and Sunday strolls through town? You know as well as I that isn't possible."

No. It wasn't. Liam remained silent, because there wasn't anything he could say.

Finally, Margaret rapped her knuckles on the carriage ceiling and turned away. "Goodbye, Liam. Whoever this woman is, I hope she's worth it."

She is.

The driver snapped the reins, the horses lurched forward, and Liam watched as Margaret's carriage disappeared down the road. He thought about Cora, alone in that tomb of a house surrounded by nothing but scattered dust motes and faded memories of happier times when her mother was still alive. Cora was like a rare, blooming flower in a forgotten winter garden. He didn't deserve her; he never would. But that wasn't going to stop him from trying. He was a thief, after all. Taking things he didn't deserve came as naturally as breathing, and he was very good at it.

Liam's mouth kicked into a smile as he made his way home, his head filled with plans, his blood fueled with determination, and his heart brimming with hope.

9

Liam hauled his duffel bag from the trunk of his car on Friday evening and charged toward Cora's front door. This was exactly where he belonged, and he couldn't wait to be with her. *Live* with her. Get her to trust him and need him and want him. He stopped short on the doorstep. No, not want him. She wasn't going to want him in this lifetime, and he'd do well to remember it. The eager anticipation he'd been feeling soured in his stomach. He pounded the door with his fist a little harder than necessary.

"I'm coming, geez!" Cora opened the door. She'd already changed from her work clothes into a blue strappy sundress that showed off her shoulders. With her hair loose around her face, tumbling down her back, she looked younger and softer, and more like the Cora he remembered from the past. A bittersweet pang of regret stabbed right through the heart. He'd missed her so much. If he felt this way every time he looked at her, living here was going to be the death of him.

"You don't have to bang the house down," she said, swinging the door wide. "I think even old Mrs. Gilmore next door must've heard you, and she's half-deaf."

"Sorry." Liam stepped inside and set his bag on the tiled floor. "I didn't realize."

"It's all right," she said with a sigh. "These walls are just paper-thin. So, if you plan on singing opera in the shower like my last roommate? Please don't."

Angel greeted him with a soft meow, then sniffed at his duffel bag. After deciding it was beneath his dignity to give it any further notice, he began to purr and nudged Liam's leg with his head.

"I still can't believe my cat actually likes you." Cora shook her head in awe. "You must smell like catnip, or something."

"Or he could just be a very smart animal."

"Or very dumb." She gave him a cheeky grin. "Come on, I'll show you your room. Is that all you have?"

"Yes." He hefted his bag and followed her down the hall. So far, the duffel from the angels had everything he seemed to need—appropriate clothing, pairs of shoes, toiletries and even a wallet with actual funds. It wasn't a great deal of money, but he couldn't complain. As mysterious and aloof as the angels were, at least they weren't stingy with basic necessities.

"But what about all your stuff?"

"I travel light." By modern standards, it probably seemed that way to her. She had no idea that the duffel bag contained more than he'd ever owned before.

Cora paused at the door on the right. "But surely you

have things from your last place. Clothes. Dishes. Neon beer signs, at the very least?"

He paused. "I have all that stuff, but it's…put away."

"Oh, right." She nodded as if that made all kinds of sense. "Well, here's your room. My roommate left her bed and linens when she moved out, so you're welcome to them, unless you want to get your own out of storage."

Liam dropped his bag on the floor. The room was more luxurious than anything he'd had in the past. It had wall-to-wall carpeting and cheerful blue curtains in the window. The bed looked much nicer than the lumpy motel mattress he'd been sleeping on, and it was worlds better than the straw pallet he'd had in his brother's house. There was even a small table with a drawer and a lamp in the room. "This is perfect."

Cora let out a huff of amusement. "I'm not sure I'd go that far, but I'm glad you approve."

"Where's your room?"

"Right next door."

"Even better," he said under his breath.

"Hmm?"

He cleared his throat. "This room. It's even better than the motel."

"Well, I hope you're not a snorer, because I wasn't kidding when I said these walls were thin." Her grin was contagious, and for a few heartbeats they stood smiling at each other just like they had in another life. Liam wondered if she felt that same pull—the strong connection they'd forged over a century ago.

When his phone began to ring, she seemed to catch herself. "I'll just go feed Angel and let you get settled."

After Cora left, Liam pulled his phone from his pocket and sat on the bed. The name Margaret flashed across the screen. *Damn*. If he was going to focus on his task with Cora, he'd need to eliminate distractions, and Margaret was definitely a distraction. As alluring as she was, Liam couldn't carry on with their affair. If Margaret was anything like the woman he remembered, he'd have to be very gentle about letting her down. Even though he loved Cora, he still cared about Margaret and he didn't want her to get hurt. It would all just be easier if she wasn't in the way.

Liam took a deep breath. "Hello?"

"Hey, sailor." He could hear a smile in Margaret's voice. "I've got good news."

"And what's that?" He leaned back on the headboard with a sense of unease. Letting her down wasn't going to be easy.

"My husband's going out of town next weekend, so you and I have plans. He said he won't be back until Sunday night. You can stay all weekend, and we can catch up on that breakfast you missed the last time."

Liam prepared to let her down as easy as he could. "Margaret, I just moved into my new place, and—"

"Really?" she said excitedly. "That's great! Where are you living? Close to me, I hope."

Liam sighed. He might as well just tell her the truth. "Not really. I'm on the other side of town from you."

"Liam," Cora sang out from the kitchen. "I'm making spaghetti for dinner. Want some?"

"Uh…" he paused and tried to cover the phone with his hand, but he knew Margaret heard "…sure."

"Who was that?" Margaret's voice was sharp. Alert. He could practically feel her bristle. *Christ.* Here we go.

"That's Cora," Liam said with a sigh. "My new roommate."

"Really," Margaret said flatly. "Funny, you never men-

tioned having a roommate. Never even mentioned looking for one."

"The opportunity came up suddenly. She just happens
to work at my new precinct, so it made sense to move in
together."

Margaret didn't say anything for a few moments. Liam
got the feeling she was reeling from the information and
trying to gather herself together. She had a strong jealous
streak, but she was a married woman. She didn't have
much of a leg to stand on when it came to lecturing him
on his choices with other women, and she well knew it.

"That's great," she said. "You can tell me all about it
when you come over next weekend." Liam heard a man's
voice call out to Margaret. "John's home," she whispered.
"I have to go. I'll talk to you later." Then she hung up before Liam could say anything further.

He tossed the phone on the nightstand and sighed. That
conversation wasn't productive. He'd have to call her back,
and soon. But first, he needed to see what this spaghetti
business was all about. It warmed his heart to think of
Cora making him dinner. His sweet, kind, caring woman.
Smiling, he headed for the kitchen.

The next morning, Liam paced the living room, glowering at Cora. Her curvy body was on full display for the
entire world to see. And apparently, she didn't care.

"You can't be serious," he said for the second time,
scowling at her outfit.

Cora lifted her chin stubbornly, then pulled an elastic
band from her wrist and began gathering her hair into a
ponytail. "No, *you* can't be serious. I don't know where
you get off thinking you can tell me how to dress on my
morning run. What is this, the 1800s?"

"Clearly not," he scoffed, gesturing to her clothes.

Cora finished pulling her hair back, then bent to pull on her running shoes. The tiny black shorts she wore rose up a little higher on her backside, leaving her spectacular legs on full display. God, she was magnificent. All toned curves and golden skin. Liam's fingers itched to touch her. He couldn't drag his gaze away. Unfortunately, that meant no other man would be able to look away, either.

"At least zip your top up, woman," he said moodily. Her sweatshirt hung open to reveal a tight tank top that left nothing to the imagination. "You can't go bouncing down the street with it hanging open like that. It's indecent."

"Oh?" Cora arched a delicate brow, her blue eyes flashing fire. Then, keeping her gaze on his, she deliberately peeled off her sweatshirt and tossed it on the sofa. "In that case, I'll just leave it here."

"Cora." Liam pinched the bridge of his nose. "You're killing me."

"Well, the feeling's mutual. And for the record, I don't *bounce down the street*. It's called running. What is up with you, anyway? You really need to ease off the pedal. These are just basic workout clothes, and that's exactly what I'm about to do. Work." She pointed toward the door. "Out."

Liam growled in frustration as she breezed out the door with her head high and her ponytail swinging.

He followed her into the yard, searching both sides of the street for men with wandering eyes. "Maybe I'll just come with you."

"Like hell you will," she said, grabbing one foot and then the other behind her to stretch her legs. "This is my time, and I don't share it with anyone. Why don't you make yourself useful and fix that lawnmower while I'm gone?"

The strange machine was propped against a tree in the front yard. Liam didn't know the first thing about using it, let alone fixing it.

"See you later, Sergeant Clothes Police." She saluted, then bounced off down the street.

Liam watched her go until she disappeared around the corner. Twice, he began to follow her, then turned back. If he was going to win points with Cora, he had to be careful and give her space. It was just so damned difficult. He walked over to the lawnmower and gave it a swift kick. It wobbled, then tipped over on its side.

A black sports car pulled up to the house, and Liam's glower grew even darker when Finn Walsh stepped out of the car. What the hell was he doing here? As far as Liam knew, Finn and Cora weren't close friends. And why did he have a fast car? It was wasted on a man like him.

Finn gave Liam a nervous smile. He wasn't wearing a suit and tie today, but he might as well have been. He still stood with that same stiff posture, and his gray, perfectly creased slacks were almost the same shade as his collared shirt.

"Hey, Liam. Is Cora around?"

Liam pretended to examine the lawnmower because anything was better than having to look at Finn. "You're out of luck, man. She's not here."

Finn came to a stop beside him. "Is it broken?"

"Why?" Liam asked. "Can you fix it?"

Finn bent to examine the underside of the lawnmower. "I know a thing or two about these. I used to have a pretty lucrative business mowing lawns when I was a kid." He looked at Liam and chuckled like they shared a funny joke. "Mind if I give it a try…?"

Liam gave a careless shrug. "Have at it."

Forehead creased in concentration, Finn began tinkering with the machine. The way he handled it with such familiar ease grated on Liam's nerves for an entire five minutes before Finn set the thing upright again.

"Okay, let's give it a whirl." Finn pulled the cord. The engine sputtered, then rolled into a smooth, loud rumble. He shut the engine off and slapped his hands together, smiling. "That ought to do it."

A curt nod of thanks was the best Liam could do.

Finn went to the trunk of his car where he withdrew a towel to wipe off his hands. Then he walked back to Liam, looking nervous all over again. "So, uh, any idea when Cora will be back?"

"She'll be gone a long time." Liam gave him a cool, assessing look. "Why are you here?"

"Uh..." Finn's gaze darted around, then he pulled something from his pocket. "It's just that I came to give her this."

A gold chain dangled from his fingertips, sparkling in the sunlight. There was a carved rose pendant hanging from it. Liam's eyes narrowed with suspicion. *Cora's necklace.*

He wanted to rip it from Finn's hand. He hated the idea that Finn was holding something so dear to Cora's heart. "Where did you find it? We went back to the bar and asked around, but nobody had turned it in."

Finn rubbed a hand over the back of his neck. "I found it that same night, but the clasp was broken. I got it fixed for her."

Liam clenched his jaw, liking the man less and less. It was a genius move on Finn's part. Cora would be grateful to him. "What do you mean, you found it that night?"

"When she lost it," Finn said. "I found it against the

wall behind one of the booths after you all left. Someone must've accidentally kicked it across the floor. But since it was broken, I just thought I'd have it fixed to surprise her."

Jealousy gripped Liam hard, he struggled to keep it from overtaking his good sense, but he failed. Try as he might, he couldn't get the image of Finn and Cora together out of his head. This man was her future, and Liam hated him for it. "Let me see if I understand you correctly. You found her necklace, but didn't tell her right away?"

"Yes, but I wanted to—"

"And you let her *worry* all this time?" Liam interrupted. "Just so you could have the pleasure of surprising her?"

The sudden look of alarm on Finn's face was almost comical. Liam decided to run with it. He shook his head and kept his expression grave. "Man, I'm afraid she's not going to be happy knowing you lied to her."

"I didn't lie," Finn said in a rush. "I didn't even find it until after she left."

"But you could've called her right away, since you knew how upset she was," Liam said. "And you didn't, did you?"

Finn stared around the yard, wide-eyed, as if looking for absolution. "No, I guess I didn't."

Liam gave an exaggerated sigh. "It's been eating away at her for days. I'm not sure it's going to sit well with her knowing you kept something so important from her."

Finn looked utterly dejected. "I didn't think about it that way. I never meant to upset her. Just… Take it, will you?" He thrust the necklace out and accidently dropped it in the grass.

Liam bent to pick it up and stuffed it in his pocket.

"Can you do me a favor and just tell her you found it?" Finn asked. Was that sweat forming on his brow? His voice shook with nervousness. "I'd hate for her to be mad at me."

Liam let him stew for a few moments, enjoying the show. Finally, he nodded.

"I'm going to get going," Finn said quickly. "Thanks."

Liam absently fingered the necklace in his pocket as Finn drove away. "No, thank *you*." The man wasn't all that smart, for an attorney. For the hundred-thousandth time, Liam wondered why the angels had chosen Finn Walsh for his beloved Cora. They were as different as night and day. Finn had no redeeming qualities to recommend himself to someone as perfect as her. So what if he could fix a lawn-mowing machine? Any idiot in this century could probably figure it out. He walked over to the lawnmower and gave the cord a yank, just to see how it worked. Nothing happened. Frowning, he tried again. Nothing. He growled with frustration. How had Finn done it?

A figure down the street caught his eye, and he wouldn't have been able to look away if his life depended on it. Cora jogged toward him, her skin glowing, her eyes bright, her beautiful curves bouncing intriguingly in that devil of a running outfit.

She came to a stop in the yard, breathing heavily, then bent over to catch her breath. "Did you fix it?"

Liam flicked a glance at the green mower. Should he tell her the truth? Nah. He couldn't betray the man's confidence, after all. Liam just gave her a noncommittal shrug. "Give it a try."

Cora jogged over, pressed the lever on the handle, then pulled the cord. Sure enough, the lawn mower purred to life. Liam made a mental note to activate the lever next time.

"This is awesome." She shut the mower off, her smile so warm and genuine, he wanted to bask in it for as long as he could.

"I have another surprise for you." He pulled her necklace from his pocket.

"Oh, my God!" Cora erupted into a squeal of glee. She took the necklace and stared at him, wide-eyed. "Where on earth did you find it?"

"It was in the grass." Not a lie.

"The grass?" She looked mystified. "It must've fallen off my neck when I walked out to my car. You have no idea what this means to me. Thank you so much!" She threw her arms around his neck.

Liam sucked in a sharp breath. The shocking snap of pain intensified with every second her skin touched his. It radiated outward in all directions until he felt like a live wire. But this was the closest he'd come to her in almost two centuries, and he desperately wanted to feel it. Happiness rocketed through him, and for a split second it was almost enough to eclipse the pain. *Almost.* The conflicting feelings at war inside him were so acute, so blazingly strong, he stumbled backward, and she giggled.

It was agony and ecstasy. He'd forgotten what it felt like to be on the receiving end of Cora's admiration—that light-as-air weightlessness. In the scant three seconds he could endure her embrace, the past came crashing back in a tidal wave. Her sweet scent. Her warm, glowing skin. The tickle of her hair against his face. God, he loved this woman. When she laughed, he could feel it radiating through his chest.

But the pain poisoned everything. It seeped through until all he could feel was the intensifying, blistering burn. Liam gripped her upper arms and shoved her away.

Confusion and hurt flashed across her face.

"I'm sorry," Liam choked out. "I'm just not…" What

could he tell her? I'm not used to your touch burning me from the inside, out?

"No, it's fine. I get it." She was still breathing heavily from her run, but she crossed her arms and took a step back, hugging herself. Her face flushed pink. "I'm sorry. I'm just really glad to have my necklace back. Thank you." Her voice was cool and composed again. Liam hated it.

He struggled to explain. "Cora, I didn't mean to push you away. I don't want to give you the wrong idea, it's just—"

"Totally cool." She held up both hands. "To be honest, I don't know what came over me. I'm not usually a huggy person." She gave a self-deprecating laugh. "I guess you just seem familiar to me, or something."

"Do I?" Liam held his breath. Did she somehow feel their connection, even in this life?

"Yeah, it's so weird," she mused. "Sometimes, when I look at you, I feel like I've known you before."

"I feel the same," he said quickly.

Her forehead crinkled. "Maybe we ran into each other at a party once before, or something."

"Or something," he murmured, wishing the angels had never bestowed their goddamned blasted, bloody "training wheels" on him. Wishing she could wrap her arms around him once more, smiling at him as if the sun rose and set by his command. She used to look at him like that. If only she'd see him that way again.

Cora broke the intimate mood with a careless shrug, then gave him a playful punch on the shoulder. "Anyway, thanks for finding my necklace, O'Connor. I owe you one." Then she walked back into the house, taking all the happiness with her.

10

Cora parked her car alongside Liam's at the precinct on Thursday morning. It figured he'd arrive before her. From what she'd seen, he had a lead foot, speeding whenever he got the chance. She'd tried to warn him to slow down, telling him he was setting a bad example for civilians, but he'd just given her that wicked smile—the one Suzette swooned over. And Cora had to admit, Liam could charm his way into a locked bank vault with that smile. In the past four days since he'd moved in, he'd even managed to charm old Mrs. Gilmore, her grumpy neighbor, into baking him a pie. If that wasn't some kind of dark magic, Cora didn't know what was.

Even she wasn't immune. She was still a little embarrassed that she'd thrown herself at him when he'd found her necklace. What had gotten into her? She never impulsively embraced people she'd just met, but it had felt like the most natural thing in the world. It wouldn't have been so embarrassing if he hadn't reacted the way he had. Cora cringed, remembering how he'd shoved her away. *I don't want to give you the wrong idea.* God, she'd felt like such a fool. He'd made it very clear he wasn't into her, and that was all fine and good. She wasn't into him, either! It's not like she'd deliberately *meant* to plaster her body against his rock-hard chest. Feel his powerful arms embracing her. His large, warm hands gripping her lower back. Who wanted that? Not her.

Cora shoved the humiliating memory aside as she slid past Liam's car in the lot. He'd asked her to carpool with him to work, but she'd declined. Even though they were now officially roommates, she still wanted—needed—her freedom. Something about his presence in her life confused her, and it wasn't just because of that odd sense of familiarity. It was something more. She had the strangest feeling he wasn't what he seemed. Normally, Cora trusted her instincts one hundred percent. They'd always served her well. But this time, she had no idea what to think. One minute, she thought Liam was a decent guy because he offered to mow the lawn, and the next minute, he annoyed her because he forgot to mow it and started watching TV instead. He also left dirty dishes around the house and propped his boot-clad feet on her coffee table. No amount of charm was going to make *that* okay. And always, always, he seemed to be hiding something. Waiting for something. But, what?

Cora made her way to her office desk and was just settling into her chair when Captain Thompson poked his head out of his office.

"Cora, Liam. A moment."

Liam looked up from whatever he was doing on his

computer. He had a pile of paperwork on his desk that seemed to be growing every day. She wondered when he was going to get to it. If he was as lazy with his work as he was at keeping house, it was going to be a while.

"Everything good with you two?" The captain asked as they entered his office. He took a seat at his desk. Stacks of paper were scattered across the scarred mahogany top, along with a bottle of Tums, a Diet Coke and a half-eaten Egg McMuffin. Breakfast of champions.

"Yes," Liam said before Cora could answer. "Things are going great."

Captain Thompson forged ahead, barely waiting for Liam to finish his sentence. "A call just came in. The mini-mart on First got robbed sometime in the middle of the night."

"Do you think it's related to the incident at the Gas n' Go?" Cora asked. They still hadn't caught the thief, and the mini-mart was in the same neighborhood.

Thompson leaned back in his chair, linking his hands behind his head. "Could be. The owner at the mini-mart got a partial look at the guy on his camera feed, but it's not much to go on. Appears to be male, about six feet tall, possibly dark hair. You two check it out, then head down and ask around. There's an apartment building near the mini-mart. Maybe someone saw something."

"Knock-knock," someone sang out from the doorway.

Captain Thompson glanced at the door and sat up straighter. "Alice. I wasn't expecting you this morning."

His wife, a pretty blonde woman with heavy makeup and lethal stiletto heels, floated into the room on a river of Chanel No. 5. A designer bag was slung fashionably over her shoulder, and she was wearing a silk shift dress that screamed, "Dry Clean Only." Alice Thompson was one of those women who looked high-maintenance, with the long acrylic nails, the out-to-there lash extensions, and highlights too perfectly spaced to ever be natural. She had bleached-white Hollywood teeth, a salon tan and an impressive chest that Cora suspected Mother Nature hadn't given her. But none of that mattered because Alice looked good, and she knew it. And more power to her, Cora figured. When you work that hard at something, you might as well be proud of it.

Alice strolled in with her megawatt smile on full blast. "Sorry to interrupt, hon. I was just heading to the mall and had a quick question."

The captain jerked his chin at Cora and Liam. "That will be all."

They started to leave when Alice placed a hand on Liam's arm. Was she squeezing his biceps? "You must be the new officer from Raleigh."

"Aye," Liam said carefully, glancing at the captain. Liam seemed uncomfortable with Alice's attention.

"Liam O'Connor," Thompson told her. "I mentioned him to you last week."

"Of course." Alice slid her hand from Liam's arm a little too slowly. Her gaze flicked over his body lightning quick. If Cora hadn't been standing right there, she'd have missed it. Poor Captain Thompson. No wonder he kept antacids on his desk the way the receptionist Mavis kept M&M's. Maybe his marriage wasn't as seamless at it appeared. Then again, maybe Alice was just one of those flirty-by-nature types. Did she treat all men this way?

Otto ambled past the office window, his paunchy belly looking larger than usual. He grinned and waved at Alice, but she didn't respond. Otto wasn't even a blip on her radar. So, that answered that.

"You and Boyd grew up together in Ireland?" Alice asked Liam. "He told me you two used to get into all kinds of trouble when you were kids."

"That we did." Liam shifted closer to Cora. "But it was a long time ago." Cora wondered if he even realized his Irish accent had grown thicker. He'd said it popped up once in a while, and she wondered if it happened during moments of strong emotion. Maybe Alice's covert attention bothered him more than he was letting on.

"Well, we all must have drinks one of these nights," Alice said smoothly, batting her eyelashes. "So you guys can tell me all about the good old days."

Liam murmured some kind of agreement, then took off down the hall.

Cora followed him back to his desk. "You got out of there fast. Is something wrong?"

"Nothing," he grumbled, shuffling the papers on his desk without appearing to read them.

Cora cocked her head, eyeing him thoughtfully. "Do you know Captain Thompson's wife, Alice?"

He didn't meet her eyes. "Why do you ask?"

"You just seemed a little standoffish back there, almost as if you didn't like her. People don't usually form such sudden opinions unless they've known a person before."

"Never met her in this lifetime," he said firmly. "She just rubs me the wrong way."

"Yes, I saw that," Cora teased. "Just be glad the captain didn't."

Liam gave a dismissive shake of his head. "Let's have a look at the video footage so we can get on the road."

Back at Cora's computer, they watched the grainy, black-and-white video clip of a man in a hooded sweatshirt pulling money from the mini-mart till.

She replayed it two more times before sitting back with a sigh. "There's no way we can identify him with this. All we've got is a male, possibly Caucasian, around six feet tall. It could be you, for goodness' sake." She pushed away from the desk. "You weren't out robbing shops last night while I slept, were you?"

"No," Liam said absently, examining her computer mouse like he'd never seen it before. He set the mouse on her desk and began rolling it, watching the cursor drag across the screen. "If I were out robbing shops, I wouldn't be that sloppy."

"What do you mean?"

"The man didn't plan it out well." Now Liam was studying the mouse, turning it over in his hands. For some reason it intrigued him. "He's got no place to put the money, for one thing. Did you see how he stuffed it down his shirt before running out? What kind of an idiot doesn't bring a bag to a robbery? And his sweatpants didn't appear to have pockets. Either he was very drunk, or just very stupid and decided to rob the shop on a whim." Liam scoffed. "*I'd* never carry out a robbery like that."

Cora stared at him. Suddenly, a fragmented memory of a dream she'd had the night before flickered through her mind. Liam in ragged clothes, half-hidden in shadow, climbing over a windowsill. The dream vision of him had been so vivid, she was surprised she'd forgotten it. Even now, she could practically see the ghost of it superimposed over the man beside her.

He put the mouse back on her desk and stood. "Ready to get out of here?"

She blinked. Like morning mist in sunlight, the dream memory evaporated until all Cora saw was him, standing in front of her in his collared shirt and blue jeans. She shook her head to clear it. It was definitely time for caffeine. "Yeah. But first I need—"

"I know, I know," Liam said with an exaggerated sigh. "Coffee."

She gave an unapologetic shrug. "Always."

Questioning the owner of the mini-mart proved to be a dead end. He knew nothing beyond what the video footage conveyed. Cora and Liam visited with the tenants whose apartments were in the vicinity, but no one had seen anything. The mini-mart was in a run-down section of town, and several of the streetlamps were burned out. It wasn't likely anyone could've had a clear view, even if they had witnessed the robbery.

Cora reluctantly walked back to her car with Liam. An entire morning gone, and nothing to show for it. She was just about to suggest lunch when someone about a block away gave a high-pitched screech.

Cora spun around and saw a man in a black hoodie sprinting down the street with a purse in his hand.

"Stop!" An old woman was hollering and pointing after him. "He stole my bag!"

Liam shot off after the man, and Cora followed a split second later.

The man ran for a good two blocks before he turned into the alley between the butcher shop and the pet store. By the time Cora rounded the corner, Liam was already at the end of the alley. There was a tall chain-link fence, so the alley was a dead end. The man was nowhere to be seen.

"Where'd he go?" Cora asked, out of breath. Liam had only been a few seconds behind the man. He couldn't have climbed the fence that fast.

Liam shook his head, then started back toward her.

Suddenly, a dark figure bolted straight at Cora from

behind a dumpster. Instinctively, she raised her hands to block him with her body. He slammed into her with all his weight, trying to get past her. She staggered backward, but stood her ground and gritted out, "You're not going anywhere."

She was dimly aware of Liam running toward them, shouting.

"I don't want any trouble, lady," the man said. "Out of my way, and no one gets hurt." He tried to push past her again, but this time she used his momentum to trip him up, twisting at the last second.

The man fell, and she started to reach for her gun.

"You asked for it." He jumped up and slid something shiny from beneath his sweatshirt. Before Cora had a chance to react, he lunged at her.

Liam was on him before Cora could blink. In one swift move, Liam knocked the knife from the man's hand and slammed him to the ground with a loud *crack*. Blood spewed from the man's broken nose. He began to howl.

Cora took a shaky breath and glanced down at her jacket. The fabric was sliced right over her heart. If Liam's timing had been one second off...

Liam cuffed the man, then glanced over at her, taking in her shredded jacket. His dark eyes met Cora's and something powerful passed between them.

She swallowed hard. She couldn't find words. Just like that, he'd saved her life. Adrenaline pumping, she jerkily reached for her phone, but Liam was already calling it in. He held the man down with a knee to his back, never taking his eyes off Cora's face.

"You okay?" Liam asked after he'd made the call.

She nodded.

The man continued to howl, but Cora barely heard him.

She was too caught up in the feelings at war inside her. Liam had just saved her life. All those things that annoyed her about him were fading away. She felt an odd, fluttery sensation in her chest. Little by little, the adrenaline rush began to wear off, and a warm, melty feeling replaced it. She knew exactly what it was. *Trust.* She recognized it because it was not something she felt often. Somehow, in just a short amount of time, he'd slid past her normal defenses which shouldn't have been surprising, since nothing about him felt "normal." She couldn't explain her feelings, but she couldn't deny them, either. For the first time since she'd met him, something began to shift inside her, as if she were making room in her life for him to stay.

11

The next evening, Liam sat on the living room sofa with Angel purring in his lap. The cat was completely comfortable. His eyes were half-closed, his claws rhythmically kneading Liam's leg. Normally, Liam would've noticed the sharp talons digging into his skin, but he was too busy trying not to stare at the glorious vision of Cora adjusting her stockings in front of him. The dress she was wearing looked like a piece of black silk wrapped around her torso, hips and thighs. Nothing else. Not even sleeves!

"So that's how I adopted Angel from the animal shelter," Cora was saying, smoothing the top of her stockings and letting the hem of her dress fall back into place. She came over to the couch and sat beside him, giving him her back. "Can you clasp the hook and eye above my zipper? I can't get to it."

Liam eyed the soft golden waves cascading down her

back. This close, he could smell the sultry, vanilla scent of some exotic perfume. It was excruciating not to be able to touch her. He bounced his knee up and down in agitation.

Angel mewled in protest and hopped onto the floor.

Cora swept her hair over one shoulder. "It's right at the top."

Like a man in a trance, Liam reached out, his hands hovering over her creamy skin. *Jesus wept, this woman.* No man could be expected to resist this. A lone curl dangled near her shoulder blade. He carefully lifted it out of the way, sliding the silken strands between his fingers. Apparently, the angel's curse only came into effect when he touched her skin. Thank God for small mercies. He held the lock of hair between his fingers and closed his eyes.

"Liam?"

"Hmm?" He was one heartbeat away from sliding his hand into her hair. Cursing under his breath, he tried to block the memory of what it felt like. It was so damned hard to play this role the angels foisted on him. It was—

"Pure evil," she said with annoyance.

He dropped her hair as if it were on fire. "What?"

"Whoever designed these hook and eye clasps did it just to torture people. They're impossible."

Liam fumbled a couple of times. The intimacy of the moment was not lost on him, even though she treated it like no big deal. There was something intensely private about helping a woman dress, even in such a small way. The fact that she thought nothing of it bothered him, and he suddenly wondered who else had had the privilege of seeing her like this. The thought darkened his mood, and he finally managed to secure the tiny hook without touching the skin on the nape of her neck. Then he shot off the couch and began to pace. "Who is this man you're going out with tonight, anyway? Tell me about him."

"I can't," Cora said, flicking her hair back over her shoulders. "Suzette set us up. It's a blind date."

Liam stopped pacing in surprise. "He can't see?"

"Oh, ha ha." Cora threw him a look. "You're not funny, you know. He's a surgeon, so his vision's just fine."

"But—"

"I can't tell you much, because we've never seen each other before."

"A *blind* date," Liam mused. His brows drew together as he committed the odd phrase to memory.

"Relax," Cora said. "He's a doctor from the medical spa where Suzette works. She said he's polite, good-looking and financially stable. As far as date material goes, that pretty much checks all of my boxes. So when he gets here, you're going to be civil."

Liam scoffed. "I'll make no such promise."

"Then you're going to be invisible," she said, pointing down the hall to his bedroom. "You're my roommate, not my bodyguard. I can't have you scaring away my dates."

Oh, yes you can.

The doorbell rang and Cora stood, smoothing her dress. Her legs looked a mile long in the strappy heels she was wearing.

Liam frowned. "Perhaps you should wear something more comfortable, like your running shoes."

"Are you trying to give me fashion advice again?"

"No, it's just… Those heels have to be hell on your feet."

"Nonsense. The higher the heels, the closer to God." She tossed her hair with a sassy smirk and sauntered toward the door.

Liam cursed the damned shoes. The sway of her hips

was mesmerizing. This woman could tempt a saint. "Let me get it."

She spun and pointed at him. "You stay where you are. And stop glowering like that."

A few moments later, a tall man followed Cora into the living room. He had blond hair, a strong build, and he was saying something that made Cora laugh.

Liam hated him on the spot.

"Don, this is my roommate, Liam," Cora said, gathering her coat and purse.

Don's grin showed too many teeth, and his blond hair had unnaturally bright streaks in it. He walked over to Liam and held out his hand. "It's nice to meet you."

Liam shook hands, imagining punching the man's lights out if he tried anything with Cora. *Don't even think about hooks and eyes, or* blind date *is going to take on a whole new meaning.*

"That's…quite a grip you have there," Don said, pulling his hand away.

Liam kept his voice deceptively mild. "What are your plans for the evening?"

"Don't answer that," Cora said in exasperation. "My roommate's just being nosy. Come on, let's go."

They were out the door and gone a heartbeat later.

Liam drew the curtain and watched the man lead Cora to his black convertible. It was one of those sleek sporty cars that flew like the wind. Now he really hated him. Watching Cora go off with another man not only felt wrong, it *was* wrong, considering that man wasn't the illustrious Finley Walsh. But how was he to stop her from doing what she wanted? This new version of Cora was so different from the woman he remembered. She was headstrong and opinionated, and while a large part of him loved seeing her become the strong woman she'd always wished she could be, another part of him felt at a complete loss. How was he ever going to coerce her into falling for any man, let alone a milksop like Finn?

Liam stood at the window for a long time after they drove away.

Angel brushed against his legs, and he glanced down at the cat. "Now what do we do?" He supposed there was nothing left to do but wait for Cora to return. This was his life now. Reduced to hovering at windows like a dried-up old lady's maid.

His phone rang and he pulled it from his pocket. *Margaret.* Of course. She'd been calling him on and off for days. He had to break things off with her, and he couldn't put off the conversation any longer. Sighing, he walked back to the couch and slumped on the overstuffed cushions.

"Hello."

"Liam, where've you been? I left messages."

"I know, I've been busy with work. I've been meaning to call you so we could talk."

"Good. Because John leaves tomorrow afternoon for his trip. I was thinking you could come over around six and we can try that new restaurant down the street. You know, the steak house near the university bar that everyone's raving about? I went ahead and made reservations for us. They say it's impossible to get in at the last minute on a weekend."

"Margaret, I don't think that's a good idea."

"Why? Too crowded? I guess we could try that hole-in-the-wall Italian place around the corner again. I heard it's under new management and the food's gotten a lot better. But we just have to be careful with PDAs because I don't want anyone talking."

"PDAs?"

"Public displays of affection. If we're eating out so close to home, it has to look like a business dinner." She lowered her voice to a sexy purr. "That's not to say we can't play footsies under the table, though."

"I'm sorry, Margaret," Liam said with reluctance. He searched for a way to let her down easy, but he couldn't think of a way to do it. "I can't."

She was quiet for a few moments. "What do you mean?"

Liam took a deep breath, then let it out slowly. "Margaret, I've been thinking about this thing we've been doing."

She let out a shaky laugh. "This doesn't sound good."

"I think we should take a break for a while."

"From me?" Her voice was softer and higher pitched.

It made him feel worse, but he couldn't carry on with her any longer. It wouldn't be fair to her or him. He was in love with Cora. That hadn't changed, even though everything else had. When you loved someone—truly loved them—the entire world could crumble down around you and that love would still be standing strong. Love always survived, even when nothing else did. He was living proof of that. "I'm sorry, Margaret."

"You don't…want to see me anymore?"

"It's not that I don't care for you," Liam said. "I truly do. I want you to be happy. It's just with this move and my new job, I have a lot of other things to focus on, and I can't do with the distraction right now."

Margaret's huff of laughter was tinged with bitterness. "I'm a distraction? I teach botany at the university, Liam. I manage coursework and detailed lectures. I grade papers for hundreds of students. I've never thought of you as a *distraction*."

"You're brilliant, though, so maybe it's just easier for

you to juggle everything." Liam tried to joke. "And you've said yourself I'm not that smart."

She wasn't amused. "Does this have something to do with that woman you just moved in with? It does, doesn't it? If nothing else, you could at least be honest with me."

"I am being honest," Liam lied. "This has nothing to do with her." Lies upon lies. Every move he made had to do with Cora. "I'm truly sorry, Margaret. We just can't carry on like we have been. It isn't right to your husband, anyway."

He heard her suck in her breath. "My marital status never seemed to bother you before. I was honest with you from the beginning. I told you John was much older than me. I told you we make our marriage work, but I needed more. You said you understood that. Just last month you suggested we take a secret trip to the beach together. You weren't too worried about my husband then."

Liam closed his eyes and pinched the bridge of his nose. Dammit, it felt like the angels were setting him up for failure once again. Why would they plant those ideas into her head? "You're right. Everything you're saying is right. I wasn't thinking when I said and did those things. But now I am, and I just can't do it anymore, Margaret. I won't."

Seconds ticked by. A car drove past the window and Liam watched the headlights slide across the living room wall.

"Yeah." Margaret's voice was carefully neutral. "Yeah, okay. I mean, if it's soured for you, it's better to part as friends."

"It hasn't soured." He didn't want to hurt her. "I just..." *Need to focus on saving my soul from everlasting damnation.* "I've got some things to take care of and I have to be able to focus."

"Focus?" A brittle laugh. "No problem, Liam. Good-bye." The phone clicked and she was gone.

Liam tossed his phone to the sofa cushions and leaned back with a heavy sigh. He did the right thing. He knew it, but he still felt guilty for hurting her. Even though their relationship in this era wasn't actually real, he still *knew* Margaret from before. At her core, she was the same passionate woman who cared more than she liked to admit. She couldn't help it now if she believed they had a relationship. It seemed wrong for the angels to meddle in innocent people's lives the way they did. Liam never spent much time thinking about the afterlife because living in the moment had been so crucial. Hunger had been all-consuming, and all his focus had been on survival. But when he had thought of angels, he'd always assumed they were noble, celestial beings full of light and love and forgiveness. How, then, did they justify forcing false memories on people and bestowing strong feelings in them that were not based on reality? He didn't understand it. But then, there was not much about this mission that made sense. Whatever the reasons were for Cora needing to embrace her true soul mate, Finn—Liam grimaced just thinking of the man—they had to be monumental.

It was just past ten o'clock when the front door opened. He'd been dozing on the couch with the pretense of watching TV, but really he was waiting for Cora to get home.

She stalked into the living room, her lips pressed into a hard line, and tossed her coat onto the sofa arm. "That's the last time I let Suzette set me up on a blind date."

Liam sat up fast. "What did he do?" He jumped off the couch and started toward the door. "If he tried anything, I'll—"

"No, it's fine," Cora said with a frustrated groan. "He's gone, anyway. I couldn't get out of his car fast enough."

Liam yanked open the front door, just to make sure. Then he shut it hard, bolted it and moved back into the living room. She wasn't there. He went down the hall and stopped at her closed bedroom door. "Tell me what happened."

"It's nothing," Cora said in a muffled voice.

"Cora, if he did something to you, I need to know." He forced the next words out. "I won't do anything you don't approve of. I just want to help."

"It's not anything you can help with, Liam. The guy was just a schmucktacular dillhole."

He mouthed those words, saving them for later.

"That level of asinine has no cure." She opened her door and was wearing a pair of flannel pajama bottoms and a blue tank with the words "I love you more than coffee, but please don't make me prove it" across the front. Brushing past him, she walked into the living room, flopped onto the sofa, and propped her feet on the coffee table. "First of all, he talked nonstop about himself. Ugh!"

Liam felt nothing but smug satisfaction as he joined her in front of the TV. "A tragedy, indeed."

"No, you don't understand." Cora raised her hands for emphasis. "Like, from the moment we left this house, all through the ride to the restaurant, and all through dinner, he barely let me get a word in edgewise. I had to listen to a recount of all his many accomplishments. His tennis championships. His Plastic Surgeon of the Year award. His deer hunting trophies." She rolled her eyes. "Oh, and let's not forget his amazing prowess in the bedroom."

Liam scowled. "What the bloody hell?"

"I know, right? What kind of man tells a woman on

their first date that he's got a reputation for being amazing in bed? He actually said I could check his references. And I don't think he was kidding."

Liam rolled his shoulders in agitation. "He needs a swift kick to the bollocks."

"Believe me, I was tempted," she said with a laugh. "I mean, the table was small, and I was sitting right across from him. It would've been so easy."

Liam grinned, enjoying the picture that painted in his mind. He suddenly appreciated Cora's lethal stilettos much more than before.

Cora sighed and hugged a throw pillow. "The worst part was during dessert, when he sat back and started analyzing my face and body. Then he—" she made air quotes with her hands "—'did me a favor, free of charge' by giving me his professional opinion on what I needed to fix. Apparently, I don't need a boob job. But, while my face is symmetrical enough, I might want to consider collagen injections to inflate my lips like the Hollywood crowd."

"Bloody asinine half-wit," Liam muttered.

"It's not that I have anything against plastic surgeons," Cora continued. "I know they can't help seeing flaws in other people, because that's their job. When I was in high school, I broke my nose falling off a climbing wall in gym class, and I always wished my nose was a little straighter, so when the surgeon mentioned he could take care of it, I agreed. I understand these doctors do helpful work sometimes, it was just hard sitting there tonight under such critical scrutiny. On a *first date*." She shook her head and sighed. "Oh, and pro tip? Never tell a girl she could stand to lose a few pounds. It doesn't go over well."

Liam clenched his teeth together, wishing he'd shoved the man out the door the moment he'd arrived that night.

"You're perfect exactly as you are, Cora. Don't let that... *schmucktacular dillhole* tell you otherwise."

She smiled softly at him. "I'll never see him again, so it doesn't matter." Her hair tumbled around her face and shoulders, and she looked completely relaxed and utterly enchanting.

The sudden urge to gather her into his arms was so strong, he had to squeeze his eyes shut.

"What's the matter?"

He shook his head. "I'm just sorry you had to go through that. I should've saved you the trouble and kicked him out when he got here. I wanted to, you know."

"Oh, I had a feeling." She threw him a reprimanding look. "I thought my dad was overprotective, but you make him look like a walk in the park. You've got to ease up a bit, you know? For both our sakes. In spite of what you seem to think, I can take care of myself just fine. I've been doing it for a long time." She gave him a playful shove on his shoulder, then got up and walked into the kitchen.

Liam didn't respond, because there wasn't anything he could say that she'd like to hear. He'd fallen in love with her almost two centuries ago, and he'd loved her ever since. There was never going to be a time when he didn't care about her well-being.

"I'm making popcorn," she announced. "And then you and I are going to talk about this ball tomorrow night. Do you have a tuxedo or formal suit you can wear?"

"I'm sure I'll have something." He hadn't even thought about it. The duffel bag held many things, but he knew for a fact there was no fancy dress suit folded up in there. If he had to, he'd go out suit hunting tomorrow.

"Good. Then that's solved. Now I need to watch something fun and silly to cleanse my palate from this whole disaster of an evening."

Soon Liam found himself watching some movie about treasure-hunting children who called themselves "goonies." While the topic of treasure was always high on his list, he was more interested in enjoying Cora. Her smiles and easy laughter were like a balm to his soul. Even threatened with the fiery pits of hell, he had no idea how he was ever going to give her up. And if he did manage to win his way back into heaven, would it even matter, if she wasn't there to share it?

12

"**A**bsolutely not." Liam stood in the kitchen the following evening, arms crossed and feet planted firmly. "Not even for all the gold in King Solomon's mine." There was no way in hell he was going to wear the blue silk tie Cora was trying to foist on him.

"But everyone's dressing up tonight. You'll need this." She held a cup of coffee in one hand and the tie in the other. Her bare feet peeked out from beneath the hem of a long bathrobe. The gala was in less than an hour, and Cora had been about to dress when she'd surprised Liam with her "gift."

"I told you, I don't like having things around my neck," he growled.

"Don't be ridiculous," she said in obvious exasperation. "It's a tie, not a noose."

A cold chill skittered down his spine. "I appreciate the

thought, but as I said before, you'll never get that evil thing around my neck."

"You have to," she insisted. "It's the dress code. Most of the men will be wearing tuxedos, and you're only in a suit." She looked him up and down. "It's a really good suit, but still."

Liam pressed his mouth into a hard line. When he woke up that morning, the black designer suit and shirt had been hanging in the closet. It fit him perfectly, as did the leather dress shoes he'd found beside the door. The angels gave him all kinds of reasons to be annoyed, but their impeccable taste in clothes was not one of them. "I won't do it, Cora. And if it means I won't be fit to attend, then so be it." He glowered at her in stubborn silence.

It was a contest of wills. Neither one of them was willing to budge.

Cora let out a frustrated groan and tossed the tie on a kitchen chair. "I'm not in the mood for this. Going to this ball was your idea. If you're too stubborn to even wear a tie—a tie that I went out of my way to buy you—then why should I bother?" She plunked her coffee cup on the table. "I think I'll just throw on some jeans and maybe go to the movies, or take a nice scenic drive instead."

Liam watched her storm down the hall to her bedroom. Swearing under his breath, he went to his room and slammed the door.

Angel let out a meow of protest. The cat was stretched out on Liam's pillow, glaring at him with feline reproof.

Liam paced the room in agitation. Forget this garbage. He'd tried to get Cora and Finn together, but if she chose not to go because he refused to wear a bloody tie, then it wasn't his fault. He rubbed his throat and sucked in a deep gulp of air. Just the thought of the fabric cinched against his skin made his hands clammy and his vision grow spotty. "Dammit all to hell," he muttered.

"You just might," a bored·voice said from behind him.

Liam spun around to see a roiling wall of mist where his bedroom wall should have been. The blond angel stepped through the mist followed by the dark-haired one.

Liam was in no mood. "Aye, I'm well aware. But she's stubborn as the day is long, that woman. I've tried to set her up with Finn, but now she says she won't go because of a stupid necktie."

The blond angel shrugged. "She doesn't have to go."

"Oh." Liam blinked. "Good." Now he wouldn't have to watch Finn bumble around trying to win Cora's attention. Maybe his argument with her tonight was a blessing in disguise. Maybe they could just spend another delightful evening watching TV together like last night.

Cora's cat leaped off the bed and padded over to the angels. The dark-haired one held out his hands and the cat jumped into his arms, purring.

The blond angel watched this with mild disapproval, then turned his attention back to Liam. "We've information to relay that might be of some interest to you. A disaster will happen tonight at Margaret Brady's house. Cora is going to die there."

Liam's head snapped up, his heart thumping. *"Die?"*

"Unless," the angel continued, "she goes to the gala with Finn, as planned."

"I thought you said she didn't have to go," Liam said, struggling to keep his voice down.

"Well, she doesn't," the blond angel said coolly. "I suppose that's up to you."

Liam let out a growl of frustration, his mind reeling with thoughts of Cora dying in some horrible way. Earthquakes. Gunfights. Explosions. "What's going to happen at Margaret's house?" he demanded. "What kind of disaster?"

"Irrelevant." The angels floated backward and began to fade into the mist.

"Wait!" Liam moved toward the mist and shoved against it. It stretched like a rubber band, then bounced back.

They were gone, but the blond angel's voice could still be heard, echoing from very far away. "It's a simple course of action, rogue. Either ensure Cora's safety by seeing that she goes with Finn tonight, or she will end up dead like she has in every lifetime, and your task will be over. It's your choice."

Liam clenched his hands into fists, breathing shakily. Like hell it was a *choice*.

Right before the mist solidified, a pair of arms poked through to place Cora's cat back on the floor. The feline gave a lazy yawn, unbothered by the fact that he'd just straddled the line between this world and the next.

Liam pounded the wall in frustration, startling the cat. He glared down at the sulking feline. "Really? *That's* what bothers you?"

The cat just twitched an ear and turned his back, unimpressed with Liam's tantrum.

Liam began pacing his room again. Whatever disaster was going to befall Cora at Margaret's house, he had to stop it. If Cora's life was in danger, there was only one thing he could do. Determined, he threw open his bedroom door and barely refrained from banging on hers. "Cora."

"I'm busy," she called out.

He gripped the doorframe and took a deep breath to calm down. Then another. "Okay. I'll wear the tie," he managed. "You're right. It's not a big deal. I know you didn't even want to go in the first place, but it would mean a lot to me if you did. Please."

Silence.

Was she going to make him beg? He'd do it, if he must. Anything to keep her from heading into a fatal disaster. "Cora—"

She cracked the door open, her cerulean blue eyes staring at him with reproof.

"I know you bought me that tie as a gift," he said quietly. "And I didn't thank you for it. I'm thanking you now, and I'll happily wear it if you come with me tonight. I'm sorry I reacted the way I did. It was foolish of me. I don't know, maybe I'm just nervous about getting out there and meeting so many new people. This transition has been hard for me, too. I've never been more out of my element than I have since I arrived here in Providence Falls." Truer words had never been spoken.

"Not even when you first moved to the US from Ireland?"

Liam paused. "This is much different." *Because it's real.* "Look, I know you were just trying to help me. Will you forgive me and come with me tonight?"

She studied him as if she was trying to make up her mind.

"Please?"

"Fine," she said with a sigh. Then added, "Let me get dressed," before closing the door.

Liam leaned his forehead against it and closed his eyes. *Thank God.* Now, he just had to make sure the evening went according to plan.

It was eight o'clock when Finn called to tell them he was on his way. Cora floated out of her room in a long white dress with sparkly straps that crisscrossed in back. Liam blinked at the vision before him. She was incandescent. Ethereal. She looked so beautiful, it was almost enough to eclipse the turmoil eating him up inside.

When he finally found his voice, all he could manage was, "You look…very well."

She blushed and waved him off just as the doorbell rang.

Liam pulled on his suit jacket. He had another plan to execute, and he needed to time it just right. As usual, the angels hadn't been forthcoming with much information about the upcoming disaster at Margaret's house. All he knew for certain was that something horrible would happen. He'd made sure Cora was going to be safe, but what of Margaret? Liam couldn't walk away to a party with Cora knowing he'd be leaving Margaret in danger. He still cared for Margaret, and he'd not let her walk innocently into a disaster if he could help it.

"Here." Cora handed him the tie. "If you need help tying it—"

"I don't." He slid it into his pocket as she answered the door. He had no intention of wearing the damned thing, but she didn't have to know that.

Finn walked into the house in a black tuxedo, his hair shellacked with more pomade than usual. One glimpse of Cora and he looked stunned. With his face flushed red, he kept trying—and failing—not to ogle her in the filmy white dress. She chatted away as she gathered her purse, oblivious to Finn's reaction.

"Hey, Liam," Finn said when he managed to find his tongue.

Liam tilted his chin up in acknowledgment. It was the most he could manage. Even if Finn was going to play a big part in saving Cora's life tonight, Liam didn't have to pretend to like him for it.

Cora slid a sparkling shawl over her shoulders. "Okay. Ready when you guys are."

It was now, or never. He pulled his phone from his suit pocket and pretended to read the screen, frowning. "Damn." He stared at his screen a little longer, just for good measure. "Something just came up. You two go ahead of me. I'll be right behind you. Twenty minutes, at the most." It was an outright lie, but he was willing to say whatever it took to make her leave with Finn and go to the gala. Anything to keep her out of harm's way.

"What?" Cora gave him an incredulous look. "No! What do you mean something came up?"

Liam shook his head and pasted on his best apologetic smile, the one he used during sticky situations when he needed to soften someone up. "It's just a small personal matter I need to attend to, but don't worry. I won't be long."

Cora placed a hand on her hip and narrowed her eyes. Her instincts were razor-sharp, and even though they didn't serve Liam's purpose, he couldn't help admiring her for it.

Finn, on the other hand, was all too happy to jump on Liam's idea. He couldn't wait to get Cora all to himself, the bastard. "Sounds great. We'll see you there in a few minutes." He held the door open for Cora, all starry eyes and sappy grin. "Ready, Cora?"

She glanced uncertainly at Finn, then back at Liam.

"I'll text you when I get there," Liam assured her. Another lie. There would be no texts because he had a mission to accomplish, and he needed Cora out of the way. When he saw the tentative trust in Cora's eyes, he almost hated himself for it. Why did this have to be so damned hard? He was going to let her down tonight, and there was nothing he could do about it if he wanted to save her.

By the time he waved goodbye to an ecstatic Finn and

an uncertain Cora, it was already eight thirty. Liam waited until they drove away, then flew to his car, gunned the engine and sped toward disaster.

13

The humid summer air was thick as molasses that night, making Liam's suit cling uncomfortably as he leaned against the lion statue across the street from Margaret's home. The streetlamps cast warm puddles of light along the sidewalk in front of her building. Her shiny bay window overlooked the park, and a multitude of flowers spilled from clay pots leading up to the front steps. If he didn't know better, he'd say the place looked as peaceful and idyllic as a drawing room painting, but according to the angels' cryptic message, that was all about to change.

All the lights were on in her home, which meant she had to be there. He scanned both sides of the street, hating that he had no idea what kind of danger was lying in wait. He didn't even know when the disaster the angels foretold would take place. Every person walking along the avenue appeared to be a threat. After being subjected to television for days, Liam's imagination was spinning with visions of house fires and drive-by shootings and serial killers. Just the idea of Margaret being attacked by a knife-wielding man in a hockey mask was enough to send him darting across the street to her front door.

He rang the doorbell, preparing to do whatever it took to get her the hell out of there.

Margaret answered, her face flushed and eyes bright. She held a glass of wine in one hand, and her mouth opened in surprise when she saw him. "What are you doing here?"

"I need to talk to you." He tried to step inside, but she stood her ground and blocked the doorway. Margaret was much shorter than him, but her rigid posture and fiery expression would make even the Bricks proceed with caution.

"I think you said enough last night on the phone." She clutched the wineglass close and lifted her chin stubbornly.

Damn. He'd seen that look on Margaret's face before. This wasn't going to be easy. "Will you please hear me out?"

"I'll hear you out*side*." She hiccupped, then gave a slow, owl-like blink, and he realized she was tipsy. It didn't take much for her. Back in his time, they'd often gotten drunk on fancy wine from her cellar while her husband was away. Three glasses and she was gone. A plan unfurled in his mind. At first, he'd thought to make up a story about a dangerous gang in the neighborhood so he could convince her to leave with him. If that didn't work, he'd planned to take her by force, but it was Saturday night and the streets were busy. There was a popular university bar right around the corner, and people would surely witness a man carrying a kicking, hollering woman to his car. Luckily, it wouldn't be necessary. She'd given him a much better idea.

"Please, Margaret," Liam said softly, adding the soulful

look that usually did the trick when he was seeking for-giveness from feisty females. "Just for a moment."

She took another sip of wine while he waited, then fi-nally gave an exaggerated sigh and stepped aside. "All right, fine."

Liam followed her through the foyer and into the liv-ing room. Like her bedroom, it was decorated with up-scale furniture in rich fabrics with floral and leaf patterns. There was a potted palm tree in one corner, and a large vase of freshly cut roses on a side table. A chandelier on the vaulted ceiling cast a warm glow throughout the room, and soft music played from speakers set into the walls. Everything about Margaret's home was tasteful, exquisite and refined, just like her.

She walked over to a bar against the wall and refilled her wineglass. "Well? What's so important that you had to interrupt my evening?"

"I came to apologize," Liam said quietly. "I thought about what I said to you on the phone, and I'm sorry if I hurt you."

She tried to feign indifference, but Liam saw right through it. "If you've come all the way across town to tell me you're sorry for hurting me, I assure you, I'm fine." Except she wasn't. Her face was paler than usual, and she looked like she'd lost sleep.

"Let me take you out tonight," he urged. "If you'll give me the chance, I'd like to explain things."

She took another gulp of wine. "Why don't you tell me the truth about this sudden roommate of yours? Go on. I can handle it."

I doubt it. "If you come out with me, I'll answer any questions you have."

She set her glass on the bar and crossed her arms. "You

know, I've never asked much of you, Liam. I'm aware you have your secrets, and I never asked you to share them, but breaking up with me on the telephone?" She gave him a disappointed-teacher look that was so effective, Liam could just imagine her university students cowering behind their books. "I thought I meant more to you than that."

"You do," he assured her. "If you had any idea what I'm going through—"

"That's just it," she interrupted. "I never know because you never share. I didn't even know you were moving in with another woman. Think about how messed up that is, considering we've been sleeping together for months. You never willingly offer up any information about yourself, and I always have to find out by accident. I don't know anything about you besides your story of moving here from Ireland and joining the police force." She began ticking things off on her fingers. "You don't talk about your childhood. You don't tell me about your family. You don't share any of your feelings unless they're between the sheets."

Liam arched a brow. "You never seemed to have a problem with that before."

She gave an exasperated sigh. "I'm talking about everything else. I don't even know your middle name. It's like you have another life I'll never be a part of because you insist on keeping me at arm's length."

He scoffed. "If we're going to be pointing fingers, let's not forget that you're *married.*" He shouldn't have said it. He knew it. But he couldn't help himself. Margaret always did know how to get him worked up. All the more reason for him to walk away from her and concentrate on Cora, who was sweet and kind and comforting as a summer breeze. And he *would* walk away, but not tonight.

He studied the angry woman standing in front of him.

By the looks of her, she was three seconds away from tossing him out.

Tread carefully, man. When riled, Margaret can be as cold as a winter squall.

She pursed her lips.

When you're locked outside.

Lightning flashed in her stormy gray eyes.

With no coat on.

"I don't have to listen to this," she burst out. "I'm not in the mood tonight, Liam. I've got papers to grade. You know, stuff to *focus* on, like you. Maybe some other time." She turned and started down the hall. "Or maybe not."

He caught up to her and laid a hand on her shoulder. "It's just dinner, Margaret. That's all I ask. You don't even have to talk to me if you don't want to. I wouldn't even blame you for giving me the silent treatment. I'll do all the talking."

Her back was rigid as she faced the front door. The clock on the hall table chimed nine. For all he knew, the disaster—whatever it was—could strike at any moment. He needed to act fast. It was time to grovel. It seemed that was the theme for the evening. "Please. I hate the way things ended with us last night. Let me make it up to you."

She slowly turned to face him. Her expression softened, and Liam felt a surge of triumph. "Are you apologizing to me, Liam O'Connor?"

"Absolutely." He reached out and took her hand. "And I'll apologize as many times as you want if you'll just come with me. I know I don't deserve it, but it would mean a lot to me if you did."

The tension left her shoulders in tiny increments, until her mouth began to curve up like a sultry feline. *There* was the woman he knew.

Liam breathed a sigh of relief. Crisis averted. Now that he was back in control—

Suddenly, Margaret lurched forward, gripped the back of his head and stamped her mouth on his.

His brows shot up in surprise. He gripped her waist, stumbling back until he hit the edge of the hall table. Margaret cupped his face with her hands, pouring all her pent-up frustration and desire into the passionate kiss. She tasted like wine and sin and dark, sexy promises, and for a hot minute Liam's brain short-circuited and he was lost in the familiar, all-too-enjoyable sensation of Margaret Brady's delectable body pressed against his.

She ran her fingers through his hair, then down his neck, then under the shoulders of his jacket. It slid off and fell onto the table behind him. Her smoky-gray eyes were hot and bright with lust. Pulling away, she yanked at the hem of his shirt then slid her hands under it. "I want it quick and dirty," she panted against his mouth. "Right here. Up against the wall, like last time."

Holy mother of— "Wait."

"No. You pissed me off yesterday, so now I demand payback. I want angry makeup sex." Her wicked smile was like a siren's song, and she dropped her voice to a sultry purr. "You like it fast and hard. Remember?" She kissed him again, biting gently on his lower lip. Then she sucked it to soothe the sting, trailing her fingertips down the hard ridges of his stomach. Heat spiraled through him. *Hell and damn*, the woman could kiss. When she started grappling with his pants, he finally came to his senses. If he didn't pull himself together, he was going to be in even more trouble than he already was.

He pulled back just enough to focus on her face. "Margaret, hold on."

"Mmm?" She looked at him through languid, wine-hazy eyes, her chest rising and falling. The tip of her tongue darted out to wet her lips.

Liam swallowed hard. *Think!* "I made a reservation for us at a nice restaurant across town. And as much as I enjoy this—" at least that wasn't a lie "—we have to get going or we'll lose our spot."

"Can't we just skip it?" She leaned forward and licked the skin at the base of his neck, her expert hands already unbuckling his belt.

He gripped her hands and dialed up the charm. "If you want me to beg, I will. Please, Margaret. Come with me, first, and let me spoil you. I promise you won't regret it." He added another "please" at the end, just for good measure. *God's teeth*, this woman was making him work for it. He hadn't groveled this hard in…well…maybe ever. Liam looked at her beseechingly.

She tipped her face to the ceiling and muttered, "He had to bust out the puppy dog eyes." Then she blew out a frustrated breath and said, "Fine, but let's make it quick. There are a hundred other things I'd rather do with you tonight."

A…hundred? Liam swallowed hard, trying not to imagine what those things might entail. Now was not the time to go spinning off into the weeds. Grabbing his discarded jacket off the console table, Liam pulled it on and followed her out into the night. He drove toward the only place he could think of, a diner on the corner near his old motel. He'd only seen it in passing, but there was a bar inside, and if he was going to carry out his plan, drinks would be necessary. Margaret would hate the place, but at least they'd be far away from her house, and that was all that mattered.

Liam's phone chimed as they left Belltown Heights behind and pulled onto the highway. Cora had been texting him for the past fifteen minutes, but he was ignoring her. He didn't even want to think about how annoyed she must be. Could he blame her? He'd stuck her with Finn for the evening. That, alone, was grounds for severe punishment. He'd just have to think of a way to make it up to her later.

"Your phone's beeping," Margaret said drowsily. She'd been quiet on the drive, and Liam wondered if she was growing pensive because of the rift between them, or if it was the direct result of all the wine she'd had.

"Someone from work," he said. "I'll check it when we get to the restaurant. We're almost there."

Margaret perked up as he took the freeway exit to the old motel. Then her shoulders began to sag as she stared out the window at the crumbling sidewalks and run-down storefronts. "Where are we going? This is kind of a seedy neighborhood for a fancy restaurant."

"I never said it was fancy, did I?" He drove past a pipe shop with bars over the windows, then pulled into the parking lot of the restaurant. The lot was empty, which meant business was slow for a Saturday night, but that came as no surprise. The diner looked older than dirt, with hazy glass windows and cracked pleather booths.

"Shag's Diner?" Margaret read the weathered sign above the building with trepidation. "You said we were going to a nice restaurant."

"Think of it as an adventure," Liam said brightly. "I heard the food's really good here." He'd heard no such thing, of course, but what's another lie when he'd already told so many? Liam jumped out of the car before she had a chance to protest and led her into the restaurant. It smelled like fryer grease and mop water.

She wrinkled her nose, carefully stepping around the dusty fake plant near the front door. Some song about a hotel in California played over the radio, punctuated by the occasional clanking of dishes and the low hum of conversation from the bar.

"Y'all can sit wherever," a server hollered from the kitchen.

Margaret shot him a look. "You made a reservation, huh?"

"Come on." He forced a playful smile and nudged her with his shoulder. "It'll be fun to try something different." He chose a booth in the corner of the bar.

The grizzled bartender was hunched over the counter talking to a woman with teased and sprayed hair. He flicked a glance at them. "Whaddya want?"

"Two Long Island iced teas," Liam said firmly. Cora's friend Suzette had said those drinks knocked her flat on her ass, so Liam had high hopes for Margaret. His plan was simply to get her as drunk as possible until she passed out. It wasn't one of his finer moments, but it was the best he could come up with on such short notice. He had to keep her out of the house and safe until morning.

Margaret began to sputter a protest over his choice of drinks just as a server came up and slapped plastic-coated menus on their table. The woman was about as old as Liam, give or take a century, with poufy gray hair and spackled-on makeup. There were deep lines around her mouth and her clothes smelled faintly of cigarettes. "Today's specials are the Spam n' Egg Scrambler and the Double Shag Burger Bucket."

Margaret looked a little queasy. "Do you have anything gluten-free?"

The lady let out a squawk of laughter. "This ain't IHOP, honey. We don't do that hoity-toity stuff here." She shuffled away, leaving Margaret staring forlornly at the menu.

Liam gave her an encouraging smile. "Live on the edge?"

"I don't want to live on the edge. I like my comfortable bubble." She pushed the menu away with a sigh just as the bartender set two tall drinks in front of them. Reaching for hers, she took a long, slow sip. *Game on.* "So. Tell me about this new woman you're living with."

Liam braced himself. "What do you want to know?"

Margaret's outward expression was calm, but the storm brewing in her gray eyes ruined it. "For starters, how long have you been seeing her?"

"It's not like that, I told you." If only Margaret's assumptions were correct. Unfortunately, she was almost two centuries off target.

"Then how exactly is it?" Margaret shot back. "What the hell am I supposed to think, here, Liam? A couple of months ago you told me you were transferring to Providence Falls, and I was thrilled because I thought it meant we'd see each other more often. Then, out of the blue, I find out you've moved in with another woman. Forgive me if I've come to the conclusion that you're in a relationship with her, but I've examined the facts. I'm a botanist, remember? I like to call a spade a spade." She fixed him with a steely glare. "Who is she?"

"Her name is Cora McCleod," Liam said calmly. It wouldn't do to get Margaret all riled up, so the more apathy he could feign, the better. "She works at the station, and her father is old friends with mine. That's all. It just so happens she had a room for rent, so I moved in. *Temporarily,*" he emphasized, since, come what may, it was the truth. "I have no plans to stay there beyond three months."

Margaret's posture eased slightly. "And after that? Where are you looking to go?"

"I'm hoping to move someplace…to the north." If he was very lucky.

Margaret shook her head and reached for her drink. "The south end of the city is a more desirable location. If you're looking for someplace permanent, it's definitely the hot spot. That's where you want to end up."

Not if he could help it. Liam scanned the menu, while Margaret asked more questions about Cora. He was very careful to provide neutral, uninterested responses, and after a few more minutes, she seemed somewhat mollified. Then she launched a new attack and began asking a slew of personal questions about Liam's life. He braced himself and dove in.

For the next hour, he told her everything and nothing. Without revealing the truth about the angels and his reincarnated soul, he told her about growing up in Ireland, describing the landscape and the weather. He told her how Hugh was his own father's partner on the police force, and he even told her about how he knew Boyd Thompson when he was a boy. And on it went. She asked questions, and he supplied her with more drinks and silly stories about his childhood.

"I can't believe you got lost in the woods for three whole days," Margaret said with a hiccup, finishing off her second Long Island iced tea. They'd settled on sharing a basket of French fries and a grilled cheese sandwich, both of which she hadn't touched. "Weren't the police looking for you by then?"

He wanted to laugh. The sheriff had far more important things to worry about than a poor farmer's kid who'd gone off on a wild woodland adventure. "No one found me, but I eventually followed the river and made my way home."

She dropped her chin in her hand. "How old were you, again?"

"Five." Liam signaled the bartender for another drink.

"Your mom must've been going crazy."

"She was out of her mind with worry. She said I was the sole reason for her gray hair because I was always running off and doing things I wasn't supposed to. My dad was so angry." Liam chuckled at the memory. "He gave me a thorough lashing, and believe me, I thought twice the next time I—"

"But, I thought you didn't have a dad," Margaret interrupted. "You said your father was here in Providence Falls while you grew up in Ireland, and he wasn't a part of your life back then."

Dammit. Even deep in her cups, the woman was sharp.

Margaret tilted her head in confusion. "Did you mean your stepdad?"

"Yes," Liam lied smoothly. "My mother eventually found another man, and we called him that."

"*We?* I thought you didn't have any brothers or sisters."

"Right." He waited as the bartender set Margaret's drink on the table. "I meant 'we' as in, my mother and me."

Margaret narrowed her eyes, and for a moment Liam thought his ruse was up. But before she could ask him any more questions, she swept her hand out and accidentally knocked over a glass of water. "Oops." She giggled and yanked a handful of paper napkins from the dispenser on the table.

The bartender brought over a dirty dishrag and mopped up the mess. Margaret gave him an overblown drunkard's apology, which made Liam smile, even under the circumstances. She may be plastered, but she was ever the proper lady.

Liam checked the time. It was almost ten. He still had hours before he could safely take her home, so he needed to drag this out. "Your turn, Margaret. Tell me something about you."

She waved a hand, and this time Liam grabbed her drink glass so it wouldn't topple over. "You know everything there is to know about me."

Not true. Margaret always played her cards close to her chest when it came to details about her private life. Liam often wondered about her marriage, and how much she and her husband actually shared. Like a bed, for example. Back in Liam's time, Margaret had hated her husband, so he'd always just assumed they didn't have a physical relationship. But maybe that assumption was his own pigheaded pride getting in the way of reality. Back then, when Liam began the affair with her, he didn't like to think she was sleeping with anyone else, even if that person was her legal husband. But in this life, Margaret seemed much more content in her marriage. Maybe even happy.

"Then tell me something I don't know," Liam urged, taking a bite of the grilled cheese sandwich. The food had gone cold, but it was still damned delicious. From the curl of distaste on Margaret's face, she did not agree. People here were a lot pickier with their food, he'd noticed. And so cavalier about letting it go to waste. He still wasn't over the shock of it, to see entire plates of food scraped into the trash at the end of a meal. It felt criminal. Cora had teased him about always finishing what was on his plate, but he couldn't help it. So far, all the food he'd tried was amazing. If his family could see him now...

He set the sandwich down as guilt washed over him. The thought of his little niece and nephews, pale and thin, faces pinched from lack of nourishment, turned his stomach. That he could be sitting here eating and drinking his fill while they went hungry seemed almost sinful. But they weren't going hungry, were they? They were dead and gone. A bleak mantle of despair began to settle over him. Liam ran a hand across the back of his neck, as if to shove it away. Then he focused his attention back on Margaret. She'd never had to worry about food and shelter. She'd been wealthy back then, and all her unhappiness came from the vile old man she'd been married to. Now she seemed healthy and content. Maybe in this life her husband, John, was a decent man, after all.

Margaret leaned her head back and smiled lazily. "Well, you know I teach botany. I enjoy gardening. Travel. Cooking." She lowered her voice to a sultry purr. "Collecting silk lingerie."

Liam shook his head. Those were all superficial things. "Tell me a secret. Something you've never told me before."

She laughed. "Like what?"

"Do you love your husband?" The words barely left his mouth before he was cursing himself. Why the hell did he ask her that? John Brady was the last person in the world Liam wanted to talk about. He'd despised the man back in his old life, and the feeling had been mutual. Even if John Brady was a good man now, Liam still didn't want to hear Margaret gush about him. He absently rubbed his throat, annoyed with himself.

Looking as surprised as he was, Margaret hesitated, then sucked back more of her drink. "I'd rather not talk about John."

Fine. Liam felt a gritty prickle of annoyance just hearing her mention the man's name. It was disturbingly close to jealousy, which was ridiculous because he had no right to be jealous. Maybe the one drink he'd been nursing was muddling his brain. "All right. Then what do you want to talk about?"

She gave him a wicked smirk and slid her foot up the inside of his leg under the table. "Let's get out of here." Those "hundred other things" she'd mentioned earlier were dancing in her eyes. Liam wondered what it would be like to step right in and take a spin around that dance floor. Exactly how many did this woman know? Would they be new to him? Regardless, he'd always been a quick study, so he felt confident—

"Do you want to?" she asked impishly. Her foot was making its way closer and closer to its target, which brought all Liam's thoughts to a screeching halt. He needed to shut this down now, or there'd be hell to pay.

"It's early yet," he managed, shifting to lean against the wall so her foot fell away. "Tell me more about your silk lingerie collection."

"I could just show you." Chin resting on her hand, she blinked sleepily. "Actually, I think I really do need to go home."

He had to think of a way to stall her. Anything! She was not going home tonight. Even if he had to handcuff her to a chair. He stared out the window at the neon motel sign across the street, mind spinning up another plan. Glancing back at her, he gave her a roguish smile. The kind that promised all sorts of deliciously wicked things, if the woman was willing. "Margaret, I have a crazy idea."

"No." She laughed, shaking her head a little longer than necessary. She was well and truly drunk. "No more of your crazy ideas. This restaurant excursion was more than enough for one night. I need a bed."

Liam leaned forward and said, "My thoughts exactly." He signaled for the check and paid, then led the giggling

Margaret across the street to the motel. After paying a bored receptionist who couldn't be bothered to glance up from his phone, Liam led Margaret into one of the shoddy motel rooms on the second floor.

"God, I can't believe you talked me into this," she said with a laugh. Her steps were unsteady as she spun in a slow circle. "I don't even remember the last time I stayed in a place like this. The air is so stale in here. It smells like—"

"Adventure," Liam said jovially.

"I think your idea of adventure is a little different than mine." She plunked herself down on the edge of the creaky bed, then kicked off her shoes. "I do hope you came prepared, Indiana Jones."

"For?"

She smiled coyly and began unbuttoning her shirt. "Adventure?" When Liam gave her a blank look, she rolled her eyes. "Condoms. You do have some, don't you?"

"Ah." He shoved his hands into his pockets. "Well, no. I didn't think about it."

Margaret groaned and flopped on the bed with her arms outstretched. "Worst. Date. Ever," she said to the ceiling.

"Why don't you wait here?" Liam offered. "There's a convenience store on the corner. I'll run over and be right back."

"Bring me some water, too," she mumbled, rubbing her temples. "And Tylenol. The room is spinning."

"Here." Liam coaxed the bleary-eyed woman under the stiff bedsheets. For a moment he was afraid she'd protest and demand to be driven home, but the drinks had done their job. He brushed the hair back from her face and whispered, "I'll be back before you know it."

When she snuggled down with a yawn, he quietly

turned off the light and left the room, shutting the door behind him.

Now what? He just had to waste a few more hours until early morning when it would be safe enough to take her home. He slowly walked down the flight of stairs and past the ancient motel pool. His phone beeped, and another angry text message popped up on his screen. Cora had tried calling him a couple of times during dinner, but he'd ignored her.

Thanks for sticking me with Finn and not even bothering to show up.

Liam crossed the street to the convenience store and slumped on a bus stop bench. It was as hard and unyielding as the final text from Cora.

Don't bother asking me for any more favors.

She seemed to have given up on him. He couldn't blame her. If only she understood what was at stake. If only he could tell her. By tomorrow, he'd have two women mad at him: Cora for abandoning him to the dullard, and Margaret for coercing her into a terrible dinner followed by a drunken crash in a cheap motel. Sooner or later Margaret was going to realize he'd never actually said he wanted to get back together with her. All he'd promised to do was explain things. He'd been purposefully evasive about their relationship, and the only reason she didn't call him on it was because she'd been knocking back those drinks, and her mind had been fuzzy.

Cursing under his breath in frustration, he jerked upright on the bench and ran a hand through his hair. A fine kettle of fish he was in, and all because the angels had to be vague and secretive. He stood, pacing back and forth on the street, brooding, until he finally stretched out on the cold metal bench and tilted his face to the sky. No stars were visible. They were no match for the ambient city lights.

A sharp, bone-deep longing for home gripped him. He missed the cool, crisp air from the fields back in Ireland. The loamy scents of damp earth and woodsmoke and green things growing. He missed twilight when the fields and forest were bathed in shadows and everything, even the harsh realities of the dilapidated cottages and failing crops, appeared softer around the edges. Those moments at the end of the day, right before the evening shattered into a million stars, were Liam's favorite. He would sit on the crumbling stone wall and imagine what it would be like to be anywhere else. To be someone else…

14

Kinsley, Ireland,
1844

"Look sharp!" an angry voice yelled from the muddy thoroughfare.

Liam glanced up from where he'd dropped a coin to see a sleek carriage pulled by two shining horses barreling toward him. He jerked back with a curse and landed in the mud.

"Bloody lackwit," the driver barked as he pulled the horses to an abrupt stop. The carriage wheel missed Liam's body by a hair's width.

For a few stunned moments, all Liam could do was suck in air, grateful to still have his limbs intact.

"Giles, what is the holdup?" a man's sharp, annoyed voice asked from inside the carriage.

"Nothing of concern, sir," the driver said. "Just a peasant. We'll be on our way directly."

Margaret Brady's husband peered out of the carriage. He

had cold, black eyes without a spark of warmth or compassion, and a disapproving slash of a mouth. With his pallid complexion and sagging jowls, it was no wonder Margaret was always happiest when he was away on business. He looked down his craggy nose, sneering when he spotted Liam on the ground. "Next time don't bother stopping, Giles. A moment of my time is more valuable than an entire lifetime of one such as this."

A woman murmured something from within the carriage. Though it had been a few weeks since Liam had ended things with her, he still easily recognized Margaret's low, throaty voice.

"My dear," the old man said coldly, turning to face his wife. "Do not waste your concern. These peasants are like vermin. One may fall, but there will always be more." He rapped on the ceiling, and the carriage shot off down the road.

Unfeeling rat bastard! Liam pushed himself to his feet. What if he hadn't moved away in time? He could've been maimed, which would almost be worse than being killed. The last thing his brother's family needed was an invalid. Another helpless mouth to feed. He slapped mud and dust from his clothes as the carriage turned on the corner and disappeared. Poor Margaret Brady. Even in his anger at being nearly run down, he pitied the woman. Her vile husband had a frozen wasteland for a heart, and Liam would take an eternity of digging in the mud and scrabbling for food over having to live with that devil's spawn.

He glanced down at the single coin he clutched in his hand, then dropped it into his pocket, adjusted his shirt and continued toward the apothecary. It had been a bad week. His young nephew was sick again, and they couldn't afford the dram of medicine he needed. His brother had twisted an ankle, making it difficult for him to work the field. Liam had taken over his brother's share of duties, in addition to his own, which left him little time for schemes with Boyd and the Bricks. Exhausted and distracted, he'd almost gotten caught picking the pocket of a wealthy traveler who'd had too much to drink the night before at the Goose & Gander. Luckily, the Bricks had started a fight, and Liam had been able to escape before the man's valet could catch him.

Now he stepped into the apothecary shop, determined to make at least one thing better. He put his only coin on the counter and nodded to the white-haired man hunched over a book. "Morning, Seamus. I'll need some of that tea for a cough, if you've got it."

The old man shuffled over to a line of glass jars and measured herbs into a paper sleeve. "Will this be for your brother's boy young Jamie O'Connor again?"

"Aye," Liam murmured, knowing he needn't say anything further. If there was one thing old Seamus was good at, it was talking. He rarely required a response.

"Poor wee thing, with the coughing sickness. Make sure to tell your brother's wife to steep it good and long, and to give it to the child just before sleeping."

"I will."

"Coughing ailment." The old man clucked his tongue and continued to ramble. "Not an easy fix, that. Most unfortunate. Especially when you're as young as wee Jamie. Some people are just born that way, you know, and there's no doing for it. When my Jenny was alive, she used to always say it was in the bones, and the only true relief for someone with a lung affliction was the peace that comes from God's grace in heaven after death."

"Right." Liam would be sure not to pass on that bit of information to his brother's wife. He thanked the old man and left the shop, slowing to stare into the bakery window that was two doors down.

The warm, yeasty scent of fresh baked bread wafted onto the street. Liam's stomach grumbled as he stared at the loaves stacked onto a tray beside a plate of currant buns in the window. He slid a hand into his pocket, now empty, but for the packet of his nephew's medicine. In a different world, he thought hungrily, in a different life—were he a different man—he'd waltz right into that shop and buy up the entire window display. He'd carry all of it straight into his brother's hut and toss armfuls of fresh bread and cakes onto the table, just to watch the little ones' faces light up with joy. *If only.*

Liam tore his gaze away from the display and began to walk on, just as the door flung open, cracking him in the face.

"Oh! Goodness, I'm so sor—" A soft, feminine gasp. "It's you."

Liam stood stunned, rubbing his forehead. The sight of the beautiful Cora McLeod standing before him was like a dream. She looked out of place clutching a bakery bag to her chest against the backdrop of muddy streets. Today she was dressed in a prim, gray woolen gown, and her glorious hair was, unfortunately, bound tight and tucked under a bonnet. But nothing could dull her bright blue eyes, now looking at him with a mixture of surprised delight and concern.

It made him want to laugh from the sheer wonder of

being this close to her again. "Why is it that every time we meet, I get injured?"

"I'm so sorry," she repeated, fluttering a hand and looking around. "Do you need to sit down? I should've paid better attention to where I was going. Nanny's always reprimanding me for walking too fast. She says a lady should only take mincing steps and never rush anywhere because it rather denotes a lack of poise."

"Nonsense." Liam gave her a lopsided grin and leaned a shoulder against the wall. "I think there's something quite dignified about a sea captain dashing off in a hurry. No telling what kind of adventure awaits her."

Cora raised a gloved hand to her mouth and giggled, her gaze alight with the same spark of mischief and amusement he remembered so clearly from their last encounter.

Liam had missed her so much since that night he'd crawled through her window. He'd tried—and failed—not to think about her because he knew it would do him no good. The very thought of ever speaking to her again had seemed nigh impossible, and yet here they were. He'd have endured far more than a crack on the face for a stroke of luck like this.

"Are you heading to the bakery?" she asked.

If only. "I've been to the apothecary. My young nephew is sick."

Cora's smooth brow creased with concern. "I'm so sorry. How old is he?"

"Jamie's only five, but he'll be on the mend, soon enough," Liam said.

"Do you have just the one?"

"No. My brother and his wife have three children. Aside

from Jamie, there's Bridget who's not yet four, and baby Daniel, born this past spring."

"How lovely to have such a big family," she said wistfully. "I imagine there's never a dull moment."

She wasn't wrong, but he doubted her view of his family life matched the reality. "What are you doing here this morning?"

"Currant buns." She held up her bag with a grin, then she lowered her voice and glanced around, as if she were about to impart secrets of dire importance. "My nanny is just in there." She pointed to the milliner's shop three doors down. "And I think she only gave me leave to visit the bakery for a moment without her because, well…" Was that a blush? Liam wanted so badly to lay a hand against her soft cheek to feel the warmth of it. Instead, he balled his hand into a fist and crossed his arms, nodding for her to continue.

"You see," Cora said in an almost-whisper, "I think she has a fondness for the old shopkeeper in there. She often lingers at the ribbon counter, and I know she's not interested in ribbons, because she says they're only for frivolous young girls. But the man always dances attendance on her whenever we visit, so it's quite possible he feels the same. Only I do wonder how they'd ever get on because she is very hard of hearing and his eyesight is rather poor. But perhaps between the two of them, their strengths are complementary."

Liam grinned down at her. He loved how animated and lively she became when she talked. Once again, he found himself wishing he could be someone worthy of her company. But the differences in their lives were split by a chasm so wide and deep, the only way he could ever bridge the gap was if a pair of angels plucked him from this life and dropped him into another. It was never going to happen, so he was well and truly stuck. He brushed the depressing thought aside and said, "Well, I, for one, find myself eternally grateful for your nanny's sordid love affair because it has allowed me the opportunity to see you again."

Cora blushed a second time, then glanced down at the bag in her hands. "I was wondering if we would. I often hoped to run into you." She looked up at him shyly. "I do believe meeting you was the nicest, most interesting thing that's ever happened to me, Liam O'Connor."

Liam's heart pounded in his chest because he felt the same way, and hearing his name on her lips made everything feel possible. He swallowed hard. "I've thought of you often since then. I enjoyed talking to you very much, even though the circumstances were…unusual."

"I'm always there, you know. If you wanted to—" She paused and seemed to gather her courage, then looked him square in the face because she was so much braver than she believed. He could see that about her, even if she couldn't. "I mean, if you wanted to visit me again." Then she rushed to add, "I wouldn't want you to climb the wall outside my window, of course. That's far too dangerous."

"Yes. I prefer my head attached to my shoulders," he said with a smile, though he'd risk it a hundred times if she was really saying what he thought she was saying.

"But I suppose," she said tentatively, "you could toss a pebble at my window?" If Liam thought she'd been blushing before, he was dead wrong, because now her gaze slid away and her face was positively scarlet. But she lifted her chin and forged on. "It was in a book I read recently, you see. Whenever two marauders needed to communicate, they tossed pebbles at each other's windows to alert the other party that the smugglers were coming."

"I find myself quite intrigued with your taste in books, *and* your attempt to lure me into piracy," Liam teased. "I accept your proposal, Captain Cora."

She looked surprised. "You do?"

"I'd be a fool not to."

Cora beamed, but before she could speak, the milliner's door opened and a woman with thinning, gray hair stepped out. She had a tight bun at the nape of her neck, a severe face stamped into a permanent frown and a dress the color of wet mold. If this was Cora's nanny, then it was no wonder Cora's wardrobe lacked allure. This woman looked as enticing as a mud puddle, and just as chilly. Liam imagined she chewed snowflakes for breakfast.

"I have to go," Cora whispered. "Here. For your nephew." She pushed the bag of currant buns at him.

He stepped back, catching it to his chest as she hurried past on a lavender-and-sunshine-scented breeze.

Liam watched her slow her pace to match that of her aging nanny. She glanced back once and gave him a secret smile.

He stood there even after they'd rounded the corner and disappeared. It was long moments before his heartbeat returned to normal. And longer still before he realized that a miracle had just fallen into his lap. Cora McLeod, the beautiful squire's daughter, wanted to see him again. *Him.* Liam made his way down the street, mulling over his sudden stroke of luck. For the first time all week, he heard the birds singing in the trees as he walked along the edge of the woods. He noticed the damp grass sparkling like diamonds in the sun as he crossed the overgrown field toward his brother's home. And when he thought about stealing out in the middle of the night to visit Cora again, the whole world bloomed bright with possibilities.

Providence Falls,
Present Day

The sound of a car screeching around the corner yanked Liam out of his reverie. The smell of exhaust fumes had him coughing as he lurched upright on the bench. Never in his wildest fantasies could he have dreamed up a place like the city of Providence Falls. He was so far out of his depth. Even as an expert liar, it was difficult for him to navigate the murky waters in this place. The angels had neglected to add so much important knowledge. The common social rituals like public courting with no intention of marriage, eating food for no reason other than boredom or running without trying to get anywhere. And there were too many confusing cultural references to ever catch up. Blind dates weren't blind. French fries weren't French. It was exhausting! He blew out a frustrated breath. Liam realized he had too much to learn, and three months would never be enough.

A guttural shout followed by a scuffling sound drew his attention. He glanced toward the alley beside the convenience store. Several feet from the ATM, a man in a dark hooded sweatshirt shoved an old man against the wall, then punched him in the gut.

The old man doubled over on a choked cough, holding his stomach with both hands.

"The cash," the attacker snarled. "Or you're gonna get

it worse, gramps." He snaked a hand into the old man's pocket and yanked out his wallet.

Without thinking, Liam vaulted over the back of the bench and barreled straight into the attacker from behind, grabbing him in a bear hug.

The man tried to throw him off. When that didn't work, he jerked his head back, hitting Liam in the face.

Pain cracked across Liam's cheekbone. His grip on the man loosened for a split second, and the attacker turned and punched him in the jaw. Liam's head snapped back, his ears ringing as he fell, but he managed to knock the wallet to the ground.

The attacker dove for it, but Liam kicked it, sending it skidding into the wall beside the old man. The attacker let out a guttural curse, and by the time Liam got to his feet again, the man was already running, disappearing into the night.

Liam braced to run after him when an unsteady groan drew his attention. The old man clung to the wall.

"Are you all right?" Liam walked over to help him.

"He—he tried to steal my wallet," the man grunted.

"Aye, he tried, but he didn't succeed. You're lucky he didn't do worse." Liam helped steady the man, scooped the wallet off the pavement and handed it to him. "Do you need me to call for a doctor?"

"No, no." He waved a shaky hand. "None of that nonsense. I'm tougher than I look." He leaned his back against the wall, breathing heavily. "If I were thirty years younger, I'd have given him a knuckle sandwich he'd never forget."

"Sure, you would've." Liam tried to sound convincing as he sized up the old man.

Watery brown eyes squinted at him from a road map of wrinkles. "Believe me, boy, he'd have been down for the count. I used to box back in my day. Fought in two wars. Raised four children. Survived cancer and even my wife." He tapped a gnarled finger to his temple. "I still got the fight up here. It's just these old bones that slow me down now." He stared off into the dark where the attacker had disappeared. "It's a damned shame this neighborhood has gone to hell."

"Oh, I wouldn't go that far." As a man whose soul dangled right over the threshold of that fiery underworld, Liam felt qualified to make the distinction. "Men like him are everywhere, even in good neighborhoods. This place doesn't look all that bad." No demons. No tortured souls screaming in agony. No fiery pits of doom. "I can think of worse places."

The man snorted. "The whole world's changed, son, and not for the better. People nowadays got their fancy beeping computer gizmos, always face down in their phone screens and never looking each other in the eye. Never paying attention to what's *real*. What's around them. You're young now, so you don't understand, but trust me, the world isn't like it used to be."

"Oh, I believe you." Liam stayed with him, waiting until the old man's breathing evened out, and his face returned to a normal shade.

"Time flies," the man said, shaking his head. "And one day you wake up and look around and wonder where the hell you are."

That was God's truth. Liam stared up at the murky sky. "You sure you don't want me to call a doctor?"

The old man let out a grunt of dismissal and pushed away from the wall.

"I'm a police officer," Liam explained. In the heat of things, he'd almost forgotten. "I can call it in right now, if you want to report it." Liam pulled his phone out of his pocket and held it up. "With my fancy beeping computer gizmo."

The man waved Liam away. "Off with you, son. I don't need to waste your time. That man is long gone, and I got my wallet back."

"Let me at least walk you home."

"No need." He pointed to an old car parked along the sidewalk. "That's my car right there. You should get your own face looked at. You're going to have quite the shiner in the morning."

Liam pressed his fingers to his face and winced. Nothing was broken, but he'd be badly bruised.

"Good night, son, and thank you." The man began walking to his car, then turned back. "Keep your eye out for wolves in sheep's clothing. We've got thieves among us, boy. They're everywhere. Masquerading as nice, honest folk like us. But you already know that."

"Yes, I do," Liam murmured. He watched the man drive away. Then he checked the time on his phone and headed back to the motel room. Margaret was passed out cold, and from the sound of her soft, kitten-like snores, he knew she wouldn't be waking up anytime soon. There was only one bed in the room, so he dropped into the upholstered chair in the corner with a heavy sigh.

He dialed Cora's number, unsure what he was going to say. When the call went to voice mail, he was relieved. For the next several minutes he tried to come up with something to tell her, then just texted a quick apology that was far from adequate. Finally, too tired to think, he shoved the phone back in his pocket and closed his eyes.

15

Finn drove Cora to the Davenport Estate, located in the foothills thirty minutes outside of Providence Falls. It was surrounded by acres of beautifully manicured lawns, rose gardens, a renowned golf course and a vineyard. Cora's father and Finn had gone golfing there many times over the years, but she'd only been once for a friend's wedding. Built in the late 1800s by a wealthy railroad baron for his wife, the Davenport now served as a hotel and resort famed for its destination weddings and events like the evening's Bread for the Hungry charity ball. The palatial estate had ivory stone columns in front, a circular drive with a giant three-tiered fountain, and a sparkling ballroom that looked like something straight out of a fairy tale.

The place was so picturesque, Cora should've been charmed, but she wasn't. Instead, she was roiling in a stew of frustration and resentment because she'd been at the gala for hours now, and Liam still hadn't arrived.

"He's kinda sexy in a sort of nerdy superhero way, you know?" Suzette was sitting at one of the round dining tables, studying Finn as he walked toward the buffet line.

Cora tilted her head and tried to imagine Finn Walsh in a cape with a giant hammer. He had the nice height and the broad shoulders, but he was just too clean-cut to give off that exciting superhuman vibe. "Nope. I don't see it."

"I'm not talking *beefcake* superhero," Suzette explained. "But like a Clark Kent-in-glasses type, with the hidden sexiness that you discover once the clothes come off. Or one of those hot, genius scientists, you know? The kind who do important things in those labs with the bubbling test tubes."

"Oh, you mean the evil villains with the maniacal laughter? Yeah, those guys are irresistible."

Suzette rolled her eyes and adjusted the rhinestone strap on her black cocktail dress. "You've got no imagination."

"What about you and Rob Hopper?" Cora asked, changing the subject. "He's been cornered by that blonde woman over there near the punch bowl, but I swear he's been staring at you for the past ten minutes." Rob was smiling politely at a woman who seemed to have had too much to drink. She was practically falling all over him, and oblivious to the fact that his attention wasn't on her.

Suzette gave Rob a cursory glance, then made a sound of disgust. "Not in a bajillion years." She tossed her hair over her shoulder, then stole a couple more glances in Rob's direction.

Cora checked her phone again. It was almost midnight, and Liam hadn't bothered to respond to a single one of her texts. Unbelievable. She gritted her teeth and tossed her phone back on the table.

"Scowling like that causes premature wrinkles, you know." Suzette plucked a chocolate from the dessert platter in the center of their table and popped it in her mouth.

"I'm just super annoyed at Liam. He's the one who wanted to come to this thing, and he hasn't even bothered to show up."

"*I* showed up," Suzette said around a mouthful of hazelnut truffle.

Cora reached out and laid a hand on her friend's arm. "And for that I am forever in your debt. I shouldn't have asked you to come at such short notice." After two hours making stilted small talk with Finn, Cora had finally called in Suzette for backup.

"Hey, it wasn't a hard sell. I never miss a chance to get dolled up and drink free booze. But I'm surprised Finn annoyed you enough to send out the emergency girl code Bat-Signal. He doesn't seem that bad."

"He really isn't," Cora said in exasperation. "I think I was just pissed off at Liam for not coming like he said he would, and I wasn't in the mood for conversation."

"Well, in your defense, the conversation hasn't exactly been dazzling. Finn's cute, sure, but the nerd factor is strong with that one. I heard him quoting *Star Wars*. And when I got here, he was telling you all about his rock collection."

"Geodes."

"Oh, excuse me. *Sparkly* rock collection. I thought any second he was going to bust out with, 'One time, at band camp…'" Suzette's hazel eyes sparkled with laughter, and she took another sip of her drink. "Still, all that aside, I like him for you."

"Oh, not for *you*?" Cora teased.

"Please. You know I only go for the superhot, emotionally unavailable bad boys."

"Maybe you should try a nice guy, for a change."

"Where's the fun in that? Speaking of hotties, where *is* that new roommate of yours? I was looking forward to getting a glimpse of him all decked out à la James Bond."

Cora's gaze flicked to the entrance of the ballroom. Captain Thompson was standing there in conversation with the mayor, while his wife, Alice, looked bored, but beautiful in her gold sequined cocktail dress. "I have no idea why Liam hasn't arrived yet, but he'd better have a damned good explanation."

"Maybe he really is an international superspy like 007, and he's off saving lives," Suzette said dreamily. "Maybe he's sitting in his lair right now with, like, a white Persian cat on his lap."

"Um, I'm pretty sure that guy was the villain."

Suzette shrugged and lifted her champagne glass. "See? I always go for the bad boys. It's a problem for me."

Cora pointed to the dessert tray. "Give me one of those, will you?"

"Good plan. Chocolate makes everything better." Suzette slid the silver platter closer.

The orchestra struck up "The Blue Danube" waltz and people began swooping and swirling across the dance floor. Most of them were older couples, which made sense. Cora didn't know a single person her age who actually knew how to ballroom dance like people did in the movies. But as she watched the elegant couples whirling around the floor, she secretly wished she'd learned.

Finn returned to the table with a plate of berry tarts

dusted with sparkling sugar. He offered it to Cora. "I thought you might want some."

"Thanks," Suzette said happily, snagging a tart.

Finn set the plate down, then said to Cora, "Would you like to dance?"

Cora had a miniature cherry tart halfway to her mouth. "Oh, I'm—"

"Yes, she would." Suzette swiped the pastry from Cora and put it on her own plate. "You need to dance. It's a good stress reliever. Go. Shoo!" She waved her hands at both of them.

"Thanks a lot," Cora mumbled under her breath.

"I'll be over here if anyone needs me," Suzette sang out.

Cora followed Finn to the dance floor, and he drew her into position, placing his hand on her lower back. Warmth tingled through her with the unexpected contact of his large hand on her bare skin. Her gaze flew to his, but he was looking beyond her. She could see him swallow, and a muscle clenched in his jaw. He seemed nervous.

"Is everything okay?" she asked.

He nodded without making eye contact and said in a husky voice, "Everything's great."

Before she had a chance to ask anything further, he swung her into the waltzing crowd. Cora gasped in surprise as she tried to keep up. Finn expertly maneuvered them through the dancing couples, occasionally twirling her until Cora found herself caught up in the gaiety and laughter. She was a miserable dance partner, that was abundantly clear, but she was never one to shy away from a challenge. On their second time around the floor, she gave him an apologetic smile. "I think that's the twelfth time I've stepped on your foot."

· He gave her a warm smile. "I didn't notice."

"Liar," she said with a laugh. "You can send me the doctor bill on Monday."

A visibly intoxicated couple came lurching toward them, and Finn effortlessly switched directions. Cora stumbled, and he pulled her against his hard chest, lifting her off her feet until they were out of danger, then setting her back into the dance as smoothly as if it had never happened.

"Where did you learn to do this?" she asked, a little out of breath.

"My mother took ballroom dance lessons when I was a kid. She talked my father into it, and he made me go, too. She said it was an important skill to learn, but I think my father just figured if he had to suffer through it, so should I."

Cora giggled as he spun her around, her mood lifting. Finn might be on the stuffy side, but the man could dance. Who'd have guessed? He had a superpower, after all.

"My father tried to put me in dance class when I was little," Cora said. "It was a disaster. The ballet instructor told my father she wasn't skilled enough to teach wild animals."

Finn let out a bark of laughter. "I doubt you were that bad."

"Oh, I really was," Cora assured him. "I was so bored, I refused to do the exercises. Instead, I pretended I was a tiger, and the other girls were sheep. Every time the teacher had us line up and 'float across the floor like a spring breeze,' the rest of the kids did the floating, and I did the stalking and pouncing."

Finn's warm laughter was contagious.

"I lasted one and a half classes before she booted me out," Cora continued. "My poor dad. After that, he tried to put me in piano lessons, Girl Scouts, peewee cheerleading and whatever else he thought little girls should do. I think it was a side effect of us losing my mom when I was so young. He was kind of at a loss with how to handle me."

"And I'm guessing none of those activities appealed to you?"

"Not a single one," Cora said with a sigh. "I was all about karate, rock climbing and trips to the shooting range."

Finn smiled and pulled her closer as he maneuvered them in a tight circle to avoid one of the dining tables at the edge of the dance floor. He smelled clean and woodsy, like a hike through the forest after it rained. Cora could feel the warmth of his chest, and the strength of his large hand gripping her lower back. She was surprised to realize how comfortable she felt in his embrace. It was…nice.

"So how'd you talk your dad into letting you do those things?" Finn asked.

"Oh, it was an uphill battle. It took me years to convince him I wasn't going to be a Junior League debutante. But eventually, he figured out I was as stubborn as he was, so he let me go my own way." Then Cora glanced up and added, "Within reason. He was still ridiculously overprotective, but he did teach me how to shoot. I think he was glad when I decided to join the police force because at least it was something he understood."

"It's amazing what you do," Finn said with feeling. "Every day you're out there trying to make the city a better place, trying to protect the people. I can't imagine a parent not being proud of the path you've chosen."

Heat crept up the back of her neck, blooming across her cheeks. Cora glanced away, suddenly shy of Finn's heartfelt compliment. She tried to change the subject. "What about you? Aside from dance lessons, did you do any other sports growing up?"

"Varsity football and lacrosse," Finn said, before adding, "And fencing."

"Really?" Cora almost stopped in the middle of the dance floor. She never imagined him as an athlete. He always seemed more like the CEO type. The guy in the suit, watching the game from a private box up in the stands.

"And golf, too, I suppose," Finn added. "But that was more of a leisure thing I did on the weekends with my dad." A quirk of his mouth. "You seem surprised."

"I am, a little," Cora said. "I just honestly had you pegged as more of an indoor-sport type of person."

"Indoor sports." His lips twitched like he was trying not to smile. "Such as bowling or darts?"

"I don't know…" Cora glanced sheepishly up at him. "Chess, maybe?"

"Actually, I was in the chess club in high school," Finn admitted. "Captain of it."

"I knew it!"

"And I was also a Mathlete," he added with a boyish grin that warmed Cora all the way to her toes. "So, your assumptions were still accurate."

Huh. A high school jock *and* a nerd. Well that explained the muscular shoulders he was hiding underneath the tailored suit of his. Suzette's comment about him being an undercover Clark Kent type was beginning to make sense. Cora started to imagine what Finn looked like out of his suit, then a hot blush scorched across her face. What the heck was she doing? This was Finn! Her dad's stuffy golf buddy. The man whose dress shoes were shinier than hers. *Pull yourself together, McLeod!*

When the song ended, Finn walked Cora back to their table, where Rob Hopper was now trying to convince Suzette that *Fight Club* was a better movie than *Pride and Prejudice*.

"Give it up, Hopper," Cora said. "I happen to agree with Suzette, so you're outnumbered."

"What about you?" Rob asked Finn hopefully. "Surely you're team *Fight Club*. Tell them how good it is. A classic, really."

Finn looked back and forth between Rob and the two women, then chose neutral ground. "Sorry, man. First rule, remember? I can't talk about *Fight Club*."

Rob slapped Finn on the back, and for the next hour, Cora sat in comfortable companionship with her best friend, Finn and Rob. She drank more wine, ate more desserts, and, to her utmost surprise, found that she was enjoying herself.

It was past two o'clock in the morning when Finn pulled his car up to her house after the gala. Cora's mood had shifted during the quiet ride home, and she was back to brooding about Liam's no-show, but she owed it to Finn to put on a good face. She'd ended up having a nice time, in spite of everything, and Finn deserved her gratitude.

He walked her to the front door, and tension suddenly crackled in the air between them. It was dark, and the rest of the world in her bedroom community was fast asleep. The only sound was the soft rustle of leaves in the breeze, and a faint tinkling wind chime somewhere in the distance.

Cora dug around in her purse for her house key. She was aware of Finn's solid presence standing quietly beside her. What now? This was weird. It suddenly felt so...*datey*. Surely, he didn't expect a good-night kiss, or anything. Her face flushed with heat. Of course, he didn't. There wasn't anything between them except friendship. God, she shouldn't have had that last glass of champagne. Her brain had jumped the track and was zooming into the weeds.

She let out a shaky breath and pulled her keys from her purse. Dropped them. Bent to pick them up. Began fumbling with the lock. "I don't know what's wrong with this stupid thing," she muttered when the lock stuck. "I had someone come out and fix it just last week. I swear this house is falling apart. I can't wait until—"

"Here, let me try." Finn reached out to take the keys. A spark of energy snapped between them when his fingertips brushed hers.

Cora sucked in a breath.

His face was half in shadow, but she could hear the smile in his voice. "Static electricity."

She gave a shaky laugh, wondering if he was going to start explaining the science behind it. Finn was a brilliant attorney; she already knew that. But he was really smart about other things, too. And while some of the topics he chose to discuss were unusual, he was like a bright ember, glowing with intelligence and surprising charm. Funny, she'd never really realized that about him before.

The lock clicked and Finn pushed the door open for her.

Cora stepped over the threshold, her breath catching when she slid past his chest and their arms brushed against each other. She felt everything so acutely, the rasp of fabric on her bare skin, the warmth emanating from his solid body, the evergreen, spicy scent of his cologne. She turned to face him and shoved all her strange feelings into the background.

"Well, thanks for that." She gestured wildly to the street.

He cocked his head and studied her. Maybe he didn't catch her meaning.

"The um, the gala. For taking me. And stuff." Wow. She

was really killing it in the eloquence department. He must be astounded by her scintillating conversational skills. That's probably why he wasn't speaking. Uh-huh.

He handed back her keys and she took them. This time, when their fingers brushed, a languid, lazy warmth slid up her arms, spiraling through her limbs. A lock of hair dangled from her updo and fell into her eyes. She shoved it away, but it fell right back again.

Very slowly, Finn reached out and tucked it behind her ear. It was an oddly endearing gesture, the kind of thing someone would do if they knew another person for years. But in the moment, it felt so intimate, Cora's smile began to fade. She bit her bottom lip, overwhelmed with nervous energy.

Finn's gaze flicked to her mouth.

She suddenly felt as if the world around them was holding its breath. The wind through the trees, the faint sound of crickets, everything stilled and all she could feel was the mad thumping of her heart. What was happening here?

Her cell phone shrilled in her purse, snapping her back to reality. Cora dug through it and the name across the screen was like a dash of cold water over her head. Liam. She pressed her lips together and told Finn, "I should get going. Thanks again for driving me tonight."

He ducked his head, an expression ghosting across his face too quickly for her to catch. When he glanced back up, he gave her his usual boyish smile. "Anytime, Cora."

She said good-night and shut the door, kicked off her shoes and walked down the hall into her bedroom. The phone was still ringing, and a tidal wave of resentment flooded through her. Now Liam calls her, after the whole night is over? On impulse, she sent the call to voice mail, slapped her phone on the bed and began to undress. A moment later, a text message popped up on her screen.

I'm sorry I didn't make it tonight.

That was it. No explanations, no dog-ate-my-homework excuses, just "sorry."

Her cat gave a soft meow and hopped onto her bed.

Cora sighed heavily. "It's too little, too late, amirite?"

Angel turned his back and started grooming himself.

She smoothed the fur between his ears. "Traitor."

16

It was just after five o'clock in the morning when Liam drove a very annoyed, hungover Margaret back to her house in Belltown Heights. The sun was already creeping over the horizon, painting the streets and buildings in glorious shades of warmth, but inside, Liam felt an icy prickle of apprehension. He knew evidence of a disaster waited for them back at Margaret's house, and he kept stealing worried glances in her direction.

Aside from her initial reaction at seeing his bruised face, she was quiet and withdrawn this morning, which was unlike her. She hadn't said a word since they got in the car. After a few more minutes of uncomfortable silence, she pulled her phone from her purse, then exhaled in frustration. Liam could tell from the black screen that her phone had no power. Neither did his. It had died somewhere in the early morning hours.

"Mine's dead, too," Liam said.

No response. He was beginning to wonder how long her silent treatment would last.

Finally, she threw him a sullen glance and asked, *"Why?"*

He searched her face, noting her bloodshot eyes and lips pressed together in unhappiness, then tried to lighten the mood. "Well, I've learned that when you don't plug your phone in, it doesn't charge, and that's why the screen goes—"

"Stop. Why bother with this?" She wagged her finger between them. "You came over last night and made me believe you wanted to smooth things over. But nothing's changed, has it? You aren't interested in getting back together. You never were." She paused, giving him a chance to explain, but he said nothing. Margaret made a sound of disgust and crossed her arms, staring out the window.

"I just didn't want to leave things the way they were when we last spoke on the phone," Liam said. "I hated to think that I'd upset you." More importantly, he'd been doing the best he could with the cryptic message the angels had given him, and he'd been trying to save her life.

"No, Liam. You just did it for closure. For yourself. You don't really care about me at all."

He gripped the steering wheel in irritation. "That's not true."

She held up a hand. "Don't. That whole thing last night was some messed-up way for you to feel better about dumping me, and you know what? It wasn't necessary. Truly. Because I'm done with all this. I don't need this shit in my life." Her voice hitched and Liam saw her hands clench into fists as she hugged herself. Margaret was trying to sound tough, but he knew she was barely hanging on.

Before he could say anything, he turned onto her street, and an ambulance sped past. Three police cars were parked at odd angles in front of her house, and someone had cordoned off the area near her front door with yellow tape. Police officers were coming in and out, and others were milling outside to keep spectators from interfering. This was it.

Margaret gasped and sat bolt upright in the car. "That's my house!"

Liam pulled to the curb across the street, about half a block away. Margaret jumped out of the car and ran toward the scene. She was arguing with an officer near her front door when Liam caught up with her.

"But I live here," she cried. "What happened? Why hasn't anyone called me?"

"We weren't able to reach you, ma'am."

"My phone," she said under her breath, then, "I didn't charge it. What's going on? Did anyone call my husband? He's out of town, but—"

"This way, ma'am." The officer tried to lead her away from the front door. "If you'll just step over here, I'll explain."

"No." She tried to move past him. "I want to go inside."

Liam placed a hand on her shoulder.

"Don't!" She jerked away, then rounded on him. "Tell him that's my house. Tell him!"

"I believe he knows, Margaret," Liam said in a low voice. "Wait out here for a moment, and I'll find out what's going on."

The officer led a furious Margaret over to one of the squad cars.

Liam flashed his badge and entered the house. The air

was thick with the smell of smoke, and several forensics people were busy collecting evidence in the living room.

"O'Connor." Boyd stood in the center of the chaos with a wrinkled shirt and messy hair. "What the hell happened to you?" He looked frazzled and tired, but his avid curiosity over Liam's battered face couldn't be masked. It reminded Liam of the man he used to know back in Ireland. Liam couldn't even remember how many scrapes and fights he and Boyd had gotten into growing up, but Boyd always took a feral sort of glee in the chaos of it. Even now, Liam could see that intense, almost eager scrutiny on Boyd's face. Some things never changed.

"Bar brawl," Liam said in dismissal. "What's going on here?"

Boyd waved him into the living room. "Victim's name is John Brady. Murdered sometime last night. A neighbor was taking his dog out this morning and saw the door wide-open. That crack in the front window made him suspicious, and then he smelled smoke coming from inside. He entered and found the victim like this, so he called 911."

Liam stared at the body of Margaret's husband lying on the floor between the living room and study. He'd seen dead men before, but that didn't make it easy, nor did the guilt stabbing at him because of his affair with Margaret. He hadn't actually done anything with her in this lifetime, but what did it matter? It was a terrible burden to know disaster had been looming, and now he wondered if he could've somehow saved this man, too. Or did John die because of some ripple effect of Liam kidnapping Margaret for the night? The thought hit him like an anvil to the head. He'd never know if his actions resulted in this innocent man's death.

"You okay, O'Connor?" Boyd was watching him with

suspicion. "You look like you're going to be sick. Don't tell me you're getting soft."

"No, I'm fine." Liam gathered himself together. He didn't have time to think of all the what-ifs. A man was dead, and the only thing he could do now was try to help find the murderer. He had general knowledge of police procedures, thanks to the angels, but many of the technical terms the officers used were still foreign to him. It was disconcerting and frustrating to always feel caught between two worlds. Sometimes having partial knowledge was worse than having no knowledge at all.

Liam took in the scene, doing his best to use the investigative skills he'd been given. The sleeve of John Brady's shirt was torn, and a pool of blood seeped into the hardwood floors around his head. One arm was twisted under him. His thinning gray hair was matted on one side, and there was a marble bust toppled on the floor beside him. An overturned chair lay on its side in the middle of the room, and Margaret's vase of roses was shattered across the living room carpet. Everything indicated clear signs of a struggle. A blackened metal wastebasket sat in the corner of the room. Two people wearing gloves and masks were sifting through the ashes and broken glass.

"Anything?" Boyd asked the man near the waste bin.

"Nothing yet, sir."

Boyd turned back to Liam. "It appears the killer used that bust to knock Brady over the head." He pointed to the red abrasions on the dead man's neck. "But these marks indicate strangulation. No weapon's been found."

"Motive?" Liam asked.

"The safe in the back room is wide-open."

"Anything stolen?"

Boyd shook his head. "We don't know yet. We'll have

to ask the wife, wherever she is. We haven't been able to get a hold of her this morning."

"She's outside. I saw her when I came in." Liam studied the broken glass on the carpet, careful to keep his voice neutral. As good at deception as he was, it had been a long night, and he was dead tired. But that was nothing compared to how Margaret must be feeling. Guilt weighed heavily on his shoulders, almost breaking his carefully controlled facade. He wanted to somehow comfort Margaret, but how could he, when he'd already hurt her? She'd likely see any overture from him as nothing but pity, and knowing Margaret as he did, she wouldn't want it. Still, he needed to talk to her so they could get their stories straight, but she wasn't going to be in any frame of mind to think rationally. Not after this. Liam took a determined breath and turned away from the crime scene.

Boyd was watching the people digging in the smoking waste bin with the single-minded focus of a sharpshooter. "Someone needs to get her statement."

"I'll go." Liam strode outside and made his way toward a ghostly pale Margaret who was now leaning against a squad car. Someone had given her tea in a paper cup, which she clutched in her shaking hands. Her bloodshot eyes and haunted expression made her seem more fragile than he'd ever seen her.

"Is it true?" She sounded like a lost little girl. "Is he really…"

Liam briefly closed his eyes. "I'm sorry, Margaret."

"No." She shook her head wildly, sloshing tea from her cup. "I don't understand. I just saw him yesterday and he was fine. Who would do something like this? John is a good person."

Liam started to reach for her, then stopped himself. "Margaret, where were you last night?"

She blinked at him in confusion.

He stepped closer and lowered his voice so no one would overhear. "They're going to ask you where you were. Why you weren't home. What do you want to tell them? Surely, you don't want them to know you were out all night with another man." She'd have enough to deal with over the next few weeks. The last thing she needed was the added stress of experiencing public ridicule or scrutiny. Liam knew this world was different, and people were more accepting of physical relationships in general, but he was pretty sure marriage still meant something, as did infidelity.

Margaret made an angry, choking sound that withered on the vine before it could bloom into a bitter laugh. "Of course. My husband just died, and you're worried about yourself."

He jerked his head back as if she'd slapped him. All the events of the previous night, all the strain and exhaustion, finally caught up with him. He'd told so many lies, and there were so many moving parts to the story, his head ached from it. Margaret had no idea what he'd done to keep her safe. Patience worn thin, he gritted his teeth and said, "Listen to me. Do you want to tell them the truth about us? Because I sure as hell don't give a damn. It won't be the first time people have judged me and found me wanting for the things I've done. I can weather it. It's your reputation, and that of your husband, you should consider. But I need to know how you want to do this, so we have our stories straight. Decide now. I'll back you in whatever you choose."

The look she gave him was so full of bitterness, he could almost taste it. "Don't worry, Liam. Your career is safe. I'm not going to reveal our dirty little secret. My husband is a good man. He doesn't deserve to be touched by a scandal. I'll say I was at my sister's house last night. She'll vouch for me."

An officer approached with a clipboard to ask Margaret more questions. She turned her back on Liam, wanting nothing more to do with him.

He trudged back up the steps to the house, drained and wishing he could just go home and fall asleep for another hundred years.

Cora arrived on the scene a moment later, gasping in shock when she saw his bruised face. "What happened to you?" She rushed toward him.

He almost smiled. Typical Cora. It was in her nature to care for others, even when she was angry. "Nothing. I'm fine."

"Don't give me that," she said in annoyance. "Your face looks terrible."

"As I said, nothing happened." He gave her a crooked smile, hoping to ease the tension between them.

She eyed his rumpled suit. His messy hair. The unshaven stubble on his face. "You never came home last night. If you don't tell me what happened—"

"A bar brawl," Boyd interrupted. "Let it go, Cora. You can have your domestic squabble later. I need you to focus here."

Liam was relieved when she turned away and fell into her investigator role. Boyd filled her in as Liam watched the officers bag evidence. He was bone weary, but even through the guilt and exhaustion, there was relief. He was sorry John Brady had died, but at least Cora and Margaret would be okay. They might rant and rave for the trouble he'd caused them, but at least they'd be alive to do it.

17

"I just don't get how anyone could do this," Otto said on Monday around lunchtime.

Liam was sitting with Cora at her desk as she studied something called an i2 Intelligence Analysis Platform. It was a computer program designed to help catalog and view the suspects and evidence during an investigation, and Liam had no idea how to work with it. He watched as she scrolled through what they had on the John Brady case so far. She'd been acting cool and aloof with him ever since the gala.

"I mean, who would commit that kind of crime right under our noses?" Otto muttered, slapping a bag of vending machine chips on his desk.

"Nobody cares about your stolen roast beef sandwich, Otto," Happy said with his usual pinched look of distaste.

"We're working on a murder investigation. Have some perspective."

"Easy for you to say, when it's not your lunch someone stole out of the fridge." Otto slumped into his chair and tore open the bag of chips. "I wrote my initials on the bag and everything."

Boyd called Liam and Cora into his office. He was pacing when they walked in, and his desk was messier than usual. Papers, coffee cups and crumbs littered the surface. He opened a bottle of Tums, popped several into his mouth and tossed the bottle back on his desk. "John Brady's widow has just arrived," he said. "I want you two to question her. We need to find out what type of person she is. What kind of relationship they had. Get her to talk. Maybe she'll open up and we'll learn something new."

Liam tensed. Interrogating Margaret with Cora in the same room was going to be like tiptoeing through a forest loaded with hunting traps. One false step, and he'd be doomed.

"Do you really think she killed her own husband?" Cora asked.

"That's what you're going to find out," Boyd said gruffly. His phone began to ring and he swore under his breath. "Now go."

Cora went to her desk and grabbed a notebook and pen. Liam followed her silent, brooding figure to the interrogation room down the hall.

"Are you going to talk to me at all today?" he asked as they stopped outside the door.

She didn't make eye contact. "We're talking right now."

"That's not what I mean. Look, I told you I was helping out a friend on Saturday night, and that's why I couldn't make it to the gala. That's the whole story, Cora. What else can I say to earn your forgiveness?"

"Tell me about this so-called bar brawl."

He lifted a hand to his cheekbone, which was still a mottled shade of purple and green. "What about it?"

A stubborn tilt of her chin. "Why were you fighting?"

He shrugged. "The usual reasons."

"What bar were you at?"

Liam remained silent, because the Goose & Gander was the only name that came to mind, and he knew that wouldn't appease her. Cora's cornflower blue eyes narrowed on him with suspicion. This wasn't going well.

"That's what I thought." She turned and reached for the door handle.

Liam placed his hand on the door to keep her from opening it. "Please, Cora."

"Please what?" She turned to glare at him. "Pretend your explanations are more than just flimsy excuses to hide your secrets? No, thanks."

"Let me make it up to you," he implored.

"No need."

"There has to be something I can do to make you stop talking to me in short sentences."

She straightened her back. "I'm not."

"Yes, you are."

"Not."

He pointed at her. "See?"

Cora blinked, then gave a heavy sigh. "Liam, it's my job to know when people are lying, and you're hiding something about what happened to you this weekend, but whatever. That's fine. Keep your secrets. Just don't treat me like I'm some amateur sleuth eating Scooby Snacks in the back of the Mystery Machine, all right? I've been around the block a few dozen times. It's the nature of this job. If you have something going on in your life you don't want me to know about, I'd rather you just say so. It's insulting to be lied to, especially from someone who's supposed to be on my side."

"I don't think you're an amateur, Cora," he said solemnly. "It was never my intention to treat you like any kind of snack."

Her forehead crinkled, and she looked at him like he was hopeless. "You're so weird sometimes. You know that, right?"

"I—"

"And ditching me with Finn at the gala was not cool, but it's over. We have more important things to focus on. Like a murder investigation. So, let's just acknowledge, and move on, okay? I don't want to talk about it anymore."

"So, everything's good between us?" he asked hopefully.

"Meh," she said with a shrug. "I wouldn't go that far."

"Let me make it right. I'll mow the lawn every week."

"You already agreed to do that when you moved in," she said, crossing her arms. "And you still haven't done it."

"I'll do it right after work today," he said quickly. "And I'll do all your laundry for a month."

"Oh, *hard* pass," Cora said, with feeling. "I saw you washing your shirt in the kitchen sink the other day."

He frowned. "Well, those machines are complicated and—"

"Weirdo." She tried to look stern, but her expression softened, and Liam didn't miss the way her rosebud mouth curved up at the corner. "Just forget it, Liam." She started to reach for the handle again.

"There has to be something I can do," he insisted. He

wanted her to smile at him again, and he'd do whatever it took to get back into her good graces.

Cora paused. "Actually, now that you mention it, there is something you can do to make it up to me."

"Anything," he said quickly, though the calculating look on her face made him want to brace for impact. "What do you want?"

For the first time since Saturday evening, she gave him a genuine smile. "I'll tell you later. Now, can we get back to the job?"

He followed her into the interrogation room with a sense of relief, but one glance at Margaret Brady's face meant his troubles weren't over. She looked nothing like the poised, polished woman she normally was. Her eyes were red and puffy from crying, her clothes were rumpled, and her hair looked like it hadn't been brushed for a couple of days. A heavy cloak of grief and regret clung to her slumped shoulders. Liam recognized it because he'd worn it before, himself. Margaret looked both exhausted and nervous when she glanced at him. There was a fragileness about her he wasn't accustomed to seeing. For the first time since he drove her home on Sunday, he wondered if she'd be able to stick to her alibi.

Cora and Liam took seats across from her at the metal table.

"Mrs. Brady, thank you for coming in today," Cora began, arranging her notebook on the table.

"I already told you people everything." Margaret's voice was hoarse enough to pull a carriage. "I don't know why you're making me say it all again."

"Sometimes it helps to go over things after you've had some time to process," Cora said. "You may remember things differently than you initially did."

Margaret twisted the handkerchief in her hand, not making eye contact. "Are you saying I'm a liar?"

"No, not at all, Mrs. Brady," Cora assured her. "I know this is difficult for you, but we are determined to find your husband's murderer, and we want justice just as much as you do. If there's anything else you can tell us about that night—anything at all, no matter how small—it could help."

Margaret rubbed a hand over her face and took a shaky breath. "I don't know why this happened. John wasn't even supposed to be home this weekend. He was supposed to be on a business trip. I've racked my brains trying to think of anyone who could have done this, but there's nobody. Everyone loved him. He was a truly kind person, unlike so many other men who are all about themselves." She didn't look at him, but Liam felt her accusation like a slap in the face. "John didn't play games. He was straightforward and honest. He was good at everything he did. Successful. Well respected in the community. He was the kind of man I was proud to call my husband." She paused and her face softened as if she was recalling a fond memory. "He made me truly happy."

Something sharp and clawlike twisted in Liam's chest. A snaking tendril of jealousy. This was a side of Margaret he'd never seen. In his old life, Margaret had hated her husband. John Brady had been a cold, mentally abusive man who'd treated her like something he owned. He'd neglected her for years, keeping her in that fancy house like a bird in a gilded cage, which was why it was so easy for her to fall into a relationship with Liam. She'd always said *Liam* was the one who made her happy. For a dirt-poor farmer with ragged clothes and not a penny to his name, he'd enjoyed the idea. And now, hearing her admit otherwise…

it chafed. He knew he shouldn't let it get to him, but male pride and reason did not often mix.

"Were you satisfied in your marriage?" Cora asked.

"Of course," Margaret said with conviction. "John was a wonderful husband."

Liam snorted.

Margaret's dark brows snapped together. "It's true. I was very happy with John. I've never known another man who could compare to him." This time she looked straight at Liam. "Not any man."

"Tell me something, Mrs. Brady," Liam said with false politeness. He leaned his forearms on the table and stared her down. "Did you love your husband?"

She stiffened. "I loved him very much, and he loved me. In every way."

"*Every* way?" he asked in a silky voice. Sharp jealousy twisted in his chest again, and as irrational as it was, Liam couldn't help but goad her.

Cora cleared her throat, and Liam could feel her staring at him with uncertainty, though he kept his gaze trained on Margaret.

"What are you getting at?" Margaret demanded.

Cora placed a warning hand on Liam's arm. "I think what Officer O'Connor is trying to say—"

"I'm asking if you had a physical relationship with your husband," Liam interrupted. "John Brady was decades older than you, so it's hard for me to believe he satisfied you in *every* way." An old codger like her husband could never keep up with Margaret's sexual appetites. If the past was anything to go by, she needed much more than that man could give, no matter how "truly happy" he made her.

Margaret's mouth fell open in outrage.

"I'm talking about sex, Mrs. Brady," Liam said sardonically. "You are familiar with it?"

The steely glint in her gray eyes was lethal. "You tell me, *Officer O'Connor*."

"Mrs. Brady, if you'll just give us a moment?" Cora scraped her chair back and jerked her chin at Liam to follow her.

Out in the hall, she spun to face him. "What the hell is wrong with you? We're supposed to be trying to get her to open up and talk. If you're trying to pull some good cop, bad cop thing, it's not working. You're just pissing her off."

Liam clenched his fists and turned away. He had to rein it in, but Margaret's confession made him want to kick something. He was acting ridiculous, and he knew it. He loved Cora, so none of this should matter, but his damned pride didn't seem to agree. *Fool!* Sometimes, he felt as if his old life was melting into this life, and the edges were starting to blur together. It was hard to remember that he had no actual relationship with this current version of Margaret. The angels had set everything up. This life wasn't even real for him. None of it was. In the past, Margaret had been head over heels for him. She was the one who'd first approached him. She was the one who'd sent him messages to visit whenever her husband was out of town. Her husband had been one of the wealthiest men in the county, and everything she'd wanted was handed to her on a silver platter...everything except affection. Everything but love. She used to tell Liam she wished she had a different life; she'd wished she could be someone else. Liam had felt the same about his own life. Those similarities were what drew them together in the first place. They'd been like flint and tinder in the beginning, burning hot and bright whenever they got close. Margaret had been—and still was—a beautiful woman, but Liam had always figured it was the very clandestine nature of their relationship that made it so irresistible in the first place. It had been too intense to last; they'd always known it. Eventually they'd burn each other to ash. Both of them existed in worlds that caged them in, so they'd clung to their tumultuous affair because it was an escape. Margaret never promised anything, and he'd never expected anything, and it had been fine, for a while. But that was before he'd met Cora and allowed himself to hope... Before he fell in love and everything crumbled to dust.

He sucked in a breath and let it out slowly, trying to come up with an explanation for his outrageous behavior. He barely understood it himself. Not for the first time, he cursed the angels for throwing him into this sea of confusion. "You're right, Cora," he finally said. "I just thought if I got her all riled up about her husband, she might let something slip."

Cora rocked back on her heels and the tension in her shoulders eased. "Go and take a break, Liam. Get some coffee or tea or whatever it is you need to get your head on straight."

"I'm fine."

"No, you're not. Go cool off. I'm taking it from here." She yanked open the door, stepped inside and closed it in his face.

He stood in the hall, waiting for his conflicted feelings to settle. When that didn't work, he went outside to run a few laps around the building. Running to get nowhere. Like a twenty-first-century lunatic.

A car honked on the busy street. The air smelled like hot asphalt and dust. Someone drove by with loud, wailing music on the radio. He recognized the song. It was the one about knocking on heaven's door. Liam grimaced. If only it were that easy. If only he could be certain he had a place waiting for him there. He stumbled to a stop, suddenly struck by the realization that this wasn't his place, but neither was the past anymore. There was only one desirable path left open to him, and he had to give up everything he cared about to get there. What if he couldn't do it? He felt like a rowboat lost at sea with a storm on the horizon. What if, no matter how hard he paddled, he got sucked under and couldn't find his way back up?

18

"There's nowhere to go but down," Cora called out. "The sooner you accept it, the better."

Liam threw her a look promising retribution as he prepared to do his penance.

Laughter bubbled up from Cora's chest as she watched her disgruntled roommate climb into the dunk tank. She was going to enjoy this.

The annual Summer Carnival was in full swing at the Teens in Action center, and all the volunteers were busy at their posts. Cora had been a volunteer since she joined the police force, and every year she watched the center grow in leaps and bounds. The place used to be nothing more than an old furniture warehouse, but with a lot of help from the community, it was now a fully functioning recreation facility for disadvantaged youths.

Today, the outside parking lot was set up with a popcorn stand in one corner, a DJ blasting music in another and an entire line of fold-out tables brimming with party food donated by local businesses. There was a photo booth with outrageous costumes for people to snap pictures of themselves, and several volunteers stood at grills making hot dogs and hamburgers. More booths surrounded the parking lot with everything from jewelry making and henna painting to more traditional carnival games like target shooting and balloon darts. On the grass beyond the lot there was a giant Slip 'N Slide, a Sumo wrestling ring with blow-up suits and, of course, the dunk tank.

Cora grinned like the Cheshire cat as she watched Liam climb onto the swing-out bench above the tank full of muddy water. She had to admit, setting him up as the volunteer police officer for The Tank was worth the hours she'd had to spend with Finn at the gala. Especially since—though she'd never admit it to Liam—she'd actually enjoyed herself with Finn that night. He'd been sweet and funny and engaging, and once she got past his stuffy outer shell, she realized there was something about him she found appealing. Who knew? The details of the evening had faded, but she still remembered the banked heat in Finn's eyes when he stood on her doorstep. She'd leaned into him as if there was some magnetic force drawing them together, and if her phone hadn't rung at that exact moment, she might've even done something crazy. With Finn! Cora blushed. Luckily, it hadn't gone anywhere. It would've been so awkward to face him afterward.

Some kids shouted encouragement at each other, drawing Cora's attention back to Liam in the dunk tank. He was wearing a pair of jeans and a navy Providence Falls Police T-shirt. With his dark hair waving over his forehead, and his reluctant, bad-boy smirk, he somehow still managed to look like he'd just been plucked off the pages of *GQ* magazine. It wasn't fair, really. How come he got the gorgeous-by-accident genes, and the rest of the lowly mortals had to put serious effort into looking that good? He wasn't even trying.

"Try aiming next time," a boy hollered, slapping his friend on the back. They were around thirteen years old, with oversize basketball shorts and the egos to match. Most of the kids attending the Summer Carnival today were regulars at the Teens in Action center. A lot of them just came for the free snacks, which was to be expected. For some of the kids, the food might be the only meal they got that day. Others used the recreation center as a landing spot after school so they could escape boredom or bad homelife situations. There was a gym with basketball hoops and donated sports equipment, a quiet library and study room for them to do their homework, and a main gathering hall with comfy chairs and game consoles. Many of the kids just lounged around and watched TV, hence the nickname "Teens Inaction" they gave the place, but Cora didn't care. If it kept them off the streets, it was a win.

"Here, let me try," a familiar voice said. "You're going down, man!"

Cora recognized Billy Mac in the lineup of people waiting for the dunk tank. He was grinning ear to ear as he swaggered up to the table in his ratty T-shirt and scuffed tennis shoes. A deep sense of gratitude washed over Cora when she saw how carefree and happy he seemed. She usually only saw Billy on the streets. As the years passed, he'd begun to perfect that hard "street stare" with the vacant eyes and the blank face. But with her, he still remained open and engaged, and Cora was grateful for it. She really liked the kid, though she knew from experience it wasn't good to get too attached to kids in his situation. Sometimes no matter how hard you tried, they just didn't want to be helped. But every once in a while, she got Billy to visit Teens in Action. He needed to be around good role models, and Cora had a feeling if she played her cards just right, he might even have a future mentoring the younger kids. It was still too soon to tell, but she wouldn't give up on him.

"Step on up, sir." Arthur, a retired firefighter who often volunteered there, waved Billy over. Arthur was a laid-back old man with a ready laugh and an unending well of patience. He reminded Cora of Santa Claus, with his pot-belly and bushy white beard, except instead of a red suit, he always wore denim overalls. He handed Billy three soft-balls for the dunk tank and said in a booming voice, "This is your chance to dunk one of Providence Falls' finest!"

Cora threw Liam a look of exaggerated skepticism.

Liam just nodded smugly. *Yep. That's me. Providence Falls' finest.* She couldn't help laughing. He was nothing, if not arrogant.

"Billy?" Liam feigned shock. "You wouldn't!"

"Damned straight, I would." Billy's smile was full of mischievous glee. He stuck his tongue between his teeth, aimed and threw. The ball missed the target and bounced into the grass.

"Lame!" one of the kids in line yelled.

Undeterred, Billy lifted the second ball, squinted and let it fly. Another miss.

Liam gave an exaggerated yawn and slouched on the bench, which egged the kids on even more. They began hollering and cheering for Billy to hit the target.

On the third try, Billy hit the bull's-eye with a satisfying *thunk*. The lever under Liam's bench seat retracted, and he splashed into the tank, sending the kids into a frenzy of wild hoots and laughter.

"Oh, that's tough," Arthur boomed theatrically. "How's the mud taste, Officer?"

Liam came up sputtering. He pointed at Billy with mock ferocity and said, "I'm going to hunt you down later, Billy Mac."

"Great job, Billy," Cora shouted, clapping. "You just made my day."

Liam sluiced muddy water off his face. "I'm coming for you next, woman."

"Hey, don't blame me," she said with wide-eyed innocence. "You said you'd do anything, remember?"

"Consider my debt paid." He heaved his body out of the tank and resumed his perch on the bench again. "With interest."

Billy sauntered over to Cora, his freckled face brimming with pride. "Man, that was sweet."

Cora's heart squeezed in her chest. In that moment he wasn't the world-weary street kid trying to be tough, he was just a boy at a carnival having fun. She wanted to reach out and ruffle his hair, but she refrained. "You really got him, Billy. I owe you for that."

"Yeah?" He wiggled his eyebrows and grinned. Aaand the swagger was back. "I knew you'd come around."

Cora rolled her eyes. "I meant lunch, kid."

He drew himself up to his full height. "I'm not a kid. I'm fifteen."

Exactly. "I know, but you should save all that charm for someone closer to your age. Like the girl over on that bench— Don't look!" Cora leaned forward and whispered, "She's been checking you out. I think you impressed her with your moves at the dunk tank. Okay, she turned away. Now you can look."

Billy's gaze slid sideways, his face a study in careless apathy, but his eyes lit with interest. The girl looked to be around his age, with shiny dark hair and a heart-shaped face. She had a hotdog in one hand and a book in the other. He turned back to Cora, looking like someone had just knocked him on the head with one of the softballs. "That's Katie Bradshaw," he said. "You sure she was looking at me?"

"Definitely."

"Dang." Billy swallowed hard enough for Cora to see his Adam's apple bob up and down. "People say she's stuck-up because she's always reading, but I don't know. Maybe she's just really smart." He stared at her just long enough for the girl to glance up.

Billy jerked his gaze away and feigned interest in the dunk tank where Liam was just crawling back onto the platform after having been dunked a second time.

"You should go talk to her," Cora suggested.

"Nah, I'm good."

"Think of it as a challenge," she teased. "Like a game. You can't win if you don't play."

Billy mumbled something under his breath about knowing how to be a player, then wandered off toward the refreshment table.

Cora made her way back to the dunk tank and sidled up to the edge of the cage. She tried not to notice how Liam's thin T-shirt clung to his muscular chest, or the way his wet jeans outlined his powerful thighs and lean hips, but it was like trying not to stare at a chocolate fountain at a dessert buffet. Because, come on. Anyone who could be blasé about a chocolate fountain wasn't human.

Sometimes, in rare, fanciful moments, Cora wondered what it would be like to actually date someone like Liam. Suzette seemed to think it was a grand idea, but then Cora would remind herself of all the reasons getting together with Liam was a ridiculous notion to entertain. They worked together. They lived together. He was headstrong and old-fashioned and—let's face it—pretty weird sometimes. But if she was being perfectly honest with herself, the main reason he wasn't an option pricked her pride a little bit. It was because Liam had made it obvious from the beginning that he wasn't into her. The few times she'd even touched him, he'd actually flinched. As if he couldn't stand it. Not a big confidence booster, that. And the only time she'd ever shown an outward display of gratitude by hugging him for finding her necklace, he'd grabbed her by the arms and thrust her away. So, there it was. He'd made his feelings crystal clear. Which was fine. *More than fine.* Cora lifted her chin and squared her shoulders. They were just friends, anyway. Sort of.

"Admit it, Liam," she said cheerfully, shoving all those forbidden thoughts aside. "You're having fun."

Liam grimaced, his dark hair sticking up in all directions like a porcupine. "I'll admit no such thing."

A ball went flying way off target and Cora had to duck to dodge it.

"Get out of here," Liam ordered. "These hellions don't know how to throw, and I didn't drag myself here to watch you get brained."

"They're just softballs. And, anyway, I've got good reflexes."

"It doesn't matter. You could still—"

Another ball went flying. This time, it hit the target dead center. Liam went splashing into the tank, and the kids hooted in victory. He came up growling like an angry cat. Cora linked her fingers through the chain-link cage, tipped her head back and laughed. Getting stuck on that date with Finn was *so* worth the payback.

Liam's mouth twitched as he climbed onto the perch again.

"Ooh!" Cora pointed at him. "I saw that. You almost smiled. I know you're enjoying this. In fact, I might just put your name on the volunteer list for next time."

He snorted. "It will be a cold day in hell before I come back to this—" A ball hit the target again, and down he went. Again.

Yep. Cora grinned and went in search of a drink. *Totally* worth it.

19

On Wednesday, a new development in the Brady murder case had Cora and Liam driving to the home of Isabelle Horvath, a woman claiming to be the mistress of John Brady.

"It's hard to believe the old man had a mistress on the side," Cora said, as she switched lanes on the freeway and took the next exit. Isabelle's condo was in a small bedroom community outside of Providence Falls. The scenic drive was a pleasant one, thick with maples and poplar trees lining the road. The sky was the kind of crisp, clear blue that seemed to go on forever. Even with the heaviness of the investigation weighing down on her, Cora could appreciate the beauty of the landscape. It never failed to lift her spirits, and today she was grateful for the view. "From the way Margaret Brady talked, her husband was a perfect man with no flaws."

Liam grunted a response that sounded an awful lot like annoyance.

Cora noted the rigid set of his shoulders and the stoic expression. "Liam, what's going on with you? Do you have something against John Brady? Or Margaret?"

He shook his head and continued staring out the window.

"Ever since we interrogated her… Did you know her husband? Is there something you're not telling me?"

"No." His face was grim.

She waited for him to elaborate, but he didn't. "Are you sure?"

"Very," he insisted.

"Then why are you angry?"

"I'm not," he said quickly. "I just thought the way she spoke of her husband was ridiculous. She made it out like he was perfect. *Too* perfect."

It was true that Margaret painted a rosy picture of her husband, which didn't strike Cora as odd, at the time. But what if Margaret lied? What if she really hated her husband? "You think she was singing his praises to us in order to take suspicion off herself? You think she murdered him?"

"No," Liam said firmly. "She doesn't have it in her. And, anyway, her alibi is solid."

"Unless she's lying about spending the night at her sister's place," Cora mused. They said nothing further, lapsing into silence until Isabelle's neighborhood appeared ahead of them. Cora pulled the car into a development of cookie-cutter town houses that all looked the same.

Her phone rang and she pressed the button to put it on speaker. "McLeod."

Captain Thompson's gruff voice filled the car. "Have you talked to the mistress yet?"

"No. We're almost to her house."

"We brought Margaret Brady in for more questioning. The coroner said the marks on the victim's neck indicate strangulation by a rope or something similar. Possibly a scarf or tie. There was a piece of silk fabric found at the crime scene they think might be part of the murder weapon."

Liam's sudden intake of breath drew Cora's attention to him. *What?* she mouthed.

Something ghosted across his face, too fast for her to catch, then his expression became carefully blank. He shook his head in dismissal, but his posture remained rigid.

"Looks like the killer burned most of the weapon in the wastebasket before leaving."

"Well, that's not helpful," Cora said in frustration.

"No," Boyd agreed. "But the fabric scrap might have something on it. We're waiting on forensics. We've got Margaret Brady in the interrogation room right now, and she's pretty shaken up. Seems she had no idea her husband was having an affair. Maybe this'll get her to talk. If she's hiding anything, we're going to find it."

He hung up without saying anything further. That was Thompson. He never did or said anything that wasn't completely necessary.

Liam began texting something on his phone.

"Here we are." Cora parked the car in front of Isabelle's town house, and they walked to the door. There was a faux marble planter filled with plastic flowers on the front step, and a fancy monogrammed doormat with Isabelle's initials scrolled across in curling black font.

Cora was just about to ring the doorbell, when the door swung open.

"Good afternoon, Officers." Isabelle Horvath was an attractive older woman with platinum blond hair, a petite figure and red-rimmed eyes from crying. She was wearing a gold silk wrap dress and matching kitten heels. According to Captain Thompson's briefing, Isabelle was a former beauty queen from an era when pageants were a way of life. After securing two crowns and two ex-husbands, she'd gone on to do a bit of acting in commercials, and now worked as a part-time host for a home shopping network.

Isabelle dabbed her eyes with a lace handkerchief and gave a regal sweep of her hand. "Please, do come in."

Cora got the feeling Isabelle thrived on theatrics, and she had to hand it to the woman. The house looked like a stage set. The living room was gaudy enough to be in a low-budget period film. There was an antique-style sofa with ruffled lace pillows and two ornately carved side chairs that were gilded to death. Porcelain vases held bunches of silk roses, and the millwork in the room was painted in gold filigree. Apparently, Isabelle had a thing for eighteenth-century France. The place looked like the Palace of Versailles' cheap drunk cousin.

Cora introduced herself and Liam as they took their seats on the uncomfortable side chairs.

"I apologize for not being at my best," Isabelle said with a sniff. "I'm sure you can understand the news came as quite a shock. May I offer you some coffee or tea? Perhaps wine?"

Liam perked up like he was on board with that last option, so Cora spoke fast. "We're fine, Mrs. Horvath. We'd hate to take up too much of your time, so if you don't mind, I'd like to ask you some questions about John Brady."

"Of course." Isabelle's eyes suddenly filled with tears and she sniffed into her handkerchief. The sniffs escalated into sobs, and for the next couple of minutes, Cora and Liam waited for her to gather herself together.

"Can you tell us how long you were seeing John Brady?" Cora asked gently.

"Almost two years," Isabelle said with a hiccup. "We met at a cocktail party hosted by a mutual friend."

"And were you aware that John was married?"

Isabelle's delicate face grew marble hard, and her chin jutted out. "Of course, I knew he was married. It's not like he could've made it a secret, even if he'd wanted to. The local magazines always have photos of him and his wife at charity events."

"Can you tell us where you were on the night of June 15?"

"I was here, with John." Isabelle's voice wobbled, but she took a shaky breath and forged on. "We were supposed to spend the weekend together, but w-we had an argument."

"What did you argue about?" Cora asked.

"John and I were talking about our upcoming trip to Cabo. We've gone for the past two years when his wife attended her annual retreat. But he said he couldn't make it this time because of some last-minute function they had to attend at her university. I got mad and started asking him if he was ever going to leave her. Because he always made me think he would, you know?" She looked to Cora for validation.

Cora nodded in encouragement, noting that Liam was staring at Isabelle with obvious distaste.

"Go on," Cora said.

"John used to tell me that he liked that we had so much in common. He said his wife was always on the go, like a race car. He said she was young and energetic, and he enjoyed the way he and I could just relax together because I was more his speed." Isabelle let out an unladylike snort. "His wife was racy, all right. She had affairs all the time."

"What makes you say that?" Liam asked sharply.

Isabelle looked at him in surprise. "Well, John said it. He suspected she had lovers over the years, but he never confronted her about it. I don't know why he stayed with her. He said they had a comfortable relationship and that it worked for them, but I never understood it. I mean, who wants to be with a cheater, you know?"

Cora gave Isabelle a polite smile, ignoring the whole pot and kettle thing.

"Anyway, John and I started arguing about the future. He said he just needed more time to sort things out, but that's when I realized. I just knew he'd never do it! He was never going to leave her. A woman can tell when a man's lying. It's an instinctual thing we're just born with, but I ignored all the signs. So, we argued some more, and then I got mad and said I wanted to break up. I said I was done for good this time. Then I kicked him out."

Cora scribbled something on her notepad. "What time did he leave your house?"

Isabelle dabbed her eyes again. "Around twelve thirty, I think."

"Can you tell us what state John was in when he drove away?" Cora asked.

"He was freaking out." Isabelle's beauty pageant facade was beginning to crack. Her pink frosted lips mashed flat, and for the first time during the interrogation, Cora felt she got an accurate view of the woman underneath the shiny veneer. "I was good to him for years, and he knew he was lucky to have me." Isabelle's face grew sullen and she smoothed her hair. "Margaret's not *that* good-looking. She might be young, but she's as boring as a lump of clay. No substance to her. I've no idea how she even became a botany teacher at the university. My guess is that she slept her way into the job. I wouldn't be surprised. Though I can't imagine what would entice any man to want to be with her. She's like one of those clueless airhead types, you know?"

"I think I do," Liam drawled. He looked outright disgusted with Isabelle, but the woman seemed too preoccupied with her own story to notice.

"Anyway, that's all I know," Isabelle said, fluttering her handkerchief. "After I made him leave, he called my phone five times, but I refused to answer. He left two messages begging me not to be angry. On the final message, he said he was going to bring me something to make it up to me. And that was it. That was the last I heard from him." She started crying again, and Cora shuffled through her notes, waiting for Isabelle to get herself under control.

"I should've answered my phone," Isabelle sobbed. "But I was still mad at him, and I thought I'd have time to talk to him later. If I had known I'd never seen him again..." More tears.

Cora wrapped up the meeting ten minutes later, happy to leave Isabelle's gilded palace.

Liam was silent on the drive back. He stared moodily out the window, checking his phone every few minutes.

"Talk to me," Cora demanded.

"About?"

So, he still wanted to pretend nothing was wrong. Well, too bad. She was sick of the secrecy. Something was eating at him, and before the day was over, she was going to get to the bottom of it. "Okay, let's start with Isabelle

Horvath. You were glaring at her like she kicks puppies or something."

Liam scoffed. "I did not care for her at all. She's a vain, petty, jealous woman. Like a shallow aristocrat sitting in her flashy house, full of overblown self-importance. A shrew is a shrew, no matter how finely dressed." He slumped in his seat and added, "No amount of money can hide that."

"Geez. Tell me how you really feel," Cora said. When he continued to scowl, she asked, "Do you think she could've killed him?"

"No. She's the size of a teacup, and John was a big man. The killer would have to be someone with considerable strength. Character flaws aside, I don't see her as the murderer."

"I don't, either, but we can't rule her out just yet. I'm curious to see what Captain Thompson finds out from Mrs. Brady today, now that they've identified the possible murder weapon."

Liam grunted something in acknowledgment and Cora could practically feel the tension rolling off him in waves.

"You have to tell me what's going on," she blurted in frustration.

"Nothing's going on, Cora." He stared out the window. The trees grew so close together along the highway, it was like driving through a tunnel of green leaves and dappled sunlight. Liam's knee bounced up and down and he wouldn't look at her. "Trust me, I'm fine."

Trust him? She almost laughed. Sitting there with his fist clenched tightly around his phone and his jaw set, he couldn't have appeared *less* fine. "How about you trust me?" she countered. "If there's something going on, maybe I can help."

"I do trust you," he said with feeling.

Finally, an answer she believed. "Then why won't you talk to me?"

Liam's mouth opened like he was going to speak, then he changed his mind.

Cora's phone rang again, and this time when she answered, Captain Thompson's voice boomed through the car like angry thunder. "Where are you?"

"We're just a few minutes away," Cora said in alarm. "What's going on, Captain?"

"A hell of a lot. I want you and Liam in my office the minute you get here, do you understand?"

"Yes." He hung up before she had a chance to ask anything further. She looked at Liam in confusion. "I wonder what that was about?"

When he didn't respond, she lapsed into silence, mulling through Isabelle's interview in her head. If everything Isabelle said was true, then John had been in emotional turmoil that night. He'd told Isabelle he was going to get something that would make it up to her. According to Mrs. Brady's account, several pieces of very expensive jewelry had been stolen. Maybe John drove home, knowing Margaret was away at her sister's place for the night, and he intended to bring Isabelle some of that jewelry. But if that's what he'd tried to do, why did he end up dead in his own house?

20

Mavis was filling the candy bowl on her reception desk when Liam reluctantly followed Cora inside the station. Ever since first arriving at the crime scene, he'd felt like there was a countdown clock and a swinging blade above his head. And after the confrontation with the distraught Margaret in the interrogation room, Liam knew it was just a matter of time before she crumbled and admitted to their affair. He should have been up-front about it from the beginning, but she'd been so devastated, and he'd been trying to save her from the backlash. But Boyd had sounded furious on the phone just now, and since Margaret had been called in for questioning again, Liam suspected Boyd knew about his affair with Margaret. Liam had tried texting her from the car, but she'd ignored him. She'd been ignoring him all week. He couldn't blame her.

"Good afternoon," Mavis sang out cheerfully. Her rosy-cheeked smile was contagious. Today she wore a heavy dose of fruity perfume and a sweatshirt with a birdhouse embroidered on the front. "Candy? It's caramel creams."

Even with one foot in a handbasket headed straight to hell, Liam couldn't help but smile back at the receptionist. Mavis radiated warmth and good cheer. She reminded him of the village baker's wife from his home back in Ireland.

Cora hurried past the front desk. "No, thank you."

Liam snagged a piece of candy and winked, leaving Mavis to giggle-snort after him.

When they entered Boyd's office, all sense of cheer vanished. Boyd's face told Liam he was in trouble.

"Anything you want to tell me, O'Connor?" Boyd's voice was razor-sharp.

Liam didn't answer right away. He was trying to figure out how much Boyd knew. From the looks of it, a lot. How was he going to spin out of this one?

"Something you *maybe* forgot to mention?" Boyd pressed.

Cora's head swiveled between them. "What's going on here?"

Christ, here we go. "What do you want to know, Boyd?"

Boyd slammed his hand down on his desk, sending papers flying. "You will address me by my title like everyone else. I demand respect in this office, and though you've already demonstrated your lack of respect for this investigation, you will not forget that I'm your superior here."

Liam held his tongue, but just barely. In the past, Boyd never would've spoken to him like that. They were on equal footing back then, and this new attitude did not sit well with Liam. He crossed a heel over one knee and relaxed into his chair. He knew his casual attitude would only incite Boyd further, but he was already in hot water. Might as well enjoy the swim. "Sorry… *Captain*."

Boyd's face grew so red, it almost turned purple. Liam got a sense of satisfaction from watching the man forcibly reel in his emotions. Boyd's chest rose and fell, and a muscle throbbed in his temple, but instead of exploding in anger like Liam expected, he somehow managed to keep it together. "Tell me about Margaret Brady," Boyd demanded.

Cora glanced at Liam in confusion. He could practically see the wheels spinning in her head.

"What did Margaret tell you?" Liam countered. Never reveal your hand too soon.

"Oh, no. You don't get to ask the questions." Boyd crossed his arms over his barrel chest and his voice rose until he was almost shouting. "I want to know why you neglected to mention you were *having an affair* with one of our prime suspects."

Cora gasped at Liam. "You and Mrs. Brady?" The accusation and look of betrayal on her face was too much, and he had to look away.

"Yes," Boyd answered. "According to the widow, they've been seeing each other for *months*."

"But, how?" Cora asked. "You've only just moved here. When did you meet?"

"While she was at a conference in Raleigh a few months back," Liam said wearily. "But it has no relevance to the murder. I've never even met her husband." At least, not in this lifetime.

"According to Mrs. Brady, you two were on a date the night of the murder," Boyd said. "She claims you decided to follow up dinner and drinks with a stay at a motel across town." He turned to Cora. "Did you know about this?"

"No," Cora said, clearly in shock. "I had no idea." Her

voice dripped with resentment. Liam could practically feel her eyes boring into the side of his head.

Boyd shot her a skeptical look. "Funny you wouldn't know, McLeod, considering you live with him. You being cozy roommates, and all—"

"Just roommates," she stated. "That's all. And I'm beginning to realize I know nothing about him." There was no mistaking the bitterness in her voice. "He hasn't told me any of this."

"Mrs. Brady broke when we told her about Isabelle Horvath," Boyd continued. "She never even suspected her husband was cheating, probably because she had her own affair to worry about." He stared Liam down. "Which brings us to you. Where were you on Saturday night during the time of the murder, O'Connor?"

"With Margaret," Liam said. "We went to dinner at a place called Shag's Diner. It wasn't planned, we just ended up there."

"You expect me to believe you took a rich man's wife like Margaret Brady to a roach-infested dive like Shag's Diner on a *whim*?"

Liam shrugged. "She wanted to go somewhere different."

Boyd sneered. "Try again, O'Connor, because I'm not buying it."

"It's true," Liam insisted. "I took her there as a sort of joke, and we ended up staying. Margaret had one too many drinks at dinner, so we decided to get a motel room for the night." It sounded seedy, even to him. He couldn't even look at Cora, and he could only imagine what she thought of him right now.

"You really roll out the red carpet for the ladies, don't you?" Boyd said scornfully. "A real prince."

Liam clenched his fists, fighting against the urge to haul Boyd across the table by the shirt collar and pummel him. He wasn't accustomed to being on the receiving end of Boyd's derision. Boyd was a hothead with a temper in the past, but they'd always been on the same side, and Boyd usually followed Liam's lead. For the first time, Liam was beginning to realize just how much he actually disliked Boyd, and he wondered if their thieving life back in Ireland had been the only shared common ground that brought them together.

"Mrs. Brady says she passed out, and when she woke up you looked like that." Boyd gestured to the fading bruises on Liam's face. "She says you told her a story about getting beat up near the ATM, but she can't prove it. She has no idea how long you were gone." It was obvious from the look on Boyd's face he was leading up to something. "Care to tell me what really happened on Saturday night?"

"Exactly that, as she said." Liam sat forward in his chair and continued in measured tones. "I went for a walk and ended up sitting on the bench near the store by the ATM. An old man was getting walloped by some guy who tried to steal his wallet."

"Is that right?" Boyd wasn't even trying to hide his skepticism.

"It's the truth," Liam said coolly. "When I intervened, the man attacked me, we threw a few punches, and then he ran away."

"What did he look like?" Boyd asked.

"It was dark, and the streetlight was out, so I didn't get a close view of his face. He wore a hooded sweatshirt. I wasn't able to see much, except that he was about my height."

"And the old man? I don't suppose you happened to catch his name or where he lives?"

Liam shook his head. "I only spoke to him briefly before he got in his car and drove away."

"Why didn't you call it in?" Boyd asked.

"The old man said not to bother. I got his wallet back for him, and that was it."

"And afterward? You just moseyed on back to Mrs. Brady at the motel and chose to sleep in the chair? She said she didn't believe you ever got in bed with her that night. Were you two fighting?"

"No," Liam said with annoyance.

"So, what? You just didn't feel like cuddling?"

Liam narrowed his eyes. "I'm not the type of man who takes advantage of a woman when she's passed out drunk."

"Even so, it strikes me as odd that you wouldn't join her in bed. Unless, of course, you never slept. Maybe you weren't really there for most of the night. Maybe you were across town at Belltown Heights."

"I was across the street," Liam said through gritted teeth.

Boyd kept talking like he hadn't heard him. "Maybe you were tired of Mrs. Brady's marital status and decided to pay her husband a little visit."

Liam snapped. "If you think I had something to do with that man's murder—"

"That's exactly what I think," Boyd roared. "Where the hell were you, Liam? What else aren't you telling us? Because your track record's looking pretty dismal right now. You've already proven you're a cheater, and you've withheld important information from this investigation, so that makes you a liar, too. Maybe the answer here is

270 JUDE DEVERAUX and TARA SHEETS

simple. Jealous lover offs the husband so he can have the woman all to himself."

"Captain," Cora blurted. She glanced worriedly at Liam, then back at Boyd. "I don't believe Liam would do something like that."

"See, now that makes me question your judgment, McLeod." Boyd turned from her and stared Liam down, his expression hard as stone. "Unless you can find that old man or get a statement from some other witness to vouch for you that night, you're a suspect. I don't want to see your face for the next week." He smacked his hand on the desk. "Get out."

"Captain," Cora said in shock. "I think—"

"Not a word." Boyd pointed at her. "Unless you want to join him."

She straightened her spine and stood. "No, sir."

Liam stared at Boyd with contempt and slowly rose from his chair.

"Out," Boyd spat. Then he jerked a chin at Cora. "Back to work, McLeod."

Liam walked stiffly out of the building. This time, Mavis's cheery disposition at the front desk did nothing to alleviate the cloud of gloom settling over him. He drove back to the house with frustration roiling in his gut. He felt like a fly caught in a spider's web, and every time he made a move, he only got stuck further. He needed divine intervention to get out of this mess. Were those angels even paying attention, or were they up there on some cloud tinkering in other people's pathetic lives? Each day that passed seemed to bring Liam more and more obstacles, and his chances of success seemed farther and farther away. Did the angels even care? Twenty minutes later, he pulled his car into the driveway of Cora's house with grim determination. He'd try summoning the angels to ask for help. They'd never answered him before, but maybe today would be an exception. And if that didn't work, then he'd chase away his worries the good old-fashioned way.

21

The following morning, Cora sat at her desk at work, staring at the empty seat where Liam should've been. Her insides churned with resentment and a driving need to know what the hell had really happened with him on Saturday night. As bad as everything looked, she still wanted to believe him, but maybe that was her problem. Since the moment he'd come into her life, her feelings were in a tailspin. His very presence seemed to turn her world on its head because he was familiar to her in a way that didn't make sense. She often had strange moments of déjà vu whenever he was around. Then there were the vivid dreams about him that made no sense. Last night, she'd woken up in a cold sweat, out of breath, with her heart thumping madly. In her dream she'd been fleeing with Liam on horseback through a forest, and she'd been wearing an old-fashioned, long, flowy gown from a different era. It felt like something out of a medieval fairy tale. Later, after her heart had slowed and the dream faded, she'd chalked it up to a side effect of binge-watching too many *Game of Thrones* episodes. But even now, she could still smell the wet leaves and damp earth from that dream. She could still taste the heady rush of adrenaline and fear and longing that coursed through her veins. It had felt so *real*.

Cora scrubbed her face with both hands and went to the office kitchen for more coffee. Her phone rang, and she half expected it to be Liam. He'd been avoiding her ever since he got sent home yesterday. She checked her phone screen and answered. "Hey, Suze."

"I think my brain short-circuited last night," Suzette said. She always started phone conversations in the middle, as if they'd been talking for hours. "Or maybe I have a tumor, or some kind of weird virus that amps up the brain's Idiotic Impulse functions, or something."

"Sounds chronic."

"I'm not kidding, Cora. This is bad. I kissed Rob Hopper last night."

"Wow." Cora poured office sludge into her mug. "What happened to 'not in a bajillion years'?"

"I don't know!" Suzette wailed. "Time flies, I guess. And it wasn't a polite peck on the cheek, either. It was one of those sinful, dirty kisses, you know? The kind that taste like poor decisions followed by a walk of shame?"

Cora opened her mouth to reply, but Suzette was on a roll.

"He told me he wasn't seeing anyone else, and we got to talking about life and stuff. Then I let him take me to dinner, and then when he brought me home, he coiled those muscular arms around me like a wily snake and swooped in for the kill. And I fell for it!" She made a sound of disgust. "I almost invited him inside because, apparently, he'd sucked all the brain cells out of my head, but then he got a text message on his phone. I saw it before he could hide it. It said, 'C U tonight' and it was from someone named Trixie." Suzette's voice began to rise. "Come on, *Trixie*? If that doesn't have 'stripper pole' written all over it, I don't know what does."

"Maybe it's just an unfortunate nickname," Cora offered. "Maybe she's just a friend."

"Her text message came with a bunch of hearts."

"Well, that doesn't—"

"Followed by a peach and eggplant emoji," Suzette said flatly.

"Oh. Um… Maybe she just really loves fruits and vegetables?" Cora could practically hear Suzette roll her eyes.

"I knew going to dinner with him was a bad idea," Suzette said with a groan. "And kissing him was an even worse idea. He's probably chuckling right now, thinking he has me on the hook like all his other booty-call girls. I can't believe I almost gave in to Rob Hopper. I've been bamboozled."

"That's terrible."

"Right? He's such an assho—"

"No, I mean, 'bamboozled.' Who says that word? But more importantly, Rob's not on duty today, but when he comes in tomorrow, I can interrogate him. You want me to cuff him to a chair, stick him under bright lights, the whole nine yards?"

"No, don't say anything," Suzette said quickly. "I don't want him to think it bothered me, because then he'll just think I care. Which, I don't." There was a long pause. "I don't care."

"Right."

"Right," Suzette echoed. "So, I'm just going to pretend the date never happened. But feel free to spill some hot coffee in Rob's lap the next time you see him. Or, trip him when he walks by. You decide."

"I'll shoot for both."

"See, that's what I love about you. You're always willing to go the extra mile."

"I'm sorry about your crap date, Suze," Cora said gently.

Her friend gave a heavy sigh. "It just sucks because during dinner, I felt like we really connected, you know? Like, for once, Rob was just being himself and not the teasing playboy he usually is. But at least I didn't sleep with him. It could've been so much worse. I just need to forget it and focus on better things."

"Agreed."

"So, how's that hot roommate of yours?"

Cora groaned. "Don't ask."

"Did he do his laundry in the kitchen sink again? Whatever he did, it can't be that bad."

Wanna bet? "Let's just say, you're not the only one who's been bamboozled."

"Sounds juicy. I need details."

After promising Suzette to meet up for drinks later that evening, Cora got off the phone and walked back to her desk. She wished she could've gotten more details from Liam last night. She'd intended to talk to him after work, but he was gone by the time she'd arrived home. Well after midnight, she'd heard him come in, and she'd started to climb out of bed to confront him, then decided against it. Why should she be the one to chase him down? He owed her an honest explanation, and he needed to do it of his own free will. Anyway, she was done trying to connect with him. It was obvious he had secrets he didn't want to share, and she wasn't even sure he'd be honest with her, anyway.

She shook her head and took a gulp of lukewarm coffee as she surveyed the case evidence on her computer screen. If her father had any idea just how much trouble Liam was causing… Well. She wasn't going to tell him. Her father had been so happy to see them connect, and she didn't want to be the one who disappointed him. Let Liam do the disappointing. He was good at it.

"Earth to Cora." Otto rapped his knuckles on her desk.

She snapped her head up. "Yes?"

"Forensics got back with the report on that scrap of fabric found in the wastebasket." Otto held it up.

"And?"

"Inconclusive," he said, shaking his head. "John Brady's DNA was found in the fibers, but only one fingerprint, and it's an obvious mistake."

"What do you mean?"

"According to our records, the only clear fingerprint belongs to a man named Clyde Wilson," Otto said.

"All right," Cora said. "Let's track him down. Where is he?"

"More like, *when*. Clyde was a smuggler from the prohibition era. Apparently, the database goes back that far. I don't envy the poor soul who had to scan in all those old documents. Anyway, his record states he spent five years evading the law until he was finally caught during a shoot-out."

Cora took the report and reviewed the document. The grainy black-and-white image of the man looked like every old gangster photo she'd ever seen. "Great." She handed the report back. "Our only suspect is the ghost of a gangster from the thirties."

"Not our *only* suspect," Happy said from across the room. His face was even more sour than usual. "There's a new one that just came up, from what I understand."

Cora threw him a look. She'd never minded that Happy was standoffish and grim; it was his life and he could live it however he wanted. He was a competent police officer, and that's all that mattered to her. But today, for the first time, she found she resented him.

"Hey, I'm just stating the obvious." Happy lifted his hands. "Liam was having an affair with the dead man's wife. And he didn't tell us. You have to admit that's a big red flag."

Cora lifted her chin and turned back to her computer. "It's bad judgment on his part, but that doesn't make him a killer."

"Have you found anyone who can alibi him?" Otto asked.

"Not yet," she said. "But I will." As much as she didn't approve of Liam's secrecy, she still believed he was telling the truth about the ATM robbery. That morning she'd gone out to the convenience store across from the motel to ask around. The restaurant server and bartender remembered seeing Liam and Margaret together, but none could attest to his whereabouts during the time of the murder. What she really needed to do was find the old man who was mugged, but the likelihood of that was slim to none.

She opened her computer, staring glumly at the screen. An image of the tiny scrap of fabric found in the wastebasket had been recently uploaded. She rubbed her eyes and zoomed in on the one-inch scrap which supposedly came from the murder weapon.

It looked like silk, or... She tilted her head as the tiny diamond pattern on the fabric solidified in her mind. Her mouth fell open, and pinpricks of shock skittered up her spine. The pattern on the fabric was an exact match to the silk tie she'd bought Liam for the gala. *Liam's tie.* She shoved away from her desk and grabbed her purse.

"Hey, McLeod," Otto called. "Where's the fire?"

Cora ignored him and rushed out of the station to her car. No more waiting around. She needed answers, and Liam was going to give them to her.

Her phone rang just as she pulled off the highway toward her neighborhood. She stabbed at the button, her mind in a tailspin. "McLeod."

"Oh. Hi, Cora." Finn's quiet voice seemed far too calm for what she was feeling.

"What is it?" she demanded. God, was she living with a murderer? No. He couldn't be. He was a police officer, for God's sake. A protector of the people. She had all sorts of weird feelings around him, but she'd never gotten the evil sociopath vibe. There had to be a good explanation for why the tie she'd bought him was the murder weapon.

"Uh, is this a bad time?" Finn asked.

She tried to switch lanes, but the car next to her accelerated and narrowly missed sideswiping her door. The driver sped past, laying on his horn.

"Idiot," Cora barked.

"I'm sor—"

"Not you, Finn," she said quickly. "It's open season on the road today, and I'm like a sitting duck out here."

"I'll call back another time."

"No, that's not necessary. What's up?" She adjusted her rearview mirror and turned into her neighborhood. Liam better be home. She was getting answers even if she had to shake them out of him.

"I was just wondering if you were going to Danté's tonight." When she didn't respond right away, Finn added, "Half-price drink specials. It's Thursday."

"It is." She couldn't believe it was already day five of their murder investigation and their best suspect was a long-dead criminal. Unless, of course, Liam was the killer. Which, he wasn't. He might be full of false charm and pretty lies and whatever else, but he wouldn't flat out kill someone. Surely…

"Anyway, I'm heading over there, myself, after work," Finn said. "I thought maybe we could catch a drink, if you'd like."

"A drink." If only Margaret hadn't had so many drinks, she wouldn't have passed out and then maybe Liam would have a better alibi. Although, Margaret's story during the time of the murder was questionable, too. Nobody had actually seen her in that motel room. Maybe she killed her husband in cold blood while Liam was away. Or, maybe all Cora's instincts were wrong, and Liam and Margaret were just a modern-day Bonnie and Clyde, murdering and stealing and wreaking havoc everywhere they went. Cora rubbed her aching temple with one hand as she maneuvered onto her street. She needed some Tylenol. Or a drink. "A good stiff one," she murmured.

Finn made a choking sound. "Pardon?"

She snapped back to the moment. "Drinks! At Danté's. Yeah, that might be good. I'm meeting Suzette there later. Listen, I'm kind of in the middle of something right now. Let me call you back."

"Yes, of course. Anytime. I'll just—"

"Okay, bye." Cora hung up as she pulled into her driveway. Liam's car was parked in front of her house. She should be glad he was home, but her insides snaked with apprehension. Part of her was so sure he was innocent, but

Captain Thompson's words kept coming back to haunt her. *You're a cheater and a liar. Your track record's looking pretty dismal right now...*

When she walked into the house, Liam was sitting at the kitchen table with a bottle of whiskey and a box of Lucky Charms. His eyes were bloodshot with dark circles under them, and his hair was a tufted mess as if he'd been running his hands through it. Stubble shadowed his jawline, and his rumpled clothes looked as if he'd slept in them.

When he saw her, he raised the corner of his mouth in a sardonic smile and lifted the whiskey bottle in salute. "Ah, the beautiful Cora McLeod. Have you come to condemn me, too?" His words were slightly slurred, and his Irish accent was much stronger.

"You're drunk," she accused.

Liam gave her a crocodile smile. "Not nearly enough, my love. But I'm hoping my friend—" he glanced at the bottle in his hand "—Jack Daniel's can help remedy that." He took a swig of whiskey, swallowed and exhaled with a hum of appreciation. "Ah, that's good stuff, that is." He swung his head back to her and beckoned with his free hand. "Come, love. Join me in celebrating my unexpected holiday."

Cora dropped her purse on the kitchen counter and took the seat across from him. "You could get suspended. It's hardly a reason to celebrate."

He regarded her through heavy-lidded eyes. Wild energy emanated from him, and even though he appeared relaxed, he reminded her of a predator from one of those Discovery Channel shows. Not the kind of predator who was on the hunt, but one who was lazily basking in the sun, like a great jungle cat. He might look casual and content, but there was no mistaking the tightly coiled energy lurking beneath. It was unsettling, and maybe she should feel afraid, but for some reason, she didn't.

"You and I are going to have a talk," she said evenly. "And you're not going to leave a single thing out, this time. I want every detail about what you did on Saturday night, no matter how small."

"Of course, fair Cora."

"Stop calling me that."

He smirked. "What? Fair?"

"Your false charm won't work with me. And you can nix all the 'my love' comments, too. I want the truth, Liam. Just the facts."

Something shifted in the atmosphere between them. His voice went velvety soft, but his hand gripped the neck of the whiskey bottle so hard, Cora could see his knuckles go white. "But those are truths. Those are facts. You are gloriously fair, and you are also my lo—"

"Can you please cut the bullshit for just five minutes?" she interrupted. "In case you haven't realized, you're in big trouble, Liam. You might lose your job—and worse— you're now a suspect in this murder investigation. You could go to prison, and life as you know it will be over."

He flashed a smile that held no mirth. "This life was never mine to begin with, my heart. I'm on borrowed time as it is."

She straightened her back. "Explain that. What do you mean? Is someone after you?"

With a deep, rumbling chuckle he said, "The devil, himself, I'd imagine. Drink?" He held out the bottle.

"No," Cora said through gritted teeth. She wanted to reach across the table and shake him, but she forced herself to take a deep breath and let it out slowly. Losing her temper wasn't going to get her answers, especially when he was already arm in arm with his good buddy, Jack Daniel's. She tried a different approach. "Please, Liam. I want to help you. Can't you be honest with me and give me the truth?"

Something very close to pain flashed across his face. Cora could hear the clock ticking on the wall, each second like a lead weight adding to the heaviness that surrounded them. He eyed her up and down, then took another swig of whiskey straight from the bottle, his gaze never leaving hers. "I'd give you the world if I could, Cora."

A bit melodramatic, but it was a start. "Forensics came back today with no conclusive evidence from the fabric found in the wastebasket, other than the fingerprint of an old gangster."

"Then there you have it. Find your gangster, find your killer. Simple enough." He rose from the chair to get a bowl, a spoon and a carton of milk from the fridge before joining her back at the table.

"It would be, if the man were still alive. He's been dead for decades, so it's useless. But I took a closer look at the evidence today. The fabric looks like it came from a blue silk tie with a diamond weave." She waited for some reaction from him, but he didn't even flinch.

"It was your tie, wasn't it?" she pressed. "The one I bought you for the gala."

Liam started to pour the cereal, but she reached forward and dragged the bowl away. "Why was your tie at the crime scene, Liam?"

A muscle ticked in his jaw. "I imagine it fell out of my jacket pocket."

"How? When?"

No response. He wouldn't even meet her eyes. It irritated the crap out of her. "If you don't start talking, I'm going to walk out that door and head straight to Captain Thompson and tell him what I know."

Genuine surprise flashed across his face. "You haven't told him?"

"Not yet." Because she was batshit crazy. It went against all her training to withhold information like this, but she needed answers before she could decide what to do. "You know, my dad might think you're a great guy, but your pretty-boy wiles don't fool me for a second. Right now, I'm your best bet in helping you prove your alibi, but I'm on the edge here, Liam. *Talk* to me."

He leaned forward as if he were going to divulge a very important secret. "So, you think I'm pretty, then?"

She slammed her hand on the kitchen table. "This is not a game, dammit! Tell me why your tie was at the crime scene."

The teasing humor evaporated from his face and all that was left was pure, masculine arrogance. "I suppose it could've fallen out of my pocket when Margaret asked me for sexual favors in the hallway of her house."

Cora frowned and shifted in her seat.

"Yes, I believe that's when it happened. Margaret shoved me against the hall table and thrust her tongue into my mouth." He seemed to be enjoying her discomfort. "Or was it, the tongue first, and then the shove? Anyway, she tore my jacket off and begged me to take her hard and fast, up against the wall—"

"Liam," Cora interrupted. "I don't need details on your sex life."

"But you said you wanted every detail, no matter how small." His expression was all choirboy innocence but the wicked gleam in his eyes ruined it.

"Just go on," she said impatiently.

Liam stretched to rub the back of his neck, his muscular arms flexing. How the hell did he stay so fit? She'd never seen him go to the gym, but maybe he did. Maybe he lifted weights on the sly with his gym rat buddies. Maybe he did all sorts of things nobody knew about. What did she really know about him, anyway, other than what her dad had told her?

"All right." He regarded her with stone-cold sincerity. "I believe the tie fell from my jacket pocket when I went to pick her up for dinner. The killer must've come across it during the struggle with her husband and used it to finish him off. That's the only scenario that seems plausible to me."

"And the motel story? The ATM mugger?"

"All true," he said wearily. "Margaret had already started drinking when I picked her up that night. At dinner, she drank even more, and by the time we left the restaurant, she was half-gone. The motel was a snap decision. Once we got in the room, she sent me to the corner store to get…" He suddenly grew very interested in reading the Lucky Charms box. "Things."

"Like what?" Cora noted the high color that bloomed across his cheekbones. Was he talking about condoms? He couldn't possibly be blushing. Guys like him didn't blush. They were too busy sauntering and smoldering.

"Tell me the rest. You were heading to the convenience store." She rolled her hand, prompting him to continue.

"I didn't go inside. I chose to lie on the street bench and look up at the stars instead."

"It was cloudy on Saturday night," she pointed out. "The stars weren't visible."

"Yes, I noticed that after I lay down. I was just relaxing

for a bit, but then I heard the scuffling and that's when I saw the old man being attacked."

"So, you helped the man get his wallet back, but never actually saw the attacker's face, even though you fought him?"

"It was too dark. He ran off, and I needed to make sure the old man was okay. Afterward, I went back to the motel room and dozed in the chair until morning. Then I drove Margaret home, and that's when we saw the lineup of police cars. That's it. That's everything."

He had no witnesses to prove he was there, and a weak alibi that sounded too convenient, but Cora wanted so badly to believe him. But something still felt off, and she couldn't shake the feeling that he was hiding something. She was filled with conflicting emotions, and they weren't only directed at Liam. She'd never wavered in her responsibilities as a police officer. She'd grown up with her father on the force, and the law was like their religion. After her mother died, her father was forever teaching Cora about codes of honor and safety and rules, and a million other things he hoped would keep his daughter safe. Then along came Liam, and now here she was withholding evidence just to protect him. And she barely knew him! God, what was happening to her?

Her cat Angel padded into the kitchen and Liam bent to scoop up the purring feline who was one hundred percent Team Liam. Great. At least Cora wasn't the only one who'd gone off the deep end.

She put her elbows on the table and leaned forward. "Okay, this is how it's going to go. You need someone in your corner who can help find something to clear your name, and—God only knows why—I'm in your corner." His face lit up, and she held out her hand. "No, don't get excited yet. I'm going to try to find information about that mugger. You said he's about your height and wore a dark hoodie. This could be the convenience store robber we've been trying to catch. But, Liam, you should know that I'm at my rope's end here. I'm actively withholding information by not telling them your tie was the murder weapon, and that goes against everything I believe in. I'm putting my neck on the line for you, and to be honest, I'm not even sure you're worth it. So, I need something from you in return."

"Anything, my lo—" He paused. "Anything."

"Complete honesty. I want the whole truth. I know you're hiding something else from me." She laid her fist against her chest. "I can *feel* it."

He pushed away from the table and walked to the kitchen sink.

"If you care about our relationship at all," she pleaded, "you'll just come clean."

"There's nothing else." His back was rigid as he stared out the window.

The disappointment was crushing. So, this was how he wanted to play it. She tried one last time. "Do you promise me there's nothing else?"

Liam gripped the edge of the counter and gave a curt nod. It was as good as she was going to get.

"Swear it," she challenged. "I want you to swear that you've lied to me about nothing else."

Liam slowly turned to face her, his expression shuttered, his voice thick with some dark emotion. "Cora, I know you don't have a good reason to trust me, but I only hid my relationship with Margaret because that's what she wanted. She didn't want to taint her husband's good name, so I agreed to keep our affair a secret. I truly didn't believe it would have any relevance to the investigation, and I swear to you, I had absolutely nothing to do with John Brady's murder."

It wasn't until later, when she was driving back to the police station that she realized he'd never promised a thing.

22

"The problem with snakes in the grass," Suzette said over a bite of jalapeño popper, "is that they don't always look all scaly and gross, so you never expect them to strike."

Cora watched her friend finish her third martini, then signal a server for another. It was after eight o'clock and they'd been at Danté's for just over an hour. Finn had joined them shortly after they'd arrived, and Cora was grateful for his company. Suzette was on a roll about the pitfalls of dating unsavory men, and Finn was taking it like a champ. In fact, Cora was enjoying his easygoing humor, and even though Suzette was grumpy, he seemed to have a calming effect on her.

"Sometimes snakes look all hot and sexy, and they lure you in with those swirly, hypnotic eyes," Suzette continued. "Like the snaky dude in *The Jungle Book*, you know?"

"Kaa," Finn offered.

"Yes!" Suzette pointed her jalapeño popper at him. "Exactly. I knew you'd understand. Because you're not a snake, are you, Finn? You'd never use those big brown eyes to hypnotize anyone."

"Wouldn't dream of it." Finn caught Cora's gaze and winked. He did have rather nice brown eyes. And he was such a trooper, acting as the sounding board for Suzette's latest rant.

"Finn." Suzette looked at him in surprise. "*You're* a man."

He gave a self-deprecating smile. "Last I checked."

"Why are you single? You're cute and nice and all that stuff. Women should be falling all over you."

He took a drink of beer, a deep flush spreading up his neck.

Cora found it endearing. "Suze, leave him alone."

"What?" Suzette looked offended. "I'm paying him a compliment. He's got a lot of great qualities. I'm surprised he doesn't have a harem of dancing girls on speed dial."

"Maybe he does," Cora said. "How would you know?"

"I don't," he said quickly. "For the record."

"Why not?" Suzette pressed. "Too busy being Super Attorney defending the innocent and all that?"

Finn's mouth quirked like he was trying not to smile. The smile won out. "I suppose I just haven't found the right dancing girl."

Cora was reminded of that dance they shared at the gala. She'd even thought about it a time or two afterward.

"I'm going to the bathroom," Suzette sang out. "Tell that server to bring me another drink, will you?"

Cora waited until Suzette was out of earshot. "I think I'm just going to order her water and call it a night. She mentioned having an early client in the morning, so she'll thank me tomorrow."

"You're a good friend," Finn said with a smile.

Cora fiddled with her necklace, aware of his warm gaze on her. Something sharp caught at the nape of her neck. She sucked in a breath, frowning.

"What's wrong?"

She reached back to rub away the sting. "Oh, it's just the clasp on my necklace. There's a bit of a rough edge on it and it keeps getting caught."

"Let me see." Finn motioned for her to turn around and she did, lifting her hair off the nape of her neck. "Ah. Hold on." Warm knuckles brushed across her skin, making her shiver as he untangled the clasp.

"All better," he murmured. "I should take it back to have them fix it."

Cora turned to face him. "What do you mean?"

He opened his mouth, then closed it. Guilt flickered across his face and he blinked rapidly.

"Finn?" Cora stared at him in surprise. She'd never seen that look on him before.

"I'm sorry." He swallowed visibly. "I asked Liam not to say anything because I didn't want you to be mad at me."

She frowned. "What are you talking about?"

Finn sighed. "I found your necklace that night at the bar, after you all went home. The clasp was broken, but instead of giving it back to you right away, I took it to a jeweler to have it fixed. The day I drove it to your house, Liam was outside and, well…"

"Well, what?" she asked sharply.

Finn dipped his head in obvious remorse. "He said you'd been so distraught about losing it, you'd be mad when you found out I'd kept it from you for a few days. I should've told you immediately, instead of trying to make it a surprise."

Cora blinked at him, stunned. She *had* been upset. For days she'd felt the loss of her mother's necklace like a missing limb, but there was no way Finn could've known that. He was just trying to be kind. "Finn—"

"No, please let me apologize. I'm sorry I didn't tell you right away. I ended up giving it to Liam and just asked him not to mention I stopped by."

Cora remembered being so happy to find Liam standing in the yard, holding her necklace. *It was in the grass.* That's what Liam had said. He'd looked her straight in the face and taken the credit for someone else's good deed. He was a master at manipulation, all right. She wondered just how often he tricked people into thinking well of him. A distasteful thought suddenly occurred to her. "Finn, did you fix my broken lawn mower?"

"No. Not at all."

Well, at least Liam wasn't lying about tha—

"It wasn't really broken," Finn explained. "The carburetor cup just needed clearing. Once I did that, it was good as new."

Cora frowned.

"Please don't be angry with me," Finn said worriedly.

She wasn't used to seeing him look so…lost. Usually he seemed so steadfast and confident, comfortable in his own skin.

"I'm not," she assured him. "I'm very grateful for what you did. It was too kind of you, really."

He looked so relieved, it was almost comical, but Cora was in no mood to laugh. She was so fed up with Liam and his lies.

"If—if you want," Finn said tentatively, "I can take

your necklace back to the jeweler so they can fix that rough edge."

Cora's immediate thought was to turn him down because the idea of being without it was unnerving, but he looked so hopeful. Quickly, before she could change her mind, she unclasped the necklace, then placed it in his hand. "It's one of the only things I have left of my mother's. I've worn it since I was a little girl."

He cradled it in his hand with reverence, as if she'd just given him the Holy Grail. "Perhaps I shouldn't—"

"I trust you," she said simply. "I know you'll take good care of it for me." And she did trust him. Finn was a good person. Unlike another man who had Cora quietly fuming.

As soon as Suzette returned, Cora made her excuses to them both and headed home to confront a lying, manipulative snake in the grass.

23

On Friday evening, Liam woke to find himself sprawled on the living room sofa. On the television a woman in a hot-pink dress was raving about a special type of squeezable kitchen mop, and while Liam wasn't the least bit interested in the item she was selling, he was certainly intrigued by her enthusiasm.

His throat was as scratchy as dry leaves, and his head felt as if it were stuffed with sheep's wool. He fumbled for something to ease his parched throat, but the whiskey and few scattered beer bottles on the coffee table were empty. A bowl of half-eaten popcorn fell off his lap, spilling onto the floor as he sat up.

Angel meowed from the end of the couch, then flicked an ear at Liam.

"Save it, cat," Liam muttered, clutching his head. "I'll take no judgment from you."

The cat gave Liam a slow blink, then continued to stare with round, headlamp eyes.

"When you're a murder suspect bound for hell, and the woman you love no longer remembers you, then you can judge me. But until then, back off and let me watch Squeezy Mop in peace."

He glanced at the wall clock. It was a little after five, and Cora was bound to be home soon. He'd missed seeing her last night because he'd passed out in bed before she'd returned, but maybe that was for the best. The look on her face when she'd confronted him about the tie… It was clear as the wind she didn't trust him, and that made his insides ache worse than the time he'd cracked a rib falling from a tree.

Spotting a half-empty bottle of stale beer, Liam fumbled for it and drained it with a grimace. Then he tossed the empty bottle onto the coffee table where it rolled off onto the carpet. Time for another trip to the local market. Mental clarity was vastly overrated, he'd decided. Ever since last Saturday night, things just kept getting worse, so escapism was high on his list of priorities.

"Enjoying your downward spiral, I see."

Liam swung his head toward the television. The infomercial was gone, and in its place was roiling white mist. The blond angel leaned through the flat-screen TV like it was a window, his elbows perched on the edge.

"Blondie!" Liam said with false enthusiasm. "How lovely of you to visit. If I'd known you were coming, I'd have put out the good china."

The angel rolled his shoulders in irritation and spoke to the corner bookshelf. "He's still as arrogant as ever."

"Yes, but it's just a shield." The tall, dark-haired angel was leaning against Cora's bookshelf, casually reading the back of a romance novel. "One has only to look at this dwelling space to see the truth."

"Yes," the blond angel agreed, surveying the mess. "He is losing his sense of purpose."

"Worse," the other said. "I believe he may be losing hope."

Liam scowled and propped his feet on the coffee table. "Aye, well thanks for the diagnosis, Doctors. Any time you want to hit me with the cure, I'm ready."

"Have you tried one of these lovely books?" The dark-haired angel held up the paperback novel. "I understand they can be quite uplifting."

Liam eyed the cover of the book with suspicion. He failed to see how a bare-chested man holding a sword was going to instill hope in a situation as dire as his.

"We've come to remind you to stay the course," the blond angel said briskly. "Your true purpose of uniting Cora and Finn is more important than any of your other trivial matters."

"Trivial?" Liam growled. "Being accused of murder doesn't do much to endear me to her right now, and it would be a bit hard to play matchmaker from prison. Speaking of which, why am I still a murder suspect?"

"I should think that would be obvious," the blond one said. "Your actions put you there."

"But can't you just wave your wings, or whatever it is you do, and make it all go away? You said I should focus solely on Cora and Finn. If you help clear my name, then it would be much easier for me to—"

"We are not here to pave the way for you, ruffian." The blond angel suddenly swooped into the room, his power crackling in the air until Liam could feel it against his skin like a low-level electrical charge. It reminded him just how formidable the angels could be. If he weren't three sheets to the wind already, he might've felt a bit more fear. Good thing he had several bottles of liquid courage in him.

"Everything you choose to do has consequences, and you must bear those consequences," the blond said. "We have set the plan in motion, but we cannot interfere with free will. Your choices have led you here."

"But I was trying to save Margaret from getting hurt," Liam pointed out. By all that was holy, did good intentions count for nothing with them?

"Who are you to assume Margaret would have been in danger, at all? There are an infinite number of ways that situation on Saturday night could've gone. You forget your place, rogue. Margaret is not part of your task. Cora is."

Liam's frustration spiked. "So, you toss me back down to earth to save Cora's destiny and right past wrongs, but when I try to do good deeds like saving another innocent woman, or helping an old man who's getting mugged, I get punished for it. How is that justice?"

"Again, you fail to understand your actions have brought you to this point." The blond angel's calm, almost bored demeanor grated against Liam's nerves. "No one is punishing you."

"Aye, well, you sure as hell aren't helping me, either." Liam gripped the nearest throw pillow and hurled it against the wall.

The blond angel flicked the tip of his wing and the pillow sailed back to land neatly in the corner of the sofa. He turned to his companion near the bookcase. "He throws tantrums like a young child."

"Give him time," the other one said gently. "He can learn."

"He doesn't have time to squander."

"Why are you both here, then?" Liam said, flinging his hands in the air. "I thought angels were supposed to be messengers of goodwill, or beacons of light and hope."

The blond angel's lashes flickered, and Liam got the feeling it was the celestial equivalent of an eye roll. "We are here to remind you to focus. To stay on task because every choice you make, every action, creates a ripple effect that will steer the course of your journey. Do you understand?"

"Sure," Liam said flatly. "Actions. Ripples. Got it."

The blond angel tipped his face to the ceiling and sighed. Then he glanced sharply toward the window. "She comes."

"Goodbye, rogue." The other angel dropped an armful of books beside Liam on the sofa. His somber expression held an ocean of pity. "I do hope you find your way."

"So that's it, then," Liam said angrily as they backed into a wall of mist. "Just a 'Fine luck, you,' and off you go?"

They disappeared right before Cora unlocked the front door.

24

Cora entered her living room and came to an abrupt halt. The place looked like a fraternity house after rush week. Fast-food wrappers littered the floor, along with empty beer bottles and random articles of clothing. *Her* clothing, she realized with a start. The neatly folded stack of laundry she'd left on the coffee table that morning was now scattered on the carpet along with stale popcorn and an overturned crystal bowl. The bowl had been a wedding gift to her parents, and Cora only used it on special occasions. But, of course, Liam wouldn't know that, because he didn't really know her. And the more she got to know him, the less she wanted to know.

She plunked her purse on the end table, glaring at him.

Liam was sprawled shirtless on the sofa with his bare feet propped on the coffee table. He was wearing dark denim jeans slung low on his hips, and with his scruffy hair and bloodshot eyes, he looked like a strung-out rock star version of Dionysus after a hard night of partying. He was surrounded by a pile of Cora's favorite books, including one of her prized hardcovers, signed by the author, which was currently being used as a beer coaster. *Unbelievable.*

If she wasn't so angry, she might have laughed at the irony. When Liam first moved in, she'd actually talked herself into believing it would be good to have him around. That he would be one of those dream roommates who were trustworthy and respectful and helpful around the house. Disappointment roiled in the pit of her stomach. Somehow, whether she'd realized it or not, she'd been holding out hope that Liam would prove to be a better person, but maybe that was the biggest joke of all. Maybe he really was just a lying snake in the grass, and it was as simple as that.

"What are you doing?" Cora demanded, taking in the mess.

Liam tossed a book aside carelessly, then hooked an arm over the back of the sofa. "Searching for a diversion." He seemed different than when she saw him yesterday, more somber and broody, which gave her the feeling that she was finally seeing a glimpse of the real man behind the mask. His dark gaze raked over her. "Any suggestions?"

"Yes." She lurched forward and picked up the crystal bowl. "Clean up this mess. Sober up. Grow up." His sullen attitude, the state of her house, his obvious disregard for anyone but himself—it all came crashing down on her, and any cooling off she might've done on the drive home evaporated. "Look at yourself. You're a wreck, and the house is a disaster." She set the bowl aside and began scooping up her books. "I've been at work all day racking my brains trying to figure out a way to help clear your name, and here you are wallowing like some selfish adolescent on spring break."

"That's the second time today I've been compared to a child," he said, rising from the sofa with easy, masculine grace. "It's getting tiresome."

"Well, you are a child," Cora shot back, shoving books back on the shelf. She strained on tiptoes to reach the top. "Completely immature. A total—"

A strong, warm hand lightly settled over hers. For a split second, he flinched, but he didn't pull away. "I can assure you, macushla," he said in a husky voice. "I am very much a man."

She spun to face him, startled by the sudden intimacy of being this close to his half-naked body. The smooth, hard planes of his chest, the rippling ab muscles and powerful shoulders proved his statement more than true.

A muscle ticked in his jaw, and their faces were only inches apart. Cora could see faint lines of strain at the edges of his dark eyes, and he smelled of whiskey and woodsmoke and sunlight. It was both confusing and familiar. His gaze was so intense, he almost looked like he was in pain, or angry about something. His grip on her hand shook with some strong emotion. It was unsettling as hell, because a part of her wanted to step right into his warm embrace, like it was the most natural thing in the world. But he didn't want that. And neither should she. *Get a grip, McLeod.*

She tugged her hand away.

He looked…relieved.

Cora's face flushed with instant humiliation. *He'd* touched *her*, not the other way around. What the hell was this, some kind of ploy of his to charm her into not being angry? Well, screw that, and screw him. Just because he looked like some dark warrior from one of her favorite novels, didn't mean she was going to fall at his feet.

Liam placed the book high on the shelf, his expression now carefully neutral. When he turned away, any residual confusion she'd felt from his proximity vanished like a wisp of smoke from a snuffed-out candle.

Determined to confront him about all the lies, Cora reached for her necklace to ground her, but it wasn't there. *Gone.* A bolt of unease caught her off guard, until she remembered Finn had it. It was safe with him. She could trust Finn, unlike other people. Suddenly, everything snapped back into place.

She remembered what she wanted to say. "I spoke to Finn last night."

Liam gave a deep, throaty growl. "He's calling you on the phone now, is he?"

"No. I met him for drinks after work. I spoke to him in person."

His expression was grim—almost accusatory. As if he had the right to judge her for her choices. God, he was a piece of work. She'd come to a decision about him on the way home, and his attitude now was just going to make it easier. Cora squared her shoulders and continued. "We had quite an interesting talk."

Liam scoffed. "Anyone who finds that man interesting is either delusional or lying to themselves."

"Oh, so now *I'm* the liar? That's rich coming from you. Tell me about my necklace, Liam. You know, the one you *found in the grass*?"

"Finn asked me not to tell you," he said after a lengthy

pause. "It's not my fault he wasn't brave enough to face you himself."

"That's because you made him think I'd be angry with him," she said. "You lied to me, and—"

"No, I didn't. Finn dropped your necklace in the grass when he handed it over, and I picked it up. I told you it was in the grass. That's all I said. You chose to believe I'd found it. It's as simple as that."

"Simple," she echoed in disbelief. God, how did he even sleep at night with all the lies? "So that's how you operate. You tell half-truths, knowing full well you're manipulating people, then you pretend it's not your fault if it works. The lawn mower. Anything you want to say about that?"

He hooked his thumbs in the pockets of his jeans and gave her an arrogant shrug. That was it. No answer, no explanation, which was answer enough.

"Thought so," Cora said bitterly. "You know I asked you for the truth a few days ago, and now I think I've finally got it. Because the truth is, you're just a lying, manipulative person who cares more about covering your own ass than anything else." She wrapped her arms around her waist, hugging herself. "I should never have let you move in here. The only reason I agreed to it was because I needed someone to help pay the rent, but at the rate you're going, you aren't even going to have a job."

"Dealing with you has been a full-time job," Liam shot back. He began to pace. "Believe me, Cora, there are things you don't—"

"Save it," she snapped. "I want you out of here, Liam. Today. I'd hate for you to have to strain yourself *dealing* with me a moment longer."

"I'm not leaving you," he said fiercely. "If I'm not here

to look after you, I won't be able to guide you and make sure—"

"*Guide* me?" The utter audacity of this man! "Now who's delusional? You call this—" she gestured to the mess "—looking after me? I don't need your guidance, thanks very much. I was taking care of myself long before I ever met you, and I'm doing just fine."

"Not for long," Liam said with conviction. "You don't do so well on your own, Cora. I've seen your track record, and it's dismal. Trust me on that."

"How dare you?" The anger that had been simmering inside her since last night finally bubbled to the surface and overflowed. "You know nothing about me, Liam O'Connor. *Nothing.* As for my track record, I may not be an all-star athlete, but I can guarantee you I don't have 'murder suspect' on my list of personal stats. Who the hell do you think you are? I don't care if my father says you're a fine, upstanding—" she made air quotes with her hands "—*good* guy. Not one second has passed since the moment we first met where I've wholeheartedly believed that."

He gave an arrogant shrug. "I never claimed to be."

"That's it," she said flatly. She was so done with him. "This arrangement between us is not working, and I'm tired of trying to hide the way I feel about you."

His dark eyes pinned her in place, glittering with emotion. "The feeling is mutual."

As usual, Cora sensed he was hiding something important from her. Something she should know...or used to know, but forgot. None of it made sense. Her head began to pound and she squeezed her eyes shut, rubbing her temples to ease the ache. She took a breath to steady herself. Then another. In a quiet, surprisingly calm voice she said, "I want you to leave now."

He started toward her. "Cora—"

She held up a hand. "I mean it, Liam."

"Don't do this." His expression was so bleak, so heavy, it threatened to take her down, too. "There's too much at stake, Cora."

"You don't get to choose," she said, steeling her resolve. "This is my home. Your name isn't even on the rental lease yet, and even if it were, I'd still insist that you go. I've tried to play house with you as a favor to my father, but I can't do this anymore." To her utter shock, tears pricked the corners of her eyes.

He opened his mouth to speak, but she cut him off before she broke down. "If there's even a tiny shred of you that cares for me at all, you'll understand that I need space, and you'll give it to me. I have to work on this case, and you being here is making it too difficult. Just, go. *Please go.*"

They stood facing each other for several erratic heartbeats, but it could've been seconds or minutes or hours, for all Cora knew. In that moment, time didn't apply. It was like a river flowing over and around them, rushing inexorably forward, and she and Liam were two trees with branches so intertwined, and roots anchored so deep, they remained unmoved.

But eventually, he did move. He walked down the hall to his bedroom, and a few moments later he reappeared with his duffel bag. At the door, he paused with his back to her, broad shoulders stiff, head high like an exiled nobleman. It struck her, at once, how devastatingly alone he seemed. A hollow ache throbbed in her chest, rising into her throat, making it hard to swallow. Cora waited for him to say something—anything—but he didn't. He just opened the door, and then he was gone.

Angel gave a forlorn meow.

The clock on the mantel chimed.

And time came rushing back, sweeping Cora up and carrying her away in a flood of frustration and tears.

25

Kinsley, Ireland,
1844

The familiar sound of tiny pebbles hitting her window stirred Cora from slumber. Smiling, she threw off her blankets and floated to the window on a cloud of happy anticipation. It had been almost two months since she'd met the handsome thief who'd climbed into her life by surprise. Not long after that second encounter, he'd come back in the night to see her again. It had become a ritual for them. Whenever Liam could get away, they'd meet beyond the garden gate, sometimes walking the fields if the moon was full enough to see, other times just sitting against the stone wall, talking about anything and everything. Ever since she met him, life had gone from a dull, lackluster existence to something unbearably precious.

She threw open her window and peered down into the darkness. There was a full moon tonight, so she could just make out his smile as he stood under the trellis.

Impulsively, Cora took a rose from the vase at her windowsill and tossed it down to him. Then she spun away, drew on her dressing gown and slippers, and tiptoed down the stairs. The house was quiet as a tomb, but Cora wasn't worried about being caught. Her father slept almost as soundly as the cook who imbibed too often, and her old nanny never heard anything. The rest of the servants—few as they were—slept in a different wing of the house.

Cora made her way through the drawing room to the door that opened to the side garden. She ran the last few steps, too excited with the prospect of seeing Liam again. *Her* Liam. She'd begun to think of him as hers within that first month. Now that they'd shared their dreams with each other, she felt more connected to him than anyone else in her life, even her own father. Cora loved her father, but he'd always been stern and overprotective. She could never have told him the things she told Liam in secret. How she longed for the happier days when her mother was still alive. How she wished for freedom to travel. How she didn't want to get married right away. None of those things would have been well received by her father, or even her nanny, for that matter. They both just wanted to see her married and settled into a boring routine. With Liam, Cora could dream all she wanted because he never judged her. Liam was her only true friend.

She swung the door wide, and there he stood, with his wild dark hair and that secret smile on his face. Even in a threadbare shirt, worn boots and patched trousers, he was the handsomest man she'd ever seen.

"Hello, thief," Cora said with a grin.

"Captain Cora." He swept his hand out and gave a gallant bow. "What wild adventures await us this evening?"

She giggled. Then she flew at him and gave him a hug.

It was an impulsive thing to do. If her actions surprised him, he didn't show it. Since they'd met, he'd been nothing but a gentleman and taken no liberties. Not a single one. Cora was beginning to wish he would.

He lifted her off her feet and spun her around until she was dizzy. When he finally set her down, their quiet laughter mingled until it faded into something equally wonderful, but far more intense. He held her close, his expression more serious than she'd ever seen it. When he looked at her like that, she felt like the most precious thing in the world. Was he going to kiss her, finally? She wanted him to! What was he waiting for?

"Liam," Cora whispered, standing on her tiptoes and tilting her face toward his. "Kiss me."

He blinked and pulled back, his hands gripping her waist tightly. He looked like he was in pain. "No, Cora."

Heat scorched up the back of her neck, and she tried to pull away. *Stupid Cora!* His rejection stung like nettles. Maybe she was as naive about the world as her nanny said. Maybe he only thought of her as an interesting diversion. All this time she'd been falling more in love with him every day, and he didn't feel the same. How could she be so wrong? "I'm sorry," she said on a hitched breath. "I shouldn't have said—"

"No." He cupped her face with calloused hands, his voice thick with emotion. "It's not that I don't want to kiss you. God knows every day that passes I can't *think* for wanting you, but…" He laid his forehead against hers and whispered, "I'm a coward."

Elation mingled with confusion. He wanted her, but he was afraid? "You're the farthest thing from a coward I've ever met."

"Not true. Not when it comes to you. The more I'm with

you, the harder it is to imagine being without you." He released her and turned away. "If I kiss you, Cora, that will be it for me. You'll have my heart and my soul. And I'll have to learn how to go on living without them."

"No, you won't." She gently placed a hand on his broad back.

"It's true." He spun to face her. "You have a whole life ahead of you that doesn't include me."

"Don't say that." Tears pricked her eyes. The thought of what her father planned—marriage to his solicitor Finley Walsh—brought nothing but despair. She'd spend the rest of her days embroidering cushions by the fire, taking tea in stuffy drawing rooms and growing old listening to Finn drone on about…whatever it was he and her father talked about. She didn't even know because he rarely spoke to her. How could she be expected to cast away all her hopes and dreams for a man who knew nothing of her heart? "What if I don't want that life?"

Liam shook his head sadly, brushing a curl away from her face. "We both know these are stolen moments. We speak of dreams and adventures, but someday you'll have to move on." He grimaced. "You'll have to get married to—"

"No, I won't," Cora said fiercely. "I'll refuse. I only agreed to an engagement with Finn because my father wanted it, but that was before I knew myself. That was before I knew you." She gazed up at him with her heart in her throat. "Liam, I love you."

"And I, you," he said huskily. "But that doesn't change—"

"You said life was a series of adventures, some big and some small. Why can't we have one together? You're resourceful, and I'm braver than I look. We could run away. Leave this place. We could start a new life together and have the biggest adventure of all. I want that with you. Only you."

Liam's eyes glittered with emotion. She could tell he wanted it, too. "I'm nothing but a thief, my love."

"So, steal me away, then!"

He gave her a teasing smile. "What if you regret it? You could grow tired of me and toss me aside."

"Never," Cora said fiercely.

"I have nothing to offer you, macushla. And you deserve everything."

She took his hand. "If you give me your heart and soul, then that is everything."

Liam searched her face. "Are you sure?"

"I've never been more sure of anything in my life."

He paused for what felt like an eternity. Finally, he reached out and drew her to him. "Well, then."

"Yes?" Cora held her breath. Hope fluttered in her chest like a caged bird. "We'll go away together?"

He nodded, and his smile was like a spark of light in the surrounding darkness. "Onward we go, Captain Cora."

When he bent to kiss her, Cora was overcome by a fierce sense of joy. For the first time, she saw the future stretched out before her with glowing optimism. He loved her, and she loved him. They would carve out a life together any way they could, and it would be enough. It would be more than enough. It would be *everything*.

Present Day

Cora woke gasping. Her heart was galloping in her chest. She sat up slowly, blinking into the darkened room.

Frowning, she tried to remember the fading remnants of the dream she'd been having. Liam had been in it; she knew that much. It wasn't the first time she'd dreamed of him, but this one felt different. As usual, the harder she tried to remember the details, the faster they slipped away. All she knew for certain was that she'd been gloriously happy. They'd been laughing together. If only that were the case in real life. A pang of guilt lanced through her. She'd kicked him out when he had nowhere else to go last night. *She'd tossed him aside.* Cora groaned and dropped her head into her hands. She knew her actions were justified, but still. Why did everything with him have to feel so complicated?

The following day across the city, Liam trudged down the street heading in no particular direction. He'd been trying to figure a way out of the mess he was in, but he wasn't having any luck. Like the progression of his earthly task so far, he was going nowhere.

"Hey, brother. Can you help me out with a dollar for bus fare? I'm trying to get to my bank job." A homeless man held out his hand as Liam passed. The man wore an outdated, threadbare business suit several sizes too big. His greasy hair was pulled back in a low ponytail, and his battered briefcase looked like it hadn't seen an honest day's work in decades.

Liam wondered if the man knew how flimsy his act was, considering it was a Sunday afternoon, and most people weren't commuting to work at that time. Most bankers also didn't wear worn-out sneakers with their suits, nor did they smell like a distillery—at least, not on their way to work. After work was anyone's guess. Liam pulled money from his pocket and offered it to him.

The man thanked him, stuffed the bills in his pocket, then ambled away in the opposite direction of the bus stop. By the looks of it, he was headed toward the old liquor store on the corner, but Liam wasn't surprised. If the man needed a pick-me-up to get through his day, who was he to judge? After checking into his old motel, Liam had spent many sleepless hours pacing in agitation. He'd considered drowning his demons in a bottle of whiskey again, then decided against it. No amount of liquid sunshine was going to help brighten the dark sense of despair that now clung to him.

Getting kicked out of Cora's house felt like the final nail in his coffin. No matter how he tried to spin his situation, he couldn't think of a way back into her good graces, if he'd ever been there at all. He'd spent the remainder of the night outside his motel room on a lounge chair by the pool. Though he couldn't see the stars, it had still felt good to lie out under the open sky. The old motel had been the first place he'd stayed when he arrived in Providence Falls, and ironically, it was the closest thing he had to a home.

It was early in the afternoon now, and he was taking a walk to clear his head. Stopping at a run-down park several blocks down the street, he took a path skirting a duck pond. He ignored the Sunday joggers who zipped past in brightly colored athletic gear. This area might've been what Cora called the older "seedy part of town," but it was still far shinier than Liam's village back in Ireland. A sharp pang of sadness overcame him. So much had been lost to the passage of time. Everyone he remembered from his old life was long dead now, and there was no one left who truly knew him. Especially not here.

In the past, Liam always thought he'd had nothing. His family had been hungry more often than not. They'd barely been able to keep a roof over their heads, and they'd spent many winters huddled together, freezing in that dark, tiny cottage because they'd had to ration candles and firewood. But he'd had friends back in Ireland, rowdy and unethical as they were. He'd had family. He'd had neighbors who knew him since he was a boy. Everything there had been familiar. Liam might have come from nothing, but at least he knew where he belonged. They were all poor and destitute, but they were poor and destitute together. Here, his only connection was Cora, and yesterday when she'd sent him away, he'd felt as if his last lifeline had been severed. Her rejection had hurt worse than starving. Almost worse than… He rubbed the phantom burn around his neck, sinking onto a park bench with a heavy sigh. No. Nothing was worse than the day he'd truly lost everything.

Scraggly ducks pecked around in the grass near Liam's feet. A couple strode past, hand in hand, the woman laughing as the man pulled her closer. Liam sagged back and pressed the heels of his hands to his eyes. What now? The angels had made it clear they weren't going to help him get out of this mess. He had no idea if Cora was still on his side, but it wasn't looking good. There wasn't a single person Liam could think of who could help. Margaret was grieving the death of her husband, and she wanted nothing to do with him. He couldn't ask Cora's father, Hugh, for help. In truth, Liam barely knew the man, and even if Hugh wanted to help, he was retired and lived hours away. There wasn't much he'd be able to do.

A lone figure stood at the water's edge, tossing bread to the ducks. Liam watched as the kid sprinkled breadcrumbs.

Something about the skinny silhouette, narrow shoulders and baggy basketball shorts looked familiar.

Liam leaned forward and squinted at the kid's profile. "Billy Mac?"

The boy glanced over his shoulder, startled. His face lit up when he saw Liam, then he blushed scarlet, shoving a hunk of bread in his jacket pocket. He looked almost guilty, as if getting caught feeding the ducks embarrassed him.

Billy walked toward him with his trademark swagger. "What's up, Liam?" His normally pale face was mottled with a dark bruise on his eye that spread across his cheekbone.

"Billy, what happened to your face?" Liam asked.

"Just a scuffle," Billy said, rubbing the back of his head. "No big."

"We match." Liam pointed to his own fading bruises.

"Dang. Who clocked you?"

Liam knew he had to play this right if he was going to get Billy to talk. The boy reminded Liam so much of his brother's kids back in Ireland. Liam felt fiercely protective of him. "You go first."

Billy forced a laugh, then shook his head and stared out at the pond. "Nah. Nobody likes a snitch, you know what I mean?"

"Sure." Liam didn't want to push the kid, so instead he tried a different tactic. He eased back on the bench and pretended to watch the ducks. "This has been a week from hell, and the fight I got into was nothing compared to everything else. Talk about crazy."

Billy's eyes sparked with interest. "What happened?"

Liam shrugged.

"Did you have to shoot someone?" He came closer to the bench.

"No."

"Did you beat someone down?"

"Yes, but not as much as I wanted to," Liam said with a chuckle. "But I got in a few good hits before he ran off." He waited a beat, then said, "I'll tell you my story if you tell me yours."

"It wasn't no big thing." Billy sank onto the bench. "Albert—he's my foster dad. He and his buddies like to drink, that's all." He said it like that was all the explanation he needed.

"Ah." Liam clenched his hands into fists, casually crossing his arms so Billy wouldn't see how angry it made him. "So your foster dad did that?" He'd hunt the man down. Hell, he'd even learn the stupid computer program at the station just so he could find him. Never mind the fact that Liam might not be asked back to the station; he'd find a way to make sure that bastard never hit another kid again.

"Naw, it wasn't him. Albert's not that dumb. He knows he'll get in trouble with the state if he gets caught hitting kids, and then he wouldn't get the checks he loves so much. His friend Cecil, though." A look of true fear crossed Billy's face. "That man's the biggest douchebag on the planet."

"I've known a few Cecils, myself." Liam pulled up his shirtsleeve and showed Billy a scar from where someone at the Goose & Gander once broke a chair over his arm during a brawl.

Billy seemed impressed. He relaxed on the bench. "They call him Crack Rock Cecil because I guess he used to sell it. Of all Albert's friends, that guy is the worst. Anyway, they bet money on games and horse races and stuff, and you don't want to be around if Cecil's losing money." Billy absently brushed his fingertips over his black eye. "I was passing through the living room and I accidentally knocked his beer over the other night." Billy pretended to box a punching bag to make light of it, which just made Liam angrier. The fact that Billy was so blasé about getting hit only made it clear he'd been through it before.

"It ain't no thing," Billy said again, waving a hand. "I don't even care."

Liam could tell Billy didn't want to dwell on the bad memory, so he let it go, for now. Later he'd find a way to hunt Cecil down.

"So how'd you get yours?" Billy asked, gesturing to Liam's fading bruises.

"An old man got mugged near an ATM last Saturday night. I tried to stop the attacker, but he ran off before I could."

Billy's face paled. "That's good."

"Not really," Liam said in amusement. "He got away, and I didn't get a good look at him. He'll probably do it again."

"Right," Billy said quickly. "I just meant it's good he ran off before you got hurt worse. Like, with a knife or something."

"Aye, there's that, I suppose. But nobody saw it happen, so now I'm in trouble at work."

He scrunched his freckled face. "Why?"

Liam considered how much he should tell him. It was one thing to tell the kid about a fistfight, and another to discuss a murder case. "Something really bad went down across town that night, and because I don't have a solid alibi placing me at the ATM, it makes me look like a suspect. It's a long story, but I got sent home, and now I don't know what's going to happen."

"Dang." Billy's eyes practically bugged out of his head.

"Yeah. And there's no way for me to prove I was helping that old man, so it is what it is."

"What happens now?" Billy looked worried for him, which Liam found endearing. It was nice to know at least one person on God's green earth was still on his side.

"No idea. Probably nothing good."

Billy glanced away, fidgeting with his hands. He was quiet for a long time. They sat watching the joggers, the mothers pushing strollers and the ducks pecking in the grass. Some of the ducks waddled over to their bench and Billy pulled the hunk of bread from his jacket pocket. He appeared to be deep in thought and didn't realize he was doing it.

"You feed the ducks a lot?" Liam asked.

"Huh?" Billy's ears turned pink at the tips, and he tossed the last chunk of bread on the grass. "No. I just happened to be walking by, is all."

"That's cool." Liam kept his voice casual. "I might come around here next Sunday, same time. Maybe I'll try feeding the ducks myself."

"Why would you bother?" Billy was wearing his street stare now, the one that made him look hardened and bored, but Liam knew better.

"Why not? A man needs to think sometimes. Seems like a decent place to do it."

Billy didn't respond, he just toyed with a loose thread on the hem of his T-shirt. Whatever was on the kid's mind, it was heavy. A few minutes later, he stood and jammed his hands into his pockets. "I gotta go. See you around."

Liam watched the kid stroll away, his narrow shoulders hunched against unseen burdens. A few ducks trailed after him, and Liam smiled. Billy might pretend he didn't come around often, but the ducks told another story. The kid was a survivor, and Liam liked him. It was strange how just that short interaction with him made Liam feel less alone. He rose and took the path around the pond, determined to find a way to make things right. He still had time, and he wasn't going to give up without a fight.

26

Cora sat at a table outside her favorite deli on Monday, grateful for the awning that blocked the midday sun. While it did nothing to ease the hot, prickly frustration that clung to her every time she thought of Liam, it made sitting outside bearable, and it was much better than taking her lunch back to the office. Ever since Liam got sent home, she'd been acutely aware of his empty desk across from hers. The other officers working the case didn't talk much about his absence in front of Cora, which made things even more awkward. Liam's choices were his own, dammit, and Cora shouldn't feel responsible for him. Not in any way. That would just be…ridiculous.

She frowned, dragging a French fry through ketchup before popping it in her mouth. When she stood back and looked at all the facts, she was right not to trust him. Who could blame her? Liam had lied to her multiple times.

He withheld important information that affected their investigation. Cora blew out a frustrated breath. She still hadn't said a word to anyone about Liam's tie. Annoyed with herself, she pushed her plate away. No matter how she spun it, no matter how much she told herself he wasn't worth her time, she still wanted to help him. How ridiculous was that?

A shadow fell over her table. "Hey."

Cora glanced up, startled to see Billy on the other side of the patio railing. He was dressed in the same baggy street clothes he usually wore, but there were mottled bruises on his face.

Cora gripped the edge of the table. "Billy, what the heck happened to you?"

"Nothing." He glanced around nervously. "You seen Liam?"

"Not in the past couple of days." Cora pulled a bistro chair out. "Are you hungry? Come inside and I'll order you lunch."

"Nah, I can't stick around." Instead of his usual flirtatious swagger, he shifted back and forth on his feet and looked like he was about to bolt. "I gotta talk to you."

"Okay," Cora said carefully. Whatever he wanted to say, it had to be important.

He shook his head. "Not here. Somewhere quiet."

"We could sit in my car," Cora suggested.

"All right, but you'll have to drive so nobody sees me."

Now he was scaring her. Billy never acted this serious. "You got it." She grabbed her purse and walked Billy to her car parked along the sidewalk. He got in, and soon they were heading toward a different neighborhood.

"First I need to ask you something," Billy said, "and you have to be one hundred percent honest."

"I'm always honest with you."

"Nah, I don't mean honest as in that fake 'adult speak,' where you leave stuff out because you think I'm too young to know stuff," Billy said irritably. "I mean *real* honest. Person to person."

Cora's mouth fell open and she gripped the steering wheel tightly. She *had* withheld information from Billy on occasion, but that's because he was just a kid. Their relationship was built on harmless banter, occasional lunches and Cora trying to get him involved with the teen center. Every once in a while, Billy would let slip some information that actually did help her with a case, but she never discussed those cases with him, and she never told him things that could put him in harm's way.

"All right, Billy. I'll be as honest as I can. But I have to warn you that I'm a police officer, so there are some things I'm not at liberty to discuss."

Billy hissed something under his breath that sounded like "freaking grown-ups" followed by a few choice swear words.

"What's going on?" Cora asked. "Just tell me, and I promise you I'll tell you as much as I can."

Billy heaved a sigh and stared out the window. "How much trouble is Liam in?"

Cora almost slammed on the brakes, but she managed to keep her foot steady. "Who told you he was in trouble?"

"He did," Billy said. "I ran into him at the park yesterday. He told me he was in big trouble at work."

She was surprised Liam shared that much with him. "He did?"

"Yeah, because he's cool like that. He tells it to me straight, unlike most adults. So, I gotta know. Is he going to lose his job, or something?"

Cora's knee-jerk reaction was to remain vague, but she'd promised to stay as open and honest as possible. "I don't know, but it's looking pretty bad."

"Because he doesn't have an alibi proving he was at that ATM," Billy said.

"Correct." God, how much had Liam told him? Surely, he wouldn't have brought up the murder case.

"Could he go to jail?"

She opened her mouth to assure him it wouldn't come to that, then closed it again. How could she know for certain? She chose her next words carefully. "Honestly, I don't know. I'm trying to do everything I can to prove his alibi. Do you know something that can help him?"

Billy stared out the window for so long, she began to think he wasn't going to answer. They passed through the older part of town and headed to the university district before he finally said, "I think I might know who robbed that ATM."

Cora kept her game face on—the calm, cool one with the bland expression—but inside she was spinning like a weather vane in a windstorm.

"I overheard someone complaining about it last Saturday," Billy continued. "Saying how he tried to steal an old guy's wallet, but he got beat up instead."

"Does this guy have a name?"

Billy twisted his hands in his lap. "If I tell you, you gotta promise not to mention me. He's a real mean son of a bitch. If he ever found out I snitched on him, it would be bad. And I'm not just talking about this." He gestured to his bruised face.

Cora swallowed hard. The idea of anyone hurting Billy made her sick to her stomach. She'd never put him in harm's way or do anything to jeopardize his safety. "I swear your name will never come up, Billy. Not ever."

The tension drained from his face. Billy obviously trusted her, and it made her want to pull the car over and hug him, but she refrained. Even though she thought of him as a vulnerable kid, she knew he'd want to be treated like an adult. And hell, why shouldn't he be treated like a grown-up? He'd probably seen things she could only imagine, which was saying a lot.

"I'll give you his name because I don't want Liam to go to jail," Billy said. "Liam's cool, you know? It's not right for him to get accused for something he didn't do."

Cora pulled the car into the city library parking lot.

Billy looked like she'd just handed him a lemon and told him to eat it. "Why are we *here*?"

"Because we need a safe place to talk. You think the bad man you're talking about spends his Monday afternoons at the city library?"

For the first time since he approached her, Billy grinned. "Hells, no."

"Exactly," Cora said, smiling back. "So, let's talk."

Three hours later, Cora leaned across the picnic table at a local park, batting her eyes at a sleazeball in polyester track pants. Cecil Watmuff had slicked-back hair and a T-shirt with a medical cross and the phrase Orgasm Donor on the chest. Fun times. Honest to God, if anyone told her she'd be fake flirting with a man known as Crack Rock Cecil a week ago, she'd have laughed in their face. But, desperate times, and all that.

They were sitting at an old park by the river on the north end of the city. Though it had a playground and baseball diamond, there was an area where the trees grew thick along the river's edge, and wild blackberry bushes obscured the few picnic tables. Because of the secluded location, it was the perfect place for a man like Cecil. A shady spot for shady dealings.

Cora had chosen her approach carefully, wearing just her tank top and jeans, making sure to flip her hair a few times for good measure as she strolled past. It didn't take long before Cecil threw her a wolf whistle, and a few minutes later, Cora was sitting at his bench listening to him yammer on about himself. Man, this guy was a talker. It made her job easier because all she had to do was simper and nod. Cora's plan was sketchy, at best. Any second now, if Billy's information was correct, Cecil would break out his pipe and stash of weed. She was going to try to slap Cecil with possession charges, and then bluff like crazy during the interrogation, in hopes that he'd confess to the ATM mugging. It wasn't a solid plan, but it was more than she had when she went to work that morning.

Cecil's watery gaze slithered down Cora's body, lingering a little too long on her chest. "So, little girl." Because all women just loved being called little girl. Awesome. "You wanna party?"

Cora showed lots of teeth, hoping it passed for a smile. She twirled a lock of hair in her fingers. "What did you have in mind?"

Cecil stood up, skirted the picnic table and came to stand in front of her. She pretended to check her phone, because she was afraid she wouldn't be able to stay in character. It was one thing to flirt, but another thing having to follow through with said flirting. She knew there was a patrol car in the parking lot just one yell away. Rob Hopper was waiting on the other side of the trees, so if anything bad happened, she was covered.

"Let Cecil take care of you." He pulled a bag from his pocket, withdrawing a single joint and waving it like a magic wand. "My specialty. I call it Wings. Just a couple of hits and you'll be flying." He laughed at himself, then settled next to Cora, close enough that their thighs touched. She tried not to cringe when the stench of unwashed skin and stale cigarettes wafted over her. Thirty-seven excruciating seconds later—because she was counting—Cecil finally lit up the joint, took a couple of hits and passed it to her.

Showtime. It all happened faster than he could bat a bloodshot eye.

Lightning quick, Cora pulled handcuffs from her back pocket and snapped them on his wrist. Before he even had a chance to exhale, she was reading him his rights. Rob emerged from the screen of trees to help apprehend him. They dragged him to the parking lot and shoved him in the police car, Cecil spewing foul curses the entire way to the station.

Once they had Cecil secured in the interrogation room, Captain Thompson and Rob stood on the other side of the one-way glass to observe the questioning.

When Cora entered the room, Cecil launched into a long, cuss-filled tirade. She took the chair opposite him, waiting for him to finish. It was amazing just how much this guy liked to hear himself talk. After insulting her, her mother, her gender and the rest of the Providence Falls police force, he finally lapsed into mulish silence. Oh, miracle of miracles.

"Are you quite finished, Mr. Watmuff?" Cora asked calmly.

Apparently not. He sucked in an angry breath and started up again. Gah! She shouldn't have asked. This time he insulted the institution, The Man and the government. Cora waited patiently. When, at last, he ended his rant with his opinions on legalizing marijuana and other drugs, Cora released a heavy sigh.

"You think you're in here just for passing me a joint, Mr. Watmuff?" she asked. "We have you on way more charges than that."

Cecil let out a derisive snort, but he seemed nervous. "Nice try, lady."

Cora crossed her arms. She'd gone from "little girl" to "lady" in less than an hour. Moving up in the world. "How's armed robbery and grand theft auto sound? The Gas n' Go ring a bell?"

He looked startled, then he swallowed visibly.

A thrill shot through her. Maybe her bluff was going to pay off bigger than she'd expected. The gas station had been robbed by a man loosely fitting Cecil's description a few weeks ago. He'd managed to slip past the police by stealing a car afterward. Cora had nothing but a slim suspicion, but Cecil didn't know that. "There are cameras everywhere, you know. Catch all sorts of things when we think no one is watching. Parking lots. Traffic stops." She leaned forward. "ATM machines."

Cecil's left eye began to twitch.

"We've got you on camera, and witnesses who've identified you, Mr. Watmuff. All of it. And attacking that old man at the ATM last Saturday night?" Cora clicked her tongue on the roof of her mouth. "This isn't your first offense, either. You've got a record for petty larceny, assault, drug charges. Add all that to the rest, and you're looking at hard time."

His ashen face was like a revelation. The man wasn't the brightest bulb in the box, but he'd still been around the block enough times to make this tricky. All she had was hope and a prayer, but she went for it. Cora pierced him with a hard stare. "Lucky for you, you stepped into something larger when you tried to rob the guy at the ATM. Maybe we can work something out that would be beneficial to both of us."

Cecil's expression turned calculating. She had his attention now.

"Help us identify someone," Cora said. "And we'll put in a good word with the prosecutor about the Gas n' Go."

"Rat someone out?" The look of disgust on Cecil's face was remarkable, considering his rap sheet.

"It's no one connected to you."

"And if I don't help?"

She shrugged. "We can put in a word about that with the prosecutor, too. I'm guessing eight to ten behind bars isn't what you had in mind when you threw on your T-shirt this morning. But I can promise you, that slogan will be very much appreciated where you're headed."

Cecil's grimy hands balled into fists. She could practically see his gears spinning. They were creaky and rusted from lack of use, but spinning, nonetheless. "What do you want to know?" he spat.

Outwardly, Cora remained calm, but under the table, she began tapping her foot with excitement. Her father once joked that she'd never be any good at poker because it was her tell, but Cora never cared about cards. She cared about her job, and she was damned good at it. There was a fierce sense of pride and satisfaction that came with serving justice, and she was just about to serve up a double portion.

In the end, Cecil identified Liam as the man who intervened in the mugging, relaying the story exactly as Liam

JUDE DEVERAUX and TARA SHEETS

had described it. After that, it only took a couple of carefully placed comments to get Cecil to spill about the Gas n' Go robbery, too.

Cora left the room with a wide smile, a spring in her step and an overwhelming sense of relief. She'd done it. Not only had she apprehended the criminal responsible for the robberies, Liam was off the hook.

"Nice job, McLeod," Captain Thompson said. "Meet me in my office in ten minutes and we'll recap." His regular stoic expression cracked at the edges, and he almost smiled. It was a day for surprises.

A couple of hours later, Rob caught her leaving the kitchen and he gave her a high five. "I can't believe you got Crack Rock Cecil to confess all that."

"Well, I think him taking a few hits of that Wings blend might've helped," Cora said. "I doubt he'd have been flying off at the mouth and singing like a bird otherwise."

Rob chuckled as they made their way down the hall. "Captain says Liam's in the clear, and he'll be back soon. That's gotta make you happy."

"I knew Liam was telling the truth," she said simply. Because as angry as he'd made her, she knew deep down he wasn't a killer.

"And now you proved it. He's lucky to have you in his corner."

She forced a smile, but inside she felt like a scattered jigsaw puzzle. She was still annoyed with Liam for all the lies, but she was also glad his name was finally cleared. And she couldn't help the stab of guilt every time she remembered his face when she'd kicked him out of her house. He was new to the city and he didn't even have friends yet. The only person he'd known outside of work besides her was Margaret Brady, and Cora doubted that woman wanted to see Liam anytime soon. So, where had he gone? How was he handling the solitude?

"Liam's going to be back at work just in time to hit Danté's for Thursday night drink specials," Rob said. "We should all go celebrate."

"Oh, that reminds me." Cora stuck her foot out and tripped him.

He caught himself against the wall, then gave her an incredulous scowl. "What the hell, McLeod?"

"That's for Suzette," she said, rounding on him. "It was either that or spill hot coffee in your lap. Be glad I chose to be merciful. Why're you stringing along my best friend?"

Rob looked thunderstruck. "I'm not stringing her along. I told you, I really like her."

"What about that booty call text from Trixie, then?"

At least he had the good sense to look remorseful. "It was bad timing. I didn't want Suzette to see that."

"Well, she saw it, and now she wants nothing to do with you. In fact, she's already forgotten you exist."

Rob swore under his breath. "Our evening was going great until I got that text, and then everything exploded into a hot mess. Trixie's just a girl I used to date, Cora. It was a drunk text message and nothing more. I haven't seen her in months. You have to believe me."

"Hey, I'm not the one you need to convince. Save it for Suzette, if she'll bother listening."

Rob muttered something and charged down the hall— probably to call Suzette again—but Cora knew her friend had blocked his number. Suzette scorned was a force to be reckoned with, so Rob had his work cut out for him. Cora almost felt sorry for him, except that he was Rob, so it wasn't necessary. He'd figure out a way to get back into Suzette's good graces…after the appropriate amount of groveling, of course. Besides, Cora didn't have time to worry about Rob's problems. She had her own hot mess to deal with. Pulling her phone from her pocket, she sent a text to Liam before she could overthink it.

27

"Now, take your girl Katie over there, for example," Liam explained to Billy Mac as he shoveled a hamburger onto the boy's plate. They were standing on the grass outside the Teens in Action center on Tuesday evening, where Liam found himself grilling hamburgers and hot dogs. The pretty teenager named Katie was sitting at a picnic table reading a book, as usual.

"She ain't my girl," Billy said quickly.

"Aye, well, not yet. But see how those lads near her are yelling like banshees and swearing like sailors?" He jerked his chin toward a group of teenage boys shoving each other and posturing nearby. "Does she look impressed? No. Because they're acting like bloody fools. If you want to get the attention of a girl like her and reel her in, you have to use your brain." Liam turned to the next kid in the dinner line, filling his plate.

He'd only come tonight to look for Billy, because he knew the boy sometimes showed up for free food, and Liam had wanted to thank Billy for helping Cora yesterday. Now that he was free to go back to work, he'd thought to spend the evening celebrating, but somehow, he'd been roped into volunteering at the barbecue grill. He wasn't half-bad at it, either. Who knew?

"Easy for you to say," Billy mumbled between bites of hamburger. "What does that even mean, 'use your brain' to reel her in?"

"You have to figure out her interests. Find things you have in common with each other." Liam flipped another burger on the grill. "She's always reading, right? So, think about what you could do to put yourself in her path. Who manages the library section in the center? Maybe you could help shelve the books."

Billy gave a long-suffering eye roll. "Books."

"Yes, books," Liam said with a laugh. "You'd be surprised how far you can get with the ladies when it comes to discussing books. I once knew a girl who was obsessed with seashells from the ocean. She had a great book filled with illustrations of them."

"So, what? You just walked up to her and started talking about shells?" Billy didn't seem very impressed.

"No, I accidentally stepped on one of her seashells and cut my foot. Then she had to bandage me up, and that's what got us talking. Then she showed me a library full of books, and that's how it all began."

Billy seemed to consider it. "That's how you got the girl?"

If only it had been that simple. "That's how we became friends."

Billy took one more look at Katie, then turned away. "I guess I'll think about it."

Liam watched him wander off to hang with some of the boys playing video games. All Billy needed was a bit more confidence, but that wasn't something you could force. The kid was smart, resourceful and loyal as hell. If Liam had been around to watch his nephews grow up, he imagined they'd have been a lot like Billy. Maybe Liam would stick around the center more often to keep an eye on him. Maybe. If he had nothing else going on, of course.

A Mini Cooper drove into the parking lot, and Liam handed the spatula to one of the volunteers. "If you don't mind, I need to take a quick break." He headed toward the edge of the lot, feeling jumpy and nervous. Billy's decision to play video games with the boys suddenly seemed like a good plan, but Liam stood his ground. He wasn't a green schoolboy, dammit.

Cora got out of her car and began walking toward him with a tentative smile on her face. She was wearing jeans, boots and a fitted T-shirt, but the image was superimposed with the faded memory of the girl in silk dresses from a lifetime ago. She was different now, stronger and much more confident, but her spirit hadn't changed. At her core, she would always be the sparkling, kindhearted woman who'd bandaged the foot of a thief who didn't deserve it.

"When you texted me your location, I didn't expect you to be here," she said, stopping in front of him.

"Well, the pubs all kicked me out for bad behavior, so I had nothing else to do."

"Right. And volunteering for underprivileged kids was your only other option."

"It was either that or rob a bank, so I thought I'd try being the good guy for a change."

The teasing glint in her eyes faded. "Liam, I know you're not a bad person. I never thought you were an actual suspect, even if Captain Thompson might've been considering it."

"I'm not a very good person, Cora," he said as they walked across the grass to stand under a shady tree. "I lied to you, and it wasn't right."

"You did lie, and it hurt me."

A pang of remorse crashed over him. "I'm sorry. For all of it, Cora. I know it's no excuse, but I wanted so much for you to lo—to like me. It wasn't right to keep my relationship with Margaret from you. And it was stupid of me to take credit for the things Finn did. I guess I just wanted to endear myself to you in any way I could. When your father first introduced us, I knew that I was nothing more than a stranger to you, and I hated that. I hated it because I felt like we'd known each other for so much longer. Like we were connected way before any of this. I know that has to sound crazy." He ran his hands through his hair, tugging at the roots. Why did this have to be so goddamned hard?

"Not crazy," she said softly. "I feel the same way, even though it makes no sense. Sometimes I have these weird dreams about us, and they're so vivid, but when I try to focus on them, they fade away. But they're not dreams in the normal sense. They're more like…memories."

Liam's heart stumbled to a halt, then leaped into a gallop.

She stared off into the distance for a moment, then gave him an odd look. "Do you believe in past lives?"

Sweet God almighty. Adrenaline rocketed through his veins in a heady rush of pure joy. He barely restrained himself from pulling her into his arms. She was remembering! He opened his mouth to spill his heart out to her, to tell her how much he loved her and missed her. Angels and heaven and hell, be damned, because this was Cora. *His* Cora. The girl he loved. The girl who loved him back—

"But I know that's so stupid," she said with a self-conscious laugh. "I don't believe in any of that woo-woo stuff. Maybe I just felt those things because we've been in such close proximity, with the working and living situation."

His happiness dissolved with every word out of her mouth, until all that was left was the hollow emptiness he was growing accustomed to. Of course, she'd explain it away with logical facts. This was a different world and a different time. People no longer had room to believe in things for which they had no proof.

"Liam," she said hesitantly. "I know this past month has been difficult for us, but I want you to know I'm glad you're here. And I'm looking forward to getting to know you better."

"Same," he managed, pretending he hadn't just gone from glowing optimism to crushing disappointment in the blink of an eye. "I'm sorry I lied to you, Cora. It was wrong of me. Can you ever forgive me?"

The wind stirred a lock of hair across her cheek as she studied him. "I can, but it's going to take some time for me to completely trust you. You understand that, don't you?"

He dipped his head in remorse. "I do."

"Good," she said firmly. "Now that that's out of the way, would you like to move back home?"

Liam snapped his head up. *Home.*

When Cora smiled, it was like sunlight on his face.

He nodded because he couldn't trust himself to speak. Even if she never knew his true feelings, it was enough just to be near her. It had to be. Because no matter where they were, no matter when, Cora would always be his home.

28

Boyd was in his office poring over a stack of paperwork on Wednesday morning when Liam rapped his knuckles on the open door.

"O'Connor," Boyd said wearily. "Come in and sit down." His tie was askew, and there were sweat stains on the armpits of his shirt. Deep frown lines creased the man's forehead, and his face was shiny and flushed like it used to get after a hard night of drinking. Liam remembered that look on Boyd well. He'd seen it too many times to count.

"Looks like your week's been almost as bad as mine," Liam said.

"Worse, I can assure you." Boyd's voice remained even, but his body was rigid with tension. "Unlike you, I have a lot more than just my own ass to worry about."

"I apologize, Captain. I should've told you that Margaret and I—"

"Goddamn right, you should've told me. It's your job. I don't have time to second-guess my own officers to see if they're telling the truth. Lucky for you, Cora pulled off a miracle when she interrogated that crackhead, and he spilled about the robberies. Do you know how close you came to getting implicated in the murder of John Brady?" He shook his head in disgust. "You must have one hell of a guardian angel, O'Connor."

Liam smirked. "Two, actually."

"That's enough." Boyd's calm facade crumbled. "This isn't a joke, and I'm going to tell you right now, you'd better tread lightly with me. We may have known each other back in the day, but that doesn't mean shit when I've got an unsolved murder on my hands and the mayor breathing down my neck. He wants my assurance that this case will be wrapped up in a nice little bow before election time, but right now, I can't promise a damned thing. You came this close to getting fired. If it weren't for Cora helping to prove your alibi, you wouldn't even be sitting here."

"I know, and I'm going to make it right," Liam said. "We'll get to the bottom of this case. Whatever it takes."

"It takes you doing your job."

Cora appeared in the doorway. "Sorry to interrupt, but I think we may have a new lead on the Brady case."

"What is it?" Boyd demanded.

"A woman out here named Lindsey Albright." Cora gestured to her desk where a sandy-haired college girl sat fidgeting with her phone. She was petite and tanned, in shorts and a Providence Falls University T-shirt. "She says she was walking home from the bar near the Brady residence last Saturday night. She took a selfie with her phone on the street right outside the house. When she read about

John Brady's death on the news, she decided to bring the picture in so we could examine it."

Boyd's scowl deepened. "What's she got?"

"It's a grainy image, but there are two figures standing in the window in the background. Hard to tell, but it looks like it could be John Brady, and there's definitely someone behind him. Want me to get her information?"

"No, I'll handle it," Boyd said. "Send her in."

When Cora left, Boyd began shuffling the papers on his desk and muttering to himself. He seemed to have forgotten Liam was there.

Liam pushed his chair back and stood. "Will that be all, Captain?"

Boyd glanced up, his expression dark as a thundercloud. "Get back to work, O'Connor. And if you ever withhold information again, I'll have your ass for obstruction. That's one promise I *can* make."

Liam walked back into the pen and plunked down at his desk.

Cora brushed past him as she ushered the college girl toward Boyd's office. "We live another day," she said under her breath.

Woman, if you only knew.

He stared blankly at his computer. As usual, the glowing screen mocked him. He still didn't know how to work the damned thing. Faking it wasn't going to work for much longer, so he was going to have to buckle down and learn. Sighing, he turned the monitor off and eyed the files on his desk. He'd rather muck out a barn with his bare hands than do office work, but the angels made it clear he didn't get to choose. Still. In spite of everything, the job gave him a sense of purpose, and being close to Cora every day was the best part. He glanced around the pen, taking comfort in the routine of it all. Everywhere he looked, it was business as usual.

Otto was wiping spilled coffee off his desk. Happy was on the phone, his face scrunched into its usual grimace. Rob strode through the pen, laughing at something one of the patrol officers said.

The copy machine in the corner jammed.

Someone cursed a blue streak.

Aye. Liam linked his hands behind his head and smiled. It was good to be back.

EPILOGUE

"How much longer are you going to laze under this tree?" Cora asked, jamming a sunhat on her head.

Liam squinted up from his shady spot on the grass. She was standing over him wearing a pink sundress with a ruffled hem and a pair of flip-flops. She could've looked like a little tea cake, the way she had the day he'd climbed through her bedroom window a lifetime ago. But her long suntanned legs and bare shoulders gleamed under the sinfully short dress, so tea and cakes weren't the first things that came to mind. "You said we were coming to the lake to relax, so that's what I'm doing."

"Fine." Cora kicked off her flip-flops and grabbed a towel from a bag in the grass. "Laze all you like. But I didn't drive thirty minutes out of Providence Falls on a gorgeous Saturday afternoon just to sleep, so I'm going swimming."

"Me, too," Suzette sang out from the picnic table near the shore. "Just as soon as I finish blowing this up." She was holding a gold, glittering flotation raft in her hands. It sparkled brighter than the sunlight glancing off the clear blue lake. Cora had proposed the beach trip to Lake Allure after the weekend wrapped up with no further leads on the Brady case. According to Boyd, the selfie picture from the college girl Lindsey Albright had been a bust, so they were at a standstill. Liam and Cora tried to follow up with Lindsey for more questioning a couple of days after she visited the station, but she wasn't around. Her roommate told them Lindsey often stayed with a boyfriend over the weekend, so they'd have to wait until next week to talk to her. All in all, things with the murder investigation weren't looking good, but Cora wasn't going to give up easily, and neither would he.

Liam propped his back against the tree and grabbed a bottle of water from the cooler beside him. The air was warm and thick with the scents of summer flowers, suntan lotion and barbecue. Children's laughter floated up from the shoreline, and somewhere in the distance a radio played a song about a brown-eyed girl. Liam took a drink of icy water and tipped his head back to gaze at the canopy of leaves above him.

"Hello, thief."

Liam let out a strangled choke. Sucked some water down his airway. Coughed. "Jesus, Mary and Joseph!"

The two angels hovered in the branches above him like snowy-winged wraiths. A fine mist clung to their hair and robes.

"You two will give me a heart attack one of these days," Liam said, wheezing. "Can't you give a man some warning before you appear?"

"Heraldry and golden trumpets aren't standard in our department," the blond angel said. He was leaning against the trunk, looking more relaxed than usual. "And you won't startle to death. That's not in the plan."

"How about just showing up like a normal person for a change? A knock on the door, perhaps. A quick phone call to tell me you're stopping by. Even a message by carrier pigeon would be appreciated."

"But we aren't 'normal persons.'" The blond angel tilted his head. "Though, I suppose we can consider your request, since we'll be watching you for the duration of your time here."

"Good," Liam said. "Great." He was more than a little surprised that they could be so accommodating. Should he push his luck? Always. "And what are your names, anyway?"

The blond angel's brows drew together. "I fail to see how that matters."

"It's just that I don't know what to call you."

"You don't call us. We appear when we choose."

"Aye, I'm aware," Liam said under his breath.

"My name is Agon," the dark-haired one announced with a smile. He was sitting on a branch, swinging his legs like he hadn't a care in the world. And maybe he didn't. Maybe dealing with Liam's situation was just another boring day at the celestial office for them.

The blond angel shot Agon a disapproving look. "That's not protocol."

"It can't hurt, Samael. He may as well call us by our names."

"Agon and Samael," Liam said. "Good to know."

"Enough useless chatter." The wind ruffled Samael's blond curls and the tips of his feathers. "We've come to—"

"Let me guess. Remind me that I must remain on task?"

Samael squared his shoulders. "Yes."

"Got it. Doing it."

"I don't see Finn here today," Samael pointed out. "Cora and he are no closer to falling in love than they were the day you arrived."

"I'll get to it," Liam said testily. He didn't like talking about it. "I can't force them together every single moment of the day. Things have to unfold naturally, or she'll never go for him. She's headstrong and smart, and she won't be pushed into anything. It's going to take time."

"Which you don't have," Samael said. "You've already squandered an entire month, and you've strayed from your task on multiple occasions."

"I was a bit preoccupied with keeping my job and staying out of jail, and I managed it, didn't I?"

"Thanks to Cora and the young boy."

"But I'm still here, and I'm back living at Cora's house again. I'm free to carry on playing matchmaker, and that's what matters. On top of that, I'm even helping out with a murder investigation and apprehending criminals. Granted, I'm not in charge of your big plan. But, hey. If you want to give me extra points for good deeds, I won't say no to a little boost now and then."

Samael stared down his nose at Liam. *"Boost?"*

"Computer proficiency, for example." Liam couldn't think of anything worse than spending hours learning those machines. "Or maybe a faster car? You know, strictly for practical reasons." That red convertible he saw the other day looked very practical. He could practically envision himself in it right now. "Or, here's a boon I'd treasure above all others—take the blasted *training wheels* off, so I no longer have to feel like I'm boiling from the inside out every time Cora accidentally touches me." He glanced hopefully between both angels.

Samael's stern face grew granite hard. "We are not in the business of granting wishes."

"Hey, lazy!" Cora called form the water's edge. "Are you coming or not?"

Liam glanced toward the lake and almost swallowed his tongue. Cora was now wearing a bright red bikini. It clung to her curves for dear life and—from the looks of the flimsy straps—it wasn't long for this world. Suzette was wearing something similar in black, except her bathing top had no straps at all. Liam stood shakily to his feet, managing a feeble wave as the two women ran splashing into the water. Perhaps a quick swim would do him good. Yes, it might be just the thing he needed. To clear his head. So he could really focus on his task.

"Where are you going?" Samael asked.

Liam found he'd taken two steps toward the lake. He glanced back at the angels and cleared his throat. "I think I should go…keep an eye on them. You know, like a chaperone. To make sure they're safe."

"Somehow, that does not inspire confidence," Samael said dryly.

"Everything's fine. Don't worry." Liam gave an absent wave and hurried toward the water, picking up speed and whipping off his shirt as he went.

The angels watched Liam charge into the lake in great splashes. He cupped his hands and sent arcs of water sailing toward the girls. Suzette shrieked. Cora laughed. The battle was on.

Samael sank down to sit beside Agon. "If he truly believes everything's fine, then he's not just a thief, he's an utter fool."

Agon watched Liam and Cora with a wistful look on his face. "But all men are fools in love, are they not?"

"We are the Department of Destiny. Love is not our domain."

"Yet it drives his every action, and Cora's destiny depends on him. Truly, this is a tangle. The more he's with her, the more he wants *more* with her. How can someone like him, a thief who's only ever known how to take, learn to give up the greatest treasure he's ever had? It would take a miracle."

Samael withdrew his clipboard and checked it. "Lucky for him, there are still a few miracles slated for this century. But Liam is as headstrong and arrogant as ever. He has to learn to see past his own desires."

Agon watched as Liam tipped his head back and laughed at something Cora said. "I'm not sure he's cut from that cloth. It would require a lot of self-reflection."

"Mmm." Samael's face lit with sudden inspiration. "Or a reflection of *self.*"

Agon regarded the other angel with curiosity. Samael was ever the steadfast and stoic one, so the twinkle of excitement in his eyes surprised him, which, for an angel as old as Agon, did not come often. "Whatever do you mean?"

Samael flicked his wrist and the swirling mist appeared above them. Then he slapped Agon on the back and grinned. *Grinned!* There went one miracle.

"Come on," Samael said, floating up through the mist. "I have a plan. Our thief is about to see himself in a whole new light."

* * * * *